Someone to Wed

Mary Balogh

W F HOWES LTD

This large print edition published in 2019 by
W F Howes Ltd
Unit 5, St George's House, Rearsby Business Park,
Gaddesby Lane, Rearsby, Leicester LE7 4YH

1 3 5 7 9 10 8 6 4 2

First published in the United Kingdom in 2017
by Piatkus

A CIP catalogue record for this book is available
from the British Library

ISBN 978 1 52885 434 4

Typeset by Palimpsest Book Production Limited,
Falkirk, Stirlingshire

and bound by
ational in the UK

CHAPTER 1

'The Earl of Riverdale,' the butler announced after opening wide the double doors of the drawing room as though to admit a regiment and then standing to one side so that the gentleman named could stride past him.

The announcement was not strictly necessary. Wren had heard the arrival of his vehicle, and guessed it was a curricle rather than a traveling carriage, although she had not got to her feet to look. And he was almost exactly on time. She liked that. The two gentlemen who had come before him had been late, one by all of half an hour. Those two had been sent on their way as soon as was decently possible, though not only because of their tardiness. Mr Sweeney, who had come a week ago, had bad teeth and a way of stretching his mouth to expose them at disconcertingly frequent intervals even when he was not actually smiling. Mr Richman, who had come four days ago, had had no discernible personality, a fact that had been quite as disconcerting as Mr Sweeney's teeth. Now here came the third.

He strode forward a few paces before coming to

1

an abrupt halt as the butler closed the doors behind him. He looked about the room with apparent surprise at the discovery that it was occupied only by two women, one of whom – Maude, Wren's maid – was seated off in a corner, her head bent over some needlework, in the role of chaperon. His eyes came to rest upon Wren and he bowed.

'Miss Heyden?' It was a question.

Her first reaction after her initial approval of his punctuality was acute dismay. One glance told her he was not at all what she wanted.

He was tall, well formed, immaculately, elegantly tailored, dark haired, and impossibly handsome. And young – in his late twenties or early thirties, at a guess. If she were to dream up the perfect hero for the perfect romantic fairy tale, she could not do better than the very real man standing halfway across the room, waiting for her to confirm that she was indeed the lady who had invited him to take tea at Withington House.

But this was no fairy tale, and the sheer perfection of him alarmed her and caused her to lean back farther in her chair and deeper into the shade provided by the curtains drawn across the window on her side of the fireplace. She had not wanted a handsome man or even a particularly young man. She had hoped for someone older, more ordinary, perhaps balding or acquiring a bit of a paunch, pleasant-looking but basically . . . well, ordinary. With decent teeth and at least *something* of a personality. But she could hardly deny her identity and dismiss him without further ado.

'Yes,' she said. 'How do you do, Lord Riverdale? Do have a seat.' She gestured to the chair across the hearth from her own. She knew something of social manners and ought, of course, to have risen to greet him, but she had good reason to keep to the shadows, at least for now.

He eyed the chair as he approached it and sat with obvious reluctance. 'I do beg your pardon,' he said. 'I appear to be early. Punctuality is one of my besetting sins, I am afraid. I always make the mistake of assuming that when I am invited somewhere for half past two, I am expected to arrive at half past two. I hope some of your other guests will be here soon, including a few ladies.'

She was further alarmed when he smiled. If it was possible to look more handsome than handsome, he was looking it. He had perfect teeth, and his eyes crinkled attractively at the corners when he smiled. And his eyes were very blue. Oh, this was wretched. Who was number four on her list?

'Punctuality is a virtue as far as I am concerned, Lord Riverdale,' she said. 'I am a businesswoman, as perhaps you are aware. To run a successful business, one must respect other people's time as well as one's own. You are on time. You see?' She swept one hand toward the clock ticking on the mantel. 'It is twenty-five minutes to three. And I am not expecting any other guests.'

His smile disappeared and he glanced at Maude

3

beforc looking back at Wren. 'I see,' he said. 'Perhaps you had not realized, Miss Heyden, that neither my mother nor my sister came into the country with me. Or perhaps you did not realize I have no wife to accompany me. I beg your pardon. I have no wish to cause you any embarrassment or to compromise you in any way.' His hands closed about the arms of his chair in a signal that he was about to rise.

'But my invitation was addressed to you alone,' she said. 'I am no young girl to need to be hedged about with relatives to protect me from the dangerous company of single gentlemen. And I do have Maude for propriety's sake. We are neighbors of sorts, Lord Riverdale, though more than eight miles separate Withington House from Brambledean Court and I am not always here and you are not always there. Nevertheless, now that I am owner of Withington and have completed my year of mourning for my aunt and uncle, I have taken it upon myself to become acquainted with some of my neighbors. I entertained Mr Sweeney here last week and Mr Richman a few days after. Do you know them?'

He was frowning, and he had not removed his hands from the arms of his chair. He still looked uncomfortable and ready to spring to his feet at the earliest excuse. 'I have an acquaintance with both gentlemen,' he said, 'though I cannot claim to *know* either one. I have been in possession of my title and property for only a year and have not spent much time here yet.'

'Then I am fortunate you are here now,' she said as the drawing room doors opened and the tea tray was carried in and set before her. She moved to the edge of her chair, turning without conscious intent slightly to her left as she did so, and poured the tea. Maude came silently across the room to hand the earl his cup and saucer and then to offer the plate of cakes.

'I did not know Mr and Mrs Heyden, your aunt and uncle,' he said, nodding his thanks to Maude. 'I am sorry for your loss. I understand they died within a very short while of each other.'

'Yes,' she said. 'My aunt died a few days after taking to her bed with a severe headache, and my uncle died less than a week later. His health had been failing for some time, and I believe he simply gave up the struggle after she had gone. He doted upon her.' And Aunt Megan upon him despite the thirty-year gap in their ages and the hurried nature of their marriage almost twenty years ago.

'I am sorry,' he said again. 'They raised you?'

'Yes,' she said. 'They could not have done better by me if they had been my parents. Your predecessor did not live at Brambledean, I understand, or visit often. I speak of the late Earl of Riverdale, not his unfortunate son. Do you intend to take up permanent residence there?'

The unfortunate son, Wren had learned, had succeeded to the title until it was discovered that his father had contracted a secret marriage as a very young man and that the secret wife had still

5

been alive when he married the mother of his three children. Those children, already adult, had suddenly found themselves to be illegitimate, and the new earl had lost the title to the man now seated on the other side of the hearth. The late earl's first marriage had produced one legitimate child, a daughter, who had grown up at an orphanage in Bath, knowing nothing of her identity. All this and more Wren had learned before adding the earl to her list. The story had been sensational news last year and had kept the gossip mills grinding for weeks. The details had not been difficult to unearth when there were servants and tradespeople only too eager to share what came their way.

One never knew quite where truth ended and exaggeration or misunderstanding or speculation or downright falsehood began, of course, but Wren did know a surprising amount about her neighbors, considering the fact that she had absolutely no social dealings with them. She knew, for example, that both Mr Sweeney and Mr Richman were respectable but impoverished gentlemen. And she knew that Brambledean had been almost totally neglected by the late earl, who had left it to be mismanaged almost to the point of total ruin by a lazy steward who graced the taproom of his local inn more often than his office. By now the house and estate needed the infusion of a vast sum of money.

Wren had heard that the new earl was a conscientious gentleman of comfortable means, but that

6

he was not nearly wealthy enough to cope with the enormity of the disaster he had inherited so unexpectedly. The late earl had not been a poor man. Far from it, in fact. But his fortune had gone to his legitimate daughter. She might have saved the day by marrying the new earl and so reuniting the entailed property with the fortune, but she had married the Duke of Netherby instead. Wren could well understand why the many-faceted story had so dominated conversation both above and below stairs last year.

'I do intend to live at Brambledean,' the Earl of Riverdale said. He was frowning into his cup. 'I have another home in Kent, of which I am dearly fond, but I am needed here, and an absentee landlord is rarely a good landlord. The people dependent upon me here deserve better.'

He looked every bit as handsome when he was frowning as he did when he smiled. Wren hesitated. It was not too late to send him on his way, as she had done with his two predecessors. She had given a plausible reason for inviting him and had plied him with tea and cakes. He would doubtless go away thinking her eccentric. He would probably disapprove of her inviting him alone when she was a single lady with only the flimsy chaperonage of a maid. But he would shrug off the encounter soon enough and forget about her. And she did not really care what he might think or say about her anyway.

But now she remembered that number four on

her list, a man in his late fifties, had always professed himself to be a confirmed bachelor, and number five was reputed to complain almost constantly of ailments both real and imagined. She had added them only because the list had looked pathetically short with just three names.

'I understand, Lord Riverdale,' she said, 'that you are not a wealthy man.' Now perhaps it was too late – or very nearly so. If she sent him away now, he would think her vulgar as well as eccentric and careless of her reputation.

He took his time about setting his cup and saucer down on the table beside him before turning his eyes upon her. Only the slight flaring of his nostrils warned her that she had angered him. 'Do you indeed?' he said, a distinct note of hauteur in his voice. 'I thank you for the tea, Miss Heyden. I will take no more of your time.' He stood up.

'I could offer a solution,' she said, and now it was very definitely too late to retreat. 'To your relatively impoverished state, that is. You need money to undo the neglect of years at Brambledean and to fulfill your duty to the people dependent upon you there. It might take you years, perhaps even the rest of your life, if you do it only through careful management. It is unfortunately necessary to put a great deal of money into a business before one can get money out of it. Perhaps you are considering taking out a loan or a mortgage if the property is not already mortgaged. Or perhaps you intend to marry a rich wife.'

8

He stood very straight and tall, and his jaw had set into a hard line. His nostrils were still flared. He looked magnificent and even slightly menacing, and for a moment Wren regretted the words she had already spoken. But it was too late now to unsay them.

'I beg to inform you, Miss Heyden,' he said curtly, 'that I find your curiosity offensive. Good day to you.'

'You are perhaps aware,' she said, 'that my uncle was enormously rich, much of his wealth deriving from the glassworks he owned in Staffordshire. He left everything to me, my aunt having predeceased him. He taught me a great deal about the business, which I helped him run during his last years and now run myself. The business has lost none of its momentum in the last year, and is, indeed, gradually expanding. And there are properties and investments even apart from that. I am a very wealthy woman, Lord Riverdale. But my life lacks something, just as yours lacks ready money. I am twenty-nine years old, very nearly thirty, and I would like . . . someone to wed. In my own person I am not marriageable, but I do have money. And you do not.'

She paused to see if he had something to say, but he looked as though he were rooted to the spot, his eyes fixed upon her, his jaw like granite. She was suddenly very glad Maude was in the room, though her presence was also embarrassing. Maude did not approve of any of this and did not scruple to say so when they were alone.

9

'Perhaps we could combine forces and each acquire what we want,' Wren said.

'You are offering me . . . *marriage*?' he asked.

Had she not made herself clear? 'Yes,' she said. He continued to stare at her, and she became uncomfortably aware of the ticking of the clock.

'Miss Heyden,' he said at last, 'I have not even seen your face.'

Alexander Westcott, Earl of Riverdale, felt rather as though he had wandered into one of those bizarre dreams that did not seem to arise from anything he had ever experienced in the waking world. He had come in answer to an invitation from a distant neighbor. He had accepted many such invitations since coming into Wiltshire to the home and estate he really would very much rather not have inherited. It was incumbent upon him to meet and establish friendly relationships with the people among whom he intended to live.

No one he had asked knew anything much about Miss Heyden beyond the fact that she was the niece of a Mr and Mrs Heyden, who had died within days of each other a year or so ago and left her Withington House. They had attended some of the social functions close to Brambledean, his butler seemed to recall, though not many, probably because of the distance. He had heard no mention of their niece's ever being with them, though. William Bufford, Alexander's steward, had not been able to add anything. He had held the position for only four months, since the former steward had been let go with a generous bonus he had in no way earned. Mr Heyden had been a very elderly gentleman, according to the butler. Alexander had assumed, then, that the niece was probably in late middle age and was making an effort to establish herself in the home that was now hers by inviting neighbors from near and far to tea.

He had certainly not expected to be the lone guest of a lady who was almost surely younger than he had estimated. He was not quite sure how much younger. She had not risen to greet him but had remained seated in a chair that had been pushed farther to the side of the hearth than the one across from it and farther into the shade provided by a heavily curtained window. The rest of the room was bright with sunlight, making the contrast more noticeable and making the lady less visible. She sat gracefully in her chair and appeared youthfully slim. Her hands were slender, long fingered, well manicured, and young. Her voice, soft and low pitched, was not that of a girl, but neither was it that of an older woman. His guess was confirmed when she told him she was almost thirty – his own age.

She was wearing a gray dress, perhaps as half mourning. It was stylish and becoming enough. And over her head and face she wore a black veil. He could see her hair and her face through it, but neither with any clarity. It was impossible to know what color her hair was and equally impossible to see her features. She had eaten nothing with her tea, and when she drank, she had held the veil outward with one hand gracefully bent at the wrist and moved her cup beneath it.

To say that he had been uncomfortable since entering the room would be hugely to understate the case. And more and more as the minutes passed he had been wishing he had simply turned around and left as soon as he had understood the situation. It might have appeared ill-mannered, but good God, his being here alone with her – he hardly counted the presence of the maid – was downright improper.

But now, in addition to feeling uncomfortable, he was outraged. She had spoken openly about the desperate condition of Brambledean and his impoverished state. Not that he was personally impoverished. He had spent five years after his father's death working hard to bring Riddings Park in Kent back to prosperity, and he had succeeded. He had been settling into the comfortable life of a moderately prosperous gentleman when the catastrophe of last year had happened and he had found himself with his unwelcome title and the even more unwelcome encumbrance of an entailed estate that was on the brink of ruin. His moderate fortune had suddenly seemed more like a pittance.

But how dared she – a stranger – make open reference to it? The vulgarity of it had paralyzed his brain for a few moments. She had provided a solution, however, and his head was only just catching up to it. She was wealthy and wanted a husband. He was not wealthy and needed a rich wife. She had suggested that they supply each other's needs and marry. But—

Miss Heyden, I have not even seen your face.

It was bizarre. It was very definitely the stuff of that sort of dream from which one awoke wondering where the devil it had come from. Some other words of hers suddenly echoed in his mind. *In my own person I am not marriageable.* What in thunder had she meant?

'No,' she said, breaking the silence, 'you have not, have you?' She turned her head to the left to look back at her maid. 'Maude, will you open the curtains, please?' The maid did so and Miss Heyden was suddenly bathed in light. Her dress looked more silver than gray. Her veil looked darker in contrast. She raised her hands. 'I suppose you must see what you would be getting with my money, Lord Riverdale.'

Was she being deliberately offensive? Or were her words and her slightly mocking manner actually a defense, her way of hiding discomfort? She *ought* to be uncomfortable. She raised her veil and threw it back over her head to land on the seat of the chair behind her. For a few moments her face remained half turned to the left.

Her hair was a rich chestnut brown, thick and lustrous, smooth at the front and sides, gathered into a cluster of curls high on the back of her head. Her neck was long and graceful. In profile

13

her face was exquisitely beautiful – wide browed with long eyelashes that matched her hair, a straight nose, finely sculpted cheek, soft lips, firmly chiseled jaw, pale, smooth skin. And then she turned full face toward him and raised her eyelids. Her eyes were hazel, though that was a detail he did not notice until later. What he did notice was that the left side of her face, from forehead to jaw, was purple.

He inhaled slowly and mastered his first impulse to frown, even to recoil or actually take a step back. She was looking very directly into his face. There was no distortion of features, only the purple marks, some clustered and darker in shade, some fainter and more isolated. She looked rather as though someone had splashed purple paint down one side of her and she had not yet had a chance to wash it off.

'Burns?' he asked, though he did not think so. There would have been other damage.

'A birthmark,' she said.

He had seen birthmarks, but nothing to match this. What would otherwise have been a remark-ably beautiful face was severely, cruelly marred. He wondered if she always wore the veil in public. *In my own person I am not marriageable.*

'But I am wealthy,' she said.

And he knew that it was indeed self-defense, that look of disdain, that boast of wealth, that challenge of the raised chin and very direct gaze. He knew that the coldness of her manner was the thinnest

14

of veneers. *I am twenty-nine years old, very nearly thirty, and I would like someone to wed.* And because she was wealthy after the death of her uncle, she could afford to purchase what she wanted. It seemed startlingly distasteful, but was his own decision to go to London this year as soon as the Season began in earnest after Easter to seek a wealthy bride any the less so?

He suddenly remembered something she had said earlier. 'Did you also make this offer to Mr Sweeney and Mr Richman?' he asked her. Ironic name, that – *Richman.* His question was ill-mannered, but there was nothing normal about this situation. 'Did they refuse?'

'I did not,' she told him, 'and so they did not. Although neither was here for longer than half an hour, I knew long before that time expired that neither would suit me. I may wish to wed, Lord Riverdale, but I am not desperate enough to do so at all costs.'

'You have judged, then, that I *will* suit you, that I am worth the cost?' he asked, raising his eyebrows and clasping his hands behind his back. He was still standing and looking down at her. If she found that fact intimidating, she was not showing it. He would suit her because of his title, would he? Then why had he been third on her list?

'It is impossible to know with any certainty after just half an hour,' she said, 'but I believe so. I believe you are a gentleman, Lord Riverdale.'

And the other two were not? 'What exactly does

that mean?' he asked. Good God, was he willing to stand here discussing the matter with her?

'I believe it means you would treat me with respect,' she said.

He looked down at her disfigured face and frowned. 'And that is all you ask of a marriage?' he asked. 'Respect?'

'It is a large something,' she said.

Was it? Was it enough? It was something he would surely be asking himself a number of times in the coming months. It was actually a good answer. 'And would you treat me with respect if I married you for your money?' he asked.

'Yes,' she said after pausing to think about it. 'For I do not believe you would squander that money on your own pleasures.'

'And upon what information do you base that judgment?' he asked her. 'By your own admission you have a half hour's acquaintance with me.'

'But I do know,' she said, 'that you have your own well-managed estate in Kent and could choose to live there in comfort for the rest of your life and forget about Brambledean Court. It is what your predecessor chose to do despite the fact that he was a very wealthy man. His wealth went to his daughter instead of to you, however. All you inherited was the title and the entailed property. Yet you have come here and employed a competent steward and clearly intend to take on the Herculean task of restoring the property and the farms and bettering the lives of the numerous people who

16

rely upon you for their livelihood. Those are not the actions of a man who would use a fortune for riotous living.'

She had more than a half hour's acquaintance with him, then. She had the advantage of him. They looked speculatively at each other.

'The question is,' she said when he did not respond to her words, 'could you live with *this*, Lord Riverdale?' She indicated the left side of her face with one graceful movement of her hand.

He gave the question serious consideration. The birthmark seriously disfigured her. More important, though, it must have had some serious impact upon the formation of her character if it had been there all her life. He had already seen her defensive, slightly mocking manner, her surface coldness, her isolation, the veil. The blemish on her face might be the least of the damage done to her. Her face might be easy enough to live with. It would be cruel to think otherwise. But how easy to live with would *she* be?

And was he giving serious consideration to her offer? But he must think seriously about some such marriage. And soon. The longer he lived at Brambledean, the more he saw the effects of poverty upon those whose well-being depended upon him.

'Do you wish to give me a definite no, Lord Riverdale?' Miss Heyden asked. 'Or a possible maybe? Or a definite maybe, perhaps? Or even a yes?'

But he had not answered her original question.

17

'We all have to learn to live behind the face and within the body we have been given,' he said. 'None of us deserves to be shunned – or adulated – upon looks alone.'

'Are you adulated?' she asked with a slight mocking smile.

He hesitated. 'I am occasionally told that I am the proverbial tall, dark, handsome man of fairy tales,' he said. 'It can be a burden.'

'Strange,' she said, still half smiling.

'Miss Heyden,' he said. 'I cannot possibly give you any answer now. You planned this long before I came. You have had time to think and consider, even to do some research. You have a clear advantage over me.'

'A possibly possible maybe?' she said, and he was arrested for the moment by the thought that perhaps she had a sense of humor. 'Will you come back, Lord Riverdale?'

'Not alone,' he said firmly.

'I do not entertain,' she told him.

'I understand that this has not been an entertainment,' he said, 'despite the invitation and the tea and cakes. It has been a job interview.'

'Yes.' She did not argue the point.

'I shall arrange something at Brambledean,' he said. 'A tea, perhaps, or a dinner, or a soiree – *something,* and I shall invite you with several other neighbors.'

'I do not mingle with society or even with neighbors,' she told him.

He frowned again. 'As Countess of Riverdale, you would have no choice,' he told her.

'Oh,' she said, 'I believe I would.'

'No.'

'You would be a tyrant?' she asked.

'I would certainly not allow my wife to make a hermit of herself,' he said, 'merely because of some purple marks on her face.'

'You would not *allow*?' she said faintly. 'Perhaps I need to think more carefully about whether you will suit me.'

'Yes,' he said, 'perhaps you do. It is the best I can offer, Miss Heyden. I shall send an invitation within the next week or so. If you have the courage to come, perhaps we can discover with a little more clarity if your suggestion is something we wish to pursue more seriously. If you do not, then we both have an answer.'

'If I have the courage,' she said softly.

'Yes,' he said. 'I beg to take my leave with thanks for the tea. I shall see myself out.'

He bowed and strode across the room. She neither got to her feet nor said anything. A few moments later he shut the drawing room doors behind him, blew out his breath from puffed cheeks, and descended the stairs. He informed the butler that he would fetch his own curricle and horses from the stables.

CHAPTER 2

The Earl of Riverdale was as good as his word. A written invitation was delivered to Withington House two days after his visit. He was hosting a tea party for some of his neighbors three days hence and would be pleased if Miss Heyden would attend. She set the card down beside her breakfast plate and proceeded to eat her toast and marmalade and drink her coffee without really tasting them.

Would she go?

Maude had offered her opinion after he left a couple of days ago – of course. Maude always offered an opinion. She had been Aunt Megan's maid and Wren's since last year. But even before then she had never scrupled to speak her mind.

'A right handsome one, that,' she had said after he left.

'Too handsome?' Wren had asked.

'For his own good, do you mean?' In the act of picking up the tray from the table in front of Wren, Maude had pursed her lips and paused to think. 'I was not given the impression that he thinks himself God's gift to womankind. He was certainly not pleased to find himself alone with you, was he? I warned you it was improper when you concocted this whole mad scheme, but you never did heed anything I have to say, so I don't know why I still bother. The other two were pleased enough to be here, though both of them looked a bit unnerved by the veil. They had probably heard you are worth a bundle and hoped they were onto a good thing.'

'Mr Sweeney and Mr Richman were a mistake,' Wren had admitted. 'Is the Earl of Riverdale a mistake too, Maude? Though perhaps the answer is irrelevant. It is probable I will never hear from him again. He would not even admit to a possibly possible maybe, would he? And then he threw the challenge back at me with his idea about inviting me to some entertainment that would include others. *If you have the courage to come*, indeed.'

'And do you?' Maude had asked, straightening up, the tray in her hands. 'You never did while your aunt and uncle were alive, and you never have since. If it wasn't for the glassworks you would be a total hermit, and the glassworks don't really count, do they? You aren't going to find a husband there. And even *there* you always wear your veil.'

She had not waited for an answer to her question about courage. Which was just as well – Wren still did not know the answer two days later as she considered the invitation. A tea party. At Brambledean Court. With an indeterminate number of other guests from the neighborhood.

21

Would she go? More to the point, *could* she? Maude was quite right – she had been a virtual hermit all her life. In more than twenty-nine years she had not attended a single social function. Her uncle and aunt had entertained occasionally, but she had always stayed in her room, and, bless their hearts, they had never tried to insist that she come down, though Uncle Reggie had tried several times to persuade her.

'You have allowed your birthmark to define your life, Wren,' he had said once, 'when in reality it is something a person soon becomes accustomed to and scarcely notices. We are always more aware of our own physical shortcomings than other people are once they get to know us. You may no longer notice that my legs are too short for my body, but I am always conscious of it. Sometimes I fear that I waddle rather than walk.'

'Oh, you do *not*, Uncle Reggie,' Wren had protested, but he had achieved one of his aims, which was to make her laugh. But he had never seen her before the age of ten, when the birthmark had been a great deal worse than it was now. He did not know what she saw when she looked in her mirror.

It was her uncle who had named her Wren – because she had been all skinny arms and legs and big, sad eyes when he had first seen her and reminded him of a fledgling bird. Also Wren was close to Rowena, her real name. Aunt Megan had started calling her Wren too – a new name for a new life, she had said, giving her niece one of her big, all-encompassing hugs. And Wren herself had liked it. She could not remember the name *Rowena* ever being spoken with anything like affection or approval or even neutrality. Her uncle and aunt had had a way of saying the new name as though it – and she – was something special. And a year later they had changed her last name too – with her full approval – and she became Wren Heyden.

Her thoughts were all over the place this morning, she thought, bringing them back to the breakfast table. Would she go to tea at Brambledean Court? Could she? Those were the questions she needed to answer, though really they were one. As Countess of Riverdale, he had told her, she would not be able to remain a hermit. He would not allow it. And that was something that needed careful consideration, both the hermit part and the not-allowing part. It was a long time since she had been forced to do anything she did not want to do. She had almost forgotten that according to law, both civil and ecclesiastical, men had total command over their women, wives and children alike. She had not considered that when she decided to purchase a husband.

Purchase – it sounded horrible. But that was precisely what she was trying to do. She wanted to wed. She had longings and needs and yearnings that were a churning mix of the physical and emotional. Sometimes she could not sleep at night for the ache of something nameless that hummed through her body and her mind and seemed to settle most heavily about her heart. She had only one asset, however, with which to induce any man to marry her, and that was her money. Fortunately she had plenty of that. She was not much interested in using it to buy worldly goods. She had all she needed. She would use it, then, she had decided, to purchase what she *did* want, and she had set about making as wise a purchase as she could with no experience whatsoever in such matters. Now she had to ask herself a new question. In giving her person to a husband along with her money, would she be surrendering all her freedom too?

Were most men tyrants by nature? More to the point, was *he,* the Earl of Riverdale? It would be very easy to be beguiled by his looks. Not that she *was* beguiled by them. Quite the contrary, in fact. She had not wanted an obviously handsome man, not when she looked the way she did. It would be too horribly intimidating. The earl was more than good looking, though, more than handsome. He was perfection. But that was on the outside. What about on the inside? Was he a petty tyrant who would take her money and tuck her away somewhere out of sight and out of mind? But no. He had said just the opposite, and that was the whole trouble. He would not allow her to be a hermit.

I am occasionally told that I am the proverbial tall, dark, handsome man of fairy tales. It can be a burden. What had he meant by that – *a burden*?

Wren tossed her napkin onto the table and got to her feet. There was work awaiting her in her uncle's study, now hers. There were papers and reports from the glassworks, and since she was now the owner in more than just name, they demanded her immediate attention. She would decide later about the invitation. Perhaps she would simply send a polite refusal and retain her freedom and her money and her aches and longings and yearnings and disturbed nights and all the rest of her familiar life. There was some virtue in familiarity.

And perhaps, just perhaps, she would go.

. . . if you have the courage . . .

She looked almost vengefully down at the card beside her plate before snatching it up and taking it with her to the study.

It seemed a little embarrassing to Alexander as a single gentleman without either his mother or his sister in residence to act as his hostess that he was entertaining a group of his neighbors at an afternoon tea, of all things. However, if he was to give the guest of honor, so to speak, a chance to attend, he must consider both her single state and the distance she must travel, and an evening event would not be practical.

A number of his neighbors from the village and its immediate vicinity had already entertained him and had shown a flattering delight that he had come here and a cautious hope that he would make it his principal residence. The men had probed his interest in farming and horses and hunting and shooting and fishing. The ladies had been more interested in his views on parties and fetes and picnics and assemblies. The mothers had asked questions obviously designed to discover just how single he was, and their daughters had blushed and tittered and fluttered. He had found it all surprisingly heartwarming, considering the dreariness of Brambledean itself, and it really was time that he returned their hospitality with some of his own. A tea party was as good as anything, even if Miss Heyden did not come.

He had explained to those whom he had invited, a deliberate twinkle in his eye, that he wished them to see his drawing room in all its faded splendor so that in a few years' time, after he had done some renovations, they would be able to marvel at the transformation. The house was indeed faded and shabby, though it was not in quite as bad a condition as he had feared when he first knew he had been encumbered with it. The staff had been small when he came here and was still not much larger, but the butler and housekeeper, Mr and Mrs Dearing, husband and wife, had kept every room clean despite the Holland covers that had shrouded the furniture in the main rooms. Every surface that could gleam did so, and every faded curtain and piece of upholstery was at least dust free. There were a few structural issues – some crumbling chimneys, some damaged areas of the roof, some water seepage in the cellars, among other things, and the equipment in the kitchens was antiquated. The stables and paddocks were looking sad. Ivy had been allowed to run riot over walls.

A whole pile of money needed to be poured into the place before it could become the stately home it was meant to be, and a great deal needed to be done to make the park a worthy setting for such a grand edifice, but both could wait – and must despite the fact that they would offer employment to a large number of people who were currently unemployed or underemployed. There were more important things to be done first. The farms were not prospering, either in cultivated land or in live-stock or in buildings and equipment. Those who were employed to work them were suffering as a result. Their homes were hardly better than hovels and their wages had not been raised in ten years or more – when they had been paid at all, that was. Their children were poorly clothed and uned-ucated. Their wives tended to look haggard.

There were more than enough problems here to overwhelm him, but he had cast them all aside for one afternoon in order to host a tea party – which might, just possibly, lead to an ultimate solution to those very problems. That faint hope would come to nothing, of course, if Miss Heyden failed to come. But he was really not sure he wanted her to.

He had not warmed to her on the occasion of

his visit to Withington House, and it was not because of her looks. He had found her whole manner cold and . . . strange. Her veil and the shadowed part of the room in which she had sat without once getting to her feet had had him thinking a little hilariously of witches and witches' dens. And her marriage proposal had offended him. It had seemed all wrong, even outrageous. He had asked himself again on the long drive home in his curricle, of course, if he found it so because it was she who had offered, not he. Why would it be fine for him to make a proposal based almost entirely upon monetary considerations but was not for her? The admission that he was applying a double standard had done nothing to endear her more to him, however. She just did not seem *feminine* to him, whatever the devil that meant.

How wealthy *was* she, anyway? Very wealthy, according to her, but *very* was not a precise word, was it? He hated the fact that it mattered, that he might overlook all his misgivings about her personally if the money was sufficient. He hated what that fact suggested about him. He hoped she would not come. But a brief note arrived the day before the tea, accepting his invitation.

She was one of the last to arrive. There were eleven people already in the drawing room apart from Alexander himself, a few of them seated, most of them still on their feet, frankly looking around the room or out through the windows, all warmly cheerful and animated and happy to be there. One young lady had just executed a pirouette in the middle of the floor, her hands clasped to her bosom, and declared that the room would be *perfect* for an informal dance if only Lord Riverdale would consider using it as such. Her mother was just reproving her, but with a laughing look cast Alexander's way, when Dearing announced the twelfth guest, and Miss Heyden stepped past him and stood just inside the doorway. Alexander strode toward her, his hand outstretched, a smile on his face.

He had still been half hoping she would not come.

She was remarkably tall for a woman – only a couple of inches shorter than his own six foot one – and willowy and slender. She was doing nothing to minimize her height, as tall women tended to do. She held herself very erect and kept her chin high. She was dressed with simple elegance in a lavender high-waisted dress and a small-brimmed silver-gray bonnet with matching facial veil. A few of the other ladies had retained their bonnets too, so hers did not look totally out of place. The veil did, however. Her face was visible through it, but not the birthmark. She looked haughty and cold and remote, and it seemed to Alexander that the temperature of the room dropped a few degrees. Even her hand when she set it in the one he held out toward her – slender and long fingered – was chilly.

'How do you do, Lord Riverdale?' she said in

29

that low voice he remembered with its very precise diction.

'I am delighted you came, Miss Heyden,' he lied. 'Do you know any of my neighbors?' He was fully aware that she did not – he had been careful not to invite either Sweeney or Richman. 'Allow me to introduce you.'

Conversation in the room had all but hushed. That was partly understandable, of course. A new face was always of great interest to people who spent the bulk of their lives in the country with the same few friends and neighbors. Even more intriguing, though, was a face that ought to be at least partly familiar, since she lived no farther than eight miles or so away but was in fact not familiar at all. Of course, no one was seeing a new face even now. She did not raise the veil as Alexander took her about the room, introducing her to everyone as they went. He watched all his neighbors being polite to her but leaning back from her an almost imperceptible half inch or so, clearly disturbed by the anonymity of her appearance and the aloof arrogance of her manner despite the fact that she repeated their names and had a polite word for each of them.

There was something . . . *other* about her, Alexander thought. He could think of no more definite a word.

His neighbors resumed their hearty, good-humored conversation over the next hour and a half, during which time they were joined by the

remaining three guests. Clearly they were all gratified to have been invited and were happy to see
the inside of his home, to judge for themselves
how shabby it was, to see him in his own proper
milieu. They had come to please and be pleased,
to be amiable, to make a friend of him. Brambledean
Court and the Earl of Riverdale were, after all, at
the heart of their neighborhood, and his arrival
here had raised their hope of a more vivid, more
elevating social life than they had enjoyed for years,
or a whole lifetime in many cases. They sat or
stood and moved about freely while partaking of
the feast Mrs Mathers, Alexander's cook, had
produced with great enthusiasm and ingenuity
with her ancient equipment.

Miss Heyden sat in their midst the whole while.
At first, she was with the vicar and his wife and
a retired army colonel and his wife. Then others
took their place, clearly curious about her and
kind enough not to leave her isolated. She did not
move from the chair to which he had directed her
after introducing her to everyone. She was not
unsociable. She spoke when spoken to and listened
with a certain poise and grace. She sipped her tea
beneath her veil but ate nothing.

It was hard, Alexander discovered, not to be
aware of her at every moment. It would be unkind
to say that she was the one discordant note in an
otherwise warm and harmonious party. She was
not. But everyone who approached her somehow
became overhearty in her presence, and no one

stayed beside her for longer than a few minutes. It would have been inaccurate to describe her manner as cold. It was not. She was neither taciturn nor supercilious nor anything else a guest ought not to be. She was just . . . *other*. And it was the veil. Surely it was the veil. It all felt a bit like being at a party one of the guests had mistaken for a masquerade, and no one liked to tell her she had been mistaken. Everyone seemed a little embarrassed. Everyone made a point of not noticing the shrouded face.

One of his tenant farmers and his wife were the first to take their leave. It was the signal for everyone else, though most people seemed flatteringly reluctant to go.

'I took the liberty,' Alexander said when Miss Heyden too got to her feet, 'of having your carriage sent back to Withington, Miss Heyden. I shall do myself the honor of escorting you home in mine.'

She looked steadily at him through the veil before sitting again without a word of reply and clasping her hands loosely in her lap.

Alexander shook hands with all his departing guests, a long, slow process as each wished to thank him profusely for the invitation and the tea. Some asked him to pass on their compliments to the cook. A few hoped, as they had on previous occasions, that he would be remaining in the country and that they would see much more of him. One or two asked about Mrs Westcott, his mother, and about Lady Overfield, his sister. One tenant farmer thought the weather they had been having so far this spring boded well for the year's crops, while another, overhearing him, argued that a dry, warm spring often presaged a wet, cold summer and a poor harvest. The young lady who had performed a pirouette earlier repeated her hint that his lordship's drawing room would be quite divine for an informal dance. Her mother again told her to mind her manners. But finally they had all left and Alexander gave the order to have his carriage brought around.

Miss Heyden rose to her feet again when they were alone. 'You dismissed my carriage without consulting me, Lord Riverdale,' she said. It was a clear reproof.

He wished he had not done so. He would have been quite happy to see her on her way with the hope that he would never see her again. He would have liked her better, perhaps, if she had stamped her foot and thrown a tantrum. But her annoyance was perfectly controlled. He set his hands behind him and gazed steadily back at her. Good God, she was tall. He was unaccustomed to looking almost straight across into a woman's eyes – or what could be seen of her eyes through her veil.

'Miss Heyden,' he said, 'the last time we met you asked me to marry you. Do you not feel we ought to get to know each other somewhat better before deciding if it is what we both want? Unless, perhaps, you have already decided and wish to withdraw your offer. If that is indeed so, I shall send a maid to accompany you and an extra footman to sit up with my coachman.'

'I have not changed my mind,' she said. 'You are considering my proposal, then?'

'Considering it, yes,' he said reluctantly. 'I would be a fool not to. But I am sure neither one of us wishes to marry in haste only to repent at leisure, as the old saying goes. Shall we?' He gestured toward the doors. 'I believe I heard the carriage drawing up a moment ago.'

She came toward him and he opened one of the doors for her to pass through. As he followed her, he considered offering his arm but decided against it. It was a breach of gentlemanly manners unlike him, but there was something about her . . . It was as if she were surrounded by an invisible wall of ice. Though that was unfair. There was nothing definably icy in her demeanor. It was just . . . *other*. He had still not thought of the word for which his mind sought – if there was such a word.

He wondered suddenly if this tea had been her first social event ever. It seemed incredible when she was almost thirty. But . . . perhaps she really had been a total recluse until today. Perhaps all afternoon she had been terrified and holding herself together by pure force of will. He had challenged her to have the courage to come. Perhaps she had shown more courage than he could possibly imagine.

Perhaps she was that desperate to marry. Though *desperate* was an unkind word. *Eager*, then. Perhaps her wish to find someone to wed – to use her own phrase – took precedence over all else. The possibility made her seem more human and perhaps even a little more likable.

He offered a hand to help her into his carriage and was a bit surprised when she took it.

He had sent Maude home with her carriage. Perhaps as her presumptive betrothed he had not felt the necessity of observing the proprieties. *Was he her presumptive betrothed?* He had done and said nothing during that ghastly tea to suggest any such thing. There had been no hint to his neighbors, several of whom had been acquainted with her aunt and uncle and had commiserated with her on her loss and expressed pleasure at meeting her. None had really seemed delighted, though. But perhaps that was her fault. Undoubtedly it was, in fact.

It had been by far the worst afternoon of her life – since the age of ten anyway. She settled on the seat of Lord Riverdale's carriage, made room for him beside her, and longed for her own conveyance. She had been waiting for what seemed like forever but was actually less than two hours for the ordeal to be over so that she might collapse into it and close her eyes and feel the comfort of Maude's presence beside her. She could not do this. She simply could not. He was too male and too handsome and the world was too vast a place and too full of people.

She wanted to curl up into a ball, either on the seat or on the floor. She did not know how she was going to keep panic at bay for . . . How long did it take to travel eight miles? She could not think clearly.

'Will you lift your veil?' he asked her as the carriage moved away from the front doors.

Did he not *understand*? What she needed was an extra veil to throw over the first – to throw over the whole of herself. She wanted desperately to be alone. But there was no point in directing her anger against him. She was the one who had set this nightmare in motion. Was she going to draw back now? She had made the decision and had planned her course with cool deliberation. She raised her hands and lifted the veil back over the brim of her bonnet. But she turned her head slightly toward the window on her left side as she did so.

'Thank you,' he said. And, after a few silent moments, 'Have you always been a recluse, Miss Heyden?'

'No,' she said. 'As the owner of a thriving business, I do not merely sit at home all year long, gathering in the profits while other people make the plans and the decisions and do the work. I learned the business from my uncle and spent long hours with him at the workshop with the artisans and in the offices with the administrative and creative staff. I am a businesswoman in more than just name.'

Her uncle and aunt had indulged many of her whims and respected her basic freedom, but they had been very insistent that she be properly educated – something she had certainly not been to the age of ten. They had hired Miss Briggs, an elderly governess who had appeared to be a cuddly old dear. In some ways she was, but she had also imposed a challenging academic curriculum upon her pupil and not only encouraged excellence but somehow insisted upon it. Miss Briggs had also taught manners and deportment and elocution and social skills, like making polite conversation with strangers. She had finally been let go the day after Wren's eighteenth birthday with a comfortable pension and a small thatched cottage, to which Wren's uncle had gone to the expense of bringing her beloved sister from halfway across the country to live with her.

Wren's real education, though – or what she considered her real education – had come at the hands of her uncle himself. One day when she was twelve he had realized after taking her with him to the glassworks that a passion for his life's work had been sparked in her. *I could hardly get a word in edgewise all the way home,* he had told Aunt Megan later. *And I lost count of the number of questions she asked after the first thirty-nine. We have a young prodigy here, Meg.*

'Did you live with your aunt and uncle all your life until their passing?' the Earl of Riverdale asked.

'Since I was ten,' she said. 'My aunt took me to

his home in London – that was before he sold it – and they were married a week later.'

'You have his name,' he said.

'They adopted me,' she told him. She had not been sure it was a legal adoption until after her uncle's death, when she had found the certificate among his papers. Her father's signature had been upon it – a stomach-churning shock at the time.

There was another short silence. Perhaps he was waiting for a further explanation. 'You have a way,' he said at last, 'of turning your eyes toward me as you speak but not your face. It must be hard on your eyes. Will you not turn your head too? I saw the left side of your face when I visited you, and if you will recall, I did not run from the room screaming or grimace horribly or have a fit of the vapors.'

She wanted to laugh at the unexpectedness of his words, but turned her face toward him instead. Would she ever be able to do it with ease? But would there be another occasion? She was still not at all sure she wished to continue with this – or that he did.

'It really is not horrible, you know,' he said, after letting his eyes roam over her face. 'I can understand that it makes you self-conscious. I can understand that as a young lady you must lament what you consider a serious blemish to your looks. But it is not altogether unsightly. Anyone looking at you will of course notice it immediately. Some will even avoid any further acquaintance with you.

Those are people who do not deserve your regard anyway. Most people, however, will surely look and then *over*look. Though I noticed the first time and have noticed again now, I would be willing to wager that after seeing you a few more times I will not even see the blemish any longer. You will simply be you.'

Will, he had said, not *would*. He expected to see her again, then? She drew a slow breath. Her uncle used to say much the same thing as Lord Riverdale had just said. *What birthmark?* he used to say if ever it was referred to, and then he would pretend to start with surprise as he looked at her and noticed it. And sometimes he would ask her to look at him full face, and he would frown as he glanced from one side of her face to the other and say something like *Ah yes, the purple marks are on the left side. I could not remember.*

'And what about before you were ten?' the earl asked when she said nothing. 'Did your parents die?'

'My life began when I was ten, Lord Riverdale,' she said. 'I do not remember what came before.'

He looked steadily at her, a slight frown between his brows. He did not press the question further, however.

It was time to turn the tables on him, since it seemed she could not simply curl up in a ball on the floor and she would not give in to the panic that still clawed at her insides. 'And what about your life before you inherited your title?' she asked. She knew some basic facts, but not details.

'It was a dull but happy life – dull to talk about, happy enough to live,' he told her. 'I had both parents until seven years ago, and I have one sister, of whom I am dearly fond. Not all people are so fortunate in their siblings. My father was devoted to his hounds and his horses and the hunt. He was hearty and well liked, and rather impecunious, I am afraid. It took me a good five years after his passing to set Riddings Park on a firm financial footing again. By that time my sister had been released from an unfortunate marriage by the untimely passing of her husband and was living with my mother and me again, and I was settling into the life I expected to continue with very few changes until my demise. There was only one slight bump of unease on my horizon, and that was the fact that I was heir to a twenty-year-old boy earl, who could not be expected to marry and produce an heir of his own for a number of years. But it seemed a slight worry. Harry was a healthy and basically decent lad. You took the trouble to learn some facts about me. You no doubt know exactly what happened to bring my worries to fruition.'

'The young earl's father had married his mother bigamously,' she said, 'with the result that the earl was illegitimate and no longer eligible for the title. It passed to you instead. What was – or is – your relationship to him?'

'Second cousin,' he said. 'Harry and I share a great-grandfather, the venerable Stephen Westcott, Earl of Riverdale.'

'You did not want the title?' she asked.

'Why would I?' he asked in return. 'It brought me duties and responsibilities and headaches in return for the dubious distinction of being called *Earl of Riverdale* and *my lord* instead of plain Alexander Westcott, which I always thought a rather distinguished name.'

Many men would have killed for such a title, she thought, even without a fortune to go with it. She was intrigued to discover that it meant little to him. The deference, even awe, with which his neighbors had treated him during tea was clearly not important to him. He would rather be back at his precious Riddings Park, where his life had been dull but happy enough, to use his own description.

Before she met him she had expected him to be a toplofty, conceited aristocrat – that was why he had been third on her list instead of first. She had expected it even more when she first set eyes upon him.

She realized suddenly how very alone they were in the close confines of his carriage, and she felt again all her unease at his gorgeous masculinity. For it was not just his perfect looks. There was something else about him that somehow caught at the breath in her throat and wrapped about her in an invisible but quite suffocating way. It was something she had never experienced before – but how could she have done?

'Did you ever consider marriage before you inherited the title?' she asked him.

He raised his eyebrows but did not answer immediately. 'I did,' he said.

'And did you have anyone specific in mind?' She hoped the answer was no.

'No,' he said, and she did not believe he was lying.

'What were you looking for?' she asked him. 'What sort of . . . qualities?' It was none of her business, of course, and his answer – if he did answer, that was – could only bring her pain or discomfort. He would hardly say he had been searching for a reclusive, awkward beanpole of a woman with a ruined face and an unladylike involvement in business – and almost thirty years old, could he?

'None in particular,' he said. 'I merely hoped to meet someone with whom I might expect to be comfortable.'

It seemed a strange answer from a man who looked as he did and had had so much to offer before he inherited Brambledean. 'You did not look for love?' she asked him. 'Or beauty?'

'I hoped for affection in my marriage, certainly,' he said. 'But beauty as an end in itself? There are many kinds of beauty, many of them not immediately apparent.'

'And could you be comfortable with me?' she asked him. 'Could you ever feel affection for me?' She would not ask, of course, if he could ever find her beautiful.

He gazed at her for so long that she had to make

a very concerted effort not to turn her face away. Would this dreadful afternoon never end? 'I can only be honest with you, Miss Heyden,' he said at last. 'I do not know.'

Well, she had asked for it. Had she expected him to lie? At least he had been gentleman enough to give a diplomatic answer. If this journey did not end soon, she would surely scream. But she could not leave it alone. 'My money would come at too high a price?' she asked.

'There is great pain behind those words,' he said. 'It is your pain that makes me hesitate, Miss Heyden.'

She felt a little as though he had punched her in the stomach with a closed fist, so unexpected was his answer. What did he know about pain? Specifically *her* pain? 'It is too unattractive a quality?' she asked with as much hauteur as she could muster. She turned her head away.

'Oh no,' he said. 'Quite the contrary.'

She frowned in incomprehension. But he did not explain and there was no chance for further questions. At last, *at last,* the distance between Brambledean and Withington had been covered and his carriage was drawing to a halt outside her own door.

'May I call again?' he asked her.

She would have been a fool to allow it. She opened her mouth to say no. Her emotions were so raw she felt as though she had real, physical wounds. The privacy of her room still felt a million

43

miles away. But the whole of her future life might be hanging in the balance – in the simple difference between *yes* and *no*.

Ah, this scheme of hers had seemed so full of hope and possibility when she had concocted it. How could she even have imagined that it was possible?

'Yes,' she said as she saw the coachman outside her door, waiting to open it on a signal from his employer.

CHAPTER 3

The thing was, Alexander thought as he made the same journey four days later, that old dreams had an annoying habit of lingering long after they had no practical place in his life.

He was not made for dreams, for he had always felt compelled to put duty and responsibility before personal inclination, and the two were not compatible. He had put away dreams almost seven years ago when his father died. He had worked tirelessly to set things to rights at Riddings Park even though he had been a very young man at the time. He had made the mistake of reviving those dreams a year or so ago when Riddings was finally prospering, but then he had had to start all over again with Bramblcdean Court.

This time, however, the task was far more daunting. There were people's lives and livelihoods at stake. And the only way he could do it was by marrying for money. He had tried to think of other ways, but there were none. Any mortgage or loan would have to be repaid. Any hope of winning a large fortune at the races or the tables would be risky, to say the least. It might just as easily yield a huge loss. No, marriage it would have to be.

The dream, when he had allowed himself to indulge in it, had been the eternal one of the young and hopeful, he supposed – that vision of something more vividly wonderful and magical than anyone else had ever experienced, the grand passion and romance that had inspired the world's most memorable poetry. It was a bit embarrassing to remember now. He probably would not have found any such love anyway. But there lingered even now a yearning for something different from what he could expect, some . . . passion. It was not to be, however. Life had other plans for him.

He gazed out at the flowering hedgerows, at the trees whose leaves were still a bright spring green, at the blue sky dotted with fluffs of white cloud, at the sun warming everything below but with the freshness of spring rather than the more somnolent heat of summer. He could smell the good nature smells of the countryside through the open window, and he could hear birds singing above the crunching sound of the carriage wheels and the clopping of the horses' hooves. Life was good despite everything. He must remember that. One could easily miss its blessings when one wallowed in what might have been. Dreams were all very well in their place, but they must never be allowed to encroach upon reality.

He had been planning to go to London before Easter, though the parliamentary session and the accompanying social Season would not begin until after. The Season was often known as the great marriage mart, and he had planned to shop there this year for a rich wife – ghastly thought, ghastly terminology, ghastly reality. As though ladies were commodities. But all too often they were. He could expect to succeed. He was, after all, a peer of the realm and young. There was, of course, his relative poverty, but it really was only *relative*. A little over a year ago he had been Mr Westcott of Riddings Park, a prosperous eligible bachelor. He had been dreading the marriage mart. Was it possible he could be spared the ordeal by finding a wealthy wife even before he got there?

He still did not know exactly why he was making this journey. And why did distances always seem to shorten when one did not particularly want to reach one's destination? he wondered as the carriage turned onto the driveway to Withington House. Perhaps he ought not to have come again. There was something about Miss Heyden that repelled him. It was not her face. She could not help that, and he fully believed what he had told her, that he would soon become so accustomed to the birthmark that he would no longer notice it. It was not her height either, though the fact that she must have been close to six feet tall might have daunted many men. He was taller. No, it had nothing to do with her appearance.

What repelled him was, paradoxically, the very thing that had brought him back here. Her pain. It was very carefully guarded. It was veiled more heavily than her face was, in fact. It was encased in a coolly poised manner. But it screamed at him from the very depths of her, and he was both horrified and fascinated. He was horrified because he did not want to get drawn into it and because he suspected the pain could engulf her if her poise ever slipped. He was compelled by her, though, because she was human and he had been blessed or cursed with a compassion for human suffering.

But here he was, regardless of all the thoughts and doubts that had teemed through his mind and prevented him from properly enjoying his surroundings. It was too late now not to come. She would probably have heard his arrival, though he was not expected specifically today, and a groom was already coming from the stables. Perhaps she was out, though it seemed unlikely when she was a recluse.

She was not out. She was not in the drawing room either. She came to him there a couple of minutes after he had been shown in, her gray dress looking old and a bit rumpled, her hair twisted up into a simple and rather untidy knot high on the back of her head, her right cheek a bit flushed – and yes, he could see that detail because she wore no veil. She seemed a little breathless, a little bright eyed, and for the first time it struck him that she was more than coldly beautiful. She was rather pretty.

'Lord Riverdale,' she said.

'I beg your pardon,' he said. 'I have taken you by surprise. Is this an inconvenient time?'

'No.' She came across the room and offered him her hand. 'I was in the study adding up a long column of figures. I shall have to start again when I go back, but that is my fault for not subdividing the column and adding one section at a time. I did not expect that you would come again, and I was so engrossed that I did not even hear your arrival. I hope I have not kept you waiting too long.'

'Not at all.' He took her hand in his and let his gaze linger on her. He had clearly surprised her, and it was taking her a few moments to don her accustomed armor. It was happening, though, before his eyes. Her breathing was being brought under control. The color was receding from her cheek and the sparkle from her eyes. Her manner was becoming cooler and more poised. It was a telling transformation.

Her eyes fell to their hands, and she removed her own. 'Well?' she said. 'Did you notice today?'

That she was not wearing a veil? But then he realized what she meant – *though I noticed the last time and notice again now, I would be willing to wager that after seeing you a few more times I will not even see the blemish any longer.* 'Yes, I did,' he said. 'But it is only the third time I have seen you. I have still not recoiled, however, or run screaming from the room.'

'Perhaps,' she said, 'you are very desperate for my money.'

He drew a slow breath before allowing himself to reply. 'And perhaps, Miss Heyden,' he said, 'I

49

will take my leave and allow you to start adding from the top of that column again.'

The color had flooded back into her cheek. 'I beg your pardon,' she said. 'I ought not to have said that.'

'Why *did* you?' he asked her. 'Do you value yourself so little that you believe only your money gives you any worth at all?'

She was taking the question seriously, he could see. She was thinking about it. 'Yes,' she said.

It was the moment at which he really ought to have taken his leave. It was a devastating answer, and it had not even been given in haste. He could not possibly take on such brokenness, even if she had all the riches in the world to offer. Good God, all because of an unsightly birthmark?

'What *happened* to you?' he asked her, but he held up a staying hand even as he spoke the words. 'No. I have no right to an answer. But I will *not* marry you for your money alone, Miss Heyden. If you truly believe that you have no more to offer than that, and if you truly believe that I have nothing but marriage to offer in exchange for your money, then say so now and we will put an end to this. I will take my leave and you need never see me again.'

She took a long time answering. She receded even further inside the cool shell of herself, becoming seemingly taller, thinner, more poised, more austere – good God, the woman really did not need a veil except to hide the birthmark. She could hide quite effectively in plain sight. He felt chilled, repelled again. He willed her to say the word, and he prayed she would not.

'I think,' she said at last, 'you are a good man, Lord Riverdale. I think you deserve and . . . need more than I could possibly offer. You have been put in a desperate situation, made worse by the fact that you have a conscience. I cannot bring you anything *but* money. Go and find someone else – with my sincere good wishes.'

Good God!

She even stepped to one side, her hands clasped at her waist, to give him a clear path to the door.

He drew another slow breath and allowed it out and drew another before he said anything. *And why did he not just go?* 'Do you ever step outdoors?' he asked her. 'It is a beautiful spring day out there, even warm in a fresh sort of way. And you have what looks like a sizable and pretty garden. Come and walk there with me, and we will leave behind this tense drama we have been enacting and talk about the weather and the flowers and what is pleasant and meaningful in our lives. We will get to know each other a little better.'

She never said anything in haste, this woman. She regarded him in silence for several moments before answering. 'I shall go fetch a shawl and bonnet,' she said at last, 'and change my shoes.'

It was indeed a lovely day. Wren stood at the foot of the steps outside the front door, lifted her face to the sky, and inhaled deeply.

'Is it not a strange thing,' he said, 'that we need all the dreary rain we get in these often soggy British Isles in order to be able to enjoy the lush beauty of gardens like this?'

'I have seen pictures of lands that get almost no rain,' she said. 'Parched vegetation or outright desert. Yet even that appears to have a sort of beauty of its own. Our world is made up of such contrasts, as is life itself. Perhaps we could never enjoy this if there were not also that, or here if there were not also there, or now if there were not also then.'

'Or a perfect right side of a face if there were not also a blemished left,' he said.

She turned toward him in astonishment. He was smiling, and his eyes were laughing. But instead of being offended by his words, she was . . . arrested. *'Perfect?'* she said.

'You must have been told that before,' he said.

She had not. But then very few people had seen her. She did not like the direction this conversation was taking. 'Come and see the daffodil bank,' she said, turning to her right and striding diagonally across the south lawn.

Her governess had expended much time and effort upon teaching her to take mincing ladylike little steps, and she *had* learned. She had not marched into the drawing room at Brambledean a few days ago, for example. But she still strode almost everywhere, especially when she was outdoors, her long legs moving in easy rhythm.

He walked comfortably beside her. She did not know many men. She did not know many *people*, for that matter. But most men she had met were shorter than she. Her uncle had been a whole head shorter. The Earl of Riverdale was a few inches taller, a fact that must put him over six feet.

She really had not expected him to come again, even though he had asked if he might. He had mentioned no specific day and that had seemed significant to her. She wished she were dressed a little more becomingly, but she had scorned to keep him waiting while she changed and restyled her hair. Besides, she was wearing a bonnet now.

'That is a rose arbor beside the house?' he asked, nodding in its direction.

'Yes,' she said. 'My aunt's creation and pride and joy. She loved her garden, and her garden loved her. I could plant a row of flower seeds at the correct distance from each other and at the correct depth and time of year. I could cover them carefully with soil and water them diligently – and never see them again. In the end I suggested an equitable division of labor. She would plant and I would enjoy.'

'Do you miss her?' he asked. 'And your uncle? How long exactly has it been?'

'Fifteen months,' she said. 'I thought the pain would grow duller with the passing of time. Then I thought that once my year of mourning was over and I put off my blacks, I would also put off the worst of my grief. And perhaps that has happened.

But sometimes I think that grief is preferable to emptiness. At least grief is *something*. I have come to realize, I suppose, that they are not just dead. They are *gone*. There is nothing there where they were.'

They had walked through the copse of trees and crossed the humpbacked stone bridge, which five years ago had replaced a battered old wooden one over the stream that bubbled downhill and that she could watch and listen to for hours when she was alone. And they came to the top of the long slope that formed the western boundary of the garden. A week or two ago it had been thickly carpeted with golden daffodils and their bright green leaves. Some of them had died back, but there was still an impressive display.

'The rose arbor is lovely in the summer,' she said, 'but I have always had a preference for the bank here in spring. The daffodils grow wild.'

'And you prefer wildness to cultivation?' he asked her.

'Perhaps,' she said. 'I had not thought about it that way. But there could not possibly be a lovelier flower than the daffodil. A golden trumpet of hope.' She felt decidedly silly then. *Golden trumpet of hope*, indeed.

'Can we go down?' he asked.

'Yes,' she said. 'They look even lovelier from down there.'

He offered his hand. She hesitated. She did not need assistance. She had been up and down this bank a thousand times. She had sat in the midst of the daffodils, hugging her knees. She had lain among them, arms spread wide, feeling the earth spin beneath her and watching the sky wheel overhead. But if she was going to marry him – and that was a large *if* on both their parts, it seemed – she was going to have to grow accustomed to his acting the gentleman. Miss Briggs had taught her all about the little details of gentility – how a gentleman was expected to behave toward a lady, how she was expected to behave toward him. She set her hand in his and it closed warmly and firmly about her own as they made their sedate way down, making her feel almost dainty, almost feminine. She usually half ran down the slope. Sometimes she even flapped her arms like wings and shrieked. Would not he be scandalized . . .

Perhaps, she thought when they had reached the bottom, their backs almost touching the rustic wooden boundary fence, gazing upward – her hand was still in his – perhaps if she wore yellow, or green, or some color other than the gray or the lavender of half mourning, she would recover her spirits more quickly. Perhaps the emptiness would seem less empty. Could the color one wore affect one's spirit?

'You were very fond of them,' he said.

He was talking about her uncle and aunt again. She knew it was not just idle chatter. She knew he was trying to get to know her. He would probably want her to get to know him too. She had not thought of that in advance. She had somehow expected to choose a man almost upon instinct alone, with just a little research and very little personal acquaintance, make her offer, be accepted, marry him, and . . . And what? Live happily ever after? No, she was not that foolish. She just wanted to be married. All the way married. She wanted the physical things, and she wanted children. Plural, very definitely plural. She had not given much if any thought to getting to know her chosen husband, to allowing him to get to know her. It was almost as though she had expected their lives as a couple to begin on the day they met. No outside world. No histories. No baggage.

It would not be like that. Not with him, anyway. *I will not marry you for your money alone, Miss Heyden.* He had not ruled out marrying her. He had not even said that he would not marry her for her money. But he would not marry her *just* for the money. Which really meant that he would not marry her at all.

Do you value yourself so little . . .

'They were my life and my salvation,' she told him. 'I knew we would lose my uncle. He was eighty-four years old, and his heart was weak and his breathing was sometimes labored. He did not take to his bed as often as many men in his condition would have done, and he never complained. He was still more active than perhaps he ought to have been and his mind was still sharp. But he had slowed down considerably, and we were all

56

aware that the end was approaching. It would have been dreadfully sad, and I would have mourned him for a long time. But it would have been . . . What is the word? Acceptable? Everyone in the natural course of things loses elderly relatives. No one lives forever. But Aunt Megan's death just before his was so sudden, so totally unexpected that—' She swallowed but could not go on. She did not need to, however. Her meaning was clear, and his grip on her hand tightened in obvious sympathy.

'I beg your pardon,' she said. 'I am not the only person who has ever lost loved ones. You too have lost people you loved.'

'My father,' he said. 'He frequently exasperated me. He lived his life upon far different principles from my own. He lived to enjoy life, and enjoy it he did. Perhaps it was not until after his death that I realized just how much I had loved him – and how much he had loved me.'

By unspoken consent they began to climb the hill again, picking their way among the daffodils so as not to crush any of them.

'Your aunt was elderly too?' he asked.

'Oh, not at all,' she said. 'She was fifty-four. She was thirty-five when she took me to call upon the man who would become my uncle at his home in London. She went there to ask if he would help her find employment. She had once worked for him as companion to his first wife, who was an invalid for many years. He married Aunt Megan

57

a week later and we went to live with him. They were happy. They shared their happiness with me and adopted me. I was the most blessed of mortals. I still am. He left me a vast fortune, Lord Riverdale. You will be entitled to know how vast, of course, if you decide to take matters further between us.'

She was aware that she had left more questions unanswered than explained. He had every right, she supposed, to ask those questions, but she hoped he would not. They were standing on the bridge, looking down at the gurgling water, and she slid her hand free when she realized it was still clasped in his. She drew the edges of her shawl together. It was chillier here in the shade of the trees.

'There is something soothing about the sound of water, is there not?' he said, and she knew he was not going to ask any of those questions. 'And the sight of it.'

'Yes, there is,' she said. 'I love coming here even when the daffodils are not in bloom. There is the illusion of seclusion and serenity here. Or perhaps it is not an illusion. Perhaps it is real. What happened to your young cousin who lost his title to you last year?'

'Harry?' He turned his head to look at her briefly. 'He is out in the Peninsula fighting the armies of Napoleon Bonaparte as a lieutenant with the 95th Foot Regiment, also known as the Rifles. He claims to be enjoying the experience enormously, though he has been wounded a few times and is a constant source of worry to his mother and sisters. I would have expected no less of the boy, however. He was always full of energy and enthusiasm for life and is not the type to whine or grow bitter over circumstances that are beyond his control. Nevertheless, he must have had the stuffing knocked out of him. The changes to my life are nothing compared with the changes to his – plus the knowledge that his father deceived his mother in the worst possible way and callously caused his illegitimacy and his sisters'. I feel guilty about the outcome, as though I am somehow partly to blame for their misery. I would have refused the title if I could. Unfortunately, it was not possible.'

'And his sisters?' she asked.

'Camille and Abigail,' he told her. 'They went to live with their maternal grandmother in Bath. Camille chose to teach at the orphanage where Anna grew up – their father's only legitimate child, now the Duchess of Netherby, that is – and she married the art teacher last summer. He is also a portrait painter of some renown and came into an unexpected inheritance last year. The two of them are now living in a large manor in the hills above Bath, running a retreat house that offers quiet study time and classes in a wide range of subjects, from dancing to drama to painting to writing. It offers guest lectures and concerts and plays. Sometimes the children from the orphanage go there for picnics and parties. They have two adopted children, and one of their own is imminent. Camille has been a huge surprise to us all. There was no lady more proper or high in the instep – or, frankly, more hard to like – than she was as Lady Camille Westcott.'

'The disaster that happened to her, then, was actually a blessing?' she said.

'I do believe it was,' he agreed, 'though it seems almost heartless to say so. Her mother at first went to live with her brother, who is a clergyman in Dorsetshire, but now she has been persuaded to move back to her old home in Hampshire with Abigail, the younger sister. Hinsford Manor actually belongs to Anna, and it is at her request that the ladies have moved there. They are all still trying to come to terms with the changes in their lives, I suspect, as are the rest of the members of the Westcott family. Sometimes I feel very helpless.'

'But are you not doing the very same thing?' she asked. 'Are you not indeed one of the central figures in the turmoil?'

'The one who would appear to have benefited most,' he said. 'I often fear Harry and his mother and sisters must hate me, though to be fair they have never shown any open resentment.'

'Does the rest of the family support them?' she asked. 'Or have they been shunned?'

'Oh, never that,' he said. 'The Westcotts have rallied around – the dowager countess, my father's first cousin, and her three daughters and their families. Then there is the Duke of Netherby, whose father made a second marriage with one of the Westcott daughters. The present Netherby was

Harry's guardian until his twenty-first birthday recently. It was he who purchased Harry's commission. And there are my mother and my sister. At first, however, Cousin Viola – the former countess – and her daughters and Harry were not willing to accept any sort of support from the Westcott family. Cousin Viola felt strongly the fact that her marriage had never been valid and that therefore she was in no way related to any of us. She even calls herself by her maiden name of Kingsley. And Camille and Abigail felt their illegitimacy keenly and chose to lick their wounds in private for a while. There will, by the way, be a written test on all these family connections when we return to the house.'

She turned her face toward him and smiled. She liked his occasional flashes of humor. 'But it would be too easy to pass with flying colors,' she said. 'You have not told me the names of all the Westcotts and their spouses and children.'

'First names, last names, and title names?' he said. 'You would need a week to study.'

Wren led the way off the bridge, and they walked side by side through the copse and back out onto the lawn. She took him toward the rose arbor, though there was not much to see there this early in the year. He had been very forthcoming with her. She had offered little in return.

'My uncle was from a small family,' she said, 'and outlived those there were. He had no children with either his first wife or Aunt Megan. They were both kind enough to tell me I was all the children they could ever want.' She could almost see him debating with himself whether to ask about her aunt's connections. His face was turned toward her, though she deliberately did not look back. 'In the summer,' she added before he could speak again, 'I could find the rose arbor with my eyes closed if ever I should be foolish enough to try. Even I have to admit that roses have all the advantage over daffodils when it comes to fragrance.'

They kept the conversation away from personal topics for the rest of his visit. He did not reenter the house with her when they returned there but took his leave, assuring her that he did not need to have his carriage drawn up to the front doors.

He did not mention seeing her again.

She watched him stride off toward the stables and wished foolishly that she was normal. She was not – normal, that was. She knew it even though she had nothing much with which to compare herself except perhaps the ladies, young and not so young, who had been at his tea – amiable, smiling, laughing, talking on a dozen different topics, totally at their ease. But if she were normal, she would not have met him, would she?

Did she want to see him again? She had the strange feeling that she could be hurt if she pursued the acquaintance. She had not thought of that, had she?

Oh, she *wished* she were normal. But, alas, she was as she was.

CHAPTER 4

After spending a whole day deliberating and changing his mind and changing it back and then changing it once more, Alexander sent off an invitation to Miss Heyden to come to Brambledean alone. It was not quite proper. It was not proper at all, in fact. But there was no point in trying to organize another social event to make her coming more acceptable. He would not get to know her that way. And he needed to know her if he was to give serious consideration to marrying her.

They had made a start at Withington. It was not nearly enough, but it was a start. He wondered if she knew exactly what she would be getting into if indeed she purchased him as a husband. He needed to know what *he* would be getting into. The idea of being bought was repellent to him, to say the least.

She came to Brambledean two days later, bringing her maid for propriety's sake. It was a gloomy, blustery day, a fact that ought not to have mattered for as long as they remained indoors, but did. The maid was taken to the servants' quarters, and he showed Miss Heyden about the house. Shabby, unlived-in rooms looked even more gloomy with heavy gray clouds beyond the windows. He showed her all of it – the ancient library to which no new book had been added for half a century or more, or if one had, Alexander had not discovered it yet. He showed her the visitor salons and offices, all on the ground floor. He bypassed the drawing room on the first floor, since she had seen it already, but showed her the so-called music room next to it, though there was not a single musical instrument there. He even showed her all the rooms for which there was no specific description, as well as the dining room and the ballroom, in which it was doubtful anyone had danced for a century. He showed her some of the guest chambers and the portrait gallery on the second floor. The gallery was sadly out-of-date, and all the paintings and their heavy frames were in dire need of cleaning and restoration. He took her down to the kitchens, where Mrs Dearing and Mrs Mathers said nothing about the many deficiencies of equipment that had not been updated in goodness knew how long.

They tramped about the inner stretches of the park to the west of the house, though he gave her the option of staying indoors and taking tea in the drawing room. She had brought a heavy cloak with her and wore stout walking shoes. She also wore a bonnet, which she had kept on indoors, the veil pulled down over her face, presumably for the benefit of servants she did not know. She glanced about her as they walked, not saying a great deal, and she turned frequently to look at the house from various vantage points. She was looking critically, he could see – at the roof, at the chimneys, at the ivy on the walls. Her eyes moved to the stables and carriage house. The park was vast, not quite wild, but failing to please either as a cultivated garden or as a deliberate piece of unspoiled wilderness. It was not the sort of space in which one felt drawn to stroll for relaxation.

'It is shabby and neglected,' he said, 'though the gardeners work long hours and do the best they can. There are just not enough of them.' And there was not enough money to hire more, he might have added, though that must be obvious to her.

'Tell me about the farms, the crops, the livestock, the laborers,' she said. 'How progressive are the methods used here?'

They were brisk, businesslike questions, matched by her manner. She was studying everything with an appraising eye, he realized, and listening with an attentive ear. She was, in fact, interviewing him – as she had every right to do. He would not have invited her here, after all, if he had not been considering her offer, and she would not have come if the offer had already been withdrawn. He would have expected to have this sort of meeting and to answer these sorts of questions with the father of any lady for whom he offered, though not with the bride herself. It felt strange and wrong, and deuced embarrassing, even humili-ating. But there was no reason why she should not do business on her own account. She was obvi-ously intelligent, and just as obviously she saw no reason to hide it, to simper and gaze at him with wide, worshipful eyes and pretend to be helpless. Picturing her behaving that way was a bit amusing, in fact.

'It is a Herculean task that faces me,' he said at last. 'Do you wonder I did not want the title?'

'No, I do not,' she said. 'But you have it and that is that. I can see that you have a clear choice to make. You can either go away from here and forget all about it while your steward does his best – or his worst – to keep things rolling along as they have for many years past. Or you can marry a rich wife. But I know that with you it is no real choice at all, for you are a man with a conscience. I suspect it is not so much the house and park or even the farms that concern you, but the people involved. Actually, I more than suspect. So a rich wife it must be. But even in that you are hampered by your conscience. You could have seized the offer I made you ten days or so ago, despite my appear-ance, and thus have solved all your problems. But you could not do that. You would not – will not – marry me unless I know exactly what I am facing. Now I believe I do. And you will not marry me unless you can be sure that you can at least respect me. Do you? Respect me, that is?'

She was the strangest woman he had ever known,

and that was a vast understatement. She was the strangest person of either gender, actually. She was so very direct in her speech and manner that there was no hiding from her; there was no social smoothing of edges, no gentle way of being tactful. But he was irritated by the fact that she was frank and open about business but entirely closed up about herself.

'Miss Heyden,' he said, coming to a stop beneath a huge old oak tree and setting his back against the trunk while he folded his arms over his chest. 'My motive for considering marriage with you is perfectly obvious. But what about yours for marrying me? You appear to have everything you could possibly need, including that rare commodity for a woman – independence. Why give it all up to a virtual stranger? You told me you wished to be wed. But to just anybody? And will you please pull back your veil?'

She hesitated and then did so. He had felt that he was talking with a mirage, he realized. Now at least she looked human. 'I have grown up with a strong sense of myself as a person,' she said. 'My uncle and aunt are largely responsible for that. In addition to providing me with a strict governess, who instructed me in everything both academic and social that a lady ought to know, my uncle exposed me to all the work of running a prosperous and successful business, and my aunt encouraged both him and me. Although in many ways the bottom fell out of my world a little over a year ago, I was able to stop myself from tumbling to the depths of despair by taking the reins of the business into my own hands. I am very much in charge of it even when I am here in the country, though I have a competent manager.

'Most women, in contrast, grow up to acquire a sense of themselves as *women*. They see themselves in the expected roles of daughter, wife, mother, and hostess, devoted to the care of the men in their lives and of their dependent children. I suspect many if not most of them never really see themselves as *persons*, though I suppose some must. My aunt did, even though she took upon herself the roles of wife and mother and performed them consummately well and was very happy for the last eighteen or nineteen years of her life. If I must choose between being a person and being a typical woman of our times, Lord Riverdale, I would choose personhood without hesitation. Having experienced it, I could not easily give it up. But why can I not be both? This is what I have asked myself recently. Why can I not be a woman as well as a person? Why cannot I marry?'

He remained as he was and looked at her for long moments after she paused, her eyebrows raised, awaiting his reply. She stood a few feet away in the sunshine, tall and slender, proud, chin raised, making no further attempt to hide her face. Yes, he thought, that was what it was about her he had been unable to define thus far. She was not typically feminine. She was more a person than a woman – a strange thought he would have to ponder at his leisure. And yet . . . could she not be both? Could a woman with a strong sense of herself as a person not also be as attractive as her peers who had been raised for marriage and motherhood – and dependence?

'What if I – or another man – turned out to be different from what you expected?' he asked Miss Heyden. 'What if I were as you see me now when I am sober but turned ugly when I had been drinking and turned that ugliness upon my wife and children?' It had happened to his sister, though there had been no children.

She considered the question. 'Life is fraught with risks,' she said. 'All we can do to guard against them is make considered choices. Or we can make no choices at all and remain static in life. Even that is not really possible or without danger, though. Life changes about us and for us whether we wish it or not. I did not wish for my uncle and aunt to die. You did not wish to inherit all this.' She gestured about her with both hands.

'But if you make the wrong choice of husband,' he said, 'you will have lost everything – your independence, your money, your happiness.'

'Oh, no, Lord Riverdale,' she said. 'I would not turn all my money over to you with my person on our marriage. I am not an utter fool, or a fool at all. We would both sign a carefully worded contract before we wed.'

Sometimes he found her chilling. *Often* he found

her chilling. But would he be feeling so chilled if this were a man speaking? Her father or uncle or guardian? And what did it say about him that the answer was no? He would expect to negotiate and sign a marriage settlement with a prospective father-in-law, after all. He would expect that man to guard the future interests of his daughter.

'You would keep hold of the purse strings, then?' he asked her. 'And dole out money as you saw fit?'

'Absolutely not.' She turned and began to make her way back toward the house with her characteristic manly – though somehow not inelegant – stride. 'How would I be able to tolerate a marriage in which I had made my husband my pensioner or my slave? I would not, just as I would not be able to tolerate one in which I had been made my husband's slave. No man would marry me if I did not have money and lots of it, Lord Riverdale, but I have no wish whatsoever to buy a husband and then hold him in thrall for the rest of his life.'

They proceeded some distance in silence. 'You have explained that you wish to marry because you want to be a woman as well as a person,' he said. 'What does being a woman mean to you, Miss Heyden?' It was perhaps an unfair question. He would not have dreamed of asking it of anyone else. But she was different from every other woman he had met, and he was, God help him, considering marrying her.

70

She drew a breath, let it go, drew another. 'I want to be kissed,' she said primly, on her dignity. 'I know almost nothing of what lies beyond kisses. But I want it. All of it. And I want a child. Children. I received warmth and love in abundance from my aunt and uncle, but perversely I longed for other children. Siblings. Friends. Now everything has gone with them. I want human warmth again, but I want more than warmth this time. I want . . . Well, I do not know quite how else to put it into words. I am naive and probably sound pathetic, but you asked the question, and you have the right to an answer.'

'Yes,' he said. 'Thank you.'

Baldly put, she wanted sex. She had decided to buy what she wanted, in the belief that she could not have it any other way because of that damned facial blemish. A man could buy it easily enough whenever he wished without also saddling himself with marriage. But she was not a man despite the fact that she was a proud, wealthy businesswoman. Besides, it was not only sex she wanted. It was human warmth in the form of a sexual relationship. She wanted far more than she seemed to realize. She wanted love, and, heaven help her, she thought it could be bought.

He felt chilled – again. How could he possibly offer her a fair exchange for what she would bring him? He could appreciate her beauty and elegance despite the blemish, and he could admire her independence and intelligence. But . . . where was

71

the attraction? He could feel none. She wanted to be kissed. Even that he could not imagine doing.

'Where do we go from here, Lord Riverdale?' she asked as they approached the house. 'You have seen me. I have seen your house and part of the park and learned something of your whole estate. We have conversed and become somewhat acquainted. Will it now be your turn to visit me and then mine to come here again? Time is of value. We will both need to get on with the job of finding other partners if we are not to find them in each other. Is there some point to proceeding, or is there not?'

So she was going to press the issue, was she? But she was quite right about time. When he had come here, to see how his new steward was settling, to assess with him what needed doing and what might be done with his limited resources and what must be given highest priority, he had intended to stay only until the end of this week. He had planned then to go to London, where his mother and sister were to join him for Easter. But he had already made the decision to delay his departure until next week, after Easter, and had written to his mother. He had even added that he was not quite sure about next week. He had not explained the reason because he had not known if it was one worth sharing. He had written something vague about the press of business, and in a sense he had not been lying. It was his business to marry a wife who would give him heirs and bring him funds. It was a ghastly way to look upon his own future and that of the young lady he would marry, and for a moment he was engulfed in self-loathing.

'Miss Heyden,' he said, coming to an abrupt halt with her at the foot of the steps to the front doors and noticing irrelevantly that there was grass pushing up through the seams between each rise. 'There must be affection or the hope of some sort of affectionate regard. I will not call it love. That is for poets and dreamers. But there must be . . . affection. I cannot stomach the prospect of a marriage without. Is there any remote chance that there can be affection between us?' He could not imagine it for himself, but what about her? And if her answer was yes, was he willing to try to match her hope?

'It is what I meant by human warmth,' she said. 'I do not know if it is possible between us. I am well aware of our differing perspectives. I look at you and see extraordinary beauty. You look at me and see . . . this.' She indicated the left side of her face with one hand. 'It would be difficult for you to—'

'*Damn* your face!' he exclaimed, and then stared at her in dismay as her hand froze in place an inch or so from her cheek and her eyes widened. 'Oh, dash it all, I do beg your pardon. I did not intend that at all as it sounded. I meant—'

But he was stopped by an unexpected sight and sound. She was laughing. 'I thought you were all gentlemanly perfection,' she said. 'How delightful it is to discover that you are human. What *did* you mean?'

He remembered then the way she had appeared for a brief few moments when he had taken her by surprise at Withington – flushed and bright eyed and slightly disheveled and breathless – and pretty. And he looked at her now, surprised into laughter by his outburst, and it struck him that it was possible to feel a twinge of attraction toward her. But only when she was startled into allowing glimpses into a self she normally kept well hidden.

'Your face is just your face,' he said. 'It is not *you*. And it is not nearly as unsightly as you think it is. You have allowed it to define you, and that fact has surely not served you well. I do beg your pardon, Miss Heyden. And for my language too. But in fearing that your face will preclude you from all human warmth and affection for the rest of your life, you cut yourself off from those very things.'

'Could *you* ever feel an affection for me?' she asked.

He hesitated. 'I do not know,' he said. 'I honestly do not, Miss Heyden. And I will not feign an affection just to convince you that your face does not repulse me.'

'That is fair,' she said.

'Could you ever feel an affection for me?' he asked.

She gazed steadily at him for a few moments. 'If I could grow accustomed to your very good looks,' she said. 'But I believe I am still a bit intimidated by them.'

He was the one to laugh then, softly but with genuine amusement. Did not women – and men – usually fall in love on looks alone and discover affection or its opposite only later?

'So,' she said, 'do we proceed? Or do we not?'

There were a number of reasons why they should – and just as many reasons why they should not. He hesitated before replying. It would be a huge step to begin an actual courtship. Perhaps an irrevocable one. It was the reason he had invited her today, though – to decide if that next step could and ought to be taken. Now he was still finding it difficult to decide. But perhaps he always would. Perhaps the idea of marrying for mercenary reasons alone would always bother him. But would he ever be able to deal with the darkness that lurked just behind her surface firmness of character and mind? And would he be able to deal with her independence and success? She was a person with so many complexities – and it was probable he did not know even half of them yet – that he felt quite dizzy. But one could not go through life as a procrastinator. At least, he would not go through life that way. And one could never know everything.

There had been a reply to his letter home this morning.

'My mother and sister are on the way here from Kent,' he said. 'They were to meet me in London this week, but when I wrote to tell them I would be delayed, they decided to come here instead to celebrate Easter with me. I would like you to join us here for tea on Sunday.'

She stared at him for a long time. 'They would be horrified,' she said.

'Did you imagine when you decided to marry,' he asked her, 'that you would live the rest of your life in isolation with your husband?'

She thought about it. 'I suppose I did,' she admitted.

'It would never happen,' he said. 'Will you come?'

'We are proceeding, then, are we?' she asked him.

'With no commitment on either side,' he said.

'And I suppose,' she said, 'you would expect me to arrive unveiled in your drawing room.'

'Yes,' he said.

She turned to climb the steps ahead of him without another word.

'He must be seriously considering your proposal,' Maude said, 'if he wants you to meet his mother and sister.'

Wren, sitting beside her maid in the carriage, kept her eyes closed. How foolish she had been and how very naive. How totally ignorant of the world. Her uncle had exposed her to the business that was now hers, but it had involved no social interaction with any of his employees, now her own, not even with Philip Croft, the manager. Her uncle had tried to persuade her to mingle socially with her peers but had never insisted. Aunt Megan, more protective of her, had always supported her decision to remain behind closed doors whenever there was a chance she might be seen and behind a veil when being seen could not be avoided. Miss Briggs, Wren's governess, had never expressed an opinion, though she had been quite adamant about educating her pupil in all aspects of being a lady. There had even been dancing lessons.

But Miss Briggs had left when she was eighteen, and ten years later her aunt and uncle had died. She had been left isolated from the world and had come up with the brilliant idea of using her wealth to purchase a husband. It had seemed a wonderfully practical idea. It was almost embarrassing to realize with what naïveté she had conceived it and put it into execution. She would choose her candidates with care, she had decided – there were always people from whom to gather information – and then interview each until she found the one she wanted. She would make her offer, be accepted, and proceed to the wedding. And yes, in her imagination it was a wedding with only two people present apart from the requisite number of witnesses, to be succeeded by a married life that involved only the same two people for the rest of their days.

It was more than *almost* embarrassing. How could anyone who prided herself upon her intelligence and good sense have been so foolishly ignorant?

First he had invited her to tea with his neighbors.

Now he had invited her to tea with his mother and sister.

What next? The whole Westcott family? The relatives on his mother's side of the family? She had not even asked about them yet.

'I am not sure I can do it,' she said when Maude must have thought she was not going to answer at all. 'I am not sure I *want* to do it.'

'You are going to let yourself turn into an eccentric old maid, then?' Maude asked.

Wren smiled without opening her eyes. 'I already *am* an eccentric old maid,' she said. 'I am almost thirty, Maude.'

'You are going to allow *her* the victory, then, are you?' Maude asked.

Wren stiffened. She did not doubt for a moment to whom Maude referred. Aunt Megan had told her the story. Wren had even overheard them once when she was still a young child. *Taking her bodily away from the woman was one thing, Mrs Heyden,* Maude had been saying, *but what was the point if you cannot also take her out of the child's mind? She is going to be destroyed forever. That is what is going to happen. Mark my words. You need to force her out in the world a bit so she knows the world is not her enemy.* Both of them had ended up in tears while Wren had crept away and diverted her mind from what she had heard with some unremembered game or activity.

'I am my own person,' Wren said now. 'I run my own life, Maude, and have not sought your advice.'

Maude clucked her tongue.

'I am sorry,' Wren said, opening her eyes at last and turning her head. 'I know you care for me. So which am I to do? Go and meet his mother and sister or proceed to live eccentrically ever after?'

Maude adopted a deliberately mulish expression, crossed her arms, and stared at the back of the seat opposite.

Wren laughed. 'Oh very well,' she said. 'You win. I shall go.'

'I have not uttered a word,' her maid protested.

'You did not need to.' Wren laughed again. 'That look and the folded arms are eloquent enough, as you very well know. I shall go and make you proud, though you would not admit it even under torture. But, Maude, I *wish* he were not so handsome. He predicts that after he has met me a few times he will not even notice my birthmark. Do you think that after a few times I will not notice his good looks?'

'Whoever would want *not* to notice them?' Maude asked, exasperated. 'I could gaze at him all day long and never grow tired of the sight.'

Wren sighed and closed her eyes again. And she could see him standing against the trunk of that oak tree, looking both elegant and relaxed, his arms crossed over his chest, and so gorgeous that her insides had clenched up and made her feel quite bilious. She could hear herself telling him that she wanted to be kissed and she could imagine *him* doing it.

She wanted it. Very badly.

But he could not possibly ever want to kiss her. Her face . . .

Damn your face.

She smiled again at the memory. His words, his outburst, had been so very unexpected. And so strangely endearing.

Oh, she must not, she must not, she *must not fall in love with him.*

CHAPTER 5

Mrs Althea Westcott, Alexander's mother, and Elizabeth, Lady Overfield, his sister, arrived at Brambledean Court early in the afternoon two days later. Alexander heard the carriage and hurried outside to hand them down and hug them warmly amid a flurry of greetings.

'So what do you think?' he could not resist asking, gesturing with one arm toward the house and about the park. 'Do I dare ask?'

'Too late. You just did,' Elizabeth said, laughing. 'It must all have been quite breathtakingly magnificent once upon a time, Alex. Even now it has a faded splendor.'

'Ah, but wait until you see the inside,' he warned her.

'Poor Alex. But at least the roof does not appear to have caved in,' their mother said, taking his arm as they went up the steps into the hall.

She stopped inside to glance about, her eyes coming to rest upon the faded and chipped black-and-white tiles underfoot. 'It is a good thing I never warmed to Cousin Humphrey, your predecessor. I would have felt sadly deceived by him. He was one of the wealthiest men in England and one of the most selfish. He totally neglected his responsibilities here. Then they landed upon your shoulders with the title while all the money went to Anastasia, whom I am *not* blaming for a single moment, bless her heart. Humphrey ought to have been shot at the very least. He ought not to have been allowed to die peacefully in his bed. There is no justice.'

'At least the house is fit to be lived in,' Alexander said. 'Just. I have never yet found myself being rained upon through the ceiling while I sleep or anything equally dire. Of course, I have never slept in either of the two guest rooms that have been prepared for you.'

Elizabeth laughed again. 'But we will spend Easter together,' she said. 'We did not relish the thought of celebrating it in London while you felt obliged to remain here a while longer.'

'And it must be admitted, Alex,' their mother said, 'that we felt a curiosity to see for ourselves what you are facing here.'

Alexander introduced them to the butler and the housekeeper, and Mrs Dearing offered to take them to their rooms to freshen up before tea. They followed her up the stairs, looking curiously about them as they went.

'Have you met any of your neighbors yet, Alex?' his mother asked later when they were settled in the drawing room with tea and scones and cakes. 'But you surely have. You have been here for a while and they must have been burning with eagerness to meet the new earl and discover if you mean to settle here and marry one of their daughters.'

'I have met a number of them,' he said, 'and all have been both amiable and kind. I have been entertained at dinner and tea and cards and music, and I have been kept standing outside church for an hour after service each Sunday and bowed and curtsied to on the street. I have even entertained here. If I waited until the house was more presentable, I might not entertain for the next twenty years. I invited a number of people to a tea party one afternoon and was gratified that everyone came. They were curious, I suppose, to see just how shabby the inside of the house is. And yes, of course, almost everyone has asked about my plans. I have assured them that I intend to make this my home even though my parliamentary duties will take me to London for a few months each spring.'

There was a beat of silence. 'You intend to make your home at Brambledean,' his mother said, her cup suspended a few inches from her mouth.

'You will abandon Riddings Park to live here?' Elizabeth asked with more open dismay. 'But you love Riddings, Alex. It is *home*, and you worked so hard and so long to restore it to prosperity. This is . . . dreary, to say the least. You have hired a new steward you described to us as hardworking and conscientious. Why do you feel the need to be here yourself? Oh, but you need not bother answering. It is because of your infernal sense of duty.' She set her cup down none too gently in the saucer. 'I am sorry. How you conduct your life is none of my business. And we came here to cheer you, not to scold you, did we not, Mama? I feel compelled to say, though, that I *care* for you and *about* you and long to see you happy.'

'You do not see me unhappy, Lizzie,' he assured her. 'But there are some things I need to do here in person, not least of which is giving the people dependent upon me the assurance that I care about them, that I empathize with them, that we are all in this struggle together. I am hoping Bufford and I together can find ways to make the farms more prosperous this year even without the input of too much new money. I want to put some into much-needed repairs to the laborers' cottages and into an increase in their wages – small, perhaps, but better than nothing. Bufford wants to put money into new crops and equipment and more livestock. Together we complement each other, you see. But enough of that. I have no wish to put you to sleep. Tell me about your journey.'

They did so, and they all laughed a great deal, for Elizabeth in particular had a ready wit and an eye for the absurd. What had probably been a tedious journey, as most were, was made to sound as though it had been vastly entertaining. But his mother had something else on her mind too and got to it before they rose from their tea.

'Do you intend making a serious search for a

wife during the Season, Alex?' she asked. 'It worries me that you are thirty years old but have never given yourself a chance to enjoy life. Last year you admitted that finally you were looking about you, but then came the wretched family upset and you set aside all thought of your personal happiness again.'

'I shall certainly give myself the pleasure of escorting you and Lizzie to various entertainments when the Season begins, Mama,' he told her.

'Which is no answer at all,' she said.

'Alex.' His sister was hugging her elbows with her hands as though she were cold, and was leaning slightly toward him. 'You are not going to be looking for a *rich* wife, are you?'

'There is something inherently wrong with a rich wife?' he asked, grinning at her. 'Wealthy young ladies are to be excluded from consideration upon that fact alone? It seems a little unfair to them.'

She clucked her tongue. 'You know exactly what I mean,' she said. 'And the very evasiveness of your answer speaks volumes. It would be so very typical of you to do it. You have never ever put your own happiness first. Do not do it. Please. You deserve happiness more than anyone else I know.' There were actually tears brimming in her eyes.

'Money is not an evil, Lizzie,' he said.

'Oh, but it is when it is given precedence over happiness,' she told him. 'Please, Alex. Do not do it.'

'You may save your breath, Lizzie,' their mother

85

said, looking sharply from one to the other of them. 'You know your brother cannot be shifted once he has decided upon something. It is what is always most annoying and most endearing about him. But I do hope you will not marry *just* for money, Alex. It would break my heart. No, forget I said that. I would not impose yet one more burden upon you. Whomever you choose – and I hope you choose *someone* soon, for I am very ready to be a grandmama and drive you to distraction by spoiling your children quite outrageously. Whomever you choose I will welcome with open arms, and I will absolutely insist upon loving her too.'

'And so will Alex, Mama,' Elizabeth said. 'He is like that. But will *she* insist upon loving *him*? That is the question that concerns me. There will be any number of candidates for the hand of the Earl of Riverdale, but will they see Alex behind the title?'

'I promise not to marry anyone I hate or anyone who hates me,' he said, smiling from one to the other of them. And perhaps he ought to leave it at that for now, he thought. But Sunday afternoon would have to be mentioned and explained soon. Perhaps he ought to have invited several other neighbors too. But that would have been grossly unfair to her. 'I have invited one of my more distant neighbors to join us for tea on Sunday afternoon.'

'On Easter Sunday? Oh, that will be lovely, Alex,'

his mother said, brightening. 'But only one? Who is he?'

'She, actually,' he said. 'Miss Heyden. She lives at Withington House, eight or nine miles from here.'

'And she is coming alone?' his mother asked. 'But who is she?'

'Her uncle was Mr Reginald Heyden, a gentleman who made his fortune in fine glassware,' he explained. 'His workshops and headquarters are in Staffordshire, but he purchased Withington ten years or so ago as a country home. He was married to Miss Heyden's aunt. She lived with them until their deaths within a few days of each other a little over a year ago.'

'And he left her the house?' Elizabeth asked.

'And everything else too,' he said. 'He and his wife adopted her. They had no children of their own and apparently no other close relatives either. Miss Heyden owns and takes an active part in the running of the business.'

'She must be an extraordinary woman,' his mother said.

'Yes,' he said, 'I believe she is.'

There was another of those beats of silence, so pregnant with meaning. 'She is unmarried?' his mother asked. 'How old is she?'

'She is close to my own age,' he said. 'She has never been married.'

'And she is coming to tea on Sunday. With no other guests.' She was looking intently at him.

'No others,' he said.

'Oh, Alex, you provoking creature,' Elizabeth cried. 'Tell us the rest of this story before I come over there and shake it out of you.'

'But there is very little to tell,' he protested. 'I called upon her a couple of weeks ago – a courtesy call, you will understand, since I hope to become acquainted with all the families within a ten-mile radius of Brambledean. I invited her to the tea I mentioned earlier. We have each called upon the other once since then.'

'You are courting her,' his mother said.

'I am making her acquaintance, Mama,' he said, frowning. 'She is making mine. It happens, you know, among neighbors.'

Elizabeth got to her feet. 'We must not subject poor Alex to any more of an interrogation, Mama,' she said. 'He is not going to admit that there is something significant about inviting a single lady of his own age to take tea with his mother and sister in his own home, the provoking man. We will have to wait until Sunday, then, to see for ourselves. I would love to view the rest of the house, Alex. At least, I think I would. Will you give us the grand tour?'

'It would be my pleasure,' he said, jumping to his feet, greatly relieved. 'Shall we start with the ground floor and work our way upward? Mama, will you come too, or would you rather rest here or in your room until dinner?'

'Oh, I am coming too,' she assured him. 'I am

not quite in my dotage yet even if I do have two children past the age of thirty. Goodness, is it possible?'

She took his offered arm.

Wren liked attending church and did so regularly. It was somewhere she could be alone yet in company with other people. It was a place where no one bothered her or looked askance at her veil, yet almost everyone nodded in recognition and some even smiled and wished her a good morning. She always sat close to the back, where her aunt and uncle had sat. With their stature and wealth, they might have made a point of sitting at the front, but they had never done so.

She never paid particular attention to the words of the service and often allowed her thoughts to drift during the homily. She rather liked the way the vicar droned on in his kindly way without any fiery rhetoric or fervent appeal to the emotions of his congregation. She was not even sure she believed all the teachings and doctrines of her religion. But there was something about the church itself – and most churches she had visited – that brought her mind and her emotions and her very being, it seemed, to a point of stillness, and she wondered if that was what her religion would call the Holy Spirit. But she did not wish to give it a name, whatever it was. Names were confining and restrictive. Though they could also be freeing. *Wren*, with its suggestion of wings and wide blue skies, had somehow set her free of *Rowena* when she was ten years old. *Heyden* instead of the other name had completed the transformation.

The church was particularly lovely on this Easter Sunday, filled as it was with lilies and other spring flowers, the somberness of Good Friday flung off. But it was neither the flowers nor the joyfulness of the occasion that made Wren happy. It was that stillness, that sense of calmness at her center, that conviction that somehow, through all the turmoil of life, all was well and always would be well. It was something she needed today, for this afternoon she was going to do something she had never done before. She was going to a social event – tea at Brambledean Court – with two people she had never met before, the Earl of Riverdale's mother and sister, and she was going without her veil.

She definitely was going, though the cowardly part of herself, which could be very vocal at times, kept loudly insisting that no, she did not need to, that if he had an ounce of feeling he would not have asked it of her, that she ought to just move on to the fourth gentleman on her list and forget all about the too handsome, too demanding Earl of Riverdale.

She went. She sat with rigid spine and raised chin and clenched hands beside Maude in the carriage. They traveled in silence after her maid had informed her that she looked as if she were on the way to her own execution and Wren had snapped back at her that when she wished for her maid's opinion she would ask for it – a not very original setdown. She went without even the muted comfort of a gray or lavender dress of half mourning, but instead in her sky blue dress, the one that was embroidered at the hem and wrists and high neckline with the same color silk. It had been her favorite before she cast it aside for her blacks. And she wore with it a straw bonnet from which she had removed the veil – she had not wanted to be tempted by its presence upon the brim. She went with the sick feeling that whatever peace she had found at church this morning, she had also unfortunately left there. She could not be feeling more naked if she actually were unclothed. Well, perhaps that was a bit of an exaggeration. She tried to feel amused and failed.

If raw terror could ever be a tangible thing, then she was it.

The journey seemed endless and was over far too quickly. She felt Maude's cool fingertips patting the back of her hand as the carriage turned onto the driveway leading to Brambledean. 'You look lovely, Miss Wren,' she said. 'If you would just believe that, your whole life would turn around.'

Wren opened her mouth to snap back yet again. Instead she startled herself and her maid by leaning closer and kissing her cheek. 'I love my life just as it is, Maude,' she said not quite truthfully, 'and I love you.'

Her maid had no response but to gape.

The Earl of Riverdale must have been watching for her. The main doors opened as the carriage drew to a halt, and he came down the steps and reached the carriage door before her coachman could jump down from the box. He opened it, set down the steps, and extended a hand to help Wren alight, a smile on his face. But she would be willing to wager he was feeling far less at ease than he looked. What man would look forward to introducing *her* to his mother, after all? Had he been hoping she would lose her courage and not come?

'You have made good time,' he said. 'Happy Easter to you, Miss Heyden.'

'And did you notice today?' she asked him almost defiantly when she was down on the terrace beside him.

His smile deepened, and his eyes seemed to turn bluer, and she wondered what on earth she was doing even considering marrying him. He could have *any woman on earth*, even a few as rich as she or richer. He could not possibly *want* to marry her.

'I have noticed the elegance of your dress and the vividness of the color, which suits you perfectly,' he said. 'I have noticed that your straw bonnet suggests summertime, as the weather itself does. I have noticed that there is no veil in sight. And – ah, yes, now that I look more closely I notice that you seem to have some slight blemish on the left side of your face. The next time or the time after that I daresay I will not notice it at all.'

Some slight blemish indeed. And *the next time or*

the time after that, indeed. 'And happy Easter to you too, Lord Riverdale,' she said rather sourly, though she had been warmed by his humor.

'Come and meet my mother and sister.' He offered his arm. 'They are in the drawing room.'

She wondered if they *knew,* if he had warned them. She told him as they made their way upstairs, just because she was unnerved by their silent progress, how lovely the church had looked this morning with all the lilies, and he told her that there had been as many daffodils as lilies in their church.

'Golden trumpets of hope,' he said, and she grimaced.

'I felt very foolish after saying those words aloud when we were on the daffodil bank,' she said.

'But why?' he asked her. 'I will always see daffodils that way from now on.'

The butler had gone ahead of them and was opening the drawing room doors, both of them, with something of a flourish. Wren felt her knees turn weak and heard a voice in her head – her uncle's. He had spoken the words when she was ten years old and her aunt had taken her to his house in London and lifted the heavy veil from her face and he had looked at her for the first time. *Straighten your spine, girl,* he had said, not unkindly, *and raise your chin and look the world in the eye. If you are cringing or dying on the inside, let it be your secret alone.* All her life until then she had hunched and cringed and tipped her head to one side and tucked her chin into her neck and tried to be invisible. Now she straightened her already straight spine, raised her already lifted chin, and looked directly at the two ladies who were standing a short distance apart halfway across the room.

Everything seemed unnaturally bright. But of course, there was no veil between her and the harsh, real world.

'Mama, Lizzie,' the Earl of Riverdale said, 'may I present Miss Heyden? My mother, Mrs Westcott, and my sister, Lady Overfield, Miss Heyden.'

'Oh, my dear.' The older lady clasped her hands to her bosom and took a few hurried steps closer, frowning in concern. 'You have burned yourself.'

'No,' Wren said. 'I was born this way.' He had not warned them, then. She extended her right hand. 'How do you do, Mrs Westcott?'

The lady took her hand. 'I am very relieved that you did not suffer the pain of a burn,' she said. 'I am pleased to meet you, Miss Heyden. I have never been to Brambledean before even though my husband's cousin owned it all my married life and it has been Alex's since last year. It was a pleasure to meet some of his near neighbors at church this morning and it is a pleasure to have the chance of a longer visit with you this afternoon. Friendly connections are very important when one lives in the country, are they not?'

She was a slight, dark-haired lady with an amiable face and a gracious manner. She was of medium stature and must have been a beauty in her day. It was easy to see where her son had got his looks, if not his height. Her daughter was taller, though still more than half a head shorter than Wren. She was fairer of coloring too and pretty without being dazzlingly lovely. She was probably a few years older than her brother. She offered Wren her hand.

'I am pleased to make your acquaintance too, Miss Heyden,' she said. 'And may I offer condolences on your double loss just a little over a year ago? It must have been quite devastating.'

'It was.' Wren shook her hand. 'Thank you.'

The earl directed her to a chair and they all sat down. The tea tray and plates of food were carried in almost immediately, and Mrs Westcott poured while Lady Overfield passed around the drinks and pastries. Wren took two of the latter, struck by the thought that she was free to help herself to food today since there was no veil to make eating near impossible.

'Do you spend much time at your home in the country here, Miss Heyden?' Mrs Westcott asked. 'Withington House, I believe Alex called it. Wiltshire is a particularly scenic county, is it not?'

'It is,' Wren agreed. 'My uncle chose it after some deliberation and much consultation with my aunt when they decided a number of years ago to buy a country home. There is another house in Staffordshire, close to the glassworks I inherited, but it is in a more urbanized area than Withington House and not as attractive. I do spend time there, however, sometimes for weeks at a time. I run the business myself, you see, though admittedly the manager there, who was with my uncle for years as his trusted right-hand man, could proceed very well without me. I do not subscribe to the notion, however, that a woman must remain at home and rely upon men to take care of everything beyond its bounds.'

There. She was speaking with what even to her own ears sounded like belligerence, like throwing down a gauntlet, as though she needed to make clear to them that she was not out to snare their son and brother merely in order to cling to him for the rest of her life. That had never been her intention. She wished to wed, yes, but marriage could never be all in all to her, as she guessed it was for most women of her class. Perhaps they did not think she was out to snare him at all, however. He was, after all, an earl and an extremely handsome man, while she was . . . Well. Some people had described her uncle a little contemptuously as a cit despite the fact that he had been a gentleman. Members of the upper classes often frowned upon alliances with such people.

'Oh, I do applaud you, Miss Heyden,' Lady Overfield said with a laugh that had a pleasant gurgle to it. 'But how you must scandalize the *ton*.'

'I know nothing of the *ton*,' Wren said. 'My uncle was a gentleman, and my aunt was a lady. I am a lady. But though my uncle had a home in London before he married my aunt, he sold it afterward and always declared that he did not miss the life he had had there. I have never craved it. We divided our time between Staffordshire and here.'

'You never had a come-out Season, then?' Mrs Westcott asked.

'No,' Wren said. 'I never wanted one or any entrée into high society. I still do not. I am quite happy with my life as it is.' *Except that I proposed marriage to your son because I want someone to wed.*

She was being a bit obnoxious, Wren realized, and more than a bit stiff in her demeanor. Miss Briggs would be tutting and shaking her head and making her practice a relaxed, gracious social manner again and again and yet again. She was feeling hostile for no apparent reason, for neither lady was looking at her disapprovingly or with any haughty condescension. They were very polite – as all ladies were trained to be. But surely they must have been inwardly cringing as they asked themselves why their son and brother had singled her out for this invitation to tea. They must have come to the inevitable conclusion, and they must have been horrified. They would surely pour outrage into his ears when she was gone.

'What is your impression of Brambledean?' Wren asked the ladies in an attempt to turn the conversation away from herself. Though even that choice of topic was probably unwise since they could hardly pretend rapture over the house and park, and their very dilapidation would remind them that he was too poor to do anything about it while she had riches untold.

'Clearly it was once a stately home of great splendor,' Mrs Westcott said. 'It may be so again in the future now that Alex is here to pay attention to it. But our focus since we arrived on Thursday has been upon enjoying our time together as a family and taking Alex's mind off the challenges that lie ahead of him here.'

Wren felt rebuked as the conversation limped onward. The two ladies were perfectly well-bred, but the conviction that their good manners must mask disapproval, even dislike, grew upon Wren. And it was at least partly her fault. She was unable to relax or to cast off the defensive, faintly hostile demeanor with which she had begun the visit. She wished she could go back and start again, but would she behave any differently? *Could* she behave differently? She found it quite impossible to smile or to sit back in her chair and at least look relaxed. The Earl of Riverdale by contrast was warm, charming, and smiling. It did not seem at all fair.

When she estimated that half an hour had passed, the requisite duration for a polite visit – one of the many social graces her governess had taught her – Wren got to her feet to take her leave, assuring the ladies as she did so that she was delighted to have made their acquaintance. She thanked the earl for the invitation and the tea, and felt a huge surge of relief that it was over, that she had *done* it, however badly, something she would not have thought even possible just a couple of weeks ago – or even this morning. And it really was over. All over. No one could doubt that, least of all Wren herself. Yet despite her relief, she felt a dull ache of disappointment too.

It had seemed such a simple scheme when she had first devised it.

The ladies made polite noises back at her – she did not really listen to exactly what they said. The Earl of Riverdale accompanied her downstairs in silence and gave the order to the butler to have her carriage brought around in half an hour's time.

'Half an hour?' she said, frowning at him as he led her out onto the terrace.

'You traveled all this way by carriage,' he said, 'and have been sitting in my drawing room since then. Now you have the long journey home ahead of you. At least take a little time for some air and exercise first. Shall we?' He offered his arm.

Did he feel obliged to *tell* her, then, to put into words what had been glaringly clear up in the drawing room? Well, perhaps he was right. At least she would not then be watching for his curricle or for the arrival of the post every day for the next fortnight or so while telling herself she was doing no such thing. Some things needed to be spoken aloud.

She set her hand in the crook of his arm and felt the pangs of what seemed strangely like deep grief.

CHAPTER 6

They took the opposite direction from the one they had taken the last time she was here. There was a stretch of lawn and then a thick copse of overgrown trees and beyond that what at one time must have been a magnificent alley lined with elm trees. Alexander thought it was still impressive with the trees stretching into the distance in two straight lines and a wide grassy avenue between. The trees needed pruning and the grass needed scything, though it had been done fairly recently. Wooden benches had been placed at intervals across the alley, and a summer house at the end, which from this distance looked to be in better repair than it actually was. He must have the benches removed, Alexander thought, as they were no longer fit to be sat upon, though he liked the idea of them and the suggestion they made of leisurely walks with rests along the way, surrounded by rustling verdant greenery and a sense of remoteness and peace. There were a few daisies growing in the grass in defiance of the gardeners' scythes. He rather liked them and thought it a shame they were considered a weed.

'This is both pleasant and unexpected,' Miss Heyden said. 'I assumed that the trees marked the eastern border of the park.'

'The park is vast,' he said. 'Its size is just one more problem to add to the others, as it would take an army of gardeners working full-time to keep it pristine. But eventually it will serve the dual role of offering employment and giving enjoyment.'

'This alley reminds me of a vast church,' she said. 'It arouses the same feelings of serenity and awe. But it is different from a church in that it is alive.'

'You favor nature over art, then?' he asked. 'I have seen cathedrals that have rendered me speechless because of the artistry that has gone into every detail from flying buttresses to gargoyle heads among the rafters.'

'But there is room for both art and nature,' she said. 'We surely impoverish our lives if we forever feel we must choose between apparent opposites. Why should we? I could spend hours in a church just looking and being. And I could spend hours outdoors just breathing in the life of it all and knowing myself part of it.'

This, he thought, was a different woman from the one who had sat on the edge of her seat in his drawing room a short while ago, making labored conversation with his mother and sister. That woman had been stiff, formal, not very likable. He thought of her telling his mother that she ran the glassworks herself, that she did not subscribe to the notion that a woman must remain at home while a man took care of her needs. And he thought of her telling him that she wished to be wed, and – on a different occasion – that she wanted to be kissed. He thought of her sudden laughter when he had briefly lost his temper with her and said *damn your face*. And he thought of her gazing at the daffodil bank at Withington and calling them golden trumpets of hope.

Here and there must both be appreciated in order to experience life fully, she had said once. This and that. Then and now. Art and nature. Daffodils and roses. The woman who had sat in his drawing room this afternoon and the woman who walked with him now.

Attraction and repulsion. There was another pair of opposites.

They strolled onward, not speaking for a while.

'Thank you,' he said at last.

'For?' She turned her head, eyebrows raised.

'I know it was incredibly difficult for you to come this afternoon,' he said. 'I know it was especially difficult to leave your veil behind.'

'They do not like me,' she said.

He frowned. They were not usually either hasty or harsh in passing judgment upon people they had just met, but he knew they had not found the visit easy. She had seemed to have a wall erected about herself in the absence of the physical veil, and it had not been easy, or even possible, to get behind it. He had tried to set her at her ease by appearing to be at his ease. His mother and sister had tried to set her at her ease, and they were normally skilled at doing it because they were both naturally warm, affectionate ladies. But the conversation had limped along, sagging, sinking to banalities, never reaching the point at which it flowed without conscious prompting. It had really been quite ghastly, in fact. The half hour had seemed endless.

'Why would they dislike you?' he asked.

'Because they love you,' she said.

'I have not said anything to them about any possible connection between us except as neighbors,' he told her.

'Ah, but I do not believe either your mother or your sister is lacking in intelligence,' she said.

She was perfectly right, of course. 'They want to see me happy,' he said. 'I am an only son and an only brother, and we have always been a close family. But they are not possessive in their love. They are not predisposed to dislike anyone who might possibly end up as my wife. Indeed, they want me to marry. I am thirty years old.'

'But I am not anyone,' she said. 'You cannot pretend to believe that this visit was anything but a disaster. And I am *not* blaming your mother and sister. They were very gracious. Neither am I blaming you. Or myself. I believe I ought to release you, Lord Riverdale. Not that you have made any formal commitment to me, but it is possible you are beginning to feel some sort of obligation now that we

103

have called upon each other a few times and you have presented me to Mrs Westcott and Lady Overfield. I assure you there is no such obligation. I think we should both forget the suggestion I made when you first visited me two weeks ago. You are a good man and a perfect gentleman, and I have appreciated your attempts to become acquainted with me. But it must end here.'

They had come to a stop in the middle of the alley, and she had slipped her hand free of his arm. They stood facing each other, and he found himself frowning. She was speaking like the cool businesswoman she was, and she was looking him directly in the eye. There was not a glimmer of emotion in her dismissal of all her plans and hopes concerning him. But . . . was she hurting inside? Was it conceited of him to believe she might be? It really had taken enormous courage on her part to come here this afternoon, yet she had done it. Why? Just to end things with him? She could have done that by letter – or simply by not coming. She had not needed to put herself through this ordeal. It was all about this visit, then. He wondered how very alone and how very exposed she had felt. It had been three against one – three close family members against a woman who had none. And she had not even had her veil to bolster her courage as she had the last time she came here to tea.

Dash it all, but she was right. He did feel an obligation even though she had just set him free of it. He had invited her here and put her through such an unpleasant experience. He should take her at her word. No doubt she was longing to get back to her familiar, reclusive world. And it would be a relief to him. He really could not see himself happily married to her – or married to her at all, in fact. Yet—

'You are going to lose your courage, then?' he asked.

'It is not a question of courage,' she protested.

'I beg to disagree,' he said. 'It took a great deal of courage to invite me to your home, to make your proposal to me, to show me your face, to take tea with my neighbors, to visit me here alone, to come here again today. But since you conceived your plan, I believe you have realized that it will be virtually impossible for you to marry and continue with the almost totally isolated life you lived with your uncle and aunt. Indeed you admitted it the last time we met.'

'I have nothing more to say, Lord Riverdale,' she said.

'You met my mother and my sister today and have taken fright,' he said. 'And so you are falling back upon instinct, which is to run for cover and remain there.'

He knew he was being unfair. But surely there was truth in what he said. It was as if, having put her toe into the ocean and found the water cold, she had abandoned her intention of bathing in it.

'I am exercising my right to live my life as I choose, Lord Riverdale,' she said, all cold, straight-backed dignity. 'And I do not choose you. I withdraw my offer. I have nothing to bring to you except pots and pots of money. *Nothing.*'

It was noticeable that she had not said he had nothing to bring her, though that would seem more to the point. He clasped his hands behind him and gazed at her for several moments, trying to fathom what was going on behind all that cool poise. He might have concluded there was nothing, but her eyes wavered for a moment before she focused them steadily on his again. And he could almost feel the pain behind the words she had spoken – *I have nothing to bring you except pots and pots of money.*

'If we wed,' he said, 'I would draw from you the story of your first ten years, Miss Heyden. And while I am not a violent man by nature, I suspect I would thereby learn there are a few people I would dearly like to pound into the middle of next week.'

Her eyes widened, and she pressed a hand to her mouth while her eyes brimmed with tears. She turned sharply away and strode off to one side of the path, to stand against one of the elm trees, facing away from him, both hands spread over her face.

Oh, good God. What had he done?

He followed her, stood in front of her for a few moments, and then set his hands against the trunk, one on either side of her head. She lowered her hands and gazed at him.

She was frowning, and he knew that at least for that moment he was gazing back into the darkness he had always known was within her. She had nothing to say and he could not think of anything that would make her feel better. Apologize? But for what? Besides, the words had been spoken now, and he knew that somehow he had plunged her into some sort of hell that was associated with those hidden years of her childhood.

'You told me you wanted to be kissed,' he heard himself say. 'Let me kiss you.'

'Why?' she asked him. 'To make me feel better? You cannot deny that you are relieved to have been released from any obligation you might have felt. You saw the impossibility of it all during that ghastly half hour. You will find someone else easily enough when you go to London. Someone more . . . normal. And rich enough to rescue you from your problems.'

'Let me kiss you,' he said again, bending his arms at the elbows to bring both his face and his body closer to hers. And he was surprised to discover that he *wanted* to kiss her, if only out of curiosity.

'Why?' she asked again. And, when he did not answer, 'Yes, then. Kiss me. And then take me back to my carriage.'

He looked into her eyes for a few moments longer and then dropped his gaze to her mouth. He kissed her. Her lips stiffened against his own and then softened and then pushed tentatively back. Her hands came up to rest on either side of his waist, on the outside of his coat. He moved his own hands away from the trunk to cup her face. His thumbs stroked her closed eyelids and her cheeks – the skin on the damaged side was as smooth as it was on the other side, he discovered. He slid one hand behind her neck and up beneath her bonnet, and circled her waist with the other arm to draw her against him. She was all tall, lithe slimness. He could feel her legs, long against his own. He could feel her awkwardness too, her inexperience – he would be willing to wager this was her first kiss. It was bound to be, in fact.

But truth to tell, he was not really analyzing the embrace clinically. He was participating in it, surrendering to the unexpected sensuality of it, the equally unexpected femininity of her, the desire to go further with her, to open her mouth with his own and explore with his tongue, to let his hands roam and caress.

But it was undoubtedly her first kiss. He did not give in to his desires. Even so, she suddenly panicked. She pressed her hands almost violently against his chest, ducked under his arm, and strode back out onto the grass of the alley before coming to a halt in the middle of it.

'I beg your pardon,' he said as he followed her.

She wheeled on him. 'I permitted it. But it changes nothing, Lord Riverdale. I am going back to the terrace now.'

But now he really did feel an obligation. 'Miss Heyden,' he said, his hands behind his back again as he observed the flush in her cheek, the brightness of her eyes, her general loss of poise, 'I will be going to London during the coming week. I have obligations there. Will you come too and be my mother's guest at Westcott House? I can take rooms elsewhere. Will you come to experience some of the social life there? As much or as little as you choose? Will you meet some of your peers – or none, according to your choosing? Will you allow me to court you there, with no obligation on either side?'

'No!' Her eyes had widened with shock. 'Whyever would I agree to do such a thing? Because *you* have obligations? I have them too, I would have you know. I need to spend time at my glassworks in Staffordshire. I have a business to run. Perhaps *you* would like to come *there* and meet some of my colleagues and employees.'

'If anything were to come of our courtship,' he said, 'I believe I would rather like that, Miss Heyden. But not in the springtime.'

'I would not like to go to London at any season of the year,' she said, 'and certainly not in the springtime. And that is my final word.' She turned on her heel and strode off in the direction from which they had come.

He walked in silence beside her. He had tried. He had tried not to accept her release with too obvious a relief. He had tried to suggest a further trial of their courtship – if it ever had been quite that. Now his conscience could be clear. This was what she chose, what she wanted, and there was nothing more to be said.

Her carriage was waiting on the terrace. Her coachman stood by the horses' heads while her maid hovered outside the open carriage door. Alexander stopped a little distance away, took her hand in his, and bowed over it. 'Thank you for giving me the pleasure of your acquaintance,' he said.

'Goodbye, Lord Riverdale,' she said.

'Goodbye, Miss Heyden.'

He handed her into the carriage and shut the door after the maid had taken the place beside her. The coachman climbed onto the box and gathered the ribbons in his hands. She did not look from the window as the vehicle moved away. He watched it as it disappeared from sight, trying and somehow failing to feel relief.

All because of a damned birthmark, he thought.

What the devil had happened during the first ten years of her life? It was clearly something catastrophic.

He turned to make his way slowly back into the house and up to the drawing room.

'You look like tragedy warmed over,' Maude said.

'Do I?' Wren set her head back against the cushions, turned her face slightly away from her maid, and closed her eyes. It was a rhetorical question and Maude did not attempt to answer it.

She had wanted to fling herself at him even after she had said goodbye. For she could not do this again with someone else. It had been an idea, she had tried it, and now she knew marriage was not a possibility for her. Though that was not the real reason why there would never be anyone else, of course, and there was no point in lying to herself. She could not do this with anyone else because no one else would be him. Yet he was an impossibility.

She relived their conversation, his kiss – she had had no idea, *no idea* that it could be like that. She thought of the visit with his mother and sister. She thought of his invitation to go to London as their guest and of his willingness to step into *her* world. She could not accuse him of being unreasonable, of acting the part of the lordly male, all take and no give. She could not accuse him of anything. Quite the contrary, in fact. She had not expected him to be a kind man. One did not with the excessively handsome – strange thought. No, the lack was all on her part. She could not enter his world, and that was that.

But oh, the pain, the emptiness, the abject self-pity. She would have it in hand by the time they arrived home, but for now she would wallow in it for the simple reason that she could not stop.

If we ever wed, I would draw from you the story of your first ten years, Miss Heyden. And while I am not a violent man by nature, I suspect I would learn that there are a few people I would dearly like to pound into the middle of next week.

Wren bit her lip, her eyes still closed, and kept her composure even while she wept inside.

The drawing room was a hive of industry when Alexander returned. His mother was tatting and Elizabeth had her head bent over an embroidery frame. Both looked up to smile at him, but his mother was soon frowning.

'Alex,' she asked, 'whatever happened to her?'

'It is a birthmark,' he said.

'Oh, that was obvious as soon as I realized it was not a burn,' she said. 'It is unfortunate that it covers almost half her face, and I can understand that it must be a severe trial to her when she has to meet new people and endure the same reaction as mine each time. But I did not mean that. What *happened* to her?'

Elizabeth was still looking up at him too, her needle with its scarlet silk thread suspended above her work. 'Mama and I came to the same conclusion, that she is shut up so far inside herself that she is well nigh invisible,' she said.

He stood halfway across the room, his hands behind him. It was one of those times when he wished he were alone in the house to brood and lick his wounds in private. Though why he should feel wounded, he was not sure. A failure, then. Or just guilty. He seemed to have been weighed down by guilt for more than a year despite the fact that he knew he had nothing whatsoever to feel guilty about. He felt it anyway every time he thought of

Harry fighting with a foot regiment in Spain or Portugal and of Camille marrying a portrait painter, though she seemed happy enough with him, and of Abigail, who should have been making her come-out this spring but instead was hidden away in the country with her mother, who after almost twenty-five years of being the Countess of Riverdale was back to being Miss Viola Kingsley, mother of three illegitimate children. How could he *not* feel guilty? And now he had made the mistake of inviting Miss Heyden here when she was not ready for it. And of hurting her. He knew she was hurting.

'I do not know what happened,' he said. 'But she is sensitive about her appearance out of all proportion to the visible facts. Today was the first time she has ever gone into company unveiled.'

'It was the first time you have seen her without a veil?' Elizabeth asked in clear surprise before threading her needle through the cloth and resting her hands in her lap.

'No,' he said. 'She removed it the first time we met. She invited me to Withington House and I went, assuming wrongly that there would be other guests there too. She had summoned me in order to . . . offer me marriage. Her uncle left her very wealthy, and I suppose it is no secret that I lack the sort of funds I need as owner of Brambledean.'

'Oh, Alex.' His mother had abandoned her tatting and one hand had found its way to her throat.

'She has been all alone since her uncle and aunt died last year,' he said. 'She has always been a recluse, but during the last year I believe she has been lonely. She wishes to wed.'

'But not you,' his mother said.

'Did you say yes?' Elizabeth asked.

'I did not,' he said. 'Neither did I say no. I suggested we get to know each other better to see if there could be any other reason for us to marry apart from . . . money. She came, veiled, to the tea I gave here for my neighbors, and we have called upon each other a couple of times since. Today she came unveiled to meet you. It took great courage.'

'Oh, Alex,' his mother said. 'I feel all the sympathy in the world for her. I truly do. But it chills me to the heart to think of you married to her.'

'She was terrified,' he said. 'This was something she has never done before.'

'I fear for you,' she said. 'I *know* you are thinking of marrying for money, not for yourself but for the people here whose livelihood depends upon the prosperity of Brambledean. And I know you are kindhearted. But, Alex, she is not the bride for you. Oh, I do try not to interfere in your life. I try not to be the sort of mother who hangs about her son's neck like a millstone. But – Oh, Cousin Humphrey Westcott was a wicked, wicked man and I do not care what anyone says about not speaking ill of the dead.'

Alexander sat down in the chair closest to the door. He rested one elbow on the arm of the chair and pinched the bridge of his nose between a finger and thumb, his eyes closed. 'She has come to the conclusion that we are incompatible,' he said. 'She told me so just now before she left. She has realized that as my wife she would be compelled to move beyond the life of isolation to which she is accustomed, and she believes herself incapable of doing it.'

He heard his mother expel her breath.

'I asked her to come to London this spring as your guest at Westcott House,' he said. 'I offered to take rooms elsewhere. I thought she might be persuaded to meet a few people, attend a few social functions, get to feel more comfortable around her peers. But she will not, or cannot, do it. She has withdrawn her offer and said goodbye.'

Neither lady spoke for a while.

'And I suppose,' Elizabeth said, 'you now feel guilty, Alex.'

He opened his eyes and laughed, though without humor. 'Like you and Mama,' he said, 'I wonder what happened to her. She will not speak of it. The only emotion she showed came when I broached the subject a little while ago. I believe, though, that this whole experiment of hers has left her feeling a little bit hurt. Perhaps more than a little.'

'But that is neither your fault nor your problem, Alex,' his mother said.

He looked broodingly at her. She was quite right, of course.

'I know,' he said. 'But I hate to think I may in any way have been the cause of pain to her.'

'Are you feeling a little bit hurt too, Alex?' Elizabeth asked.

He thought about it. 'Her birthmark,' he said, 'is just the visible symbol of much deeper pain. I was relieved to see her go, Lizzie, I must confess. It was not a relationship that was developing comfortably. But she is a person, and I got to know her a little. She likes daffodils.' He frowned down at the hands he had draped over his knees. 'She calls them golden trumpets of hope but was embarrassed when she said it aloud. Perhaps I would like to be her friend, but it is too late for that. Anyway, a friendship between a single man and a single lady never seems quite appropriate. I am sorry to have clouded your day. What can I do to lift the gloom? Take you both for a walk outside, perhaps?' He smiled from one to the other of them.

'I do believe,' his mother said, 'I would prefer a quiet half hour or so lying on my bed. It has been an eventful day. But you and Lizzie go outside if you wish.'

'You may be right, Alex,' Elizabeth said, bending to put her embroidery away in the bag beside her chair before getting to her feet. 'It may be impossible for you to reach out to Miss Heyden in friendship, but it is not impossible for me. I should like to call upon her at Withington House, with your permission.'

Their mother sighed but said nothing.

'It is all of eight miles away,' he said, 'perhaps more. Are you sure, Lizzie?'

'It is good manners to return a call, is it not?' she said. 'It need be no more than that. If she freezes me out, then I shall return here with no real harm done. But perhaps she needs a friend, even if the sort of friendship I can offer can really only be conducted by letter. We ladies thrive upon letter writing, though, as you know.' Her eyes twinkled at him.

Would she freeze Lizzie out? He had no idea. But he felt a certain relief to know that she would have the chance at least of a long-distance friendship – and that she would know that she had not been as thoroughly disliked as she had thought.

'Thank you,' he said.

'And now you may escort Mama up to her room,' she said, 'and I will come up too for my bonnet. I am in need of that walk.'

CHAPTER 7

Wren was making preparations to go to Staffordshire. She had not intended it to be so soon. She loved being in the country during springtime, but, more important this year, she had set herself the task of finding a husband. That project was at an end, unsuccessfully as it turned out, but not every enterprise could succeed. That was one lesson she had learned from her uncle. Failure must be taken in one's stride just as success must be. If one kept a cool, sensible head and learned from one's mistakes, the successes would ultimately outweigh the failures. There was always something new and something challenging to look forward to. It was a bit hard to believe at the moment, it was true, for her feelings had been bruised and she had found herself for the last day or two a little broody and even a little weepy. But through this experience she had learned that for her, success was to be looked for alone and in impersonal things, most notably in her business. For that at least, she could be grateful.

A change of scenery would invigorate her and

do her an immensity of good, she had decided. She would keep herself busy doing what she loved doing and did well. Being there would enable her to speak directly with Philip Croft, the longtime manager, and everyone else. She would be able to get out into the workshops and marvel anew at the almost magical process of creating vases and jugs and tumblers and figurines out of something as airy and fragile as glass. She would be able to watch the glassblowers, the glass cutters, the engravers, and the painters and know herself in the uplifting company of true artists. She always found it a humbling experience. Whenever she was there, she wondered how she could ever bear to stay away so long.

She was in her room packing the trunk and valise she had had brought up to her dressing room. It was something she always liked to do for herself despite Maude's protests. But perhaps she was not going to be able to finish. She could hear the arrival of a carriage on the terrace below her window. Who—? No one ever came visiting. Surely it was not *him*. She did not look through the window, lest he look up and see her. She had no intention of receiving him, though it would not be the best of good manners to turn him away when he had come so far in the rain. If it *was* him, that was. But there was no one else. If only he had waited until tomorrow, she would have been gone and would not have had to worry about being rude.

It was Maude who tapped on her door and opened it at Wren's bidding. 'Lady Overfield wishes to know if you are at home to visitors, Miss Wren,' she said, looking disapprovingly at the open trunk and valise and shaking her head in exasperation.

'*Lady Overfield?* Is she alone?' Wren asked.

'Yes, she is,' Maude said. 'The earl did not come with her, unless he is stooped down and hiding in the carriage.'

How very foolish to feel a pang of disappointment. But . . . his sister? Whatever could she want? Had he not *told* her? 'Well, if you said you would come to see if I am home, as I daresay you did,' she said, 'she will know that indeed I *am* here. You had better show her up to the drawing room, Maude, and tell her I will be down in a moment.'

'I already have,' Maude said. 'You could hardly refuse to see her, could you?'

And she would have done the same for the earl, Wren supposed. 'Send a tea tray to the drawing room, will you, please?' she asked.

'Already done,' her maid said before disappearing.

Wren looked down at herself. She was wearing an old dress, a faded gray one she had worn years ago and resurrected recently to serve for half mourning. She brushed her hands over it. It would have to do. So would her hair. She checked it in the mirror. It had been twisted into a simple knot at the back of her head but was at least reasonably tidy. She glanced at the veil hanging over the back of a chair but decided against it. The lady had seen her in all her purple-faced glory, after all. She went downstairs with reluctant feet.

Lady Overfield was standing by one of the windows, looking out, though she turned as soon as Wren entered the room. She was very unlike her brother. Wren looked for some resemblance but could find none. She did not have his dark and formidable good looks or his rather formal aristocratic bearing. Her main claim to beauty was an amiable face that seemed to smile even in repose.

Wren did not greet the lady or move toward her after she had closed the door. She did not smile. She had issued no invitation, after all, and she could guess the purpose of this visit.

'I do hope,' Lady Overfield said, 'I have not come at a very inconvenient time. If I have, you must say so and I will take myself off without further ado.'

'Not at all,' Wren said. 'I was just packing. Please come and sit down.' Good manners had reasserted themselves.

'Packing?' Lady Overfield seated herself on the chair Wren had indicated.

'I have a home in Staffordshire near the glassworks,' Wren explained as she sat opposite her guest. 'It is possible to run the business from a distance since I have a competent manager who has been there for years, but I like to spend time there occasionally. I like to see for myself what is happening, to take an active part in plans and decisions for future developments, to get out into the workshop itself, partly to show my workers that I appreciate their skills. I also marvel at their talent and dedication to producing perfection. I have spent some of my happiest days there. Glassware can be so very lovely, and the emphasis with us has always been upon producing what is truly beautiful rather than just what is utilitarian and quickly made and easily sold.' She was on the defensive again. She could hear the edge of hostility in her voice.

'How very wonderful you make it sound,' Lady Overfield said. 'Do you realize what a rarity you are among women, Miss Heyden?'

Was she being mocked? Wren was not sure. Yet the lady's manner seemed warm and sincere. Perhaps she was better at dissembling than Wren was. 'I do realize it,' she said. 'I think of myself as being one of the most fortunate of women.'

A maid brought in the tea tray at that moment, and there was a pause while Wren poured and they each sat back with their tea and a ginger biscuit.

'Your long journey here was quite unnecessary, Lady Overfield,' Wren said, dunking her biscuit in her tea, which was probably not a genteel thing to do. 'You have come to warn me off. Lord Riverdale did not inform you, I daresay, that we said goodbye a couple of days ago and that I said it first. Goodbye does not mean farewell until we meet again; it means we will never meet again unless by chance. Since I live a reclusive existence here in the country at least eight miles from Brambledean and spend weeks of each year elsewhere, that chance is slim to none. He is quite safe from me – and the lure of my money.' Ah. So much for good manners. She stopped, breathless.

Lady Overfield returned her cup to its saucer before replying. 'He did tell us,' she said. 'He seemed a little sad about it, and that made my mother and me a little sad too. But my coming here has nothing to do with that, Miss Heyden. Your dealings with Alex are a matter entirely between the two of you.'

Sad? He had been sad? 'Why did you come, then?' Wren asked.

'It seemed the polite thing to do to return your call,' Lady Overfield said. She held up a staying hand before Wren could reply. 'No. I do not believe social platitudes will work with you, will they? And why should they? Why should not truth be told? I sensed when we met the day before yesterday that you were perhaps in need of a friend. I know you have been alone since losing your aunt and uncle very close to each other last year. And I know what it feels like to be alone.'

'After you were widowed?' Wren asked.

Lady Overfield hesitated. 'It was not after his death that I felt alone,' she said, 'but during. He was – Well, he was an abuser, Miss Heyden, a fact I felt compelled to keep secret, even from my family – for a variety of reasons, which I shall not go into. I did have family. I also had acquaintances galore. We were very active socially. But I felt alone and friendless at the heart of it all. I am not suggesting there is anything in common between your experience of aloneness and mine except in that one thing. And forgive me if my assumption is offensive to you. You may have numerous very close friends. Or you may not want any. You certainly may not want me as a friend.'

Wren stared at her, speechless, and without warning she was catapulted back to childhood and the constant yearning that had made it unbearable. She could remember more than once curling up into a ball in the corner of her room behind the bed, sobbing inconsolably, rocking back and forth, longing and longing for the friends of her own age she could never have. Or even one friend. Just one. Was it too much to ask? But it had been a rhetorical question, for the answer was always yes. While she had heard the shouts and laughter of other children outdoors or in other rooms, she had always remained alone, sometimes behind a locked door – locked from the other side. There had been only one child, a mere infant . . .

She had long ago suppressed any yearning for friends. She had had a safe, nurturing home instead and the unconditional love of two people who must surely have been angels in human disguise, she had sometimes thought a little fancifully. But hearing her friendless state put into words now made her need feel raw again. Her first instinct was to be defensive, for there seemed something a little shameful about having no friends. Yet this elegant, poised, smiling lady, who looked as though she could never have suffered deeply in her life despite what she had said about her husband, knew what it was like to feel all alone in the world and had been willing to share with a near stranger what must have seemed like her shame at the time.

'Of course,' Lady Overfield continued when Wren said nothing, 'I do not live at Brambledean or ever expect to do so. But if Alex makes it his home, as he fully intends, I daresay I will spend some time there. We have always been a close family, and he has been particularly good to me. I cannot offer any very close friendship, perhaps, but I do offer what I can. There are always letters with which to keep up an acquaintance. I am a champion letter writer.'

'I am forever busy with business correspondence,' Wren said stiffly.

The lady was smiling again. 'Shall I tell you *how* Alex was particularly good to me?' she asked. 'Or would you rather never hear his name again?'

'How?' Wren asked unwillingly, noticing the second half of her biscuit still untouched on her saucer and taking a bite out of it – there was no tea left in which to dip it.

'When Desmond – my husband – first hurt me very badly,' Lady Overfield told her, 'I fled home to Riddings Park. But he came after me, and my father, very conscious of the fact that I had married him of my own free will and was therefore his property and possession, to do with as he willed, insisted that I return home with him. In my father's defense, Desmond was abject with apologies and assurances that nothing like it would ever happen again. When I was even more badly hurt later – my arm was broken among other things – and fled home again, my father had already passed away. When Desmond came for me, Alex punched him in the face and sent him on his way. He returned with a magistrate, but Alex stood his ground and refused to give me up. I have lived with him and my mother ever since. Desmond died the year after. My brother is a gentle man of even temper, but no one should ever make the mistake of believing him to be a weak man. Now, do tell me about your aunt. I know your uncle was a successful businessman and that he must have encouraged your interest in the business and even, presumably, trained you to carry it on after him. But what about your aunt, whom you loved so dearly?'

How could Lady Overfield have suffered as she had without showing any outer sign of it now? How had she recovered? But *had* she? She seemed very poised and very amiable, but one could not know from such a brief acquaintance what went on deep inside another person. And why had the lady confided something so deeply personal to Wren? Because she wanted to be her friend? Was it possible? It would be very easy to shed tears, Wren thought, blinking away the possibility. Lady Overfield had chosen to confide in her.

'She was plump and placid and reveled in her

role as wife and surrogate mother,' Wren said, 'and never showed the slightest interest in the business beyond an admiration for some of the lovelier pieces that were presented for her approval. She never raised her voice, never lost her temper, never said an unkind word about anyone in my hearing. But she was as tough as old leather when aroused. When—' She stopped abruptly. 'Well. There was one time . . .'

She was relieved when Lady Overfield filled the gap. 'I wish I could have known her,' she said. 'Did she educate you or did you have a governess?'

And somehow the correct half hour for a visit slipped by unnoticed and then another while they talked on a number of subjects without any seeming effort on either of their parts. She was talking, Wren realized, and even smiling. She was warming to the first offer of friendship she had ever received. It was not until Lady Overfield glanced at the clock on the mantel, looked startled, and said it was high time she took her leave and let Miss Heyden return to her packing that Wren realized how much she had been enjoying herself.

'How time has flown,' Wren said, setting the tray aside and getting to her feet. 'I do thank you for coming. I hope the rain has not made the road treacherous.'

'It is not the sort of heavy downpour that turns a road to mud very quickly,' Lady Overfield said, glancing through the window as she stood too. She did not immediately turn to the door. She frowned, hesitated, and then turned to look fully at Wren. She drew breath to speak, seemed to change her mind, shook her head, and then smiled. 'Miss Heyden, I came to say something and then got lost in the pleasure of conversing with you. But I must deliver the speech I prepared so carefully and rehearsed so diligently in the carriage, or I shall kick myself in the shins all the way home. Alex told us that he invited you to come to London sometime this spring as my mother's guest at Westcott House. I know you refused, and I fully respect that. However, I do want to say two things. First, if your refusal was in part because you felt we would not welcome your company, you were quite wrong. Both my mother and I are very sociable beings and it would be a genuine pleasure to entertain you. Second, if you were to choose, for whatever reason, to come to town after all, we would be more than delighted to show you about London, which is certainly worth a visit, though perhaps it cannot compete with a glassworks. I would *very much* enjoy a tour of that one of these days, by the way. We would be delighted too to accompany you to any of the myriad entertainments of the Season that might take your fancy. We would be equally willing to leave you at home whenever you chose not to accompany us. There would be no pressure whatsoever upon you to do anything you did not want to do or to meet anyone you did not want to meet. There. That is what I came to say. My mother wished to accompany me this afternoon, I ought to add, but I suggested that you might feel overwhelmed if we both turned up on your doorstep. Ah, one more thing.' She opened her reticule and drew out a card, which she handed to Wren. 'It has the London address. I hope you will write to me there regardless. I promise to write back.'

'Thank you.' Wren looked down at the card. 'I shall . . . write.' She was not at all sure she would. But then she was not sure she would not. She had never before been offered friendship, even at a distance. She would never go to London, of course, but . . . she could have a friend. Perhaps see her here occasionally. Perhaps invite her to Staffordshire at some time in the future. Yes, she *would* write. It would be the polite thing to do if nothing else. 'I will walk downstairs with you.'

By the time she arrived back in her room, Maude had finished packing both her trunk and her valise. Wren looked at the card in her hand and slipped it down the inside edge of the valise. 'I was not sure everything was going to fit,' she said. 'You are a far neater packer than I, Maude. Thank you.'

'You always give me twice the work,' her maid grumbled. 'First I have to haul out everything you have packed, and then I have to do the job properly.'

Wren laughed and went to stand by the window. She gazed out and wondered if the rain would delay her own journey tomorrow. But after a few moments it was no longer the rain she saw. It was the Earl of Riverdale pummeling Lady Overfield's husband in the face and refusing to give her up, even though the law was against him and arrived on his doorstep in the form of a magistrate to tell him so.

My brother is a gentle man of even temper, but no one should ever make the mistake of believing him to be a weak man.

And he was the brother of her friend.

My friend. She whispered the words against the glass.

Alexander left for London with his mother and sister the day after Wren left for Staffordshire. He had discussed with his steward what could and would be done with the limited resources he had at his disposal. It was not much, but they could only do the best they could and hope for a decent harvest and a little more money to invest next year. The house and park must wait, though Alexander had every intention of returning there to live for the summer.

In the meanwhile he went to London because it was his duty to take his seat in the House of Lords. And because his mother and Elizabeth really ought to have his protection and escort while they were in town. They did not have to lease a house this year. Westcott House on South Audley Street, town house of the earls for the past few generations, was not an entailed property. Last year Anna had ended up owner of the London residence. But she had never wanted to keep everything for herself. She had tried to divide her fortune into four parts, three-quarters of it to be divided among her three dispossessed half siblings. And she had tried to give Westcott House to Alexander. They had finally settled upon his living there whenever he was in town, though she had informed him that her will already stated that the house was to be his and his descendants' after her time. He hoped it would be after his time too – Anna was four years younger than he.

He went to London also – of course – because he needed a wealthy bride, though the very idea was becoming more and more distasteful to him. He had not enjoyed his dealings with Miss Heyden when he had known that his only real motive for considering marriage with her was the fortune she would bring with her. He had felt . . . almost dirty, though there had been no deception involved. She had been the one to approach him, after all, because he needed money and she wanted someone to wed. Good God, they would have hated each other within a fortnight of marrying.

Perhaps. Though perhaps not. He remembered her with a bit of an ache . . .

But he shook off thoughts of her whenever they threatened to intrude and turned his mind to the future – or rather to the present of these few months in London. He did it, however, with very little enthusiasm for the mission he had set himself.

It soon became apparent that the task was going

to be far easier than he had anticipated. He met numerous young ladies in the three weeks following his arrival. This was the Season, after all, and he was the Earl of Riverdale, relatively young and single. The fact that he was not also a wealthy man, that he had inherited a dilapidated heap of an ancestral estate, could be no secret, of course. But far from deterring interest, those facts actually seemed to be an encouragement to some. Wealthy families of lower estate, it turned out, were only too willing to pay handsomely for the chance to marry one of their daughters into the aristocracy in return for a boost to their own social stature. That, some people claimed, was what daughters were for.

Alexander hated to be caught up in such crass cynicism. But the Season was not called the great marriage mart for nothing. He found it difficult and a bit humiliating to attend balls and soirees and concerts and other social events when he knew that all many people saw when they looked at him was an eligible aristocrat who must be looking for an equally eligible – and rich – bride. And, dash it all, they were quite right.

Miss Hetty Littlewood was one of many. Alexander danced with her one evening – twice, in fact, though he was not quite sure how the second one happened. Sometimes one could be taken off guard when ambitious mamas were determined enough. She was eighteen years old, fresh out of the schoolroom, blond and pretty with dimples in both cheeks, and of pleasing disposition. She was happy to chatter about the weather and other people and upcoming events of the Season and fashions. She gazed at him with wide, rather blank blue eyes, however, when he tried to speak of books she said she had read, of a play currently being performed on one of the London stages she said she had attended two evenings previously, and the music performed at a recent concert she said she had enjoyed 'more than anything,' and some of the galleries she claimed to have visited and 'adored.'

That evening was followed the morning after by an invitation to join the Littlewoods and a select group of their friends at Vauxhall three evenings hence. And the same day Mr Oswald Littlewood, a florid-faced, portly gentleman, had an acquaintance they had in common introduce them at White's Club and sat down beside Alexander in the reading room and held forth for half an hour upon his credentials, to the obvious annoyance of those who were actually trying to read the papers or even a book in peace. He was the younger son of a baron, but had ended up ten times richer than his elder brother when an uncle who had amassed a king's ransom in India – *make that a nabob's ransom, Riverdale* – died and left him half of everything.

'A good half,' he added illogically. 'And the other, lesser half did not go to my brother.' That fact appeared to please him enormously. He chuckled and rubbed his hands together.

The good Lord had apparently blessed him and

Mrs Littlewood, a considerable heiress in her own right, with only the one daughter, the apple of their eye, the joy of their days, the paragon of all daughters, who aimed to desert her doting parents soon, the little puss, by marrying a handsome gentleman of her own choosing.

'And so besotted with her are her mother and I,' the gentleman added after a hearty laugh at what he appeared to believe was a grand joke, 'that we will allow her to have her way, Riverdale. Provided he is a gentleman and respectable, of course. And provided he treats her well. We are in the fortunate position of not having to urge her to choose someone rich to support her. Indeed, if she were to choose a poor gentleman and support *him*, her mother and I would have no objection, provided he recognized his good fortune. Have you met my good wife and our Hetty, Riverdale?'

Unfortunately, Alexander had already returned an acceptance of the Vauxhall invitation. Even more unfortunately, he must allow himself to be courted. He could not afford *not* to.

And Miss Littlewood and her fond mama and papa were not the only ones – only the most persistent so far.

Wren spent two and a half busy, happy weeks in Staffordshire. She had no social life, of course, but she did not need one there. She spent her days in the workshops and the offices. She was a familiar figure and felt no self-consciousness, though she always went veiled. She pored over sketches for new products with her manager and designers and engaged them in an often vigorous exchange of views. Those discussions were never either acrimonious or obsequious. There was mutual respect among them all. She went over plans for selling the products and costing projections with the relevant persons and looked over long columns of profits and losses so that she could participate knowledgeably in discussions about finances. She suggested when she was sure of her facts that profits were such that wages could be raised again, and her suggestion was approved.

But one day she sat alone in her office, the door closed so that she could throw back her veil – no one ever entered her room without first knocking. To anyone who did enter, she would look as busy as usual, seated behind her desk as she was, papers spread before her, quill pen in hand.

She was actually drawing up two lists, one headed 'Pros,' the other headed 'Cons.' The cons list was longer than the other and easier to write.

Cons:

1. *Have never been there before, except with Aunt M when I was ten.*
2. *Do not really want to go.*
3. *Do not want to see him again.*
4. *Am sure he feels the same way.*
5. *Would not know where to go or what to do.*

6. *Lady O probably did not mean it.*
7. *Mrs W almost certainly did not.*
8. *Am perfectly happy here.*
9. *Would be just as happy at Withington.*
10. *Lots of people there. Too many.*
11. *Do not know anyone there except Lady O, Mrs W, and him.*
12. *Do not want to know anyone.*
13. *Might run into one of them there. Disaster!*
14. *Specifically, might run into her. Unthinkable!*
15. *Sleeping dogs are best left lying.*
16. *It might seem a bit desperate or pathetic.*
17. *Nothing much to put on the pro list. Means there are no real pros.*

Pros:

1. *Would exorcise some demons.*
2. *Could feel proud of myself.*
3. *Was invited.*
4. *Would actually like to see St Paul's and the National Gallery and other places.*
5. *Would be able to visit some shops that display our glassware.*
6. *Would prove I am not a coward. (Same as point 2?)*
7. *Just because. (Not a reason.)*
8. *Would see him again. (Contradicts cons.)*
9. *Just because I want to. (Another contradiction. Plus is this the same as 7?)*

The idea that after all she should go to London had been gnawing at Wren since she arrived here – no, actually since the day before she left Wiltshire. Just for a few days, a week at most. She would not have to stay at Westcott House. Indeed, she would not have to let Lady Overfield or anyone else know she was coming – or even that she was there. She could stay at a hotel. She had no fear of doing so as a woman on her own. She would have Maude and other servants with her for respectability. She had been busy and happy here, though. Why give that up? She could stay here as long as she liked and then go home to Wiltshire and be busy and happy there for the rest of the summer.

But he had suggested she go to London to stay with his mother, and Lady Overfield had repeated the invitation. The idea had horrified Wren both times. She had said goodbye to the Earl of Riverdale largely because marriage to him would drag her into the social life of the *ton*, and that was just not going to happen. So why was she even thinking of going? The cons list was almost twice was long as the pros list.

But the idea of going to London anyway had gnawed and nibbled and nudged at her until – horror of horrors – she found herself sorely tempted to go, even if just to show that she *could*. Show whom, though? Herself? Him? His sister and mother? The world at large?

It all boiled down to a question of courage, she

decided at last. And while she really did not want to go and really *really* did not want to see the Earl of Riverdale again, she also did not want to be a coward in her own eyes. Was it cowardice not to do what one did not want to do anyway? But was she being quite honest? Was it possible that she secretly did wish to see London? And was it remotely possible that she yearned to see him?

Yearned?

Wren grabbed another piece of paper and scrawled a single word almost vengefully across it.

WHY?

But staring at it brought no clear answers. Why indeed was she tempted? Because she had taken a look at herself and did not quite like what she saw? And this had *nothing* to do with her hideous face. Because Lady Overfield had offered friendship and she had never had a friend? They had actually exchanged a couple of letters each and Wren had found both writing her own and reading the answering ones a great, unexpected delight. Because he had invited her – before she said goodbye? Or was it after? She could not remember.

Because he had kissed her?

Because she could not quite forget him?

She arranged the three pages neatly on top of one another, tapped them on the desktop to even up the edges, then tore them once across and once down, dropped the pieces into the back of the fireplace behind the unlit coals, and decided that she would not go.

There.

It was done. She was not going.

Definitely, irrevocably not. Final decision, never to be revisited.

She felt very much better.

CHAPTER 8

Alexander was walking along the banks of the Serpentine in Hyde Park one afternoon a little over three weeks after his arrival in town, Miss Hetty Littlewood on his arm, Mrs Littlewood beside her.

He had been maneuvered into the walk the evening before while attending a concert with his mother and Elizabeth. They had been sitting with the Radleys – Uncle Richard, his mother's brother, and Aunt Lilian – and with Susan, their daughter, and Alvin Cole, her husband. Alexander had gone with Alvin during the interval to fetch lemonade for the ladies and had found himself face-to-face with Mrs Littlewood and her daughter as he turned from the table, one glass in each hand.

'How very good of you, my lord,' the mother had said, fanning her face as she took one of the glasses and gestured for Miss Littlewood to take the other.

And somehow during what remained of the interval Alexander had found himself agreeing that indeed Hyde Park was a delightful place in which to stroll during an afternoon, particularly the banks of the Serpentine. Miss Littlewood had apparently not been there yet, her papa not being fond of walking and Mrs Littlewood herself always a little wary of stepping out anywhere except the more well-frequented shopping streets without male escort. Alexander had responded like a puppet on a string.

And so here he was.

Miss Littlewood was looking very fetching in a peach-colored walking dress with matching parasol and a straw bonnet. She was small and dainty and smiling. And she was not without conversation since they strolled in a picturesque part of the park on a warm, sunny day, and other people were out in force, and there was much to be commented upon and rhapsodized over. Mrs Littlewood meanwhile nodded graciously to everyone about her, the tall plumes on her bonnet nodding with her as though, Alexander thought with some discomfort, she were already the mother-in-law of the Earl of Riverdale.

Even more uncomfortable was the thought that perhaps she really would be before the summer was out – or someone like her. Any parent willing and eager to give a vast dowry with a daughter, he had come to understand, wanted a great deal more in return than just a decent marriage for that daughter. He wondered if he was going to be able to do it. But he smiled at his companion and agreed that yes, the little boy approaching along the bank, trailing a boat by a string in the water behind him, was a darling little cherub.

'Oh dear,' she said in sudden distress, tugging slightly on his arm to draw him to a halt. 'Oh no.'

A girl, slightly older than the darling cherub, was skipping along the bank in the opposite direction and chose to pass the little boy on the lakeside without noticing the string. She tripped over it, fell sprawling, and scrambled to her feet, eyes blazing, mouth going into action with shrill insults, which included *silly oaf* and *clumsy clod* and *loutish imbecile*. The boy opened up his mouth and howled, pointing pathetically to his boat, which was escaping merrily along the bank, trailing the dropped string.

'Ah, help is at hand,' Alexander said just when he expected to be urged to step up to the rescue. A lady in green had caught up the string and was leaning down between the children and saying something to reduce the girl's tirade to a petulant murmur and the boy's anguish to a few injured hiccups as he reclaimed his mastery over his boat. She straightened up as two women, both nurses by the look of them, converged upon the spot from opposite directions and took ownership of their respective charges. 'All appears to have been solved.'

'Poor little angel,' Miss Littlewood said, presumably referring to the boy.

'If that girl were mine,' her mother said, 'she would be marched home without further ado and shut into her room for the rest of the day on bread and water after having her mouth washed out with soap. Her nurse would be dismissed without a character.'

Alexander scarcely heard either of them. The lady in green, tall, slim, and elegant, had been facing away from him until she half turned in order to resume her walk. She was wearing a pale green bonnet with a matching facial veil. Good God. Could it be? She moved her head fully in their direction just at that moment, stopped abruptly, and then turned right about and hurried off in the other direction – with a familiar stride.

'Pardon me,' he said, drawing his arm free of Miss Littlewood's without looking at either her or her mother – indeed, for the moment he had forgotten them. 'There is an acquaintance I must greet.' And he went after her, outpaced her within very few steps, and set a hand upon her arm. 'Miss Heyden?'

She stopped again and turned to face him. The veil had been cleverly made to look light and attractive, but it quite effectively hid her features. 'Lord Riverdale,' she said, 'what a delightful surprise.' She did not sound either surprised or delighted.

'You came to town after all, then?' he said.

'I had some business here to attend to,' she told him. 'Some London shops sell our glassware and I wanted to see them for myself.'

But had she not told him she never came to London and never would? Had that not been at the heart of the whole compatibility issue between them?

'I would love to see those shops myself,' he said. 'You must tell me where your glassware is displayed. But more important, where are you staying?' And where was her maid or her footman? She appeared to be entirely alone.

'At a quiet hotel for gentlewomen,' she said. 'I arrived in town just an hour or two ago and sought out the park for air and exercise after the long journey. I trust Mrs Westcott and Lady Overfield are well?'

'Yes,' he said. 'Thank you. Lizzie was pleased to receive your letters.' There was a pointed cough from a short distance away and Alexander remembered that he was not alone.

'You are delaying the ladies you are escorting, Lord Riverdale,' she said.

He must return to them. 'Will I see you again?' he asked. 'Tell me the names of those shops. Will you call upon my mother and sister? They would be delighted to see you. Do you have the address?'

Why was he feeling near panic over the fact that he might not see her again?

The second cough was even more pointed.

'I will call,' she said. 'Tomorrow morning. I have the address.'

'I will tell them,' he said. 'They will be delighted.' Had he already said that?

'I hope it will not be inconvenient for them,' she said.

'It will not.' He hesitated, but there was no more to be said, and he was already being very bad

144

mannered to the two ladies who were under his escort. He turned away and hurried back to them.

She had not told him the names of any of the shops. She had not named the hotel where she was staying. What if she did not turn up tomorrow?

But did it matter?

'What an extraordinarily tall lady,' Miss Littlewood said, gazing after her.

'It is very unfortunate for her,' Mrs Littlewood agreed. 'And thin too. And not at all pretty, I daresay, if one may draw conclusions from the veil. Her governess really ought to have taught her not to stride along like that, just like a man. I would be very surprised to hear that she is married.' She looked inquiringly at Alexander.

He smiled and offered an arm to each. 'I do apologize for keeping you waiting,' he said.

'Poor lady. I would simply want to die if I were that tall,' Miss Littlewood said, slipping her hand through his arm. 'I have heard it said that gentlemen do not like tall ladies.'

'It is a severe misfortune,' her mother said. 'One can only feel for her. But where, Lord Riverdale, is her chaperon?'

'I did not ask, ma'am,' he said. 'What did you think of the second half of the concert last evening? The best was kept for last, I thought. It is little wonder the cellist is much sought after.'

He had made one firm decision at least during the last few minutes. If he must marry a rich bride this spring or summer, she was not going to be Miss Hetty Littlewood. He was going to have to be more vigilant against the persistent maneuverings of her mother, though it would not be easy.

Why *had* she come? It was certainly not because she wanted to see some glassware displayed in a few London shops. Had she had second thoughts about Elizabeth's invitation? About his own? What would he do if she did not call at South Audley Street tomorrow morning? Seek out every gentlewoman's hotel in London? How many *were* there, for the love of God?

And why exactly would he do any such thing?

Wren was a famous maker of lists. They helped organize her thoughts and her time. They increased her efficiency and ensured that everything she needed to do was done in a timely manner. But the ones she had made in her office in Staffordshire had been nothing but a waste of time, for she had made up her mind even before she had started to compose them. Of course she had found more cons than pros. It was her rational mind trying to impose sense upon her emotional self. And since she did not have a close acquaintance with her emotional self, reason had mowed it down with no trouble at all. But the emotional self was the more persistent of the two. It had picked itself up, dusted itself off, and carried on regardless.

She had come.

But she had not come boldly to conquer the

world. Rather she had crept in and taken a room at a hotel for gentlewomen. Not that doing so had necessarily been a cowardly move. Having refused two separate invitations to stay at the house on South Audley Street, she could hardly now arrive on the doorstep without warning. The very thought made her cringe.

She had settled herself in her room and decided to step out for air and exercise, flatly refusing Maude's company since her maid was exhausted and needed to lie down for a while. Wren had told herself that she would pay a call upon Lady Overfield before she lost her courage. But she had lost it anyway. What if they were not at home? What if they had other visitors? What if they looked visibly dismayed to see her? They would not, of course. For one thing, a servant would give them ample warning of her arrival before admitting her to their presence. For another, they were ladies. But what if *he* was there? She had said a very definite goodbye.

Why, then, had she come all this way?

She had made her way to Hyde Park instead after asking directions. It was a part of London she wished to see, after all – she had made a list. It was one item she would be able to strike off. Tomorrow perhaps she would see St Paul's Cathedral, Westminster Abbey, the Tower of London, St James's Palace, Carlton House. Were they within walking distance of one another? And there were all the galleries and museums. Perhaps they would fill the next day. And, of course, there were the shops that sold her glassware – she must not forget about them.

What she was, she had decided as she strode into the park, was one abject, cringing, shameful cowardly creature. South Audley Street was at the top of her list – underlined. Was it going to remain there, the one item not satisfyingly crossed out as having been done?

She had found, purely by accident, one of the most famous features of Hyde Park and strolled beside the Serpentine. She had been proud of herself for one thing, at least. It was a crowded area of the park, but she had held her head high and not faltered. Oh, she was wearing a veil, it was true, but even so she was *here,* out of doors, mingling with others even if she was not stopping to speak to anyone and no one was stopping to take any notice of her. Still, she was *doing* it.

And then she *had* both stopped and spoken – to two young children who had run afoul of each other along the bank and were reacting with predictable lack of logic, the one with a shrill scold, the other with wails of protest and anger. Meanwhile the toy boat of the wailer was making its escape. She had caught up the string before it fell completely into the water and had spoken to the children. The girl had stopped scolding the boy in order to ask her if she were a witch – she had looked delighted by the possibility rather than frightened – and the boy had more or less stopped wailing in order to point out that *everyone* knew witches wore big black hats. Wren had turned away after saying that alas, she was nothing nearly as exciting as a witch, with or without a black hat. She had been feeling pleased with herself and pleased with the world.

And then—

Well, and then she had found herself looking straight into the eyes of the Earl of Riverdale no more than a few yards away. If the earth could have opened and swallowed her whole, she would have uttered no complaint whatsoever.

Foolishly, she had turned to hurry back in the direction from which she had come, her mind at the same moment catching up with her eyes to inform her that he had a young lady on his arm with an older lady in attendance. She had felt a nasty pang of something she did not stop to analyze. But he had come after her anyway and touched her arm and spoken with her, though she could not afterward remember a word of their brief exchange except that he had asked her to call on his mother and sister and she had agreed to do so the next morning. What she did remember with far greater clarity was that the lady on his arm had been very young and very pretty and that the older lady who had coughed twice had done so with a possessive sort of annoyance.

All night, between fitful bouts of sleep, Wren longed to go home to Withington. At dawn, before she slid into another doze, she decided that that was precisely what she was going to do. She relaxed and felt infinitely better.

So of course here she was the next morning walking along South Audley Street, looking for the right house number. Maude was with her this time, and because she was, Wren stopped outside the correct house when she might otherwise have walked on by, pretending not to have seen it. She was *such* a coward. She climbed the steps with firm resolution and rapped the knocker against the door.

Less than a minute later she was ascending a grand staircase inside the house behind the butler, who had acknowledged her with a bow as soon as she gave her name and had not even gone up first to ascertain if Mrs Westcott was at home. He admitted her to what was obviously the drawing room after announcing her, and she lifted her veil over the brim of her bonnet. Both ladies were on their feet – there was no one else in the room – and both were smiling. Mrs Westcott came toward her, right hand extended.

'I am so pleased you came, Miss Heyden,' she said, taking Wren's hand in a firm grip before letting it go. 'Alex told us you are in town on business. It is good of you to give us some of your time. Do come and sit down. I hope you like coffee. That is what is being sent up, but it will be no trouble at all to have a pot of tea brought too if that is what you would prefer.'

'Coffee will be lovely,' Wren said. 'Thank you. I do hope I am not keeping you from something more important.'

'Nothing could be more important this morning,' Lady Overfield said as Wren moved toward the chair that had been indicated. And then she startled Wren by kissing her on the cheek – her purple cheek. 'May I take your bonnet? Have you been very busy since you arrived in town?'

Wren removed her bonnet and sat down. Mother and daughter sat side by side on a sofa. 'I arrived just yesterday,' she said. 'I went for a walk in Hyde Park to get some air and exercise after the journey, and met Lord Riverdale there.'

'Then you must plan to be busy today,' Mrs Westcott said.

'Yes.' Wren clasped her hands in her lap and then unclasped them and spread her fingers over her skirt. 'A few London shops sell my glassware. I thought it would be interesting to see how it is displayed. It sells well, but perhaps I can make some suggestions—' She stopped abruptly. 'I did not really come on business.'

'Then you came for pleasure,' Lady Overfield said, smiling warmly. 'And there is much of that to be had in London. But allow me to tell you in person, though I did so too in one of the letters I wrote you, how fascinated I was to read about the glassworks. I had no idea how much design planning and skill and artistry are involved and how important sales strategies are. I have a great curiosity to see some of the finished products. Perhaps I may go with you to the shops?'

Their coffee arrived at that moment with a plate of sugar biscuits.

'Where are you staying?' Mrs Westcott asked after the maid had left the room. 'Somewhere comfortable, I hope?'

'At a small hotel for gentlewomen,' Wren told her. 'It is quite respectable.' She was beginning to take in the spacious splendor of the drawing room, so very different from that at Brambledean Court. A great deal of money had been spent on this house to keep it fashionable and beautiful as well as comfortable. From what she had learned before she met the Earl of Riverdale, this house had not come to him with his title and estate but had gone with the bulk of the fortune to the former earl's legitimate daughter – the one who had grown up in an orphanage and then married a duke.

'*For gentlewomen. Respectable,*' Mrs Westcott repeated with a grimace. 'Is it as dreadful as it sounds?'

Wren bit her lower lip to stop herself from laughing aloud. 'My room is like a nun's cell,' she said, 'and the landlady looks like the head nun without a wimple. There is a list of rules posted just inside the front door and on the wall in my room, and rule number one is that no person of male gender is allowed to set foot over the doorstep under any circumstances whatsoever. I amused myself last night with images of persons of the

152

female gender hauling heavy furniture up and down the stairs and cleaning the chimneys. But one thing cannot be denied. It is a very respectable establishment.'

They all dissolved into laughter and Wren felt the paradoxical urge to weep. Her uncle and she had had an eye for the absurd, and her aunt had had a hearty sense of humor. They had laughed frequently. How often had she laughed since their passing?

'It may remain respectable without you, Miss Heyden,' Mrs Westcott said briskly, offering the plate of biscuits for the second time. 'Do not tell me the mattress on your bed is not stuffed with straw, for I will not believe it. You brought a maid here with you this morning? You did not come by carriage, though, did you? We would have heard it.'

'We came on foot,' Wren said, taking another biscuit and biting into it. It was still almost but not quite warm. It was fresh and delicious. Breakfast had been a Spartan meal – toast with the merest scraping of butter already applied and no jam or marmalade, and weak tea.

'Then we will send your maid back with a carriage to pack up your belongings and her own and bring them here,' Mrs Westcott said. 'You will stay with us while you are in town, Miss Heyden.'

'Oh no,' Wren cried in some alarm. 'I would not so inconvenience you, ma'am.'

'It will be no inconvenience,' Lady Overfield said.

'You were specifically invited, if you will recall, by both Alex and me, speaking on behalf of Mama too. Alex suggested again last evening that we ask you to move in here. We agreed with him that you really ought not to be left languishing on your own at a hotel.'

'But—' Wren frowned. 'You cannot really *want* to have me here. Oh, I beg your pardon. There is only one answer you can possibly give to that because you are ladies, and you are also kind. But you know that before you came to Wiltshire I quite brazenly offered my fortune to the Earl of Riverdale in exchange for marriage. You know that the whole . . . idea of it was abhorrent to him. And you cannot deny – not if you are truly honest – that when you met me at Brambledean you were horrified at the prospect that he might marry me. I recognized the impossibility of it on that day, and I released him from any obligation he might have felt after prolonging our acquaintance for more than two weeks. I said goodbye. You will not deny, I think, even if you are too polite to say it aloud, that you were greatly relieved when he told you.'

The other two ladies sat back in their seats as though to put some distance between themselves and her. There was a brief silence.

'I was,' Mrs Westcott admitted.

'Mama.' Lady Overfield frowned.

'No, Lizzie,' her mother said. 'Miss Heyden is right. There ought to be more honesty between people. How is anything to be communicated if everyone is too polite to speak their real thoughts?'

Lady Overfield inhaled audibly but said nothing.

'I love my children quite passionately, Miss Heyden,' Mrs Westcott said. 'More than anything else in life I want to see them happy. I want to see them married and settled with the right partner and enjoying their own children as I have enjoyed mine. My heart was broken when Lizzie's marriage turned to nightmare. Now I have her with me again, and I can hope and dream for her once more. My heart was hurt when Alex's youth was torn from him after his father's death with the discovery that all was not as it ought to be at Riddings Park. He left behind the life of a carefree young man and returned home to set things to rights.'

'It made him happy, Mama,' Lady Overfield said.

'Yes, I believe it did,' her mother agreed. 'But he is thirty years old, Miss Heyden, and last year he began to dream of marriage and love and happiness. And then everything changed – for the whole of the Westcott family. Now Brambledean hangs about my son's neck like a millstone and neglect is out of the question because Alex is who he is, and loans and mortgages are pointless because they have to be repaid. Everything in me revolts against the idea of his marrying for money, but that is what he feels he must do. Yes, I was horrified, Miss Heyden. Not because of that . . . facial blemish of yours, though that is probably what you believe. And not because you were so uncomfortable when you met us that you appeared stiff and cold and unapproachable. It was because you are rich and he is poor – at least poor as far as his new responsibilities are concerned – and I very much feared there could never be any proper respect or affection between you, not to mention love and happiness. I could not bear the thought that my son would be seen as mercenary.'

'Mama.' Lady Overfield set a hand on her arm.

'No, Lizzie,' her mother said. 'Let me finish. I *was* delighted after you had left, Miss Heyden, and then dismayed when Lizzie decided that she would go to visit you. But then we came here and Alex has been besieged by wealthy, ambitious people who have daughters to be settled. There is not one of those girls who does not fill me with terrible misgivings. Not for themselves – I daresay they are sweet enough girls, who have dreams of their own. But for Alex, who deserves so much more and so much better.'

'I am sorry.' Wren could think of nothing else to say.

'I think, Miss Heyden,' she continued, 'that perhaps you have more substance than all those little girls combined. And you have no ambitious parents.'

'No,' Wren said, and it was her turn to sit farther back in her chair.

'Were your aunt and uncle ambitious for you?' Mrs Westcott asked.

'Not in the way you mean,' Wren said. 'They wanted me to be happy. My aunt desperately wanted it, but they always respected my wishes.'

'You still feel their loss,' Mrs Westcott said.

'Yes.' And something dreadful happened. Wren felt her chin tremble. She spread one hand over the lower half of her face, but it was not enough. She covered it with both hands. Her bonnet was gone, and so was her veil. 'Oh, I am so sorry.' But her voice came out all high and squeaky. She sniffed.

And then Mrs Westcott was sitting on the arm of her chair, and one of her arms came about Wren's shoulders, and the other hand held Wren's head to her shoulder. Wren sobbed until her chest was sore and wept until there surely could be no tears left. A handkerchief and then a linen napkin were pressed into her hand, and she realized that Lady Overfield was kneeling on the floor in front of her chair.

'I am so s-sorry,' she said again.

'Have you wept before?' Mrs Westcott asked.

'N-no.' She had been very stoical about the whole thing. There was no point in tears, and sometimes her grief had felt too deep for such easy relief.

'There was no one with whom to share your grief,' Lady Overfield said. It was not a question. 'But you are among friends. You must not apologize.'

Maybe not. But her words brought on yet more tears.

'No,' Mrs Westcott said, hugging her shoulders more tightly for a moment, 'I am not a friend, Miss Heyden. I am a mother, and I am going to behave like one. It is quite outrageous for you to be staying alone at a horror of a hotel, or at any hotel for that matter. Your aunt would not have liked it. Your uncle would not have allowed it, I daresay, for all that he took you into his business and treated you as an equal. We will have your things brought here immediately, and I do not want to hear any arguments. Now, Lizzie and I will show you up to your room – it has already been prepared – and we will have water fetched so that you can wash your face and look present-able again. You look a fright at the moment.'

Wren laughed – and then wept a few more tears.

'I warn you that it is pointless to try arguing with Mama when she decides to play mother,' Lady Overfield said.

Wren felt horribly embarrassed as she got to her feet. 'But the Earl of Riverdale—' she began.

'Alex is at the House of Lords this morning,' Mrs Westcott told her. 'But everything is arranged. He will go to stay with his cousin – my brother's son – and will enjoy the excuse to be a carefree young bachelor about town again in company with another. He spoke with Sidney last night and is expected. They have always been close friends. Oh, the mischief they used to get up to while they thought my sister-in-law and I were quite ignorant of it.'

'I daresay you did not know the half of it even so, Mama,' Lady Overfield said, laughing.

And while they spoke lightly and cheerfully, they were taking Wren upstairs and along a wide corridor to a guest room. 'It will be lovely having you here, Miss Heyden. We can go with you, if you wish, to see what you hope to see in London. We can introduce you to some people and take you with us to some entertainments – or not. We will put no pressure whatsoever upon you just because you are staying here.'

It seemed that everything had been decided for her, Wren thought, without her having to make the decision for herself. Here she was in a pretty room at the back of the house, overlooking what appeared to be a colorful, well-tended garden, and it was too late to say no. And she was feeling too weary to argue anyway. She was here, and Lady Overfield was her friend and Mrs Westcott was her . . . mother? And the Earl of Riverdale had already made other living arrangements for himself. Perhaps she would not even have to see him again. It would be very much more comfortable if that were so.

Liar. The inner voice spoke up despite her weariness.

'Thank you,' she said. 'You are both extraordinarily kind.'

Aunt Megan, then, was not the only kind lady the world had ever produced. Had she really believed she was?

CHAPTER 9

Ever since Miss Heyden said goodbye to him on Easter Sunday, Alexander had been telling himself what a fortunate escape he had had from what would surely have been a gloomy, troubled marriage. Perhaps the fact that he had thought it every single day since ought to have alerted him to the fact that perhaps he was not as happy about it as he thought he was.

Today he had gone to the House of Lords since there was an important debate in which he wanted to participate, but all morning he wondered if she had called upon his mother and Elizabeth and wondered what he would do if she had not. At the first opportunity, around noon, he sent off a brief note and waited impatiently for a reply. When it finally arrived, he learned she had indeed called and been persuaded to stay.

He took himself off to Sidney's rooms later, wondering what it was all going to mean. Must their courtship be considered to have resumed? Had it ever been a courtship? Did he want it to be? Was it too late now to ask himself such a question? He wondered if he ought to go immediately to pay his respects to her or if he ought to leave it until later. Perhaps they were not even at home.

It troubled him that she had come. She had left him with ruffled emotions, the chief of which had been relief that he no longer had to contend with them and try to sort them out. He wanted to be able to choose a bride with his head. The heart was too unpredictable and too capable of feeling pain and doubt and a host of other things. It was his heart that had sent him in pursuit of her in the park when it might have been wiser to let her go.

Dash it all.

The decision of what to do next was taken out of his hands. Sidney was not at home – he worked in the diplomatic service and often put in long hours. But there was a note from his mother awaiting him. Cousin Louise, the Dowager Duchess of Netherby, had called a Westcott family conference at Archer House on Hanover Square, town house of the duke, her stepson, and her own home too. Such meetings had been rare until last year. There had been a number of them after what the family collectively referred to as the great catastrophe, and then a lull. Now the summons had been sent out again, and the meeting was for this afternoon. Alexander glanced at a clock. Less than one hour from now, in fact. And, like it or not, he was head of the family.

Cousin Louise had a tendency to be overly dramatic. Alexander wondered as he left Sid's rooms again what sort of dire emergency had arisen now to necessitate the whole family's gathering together. He hoped it was nothing to do with Harry. Harry Westcott, who had been the earl for a brief time until the truth about his birth came out, was fighting out in the Peninsula and was a constant source of worry to them all. Not that they were unique in that. Innumerable families, both rich and poor, all over Britain must live with a similar anxiety. One never knew when a letter might arrive with the worst news anyone could ever receive. He hoped no such letter had come. God, he hoped not.

There must be something wrong, though, unless Cousin Louise simply wished to announce the betrothal of Jessica, her daughter, who was making her come-out this year at the age of eighteen. She had been much sought after at all the myriad entertainments of the Season so far. Alexander had seen it for himself. She was a duke's daughter, after all, with a handsome dowry. She was also pretty and vivacious. He had neither seen nor heard about any particular suitor, but one never knew.

He was the last to arrive. Cousin Louise had a mother still living – the Dowager Countess of Riverdale – and two sisters. The elder, Cousin Matilda, who had never married, lived with her mother. The younger, Cousin Mildred, was married to Thomas, Lord Molenor, and had three sons still at school. They were all there, except the boys.

The Duke of Netherby was there with his duchess. Anna was the daughter born of the first, secret marriage of Cousin Humphrey, the late earl, to a lady called Alice Snow and was his only legitimate child, as it had turned out. Jessica was there. So were Alexander's mother and his sister, Elizabeth. Absent were Cousin Viola, the former Countess of Riverdale, now going by her maiden name of Kingsley, and her two daughters, Camille, now married to Joel Cunningham and living in Bath, and Abigail. And Harry, of course.

Alexander greeted everyone and took up his stand before the fireplace, a habit of his, though he had once realized that it might be construed as an attempt on his part to assert his seniority in the family. He declined Cousin Louise's offer of a cup of tea, and conversation resumed around him. Netherby, he could see, was lounging in a chair in the far corner of the room beside a window, as he tended to do in any room, just as Alexander gravitated toward fireplaces. Perhaps he liked to observe what went on before him without having to turn his head a great deal or feel the obligation to participate. Perhaps it was an acknowledgment of the fact that he had no tie of blood to the Westcott family. He was the son of the Duke of Netherby, who had taken Cousin Louise as his second wife and fathered Jessica.

Netherby was looking as exquisitely gorgeous as ever, Alexander noticed with slight irritation, his blond hair immaculately cut into its longish style, his tailoring bordering upon the dandyish but not quite spilling over to the other side, his perfectly manicured fingers bedecked with rings. The chains and fobs and jeweled watchcase and quizzing glass that always adorned his waist were invisible today, however. He was holding a fat-cheeked, bald-headed babe nestled beneath his chin. She was sucking on her fist and – if Alexander was not much mistaken – one fold of her father's neckcloth. And if that was not an incongruous sight, Alexander did not know what was. Was Netherby not terrified of getting a spot of . . . drool upon his spotless linen? But it was an unkind thought, for Alexander had learned during the past year that despite appearances, there was nothing either weak or effeminate – or petulant – about Avery Archer, Duke of Netherby. Quite the contrary.

Alexander turned his attention to Elizabeth, who was seated close by. 'She did come, then?' he asked unnecessarily.

'She did indeed,' his sister told him. 'It took some effort from both Mama and me to persuade her to stay with us. But she is all settled in. I believe she was quite happy at the prospect of a quiet hour to herself after we left to come here.'

Why had they made that effort? he wondered. Why had he suggested it last evening? Why had he thought of little else today? Until this moment he had not thought even once today about Miss Littlewood. Or about any of the other young ladies whose mamas were aggressively pursuing him either. If he never saw any of them ever again he would really not notice. But Miss Heyden . . .

'I went to St Paul's Cathedral with her after luncheon,' Elizabeth said. 'She sat on a pew close to the back, Alex, and did not move for half an hour. She did not wander about to gape at everything, as other first-time visitors invariably do. She gazed about from where she sat, and she looked rapt, though I could not see her face clearly, it is true. She wore a veil.'

'Yes,' he said, 'she would.'

'Tomorrow morning we are going to look at some of the glassware from her workshops,' she said. 'I vastly look forward to that.'

But Cousin Louise was signaling with a clearing of the throat that the time had come for the business of the afternoon to begin. Everyone fell silent and looked expectantly at her.

'We need to decide what to do about Viola and Abigail,' she said.

'Are they not still at Hinsford Manor?' Cousin Mildred asked. 'When I heard from Viola a month or two ago she sounded quite cheerful about being back there. Their return home was well received by their neighbors, I understand.'

The late earl and his family had made their country home at Hinsford in Hampshire rather than at Brambledean, but last year Anna had inherited it and Cousin Viola had fled with Camille and Abigail to Bath, where her daughters had stayed with their maternal grandmother while she went to live with her brother at the vicarage in Dorsetshire. Anna had persuaded them months later to move back home. She had offered to give them the property, just as she had offered to give Westcott House to Alexander, and when she had been refused she had apparently informed them that she was willing Hinsford to Harry and his descendants and Westcott House to Alexander and his. Camille had remained in Bath, of course, to marry Cunningham.

'Yes, they are definitely there, Mildred,' the dowager countess said. 'I had a letter just last week. Viola did not sound discontented.'

'It is not Viola who is my main concern,' Cousin Louise said. 'It is Abigail. She is nineteen years old. One wonders how many eligible gentlemen she will meet in the country.'

'Well, there is the problem of her birth, Louise,' Cousin Matilda pointed out. 'It is unfortunate, but her illegitimacy is one of those realities that cannot be ignored. It is unlikely she will meet any eligible gentleman no matter where she is. Perhaps she will be as content to remain with her mama as I have been to remain with mine.'

'I have tried to persuade her to come here,' Anna said, sounding unhappy. 'She is my half sister, after all, and I would do all in my power to see that she was well received by all the people who really matter. *Kind* people, I mean. And *sensible* people. Abigail has done nothing to deserve ostracism. Avery would do all in his power too, and that is considerable. I am sure we all would, just as we did in Bath last summer when we went to celebrate Grandmama's birthday. Perhaps we should *all* try to persuade her to come.'

'We could invite her to stay with us,' Alexander's mother said. 'Westcott House was always her home when she was in town, after all. It would be familiar to her. Perhaps Viola would come with her. She and I have always been on the best of terms.'

'One would hate to expose either one of them to possible unkindness, though, Althea,' Cousin Mildred said. 'And we all know how many high sticklers there are in the *ton* and how much influence they wield. We would all rally around them, of course, because they are our family and we love them, but—'

'I *hate* the *ton*,' Jessica blurted out from her perch on the window seat close to Netherby. She had her knees drawn up before her, her arms wrapped about them. 'I hate people, and I hate this place. I hate London and the stupid, stupid *Season*. I want to go home, but no one will take me.'

'Jessica.' Cousin Louise's voice was both stern and strained. 'There is no call for such an outburst.'

'There is every call. I hate, hate, hate *everything*,' Jessica said, pressing her forehead to her knees.

'If hatred would solve all the world's hurts and injustices, Jess,' Netherby said on a languid sigh, 'they would all have been solved long ago. Unfortunately, it only seems to make matters worse. Your mother has called the family together in an effort to see if any workable solution can be found.'

'Well,' she said, looking up and glaring over her shoulder at her half brother, '*is* there a solution, Avery? The world in its oh-so-righteous wisdom has chosen to call Abby a bastard – and no, Mama, I will not avoid the word just because it is ungenteel. That is what she is called, just because Uncle Humphrey was mean and selfish and I am glad I never liked him and always felt sorry for Aunt Viola. I am *glad* she was never really married to him – though that, of course, means Abby and Harry and Camille are bastards. Don't tell me it is pointless to hate. Do you think I do not know that?'

Netherby looked at Anna, who bent over him and took the baby from him, leaving behind a noticeable wet patch on the lapel of his coat. He got up, swung Jessica's legs off the window seat, sat beside her, and wrapped one arm about her shoulders.

'This is the problem, you see,' Cousin Louise said, indicating her daughter. 'Abigail was to make her come-out last year but had to postpone it when Humphrey died. Jessica was overjoyed at the prospect of the two of them making their come-out together this year. But it was not to be. And now Jessica is unable to enjoy her own. She has become more and more unhappy in the past few weeks until it has come to this in the past day or two. She demands to go home to Morland Abbey.'

'She is young, Louise,' the dowager countess said. 'The young believe they can make the world a perfect place merely by wishing it or by expecting that justice will always be done. It is rather sad that as we grow older we come to understand that it can never happen. Perhaps you should do as she wishes and take her home. Invite Viola and Abigail to come and visit you there. Let the girls enjoy each other's company where the world of the *ton* is not constantly threatening them. They are both very young.'

'I would have to agree with Mama,' Cousin Mildred said. 'There will be time enough for Jessica to find a husband, Louise. She is only eighteen. She is also very pretty. And even if she were not, she is the daughter and sister of a Duke of Netherby. There will be no lack of suitors when she is ready for them.'

'I will *never* be ready,' Jessica said into the side of Netherby's neck. 'Not without Abby.'

'Perhaps we do need to consider some sort of solution for Abigail,' Alexander said. 'It is too easy, perhaps, to assume that she must be happy now that she is back in her old home with her mother. Jessica is the only one among us honest enough to confront a problem we need to help solve together, as a family. Perhaps they will agree to come for a visit to Westcott House, and perhaps we can arrange some social functions at which they will be welcomed and made to feel comfortable. Illegitimacy surely does not fall into the same category as smallpox or the plague. Collectively we wield a great deal of influence. Shall Mama write? And Elizabeth too? Shall I?'

Jessica was gazing mutely at him.

'They will probably not come,' Cousin Matilda said. 'You might as well save yourself the effort, Althea.'

'I can be very persuasive, Matilda,' Alexander's mother said, a twinkle in her eye.

'In the meanwhile,' Elizabeth said, 'why do you not come to Westcott House with us for some air and exercise, Jessica? We have a guest staying with us, a neighbor of Alex's at Brambledean. She is a rather lonely lady who lost both her aunt and her uncle, her only relatives, within a few days of each other a little over a year ago. Alex will be coming too, I daresay, to pay his respects to her, though he will be staying with Sidney Radley while she is here. He will walk you home later.'

Cousin Louise was looking at Elizabeth with obvious gratitude. Jessica was frowning. 'Is she young?' she asked. 'Or is she old? Not that it matters. I will come anyway.'

'She is about Alex's age,' Elizabeth said. 'Is that horribly old, Jessica? I beg you not to say yes, for I am older than Alex.'

'Not *horribly* old,' Jessica conceded.

'Just old,' Alexander murmured.

Five minutes later they were on their way to South Audley Street, Alexander's mother on his arm, Elizabeth and Jessica walking ahead of them.

'Poor Jessica,' his mother murmured. 'And poor Abigail. I have been trying not to think about her. I do hope I can persuade Viola to bring her to us.'

Alexander was wondering how Miss Heyden would receive him. And how would she react to meeting yet another member of his family?

Wren was indeed enjoying her time alone. She was sitting in her room, a book open on her lap. It was a spacious, light-filled chamber, the perfect place in which to relax. She was not really reading. She was thinking about the wonder that was St Paul's Cathedral and the even greater wonder of the fact that she had gone there in the company of a *friend*. And she thought of her embarrassingly lengthy weeping spell this morning, the first and only time she had wept over Aunt Megan's and Uncle Reggie's deaths. But it was not of the actual weeping she thought but of the way Mrs Westcott had been transformed into a mother figure almost as endearing as Aunt Megan herself.

She refused to feel guilty either about being here or about forcing the Earl of Riverdale out. He had asked her to come, and Lady Overfield had asked. He had met her in the park yesterday and repeated the invitation. It was as simple as that. She would stay, perhaps for a week, and see everything on her list, and then she would go home. And she would write to both ladies afterward. Friends were too precious to be squandered.

Her thoughts were interrupted by a light tap on

the door Lady Overfield answered the summons to come in.

'Ah,' she said, 'I was afraid you might be having a nap. We neglected to tell you, I believe, that you must feel free to use the drawing room or the library or any of the other day rooms at any time. You must not feel obliged to remain here when we are out. Although neither are you obliged to leave here if you do not wish.'

She smiled and her eyes twinkled. 'It is late for tea, but we are going to have some anyway. Alex has returned from Archer House with us and we have also brought young Jessica – one of our second cousins. She is eighteen years old and had a serious case of the blue devils. She made her debut into society this year – with great success, it must be added. She could probably be married thirty times over by the summer if she chose and if it were allowed. But she is desperately unhappy nevertheless, as only the young can be under such circumstances. Her cousin and dearest friend is unable to be here with her. That is Abigail, whose illegitimacy was discovered last year. Jessica wants to go home and bury herself in the country, and the whole family has been thrown into consternation. For she has reminded the rest of us that all is not well in one segment of the family and we really ought to do something about it – if anything can be done, that is. But I am rambling. We invited Jessica to come here with us for an hour or so. We told her we had a visitor staying with us, and I hope you will come down. But you must not feel obliged to.'

It was very easy sometimes to believe one was the only person who had ever suffered troubles, Wren thought, especially when one totally isolated oneself. But here was a clear reminder that in reality everyone had, even presumably pretty, well-connected eighteen-year-olds who had the world spread at their feet.

'Lady Overfield,' she said, 'I believe you are very sly.'

The lady looked taken aback for a moment and then smiled again. 'If you meet one person at a time,' she said, 'eventually you will have met the whole world. But I mean it when I say you do not have to come down. No one will think the worse of you.'

Wren got to her feet. Yes, she did have to go. She was a guest here. 'I never did mingle, you know,' she said as she smoothed out her dress and touched her hair to make sure everything was in place. 'Whenever my aunt and uncle entertained at home, I remained in my room even though they never seemed to tire of inviting me and occasionally trying some gentle persuasion.' She turned to her hostess then and smiled. 'Lead the way.'

But Lady Overfield did not immediately open the door. 'I would love to have you call me Elizabeth,' she said, 'or, better yet, Lizzie.'

'Lizzie,' Wren said. 'I am Wren.'

'Wren?'

'Like the bird,' Wren said. 'My uncle called me that when he first saw me, and it stuck. I was Rowena before then, but never since.'

'Wren,' Lizzie said again. 'It is pretty.' And she led the way down to the drawing room.

The first person Wren saw there was the Earl of Riverdale. He was standing not far inside the door, looking tall and handsome in a formfitting coat of dark green superfine with dark pantaloons and gleaming Hessian boots and very white linen. His gaze met hers with smiling eyes – he shared that look with his sister. Wren offered a hand and he took it in a warm clasp and she felt a bit as though it were her heart he had clutched. She had forgotten how . . . masculine he was.

'Lord Riverdale,' she said. 'I must thank you for inviting me to come here and for moving out so that I would not feel too awkward about staying. It was very thoughtful of you.'

'As soon as you mentioned a gentlewoman's hotel,' he said, 'I knew it must be my mission in life to rescue you. I had an instant vision of brick mattresses and bars upon the windows and a massive landlady with a large bundle of keys jangling at her waist.'

'Oh, it was not quite as bad as that,' Wren assured him. 'I do not remember the keys *jangling*.'

He laughed and she slid her hand free of his before it got irredeemably scalded. She had forgotten his laugh.

She had not forgotten his kiss.

174

'Allow me to introduce my cousin,' he said, 'or *second* cousin, to be quite accurate. Lady Jessica Archer is the daughter of the late Duke of Netherby and half sister to the present one. Miss Heyden, Jessica.'

The young lady was pretty and fair haired and youthfully slight and graceful in build, though her loveliness was somewhat marred by a slightly scowling face and a petulant mouth.

Wren smiled. 'I am pleased to make your acquaintance, Lady Jessica,' she said.

'How tall you are,' the girl said. 'I am very envious. I suppose you tower over most men, but sometimes I think that would be wonderful. There are some men I would dearly like to look down upon.' And surprisingly, considering the fact that she had delivered the greeting with the near scowl still on her face, she suddenly smiled dazzlingly and laughed with girlish glee. 'Are you not envious too, Elizabeth? Of course, Alexander does not have to fear having any woman look down upon him.'

'Being tall would certainly make it easier to look distinguished and elegant,' Lizzie said. 'However, it would be harder to hide in a crowd, and that can be a very handy thing to do on occasion.'

And that was done, Wren thought as she took a seat to one side of the fireplace. The world was being conquered one person at a time. The girl had not run screaming from the house at the sight of her.

Lady Jessica sat close by while Lizzie and her

mother sat on a love seat some distance away. The earl was standing beside them, ready to hand around the cups of tea his mother was pouring. Lord Riverdale brought their tea and then retreated to stand by the love seat again and converse quietly with the other two ladies. Wren had the feeling that the positioning was deliberate, that the others were giving their young relative a chance to recover her spirits with a new acquaintance, someone from outside the family. And perhaps they were giving *her* the opportunity to meet someone else without the comfort of her veil. As she had said upstairs, Lady Overfield – Lizzie – was very sly. All three of them were. She felt a rush of unexpected affection for them.

'You lost your uncle and aunt last year, I heard,' Lady Jessica said. 'Did you live with them?'

'I did,' Wren said. 'I was terribly fond of them.'

'And there is no one else?' Lady Jessica asked.

'No,' Wren said without hesitation. 'Just me.'

'Sometimes,' the girl told her, 'I think it would be lovely to be all alone, to have no relatives. It is not because mine do not love me, Miss Heyden, and it is not because I do not love them. Love is the whole trouble, in fact. I adore my half brother. Yet he married someone I hate, though I love her too. She was my uncle Humphrey's only legitimate daughter, but no one knew it until last year. Even she did not. Do you know what happened?'

'Some of it has been explained to me,' Wren said, but her young companion continued anyway.

'My uncle's other three children – my cousins – were dispossessed,' the girl said. 'They even lost the legitimacy of their birth. Can you imagine anything more horrible? Anastasia inherited everything except Brambledean, which is just a heap anyway, and Avery married her. They love each other dearly, and they have the most adorable baby, and I both love and hate her – Anastasia, that is. I wish I loved her entirely. I try to. It makes no sense whatsoever, does it?'

'It makes perfect sense to me,' Wren told her, and it did. 'You were close to your other cousins?'

'I *love* them,' Lady Jessica assured her. 'Well, Camille was always a bit starchy and humorless, though I was fond enough of her. Harry – he was very briefly the Earl of Riverdale after my uncle's death, you know, or perhaps you did not know – is *gorgeous*, though he is only my cousin and was never my beau or anything like that. And Abby has always been my very best friend in the world. She is a year older than I and she was disappointed last year that my uncle's death prevented her from making her come-out. I was secretly a bit glad, for that meant we could make our debut together this year. It would have been the best thing *ever*. But now she can never have a Season of her own or marry anyone respectable, and my heart is dead inside me. Sometimes I wish it had happened to me instead of to her. It would be somehow easier to bear. If I had no family, you see, I would not be unhappy. There

177

would be nothing to be unhappy about. Am I talking nonsense?'

Wren set a hand over one of hers and patted it. At the same time she caught the eye of the Earl of Riverdale, and it seemed to her that there was concern, even perhaps . . . anxiety in his look. But was the concern for her or for his cousin? He was looking directly at her, though, until he turned his head to reply to something Lizzie had said.

'Perhaps you have heard the old saying about the grass always looking greener on the other side of the hedge,' Wren said.

'It is probably no better to be without relatives, is it?' the girl said. 'I am sorry. You must be wishing you could punch me in the nose for ingratitude and insensitivity and lots of other things. Why have you not married?'

'I was perfectly happy with my life until just over a year ago,' Wren said, not pausing over the girl's lightning-fast change of subject. 'And even now I am content. I am always busy. I am a business-woman, you see. I own a large and prosperous glassworks in Staffordshire and am extremely proud of our products, which are designed more to be works of art than merely to provide a prac-tical function. I was involved in the business before my uncle died, but I immerse myself even more in it now. I do not want anyone to get the idea that I am a helpless woman and must rely upon my male employees to make all the decisions and do all the work.'

Lady Jessica's eyes were shining. All signs of petulance were gone. 'How absolutely splendid!' she exclaimed. 'Now I envy you even more. You are very tall *and* you are a businesswoman. I have never heard of such a thing.' She laughed again, that same youthful, happy sound. She was facing away from her three relatives, all of whom looked briefly their way and smiled. 'Is that a bruise? Or is it always there?'

It was her first mention of the blemish, and now it was almost an offhand remark.

'I have been stuck with it from birth,' Wren said.

'That is unfortunate,' Lady Jessica said, looking closely and frankly at the left side of Wren's face. 'I suppose you curse it every day of your life. I know I would. It is fortunate that the rest of your face and even this side if you ignore the color is so beautiful. Oh, dear, Mama would be looking very pointedly at me if she were here now, and quite rightly so. I ought to have pretended I had not noticed, oughtn't I? I am so sorry.'

But Wren found herself unexpectedly smiling. 'I wear a veil almost wherever I go where strangers are likely to see me,' she said. 'Even indoors.'

'People must *really* look at you then,' the girl said. 'They must see you as a lady of mystery. How splendid! Especially when you are so tall.' Her laughter had turned to girlish glee.

'Some London shops sell my glassware,' Wren said, raising her voice slightly and looking up to include the other occupants of the room. 'Lizzie – Lady Overfield – and I are going to find some of them tomorrow morning to look at the displays. Would you care to accompany us? If your mother will permit it, of course.'

'Oh, I should like it of all things.' She clasped her hands to her bosom and turned her head to look across the room at the others. 'Will you mind my coming too, Elizabeth? And, Cousin Althea, may I *please* stay here tonight so that I will be ready to go in the morning and Elizabeth and Miss Heyden will not have to come to Archer House and wait forever for me? There is a horrid soiree tonight that I have no interest in attending and I have told Mama so. Please may I stay?'

'We must ask your mama,' Mrs Westcott said. 'I shall write a note and Alex will take it to Archer House on his way back to Sidney's. If the answer is no, I daresay he will bring word back to us and escort you home.'

She got to her feet and went to the escritoire at the far side of the room to sit and write her note, and Lady Jessica fairly bounced across the room to suggest some of the wording. The Earl of Riverdale came to take her vacated chair beside Wren.

'You have made my mother and sister happy by coming here to stay,' he said. 'And we all appreciate your listening to Jessica's woes and helping take her mind off them. You appear to have been very successful.'

'Lady Jessica is very young,' she said, 'and clearly hurting on her cousin's behalf. Sometimes it must seem almost worse to watch loved ones suffer than to suffer oneself. One must feel more helpless.'

'You will be busy with Lizzie and probably Jessica too tomorrow morning,' he said. 'I shall be at the Lords. Will you come walking in the park with me in the afternoon, weather permitting? There are paths that are less public and in many ways more picturesque than the one by the Serpentine.'

Kind courtesy again? Or . . . what? She searched his eyes but found no answer there. She ought to say a polite no. What might have been between them had ended on Easter Sunday. She did not want to revive it – it had been somehow too painful. And surely he did not want to. She knew he had not warmed to her during those weeks of their acquaintance, and she knew equally well that her fortune in itself would be no inducement to him.

So why exactly had she come?

Why exactly had he invited her here yesterday and even asked his mother to persuade her to stay here?

'I would like that,' she said. 'Thank you.'

CHAPTER 10

Alexander spent a thoroughly enjoyable bachelor evening with his cousin Sidney. They dined at White's Club and moved on to another club, where they had a few drinks with friends and he won three hundred pounds in a card game, and then on to a private party, where he lost two hundred and fifty. By the time they returned to Sidney's rooms rather too long after midnight, they had done a great deal of reminiscing and laughing, not to mention drinking. But times had changed, they both agreed, and such evenings as this, though pleasant, were not to be craved as a regular diet as they had been ten years ago.

Alexander's mother and sister were awaiting the arrival of Cousin Louise and Jessica when he entered Westcott House early the following afternoon. They were going to a garden party together. His mother had written to invite Cousin Viola and Abigail to come to London for a week or two, she told him.

'I am not at all sure they will come,' she said. 'There is no definite event we can dangle before them as an inducement, as there was last year when we all went to Bath to celebrate Cousin Eugenia's seventieth birthday. Her seventy-first would not sound nearly as special an occasion, would it?'

'Probably not,' he agreed. 'How does Miss Heyden feel about their coming here?'

'She insists she will not be staying longer than a week,' his mother said, 'and it is very unlikely they would arrive so soon. Really, though, Alex, the more I think about it, the more I despair of their actually coming. We are living in what was their home, after all, and you bear the title that was Harry's all too briefly.'

'Wren's glassware is absolutely exquisite, Alex,' Elizabeth told him from her position by the window. 'I swear Jessica and I both gaped when we saw the display in the first shop this morning. Every piece is a work of art. I am going to wheedle an invitation to Staffordshire the next time she expects to be there. I want to watch the whole process.'

'You are going to be friends, then, are you?' he asked.

'We already are,' she said. 'Here is Cousin Louise's carriage, Mama.'

Alexander went back down with them to hand them into the vehicle and exchange greetings with the dowager duchess and Jessica.

Miss Heyden was coming downstairs as he stepped back inside. She looked elegant in a slim, high-waisted walking dress of a light blue. The brim of her straw bonnet was decorated with a veil of the same color. It did not yet cover her face.

'We are close to the park,' he told her after bowing and bidding her a good afternoon. 'I hope you do not mind walking rather than riding. One is confined largely to public areas with a carriage.'

'But it was to a walk that you invited me,' she said as the butler opened the front door and she reached for her veil.

'Will you leave it raised?' he asked her. 'We are not likely to encounter many people face-to-face, and the veil is really quite unnecessary anyway.'

Her hands remained in the air for a moment before she sighed and lowered them. 'Very well,' she said, and they stepped out onto the street. She took his arm, and he was reminded as they set out along the street of how very comfortable it felt to walk with a woman so close to him in height and with a stride to match his own. 'I am sorry to have kept you from a garden party on such a beautiful day.'

'I was not planning to attend,' he told her. 'I would prefer the alternative anyway.'

'You are gallant,' she said, and frowned as a gentleman hurried past them with a nod for Alexander and the touch of a hand to his hat brim for Miss Heyden.

'Lizzie told me you found some of your glassware on display,' he said.

'Yes, indeed.' Her voice warmed noticeably. 'In two shops, on Bond Street and Oxford Street. I found it really quite exciting. I am familiar with the designs, of course, and see the finished products all the time in the workshops and the visitor shop attached to them. But they looked somehow different and more impressive displayed here among other, competing wares. They were not by any means overshadowed. I even had the pleasure of witnessing a gentleman purchase one of our vases for his wife.'

'I hope you made yourself known to him,' he said.

'I did not.' She winced slightly. 'But Lady Jessica did. It was terribly embarrassing.' But she laughed suddenly. 'And really rather gratifying too, I must admit. He shook hands with me, as did the shop-keeper, who assured me that our glassware items never remain long on his shelves.'

'You were not annoyed with Jessica, then?' he asked as they crossed the road to make their way into the park.

'Oh, not at all,' she said, 'despite my embarrassment. She was so very happy to make the announcement, as though I somehow belonged to her and she could bask in my reflected glory.'

He had been surprised yesterday at the way Jessica had taken to her and by the way she had responded in kind. It seemed nothing short of tragic that she had been so alone through much of her life, and he wondered if her aunt and uncle had been partly to blame, if perhaps they had coddled her rather too much when they might have nudged her out of the nest when she grew up. But he must not judge. He knew so few facts. He had heard Jessica say – with great delight – that Miss Heyden must be looked upon as a mystery woman when she appeared in public, her face shrouded by a veil. But she was a mystery woman even without it, for she wore layer upon layer of inner veils. He had had only brief, rare glimpses within, and this was one of them. Her eyes were bright and her right cheek was flushed, and she looked eager and youthful and approachable.

It did not last, of course. They passed a few people inside the park gates, and each time she raised her left hand to her bonnet brim, as though a brisk wind were attempting to blow it off. She did not draw down the veil, however, and she removed her hand whenever there was no one close by. He turned them onto a wide expanse of grass and led the way toward the line of trees beyond it. A path meandered through the trees close to the border of the park and was a lovely shaded place to stroll. It was not usually much frequented, most people preferring the more open areas of the park, where they might meet friends and acquaintances and have plenty of human activity to observe.

They talked about her long journey from Staffordshire, about the Serpentine and St Paul's Cathedral and Bond Street, about Hookham's Library, which she had also visited this morning in order to borrow a few books on Elizabeth's subscription. They talked about the House of

Lords and some of the issues currently being debated there, about the wars and the weather. They passed only one other couple, and they were so intent upon what might have been a quarrel that they kept their heads down and their eyes lowered as they hurried past in a tense silence before resuming the argument just before they moved out of earshot.

'Why did you come?' Alexander asked at last. It was perhaps not a fair question, but it had been spoken aloud now.

There was a fairly lengthy silence, during which he became aware of the distant shrieking of children at play and birds trilling and chattering in the trees.

'When you and then Lady Overfield – Lizzie – asked me to come,' she said, 'I saw it purely as an invitation I would not accept. But after I had gone to Staffordshire, I remembered it more as a challenge I had missed. And I asked myself if it really was a matter of courage. I have always wanted to come to London to see the famous sites. I like to think of myself as a strong, independent woman, and in many ways I am. I am proud of that. But sometimes I am aware of the coward lurking within. My veil is one aspect of it, I freely admit. My tendency to live the life of a hermit is another, though I genuinely like being alone and could never ever become truly gregarious. I came to prove that I could, Lord Riverdale. I did not come in answer to either your invitation or your sister's.

That would have been unfair, for I had refused both. However, I did intend calling at South Audley Street to pay my respects – oh, and to prove I was not too cowardly to do so.'

'It takes courage to call upon friends?' he asked her.

'I do not know,' she said. 'Does it? I have never had friends. And are *you* a friend, Lord Riverdale? To me you were and are the gentleman to whom I once offered my fortune in exchange for marriage. I withdrew that offer when I understood that such a plan would not work for either of us. We could hardly be called friends, then, though I hope we are not enemies. We are something between the two, friendly acquaintances, perhaps. Your sister has been kind enough to call herself my friend since that day she visited me, but it was a friendship to be conducted largely at long distance by letter. Yes, it would have taken courage to call at Westcott House. And it seemed to me it might not be the right thing to do anyway. You came here to find a bride. I had no business interfering with that and still do not. But I met you here – quite by accident, I assure you – and then felt obliged to keep my promise to call upon Mrs Westcott. Then, of course, I found myself being persuaded to stay there. I hope you do not believe I maneuvered such an outcome.'

'I know you did not,' he said. 'I suggested it to my mother, and I am well acquainted with her powers of persuasion.'

'I hope I did not cause any awkwardness with the young lady you were escorting by the Serpentine,' she said. 'She is very pretty. Though I am sure I could not have been mistaken for competition.'

'That pretty young lady's mother has serious designs upon me,' he said, 'as does her father. They will turn their matchmaking efforts upon someone else, however, as soon as they understand that I am not in the market for their daughter's hand.'

'Ah,' she said, stopping and sliding her arm from his before moving off the path to look out through a gap in the trees to the sloping lawn beyond and the carriage drive below. 'You have someone else in mind, then.'

'Yes,' he said.

She gazed into the distance, tall, elegant, self-contained, unapproachable again. 'I hope for your mother's sake,' she said, 'oh, and for yours too, that she is someone who can do more than just repair your fortunes, Lord Riverdale. I hope you *feel* something for her and she for you.'

'Respect?' he said. 'Liking? A hope of affection? Those three weigh more heavily with me than fortune. I could probably limp along somehow at Brambledean with only my own resources and the hard work and innovative ideas of my steward. The farms would not thrive for a number of years, and the house would have to continue to fall into disrepair except for absolute necessities. But I could see to it that body and soul were held together for my workers and their families, and perhaps they would forgive me for a lack of real prosperity if they were to see that I was in it with them, living and working alongside them. I would not marry for fortune alone.'

'No,' she said, still gazing off into the distance, her chin held high, her hands clasped at her waist, 'you always did say that. It is something I respect about you.'

He was gazing at her rather than at the view, at her right profile, proud, inscrutable, beautiful. But appealing? Attractive? Lady of mystery. Jessica had chosen the very best words to describe her, he thought. She was unknown and perhaps unknowable. It had bothered him back at Brambledean, and it made him uneasy now. But . . . he had glimpsed something tantalizingly fleeting behind the veil. Something . . . No, he could not find the word. But something that invited him to keep looking.

She turned her head toward him at last. 'I wish you well with your courtship,' she said. 'Shall we walk onward? I am grateful that you brought me here. I like it better than the more public area by the water. There is something very soothing about a woodland path.'

And there was something about her eyes. Sadness? Yearning? 'Miss Heyden,' he said, 'will you marry me?'

Her eyes stilled on his. 'Oh,' she said, but if she

had intended to say more she was prevented by the inopportune approach of other people – three of them, one man and two ladies, trying to walk abreast on a path that was narrow even for two. Miss Heyden turned sharply back to gaze out at the park.

'Riverdale,' the man said affably.

'Matthews.' Alexander nodded genially. 'A lovely day for a stroll, is it not?' He smiled at the ladies. Fortunately he did not know any of them well enough to feel obliged to hold them in conversation. They continued on their way after agreeing that yes, indeed, it was a beautiful day.

Alexander offered his arm to Miss Heyden again and took her a few steps farther off the path among the trees. 'I will not deny,' he said, 'that your fortune would help serve my more pressing needs. You have seen Brambledean for yourself. But it is *not* your fortune alone that has prompted my offer. I beg you to believe me on that.'

'What has prompted you, then?' she asked without turning her head toward him. 'Respect? Liking? A hope of affection? You cannot pretend to love me.'

'I will not *pretend* anything,' he said. 'I try to be honest in all my dealings, but honesty with the woman I hope to marry is surely essential. No, I will not pretend to love you, Miss Heyden, if by love you mean the sort of grand passion that has produced some of our most memorable poetry and drama. But I believe I like you well enough

191

to invite you to share my life. I would hope that liking would grow into affection. But respect is the strongest factor that has led me to speak today. I respect you as a businesswoman and as a person, though it is true I scarcely know you. I sense that you will be worth getting to know, however, and I hope you can feel the same about me. I hope you do not look at me and see only a mercenary man to whom things are more important than people. I beg your pardon. This is hardly the sort of speech a woman must hope to hear from the man who is proposing marriage to her. I have not dropped to one knee. I have not brought even one red rosebud with me.'

'No,' she said.

'No, it was not the sort of speech you hoped to hear?' he asked.

'No,' she said again. 'I do not ask for roses or bended knee or the trappings of romance. They would be patently false and would arouse my distrust of everything else you have said. I know you would not marry me for my money alone. Liking and respect are perhaps a firm enough foundation upon which to base a marriage, and I both like and respect you. Thank you. I will tentatively agree to marry you.'

She was still gazing off into the distance, her eyes narrowed against the sunlight. He felt suddenly chilled. It was all very well to marry for practical reasons rather than for romantic ones. People did it all the time, and those marriages were often solid, even happy. He had resigned himself to the fact that he must do so too. But surely there ought to be more . . . warmth of feeling than this. He had just made her what was possibly the world's worst ever proposal, and she had accepted, without looking at him and without conviction. Could he blame her?

'Tentatively?' he said.

'Your mother and your sister must give their unequivocal approval,' she said.

'It is I you would be marrying, Miss Heyden,' he said. 'Our home would be Brambledean Court in Wiltshire. Theirs is Riddings Park in Kent. There is a goodly distance between the two.'

'You are a very close family, Lord Riverdale,' she said. 'They love you dearly and want your happiness before all else. And you love them and do not wish to make them unhappy. Those are things not to be scoffed at.'

'You think they will disapprove, then?' he asked her. He expected that they would give their blessing, even if it came without any real joy. 'Would your uncle and aunt disapprove if they were still alive? And would you refuse to marry me if they did?'

She thought about her answer. 'I do not believe they would have disapproved,' she said.

'Even if they had known that I do not love you and you do not love me?' he asked her.

'They would see you as a good and honorable man,' she said. 'They would want that for me. And they would trust my judgment even if they felt doubts.'

'Do you think my mother and Lizzie will not trust mine?' he asked.

'My aunt and uncle would have understood my motive as your family will understand yours,' she said. 'They are very different motives, are they not? I want marriage, a husband and family, and you are a good choice, for you do have a sense of honor. I could feel confident that you would always treat me with courtesy and respect, that you would never abandon me or dishonor me. I could feel confident that you would be a good father to my children. You, on the other hand, want to be able to fulfill your obligations as Earl of Riverdale and master of Brambledean. You want a wife who can bring you sufficient funds to make that possible. And of course you want a wife who can bear you heirs. Our families would look from very different perspectives upon the prospect of our marrying.'

'Lizzie and my mother like you,' he said.

'Astonishingly, I believe they do,' she agreed. 'But they may have reservations about my being your wife. I am not as other women are, Lord Riverdale – and I do not refer just to my birthmark. Were it not for my exposure to the glassworks, I would be a total recluse. I had a good upbringing and a good education, but all is theory and not practice with me. Just in the last couple of days, though I have mingled with no one except your mother and sister and cousin, I have seen and felt

194

my differentness. I think of that young lady with whom you were walking here. Even in the brief glance I had of her, I was aware that in addition to her physical prettiness she was warm and charming and feminine and . . . vivacious.'

'I could have proposed marriage to Miss Littlewood anytime in the past three weeks,' he said. 'She would have accepted – and I am not being conceited in believing so. I have not done it or felt the slightest wish to do so, though before I saw you again I did have the sinking feeling that soon I was going to have to choose someone not very different from her – someone whose father was rich and wanted a peer of the realm for a son-in-law. But then I *did* see you again and I knew, almost immediately, that I *could* feel comfortable with the thought of marrying you. And it is *because* you are so different from other women rather than despite that fact. I would rather marry you, Miss Heyden, than any other lady I have met, and I believe my mother would prefer it too. And Lizzie.'

'Then you must put it to the test,' she said, turning her head at last to look at him. 'They must approve. I would not be responsible for putting any strain upon such a close family. It is worth more than anything else in the world and must be preserved at all costs.'

'And yet,' he said, 'you left your own family at the age of ten and have not spoken of them since.' At least, that was one theory of what might have happened. It was equally possible that there had been some catastrophe that had wiped out all her family except her aunt.

For a moment her eyes held his. Then she jerked her hand free of his arm, turned about, and scrambled her way back to the path. She began to hurry along it, back in the direction from which they had come. He went after her. Damn him for a clumsy wretch.

'Miss Heyden.' He hurried up beside her and set a hand on her arm. She stopped but did not turn to face him.

'Sometimes,' she said, 'it is the exception that proves the rule, Lord Riverdale. That is a cliché, but often there is truth to clichés.'

'I beg your pardon,' he said, moving around to face her and taking her gloved right hand in both of his. 'I really am sorry to have upset you.' He raised her hand and held it to his lips. She was frowning, her eyes on their hands.

'I do not believe I can bring you any happiness, Lord Riverdale,' she said, and he found himself frowning back.

'Why not?' he asked. 'Happiness does not come ready-made, you know. Even a sunset or a rose or a sonata or a book or a banquet is not happiness in itself. Each can *cause* happiness, but we have to allow feeling to interact with the moment. Surely if we like and respect each other, if we make an effort to live and work with each other, to make a home of our house and a family of any children with whom we may be blessed – surely then we can expect some happiness. We can even expect moments of vivid, conscious joy. But only if we want it and work for it and never allow ourselves to become complacent or imagine we are bored or inadequate. And only if we understand there is no such thing as happily-ever-after. Not for anyone, even those who fall wildly in love before marrying.'

She had raised her eyes to his, though she was still frowning. 'If Mrs Westcott objects,' she said, 'I will fully understand. I will even agree with her. I would not want *my* son to marry me.'

'Good God,' he said, grinning suddenly. 'I should hope not.'

She must have realized what she had just said. She snatched her hand from his grasp, pressed it to her mouth, gazed at him horrified for a moment, and then – exploded into laughter. And suddenly it all felt right. All of it. She was a real person despite the layers of armor, and she had a mind and a conscience and opinions. And even a sense of humor. There was substance to her character and a sturdy sort of honesty. And if being associated with her was going to be difficult, well, so it would with anyone. He glanced quickly ahead and behind. The path was deserted in both directions.

'We are – tentatively – betrothed, then, are we, Miss Heyden?' he asked.

She sobered instantly and lowered her hand. 'Yes,' she said. 'Tentatively.'

'Then we must celebrate,' he said, and cupped her face in his hands and ran the pads of his thumbs over her cheekbones while her hands came up to clasp his wrists.

'Someone might come,' she said.

'A very brief celebration,' he said, and kissed her – and instantly remembered the shock he had felt when he kissed her at Brambledean. He had felt an unexpected surge of desire then, and he felt it again now, inappropriate as it was when they were standing on a public path in the most public park in London. Her mouth was soft, her lips trembling slightly against his own. Her breath was warm on his cheek, her hands tight about his wrists. There was nothing remotely lascivious about the kiss, but . . . There was that knowledge that he could desire her.

She drew back her head rather sharply. 'Are we mad?' she asked, her frown back. 'We have forgotten the most important thing.'

'And that is . . .?' He took a half step back from her.

'The very reason we put an end to everything on Easter Sunday,' she said. 'I cannot be a countess, Lord Riverdale. I have no training or experience. I am a businesswoman, what the *ton* refers to with some disparagement as a cit. And when I am not that, I am a hermit. And I am—' She made a jerky gesture with her left hand in the direction of her cheek.

'Ugly?' he suggested. 'Unsightly?'

'*Blemished,*' she said.

'Even though I have never recoiled at the sight of you?' he said, clasping his hands behind his back. He was getting a bit tired of this image she had of herself. 'Even though my mother and Lizzie have not? Even though Jessica has not? Cling to this image of yourself as some sort of monster if you must, Miss Heyden, but do not expect other people to endorse it.'

'I am still unqualified to be your countess,' she said. 'And incapable. Moreover, I have no wish to learn.'

'Now that is unfortunate,' he told her. 'When we refuse to learn, we often end up stunting our growth and never becoming the person we have the potential to be. But we all get to decide that for ourselves. What you will be if you marry me, Miss Heyden, is an eccentric. Eccentrics are often admirable people because they are not afraid to stand alone rather than huddle with the masses, as most of the rest of us do to a greater or lesser degree. Eccentrics at their best listen to the music at the heart of themselves and let it fill them as they dance to its melody while other people who cannot hear it gawk and frown in disapproval and mutter about straitjackets and insane asylums.'

She gazed mutely at him until she laughed again suddenly, her whole face lighting up with amusement. 'It is not a rose you ought to have brought with you today, Lord Riverdale,' she said. 'It is a pedestal upon which to set me. But only, presumably, if I choose to be at my best.'

'Shall we walk on?' he suggested, and they continued on the way back to the gates.

'What is one specific thing you would *like* me to learn, Lord Riverdale?' she asked.

'You are already doing it,' he said. 'You have met my mother and my sister without your veil. You met Jessica yesterday without it. You came out today without lowering it from the brim of your bonnet. I suppose I cannot know just how incredibly difficult all that has been for you, but I can at least appreciate your courage. I wish you would do it again and then again – one person at a time or the whole world in one shot. A drive in the park, perhaps, or a shopping excursion on Bond Street. Or an evening at the theater. Or something on an outrageously grand scale, like a ball. A betrothal ball, maybe. Or just the rest of my family, one or two persons at a time. My cousin Viola may possibly come to stay within the next couple of weeks with her daughter Abigail.'

'That is one specific thing?' she said. 'But what about you, Lord Riverdale? Presumably you too must keep learning if your growth is not to be stunted. What is one specific thing you can learn?'

'Touché.' He grinned at her. 'I can learn not to manage the lives of those around me.'

She laughed again. Laughter softened her and gave hints of the woman she could be if she could just get past whatever it was that had frozen her natural development when she was still a child.

'I shall think about what you have said,' she told

him, 'keeping in mind that you will be busy learning not to manage my life. But there will be no betrothal ball or any other. I am far too busy dancing to my own private melody, remember.'

He had felt more hopeful in the past few minutes than he had in his whole acquaintance with her. She was willing, it seemed, to open herself in small ways if not in large, and he had acknowledged his own need not to be inflexible. More important, she was capable of laughter and even of wit.

'Before anything else, though,' she said, 'your mother and sister must approve.'

It struck him as sad that there was no one on her side whose approval he must seek. No one to share the celebration of their betrothal or the planning for their wedding.

'Last year,' he said, 'when Anna had been newly discovered by the Westcott family and everyone was trying to bring her up to scratch, Netherby offered her marriage and the family swung into action to plan the grandest wedding the *ton* had ever seen. While they – we – were at it, Netherby acquired a special license and took her off one morning and married her without a word to anyone. It came as a severe shock to the family, but I have always thought it was the very best way it could have been done. Anna was new to the *ton*. She would have hated the pomp and bluster of a public wedding. And Netherby simply would not allow it. Would you like us to imitate them, Miss Heyden? Shall I purchase a special license – I could do it tomorrow – and marry you quietly? You would be my countess without any public fuss and would have my full permission to be as eccentric as you pleased for the rest of our lives.'

It was an impulsive suggestion on his part, but it was not one he expected to regret. He had to wait for her answer until a couple of ladies had passed them. As they did so, she half raised her left hand in the direction of her face but then returned it to her side. The two ladies exchanged greetings with him – he knew them slightly – took a good look at Miss Heyden, and walked on in silence until they had passed out of earshot. A few drawing rooms were soon going to be buzzing, he guessed.

'Without even speaking to your mother and sister?' she asked. 'And without any discussion of the full extent of my fortune? Without signing any sort of marriage contract?'

'I will take you upon trust if you will take me,' he said. He was beginning to feel a bit dizzy. He could be a married man the day after tomorrow, depending upon her answer.

She drew an audible breath and held it for a few moments as they approached the crowded carriage road close to the gates.

'It is a tempting idea,' she said. 'But I will not marry you without your mother's full approval, Lord Riverdale.'

CHAPTER 11

Wren went straight up to her room upon her return, removed her bonnet and gloves, and sat on the chair by the window. Fortunately, Mrs Westcott and Elizabeth had not yet returned from the garden party, and the earl had not stayed. He was, however, planning to return for dinner. She picked up her library book and opened it before closing it again and setting it aside no more than a minute later. She was certainly not going to be able to read for the next little while. Her mind was buzzing as though a whole hive of bees had been let loose in there.

She was betrothed. Tentatively.

Her dream was about to come true.

Or was it? She could not possibly be the Countess of Riverdale. He had brushed aside her misgivings by assuring her that she might be an eccentric recluse if she wished, but she did not quite believe it would be possible. Already she had met his mother and sister and cousin. Another cousin – the dispossessed former countess – had been invited to come here to stay with her daughter. If she was to be married, she would be here when they came – *if* they came – and she would remain here until the end of the parliamentary session. She would not be able to hide in her room all day every day. How long would it be before she was called upon to meet all the Westcotts – and the Radleys too, the relatives on his mother's side? And then who after that?

But why not?

Perhaps her face was not so hideous after all. Not one of the people she had met had shrieked or stared at her in horror or called her a monster or wanted to keep her confined to a room with the key turned in the lock from the other side, with netting over the window, lest someone look up from below and see her peering out. No one had called her a punishment from hell. No one had suggested that she belonged in an insane asylum or had been on the brink of sending her there.

Wren spread shaking hands over her face and concentrated upon getting her breathing under control so that she would not faint. No, of course not. No one had said or done any of those things in twenty years. But there was a certain sort of memory that seeped into one's very bones and tissues and sinews and into the deepest recesses of one's mind and being. Would she ever see herself as others saw her? Would she ever believe what they saw?

She removed her hands from her face and rested them in her lap while she looked out at the garden, at flowers and shrubs and rows of vegetables off to one side and a sort of knot garden of herbs beyond them, and breathed in the sweet air and the myriad scents that came through the open window with the light breeze.

She was betrothed. She was going to be wed. All the dreams she had ever dared dream were going to come true. And it was not going to be just any old marriage, but marriage to *him,* the Earl of Riverdale, and she very much feared she was in love with him. But why had her mind chosen the word *feared*? Because she knew her feelings could never be returned? It did not matter. He had promised liking and respect and a hope of affection, and they were good enough. From him they were good enough, for if she had learned one thing about him during their brief acquaintance, it was that he was a man of honor to whom family was of paramount importance.

Wren closed her eyes and continued to breathe in the soothing smells of sweet peas and mint and sage. She feared – and yes, it was definitely fear this time – that she would not be able to change enough to arouse any real affection in him. It was not just her face that she had hidden from the world. It was the whole of herself. Her instinct was to hide behind veils within veils, and she had done it for so long that she did not know how to cast those veils aside.

She had met four people without her facial veil. She had even gone out without it this afternoon. But could she lift the heavier veil she wore over herself? She had only ever done it with her aunt and uncle. She was well aware that she was *different*. She was not warm or open in manner and never could be. She seemed incapable of showing her feelings. She was not . . . Oh, she was not a thousand and one things other people were without any effort.

What *was* she, then? She did not want to define herself for the rest of her life with negatives.

She was a businesswoman and a successful one. She had a good head on her shoulders, and she worked well, curiously enough, with other people. She was capable of love. She had loved her uncle and aunt with all her being. She had easily grown fond of Elizabeth and Mrs Westcott. She apparently loved the Earl of Riverdale. She knew she would love their children – if, please God, they had any – with a passionate adoration *no matter what*.

Oh, God, oh dear God, she loved him. She spread her hands over her face again. But was it any wonder? He was the first eligible man she had ever met, apart from Mr Sweeney and Mr Richman, each of whom she had dismissed in less than half an hour. Perhaps what she felt was not love at all but merely gratitude.

Or maybe it was love. What difference did a word make anyway? She was going to marry him despite her misgivings about being the Countess of Riverdale. Her acceptance of his offer was still tentative, but surely his mother and Lizzie would not withhold their approval. They had persuaded her to stay here. They had said other things . . . Oh, she was going to marry him, and she did not believe she had ever been happier in her life.

To prove which point she shed a few tears before hurrying into her dressing room to wash her face.

She took extra care dressing for dinner that evening. She had stylish clothes, though she doubted she was ever in the first stare of fashion. She did not have a London modiste, but she did have one in Staffordshire who had long had the clothing of her and knew her well – her height, her size, her preferences, her personality. The pale turquoise dress she donned was fashionably high waisted and short sleeved and low necked, though not too low. Like most of her dresses, it had a narrow skirt, but flowed about her in a way that prevented her from looking like a flagpole without a flag. The hem was accentuated with embroidery in a slightly darker shade. She had Maude arrange her hair a little higher than usual even though she knew it would make her appear taller. She clasped about her neck the pearls her uncle and aunt had given her on her twenty-first birthday and looked approvingly at her image in the full-length mirror, then a bit regretfully at her face.

But it was time, she decided, squaring her shoulders and drawing herself up to a greater height, to forget about her face, at least with her conscious mind. If only it were that easy! She had almost died this afternoon when they had left behind the near seclusion of the wooded path and walked out onto the carriage drive by the park gates. There had been carriages and people everywhere. The veil on the brim of her bonnet had felt like a physical weight, and it had taken all her strength of will not to pull it down over her face. And they had certainly not gone unnoticed. Even if he had not been the Earl of Riverdale and no doubt a familiar figure to everyone in the beau monde, there were the triple facts of his height, perfect physique, and extraordinary good looks to draw attention.

But she had survived.

Now she was seated in the drawing room as the other ladies came down, dressed for dinner. Wren smiled at them. 'Did you enjoy the garden party?' she asked. 'The weather must have been perfect for it.'

'It was very pleasant,' Elizabeth said. 'It was in Richmond at one of the grand houses by the river. Both Mama and I were invited to take a boat ride. I sat at my ease in my boat, looking decorative, while poor Mr Doheny turned bright red in the face as he pulled on the oars. I was forced to deliver a monologue the whole time we were out, as all his breath was needed for his exertions. Mama was out for more than an hour with Lord Garand and he looked quite unwinded when they returned. Does that suggest I weigh a ton?'

'I believe it suggests, my love,' her mother said, 'that Mr Doheny does not know how to row a boat. Lord Garand remarked that he was dipping the oars too deep and trying to displace the whole of the River Thames with each stroke.'

They all laughed.

'And Lady Jessica?' Wren asked.

'She sat in the summerhouse with Louise almost the whole time we were there,' Mrs Westcott said, 'while hordes of young men prowled in the vicinity just waiting for her to emerge so that they could fetch her food or drink or bear her off to explore the orangery or to ride in one of the boats. She actually looked quite happy even though she ignored them all. I think the visit here did her a great deal of good, as well as the hope that Abigail will come here with Viola. I must thank you for giving her so much of your attention, Miss Heyden, and for taking her with you this morning to see your glassware. She was enchanted.'

'I very much enjoyed her company,' Wren said. And perhaps she was not so totally lacking in warmth as she feared. Lady Jessica had actually seemed to like her.

'And how was your walk in Hyde Park?' Elizabeth asked.

'It was lovely,' Wren said. 'We walked among the trees and I felt almost as though I were back in the country. You know that the Earl of Riverdale is returning here for dinner?'

'Yes, Lifford told us so,' Mrs Westcott said. 'I am glad we have no firm commitment for this evening. We will be able to enjoy his company for as long as he chooses to stay. And . . . well, and here he comes.'

The door had opened to admit the Earl of Riverdale, looking breathtakingly smart in black evening clothes with silver waistcoat and crisp white linen. He was also looking relaxed and good humored as he strode across the room to kiss his mother's cheek and then Lizzie's. He hesitated and then smiled at Wren.

'Do I take it,' he asked, 'that nothing has been said?'

Wren closed her eyes briefly.

'About what?' Elizabeth asked.

'About my betrothal,' he said, 'and Miss Heyden's. To each other. Our tentative betrothal.' Perhaps he was not so relaxed after all.

'*What?*' Elizabeth jumped to her feet.

'Tentative?' Mrs Westcott said, her hand going to her bosom.

'Ah,' he said, grinning as he glanced at Wren. 'Nothing has been said. I made Miss Heyden a marriage offer this afternoon, Mama – and yes, it was I who did the offering this time. She accepted. Tentatively.'

'*Tentatively?*' Both ladies spoke this time.

'I will marry Lord Riverdale only on the condition that both of you wholeheartedly approve,' Wren explained.

'But why would you think we might not?' Elizabeth asked.

'You want his happiness.' Wren could hear a slight quaver in her voice and swallowed.

'We thought it was clearly understood when you came to stay here,' Mrs Westcott said, 'that we were acknowledging the likelihood of a courtship and eventual marriage between you and Alex, Miss Heyden. And *Miss Heyden* no longer. You are Wren. I warned you that I was going to mother you. How much clearer could I have made myself?'

'Oh.' Wren swallowed again. This time she heard a distinct gurgle in her throat and had to blink a few times to clear her vision.

'I think, Miss Heyden,' the earl said, 'we are betrothed.'

'Yes.' She clenched and unclenched her hands in her lap.

'Come.' Mrs Westcott got to her feet and held out her arms, and Wren stood too and found herself caught up in a warm hug while Elizabeth was hugging her brother. They changed places after a few moments.

'I am very happy for you both,' Elizabeth said as she embraced Wren.

Was it possible? They had expected this? They approved it?

'And now we have something definite to talk about over dinner,' Mrs Westcott said, looking in apparent satisfaction from one to the other of them. 'We have a wedding to plan.'

Lord Riverdale exchanged a glance with Wren. 'Our wedding needs no discussion, Mama,' he said. 'I am going to purchase a special license tomorrow and make an appointment with a clergyman at some quiet church to be married the day after.'

'Just as Anna and Avery did last year,' Elizabeth said. 'I was there as a witness, Wren, and it was one of the loveliest weddings I have ever attended. Yes, such a wedding will suit both of you. Alex would hate the fuss of a grand wedding, and I cannot imagine you would be able to bear it. But please, *please* may I come as a witness? I have experience in the role.' She chuckled.

'Am I allowed a say?' Mrs Westcott asked. 'I can see it was downright foolish of me to dream immediately of a grand *ton* wedding at St George's on Hanover Square. Poor Wren. We might as well cast you into the lions' den and be done with it. And Lizzie is quite right. Alex would hate the fuss too.'

'I would,' he said. 'I am sorry, Mama. You would love to plan a grand wedding, I know.'

'There is always Lizzie,' she said. She was frowning, apparently in thought. 'I suppose over time you will inevitably meet our family, Wren, as you did us on Easter Sunday and Jessica yesterday. There are the Westcotts on the one side and the Radleys on the other. Almost everyone is here in town this spring. Would you be prepared to meet everyone at once – on your wedding day? It would still be a small wedding, just not quite as small as you intend. Or there is another possibility. You could have your private wedding and meet the family here afterward for a wedding breakfast. What do you think?'

What Wren thought as she felt pins and needles in her hands and flexed her fingers was that her life could easily spiral out of control if she was not very careful.

'Mama,' the earl said, 'I have assured Miss Heyden that I will never pressure her to meet anyone she does not choose to meet or do anything she does not choose to do. She is afraid that marrying me will force her into an unwanted social role as Countess of Riverdale. I have assured her that I will have no such expectations.'

But Mrs Westcott was right. It was absurd to think of marrying the Earl of Riverdale and never meeting any of his family apart from his mother and sister and one cousin. Wren closed her eyes briefly.

'The letter you wrote last evening has already been sent to Hinsford Manor, I suppose?' she said to Mrs Westcott in an apparent non sequitur that had them all looking rather blankly at her.

'Yes,' Mrs Westcott said. 'It went out at noon.'

'Will you write again?' Wren asked. 'You told me you doubted they would come without some specific family event with which to entice them. Will a wedding suffice? Will you invite them to come for our wedding – next week instead of the day after tomorrow? A *family* wedding, which will not be threatening to them but for which their presence will be much appreciated by the whole family – and by the bride? Yes, I will meet the two sides of the family on my wedding day. And after

213

that, I may well shut myself away at Brambledean and never meet anyone else for the rest of my life.'

Elizabeth, she was aware, had tears in her eyes and looked as though she were biting her upper lip. Mrs Westcott was still frowning. The earl was gazing very intently at Wren.

'It may just work,' Mrs Westcott said. 'We can but try. Wren, my dear, I am going to love you to pieces. Be warned.'

'Wren,' Elizabeth said, 'will you write to Cousin Viola and Abigail too and send the letter with Mama's?'

'I will,' Wren said. But what had she started? It was too late to unstart it, however. At the very least she had committed herself to a family wedding one week hence. She had never felt more terrified in her life.

The butler appeared in the doorway at that moment to announce that dinner was served.

The Earl of Riverdale offered Wren his hand, his eyes intent upon hers. 'Thank you,' he said softly. 'Do not think I am unaware of the magnitude of what you have agreed to and what you have suggested. I honor you. I only hope I can be worthy of you.'

And here she went, tearing up again. This was becoming a nasty habit. She set her hand in his. 'But I may well flee before our wedding day,' she said just as softly.

'Please don't.' He chuckled.

*   *   *

And so the chance of getting married quietly within two days of the Earl of Riverdale's proposal, almost before she had time to think about it in order to have second and twenty-second thoughts, had disappeared, entirely through her own fault. She was going to have to wait a whole week. Worse, she had agreed that the Westcott and Radley families would be invited to both the wedding and the breakfast afterward at Westcott House. She had even agreed to St George's on Hanover Square as the venue, the church attended by the fashionable world during the spring, though the congregation would be small. There was no point, after all, in seeking out an obscure little church on some equally obscure back street, as the Duke and Duchess of Netherby had done last year, since there was to be nothing secret about their wedding.

Their betrothal was announced in the morning papers two days after their walk in Hyde Park – Miss Wren Heyden to Alexander Louis Westcott, Earl of Riverdale. On the society pages, no less, where the whole fashionable world would see it and half that world, no doubt, would mourn the loss of the earl from the ranks of eligible bachelors.

The afternoon brought a steady stream of visitors, all of whom Mrs Westcott and Elizabeth entertained in the drawing room while Wren cowered in her room, writing to Philip Croft to tell him how gratifying it had been to see for herself the displays of their glassware in fashionable London shops. Elizabeth tapped on her door, however, just when she thought everyone must have left.

'Cousin Louise and Jessica and Anna are still here,' she said. 'They know how reclusive you are and will understand if you do not come down, but Jessica begged me to come and ask you anyway. It is entirely up to you, Wren.' Her smile held a hint of a twinkle. 'I know that such a lead-in is usually followed with a *but* . . . In this case it is not, however.'

Wren sighed and set down her pen. 'Do they know?' she asked. 'Has Lady Jessica told them? Or you or your mother?'

'About your face?' Elizabeth asked, coming right into the room. 'No. Why would we?'

Why indeed? Wren thought as she got to her feet. She was beginning to be a bore even to herself. So she had a very unsightly birthmark covering most of one side of her face. So what? Anyway, she was curious to meet the famous Anna – full name Anastasia – who had grown up in an orphanage only to end up a duchess with a fabulous fortune of her own. The famous Anna, who all unwittingly had caused havoc within the Westcott family.

'Lead the way,' she said with a huge sigh that only made Lizzie smile more.

Within minutes there were two more people to add to the growing list of those who had seen her without her veil. And though Wren suspected that Lady Jessica had indeed told them about her birthmark, neither her mother nor her sister-in-law paid any attention to it or – perhaps more significant – studiously avoided looking into her face. The Dowager Duchess of Netherby, Cousin Louise, was a handsome lady, somewhat on the stout side, probably in her early to mid-forties. The duchess – Anna – was slight of build and pretty and exuded a sort of smiling serenity that intrigued Wren when she considered all the woman had gone through in the last year and a half. They were polite and amiable and kind. Anna thanked her particularly for suggesting that the former countess and her daughter be invited to the wedding and for writing in person to add her persuasions to Mrs Westcott's.

'Perhaps they will come for such an occasion,' she said. 'I live in hope. Abigail is my half sister, Miss Heyden, and I long to see her again almost as much as Jessica does. And Aunt Viola is as much a part of this family as anyone else and ought to be here for Alex's wedding.' She paused then for a moment before saying, 'I am so sorry you have no one of your own to be with you. You must be missing your aunt and uncle more than ever this week. However, this is a welcoming family. I know that from personal experience. We will all be your cousins. Lizzie has the advantage of us, of course. She will be your sister.'

'Thomas – my brother-in-law, Lord Molenor – believes he remembers Mr Reginald Heyden, your uncle, as a venerable elder when he was just a young sprig about town, Miss Heyden,' the dowager duchess said. 'He will no doubt have questions for you when he meets you. And about your aunt too, though Mr Heyden was still a widower after his first marriage at the time.'

'He married my aunt twenty years ago,' Wren explained, 'and sold his London house and never came back here.'

The conversation flowed pleasantly after that, but the ladies stayed for only twenty minutes more. But now she had met five members of the family, including Mrs Westcott and Elizabeth. She could meet the rest too. It was not going to be easy, but she could do it. She *would* do it. It was her newest project, and she would not fail any more than she failed at any of her business endeavors.

And then – oh, then, she would settle into the marriage of her dreams and never meet anyone else ever again.

She almost believed herself.

CHAPTER 12

Wren was looking forward to an afternoon drive to Kew Gardens with her betrothed. There were three days still to go to her wedding, and it seemed to her that some invisible force must have slowed time to a fraction of its usual speed. Yet there was pleasure too in going shopping with her future mother- and sister-in-law and simply being at home, getting to know them better and learning to relax in their company.

Her future family had gone visiting on this particular afternoon, however, and Wren stayed behind in her room in her favorite place by the window, reading one of the books she had borrowed from Hookham's Library. The earl was not due to arrive for another hour yet. He had assured her she would find Kew Gardens lovely. She particularly wanted to see the famous pagoda.

When she heard the distant sounds of closing doors and male voices, she glanced at the clock on the mantel. He must have mistaken the time – or she had. He was an hour early. It did not matter, however. She was ready and eager to go. She got to her feet, took up her bonnet and gloves and shawl and parasol and hurried light-footed down to the drawing room.

The door was open. Wren could see that Mr Lifford, the butler, was bent over another man, who was seated in a chair close to the door. Her first thought was that her betrothed must be unwell. Too late she realized that the man was a stranger – she was already inside the room and had been noticed. Both men looked up at her, the butler in some consternation, the other man with a frown and a blank look in his eyes.

'Who are you?' he asked, jumping to his feet.

He was a very young man, tall and thin, almost to the point of emaciation. He might once have been very good-looking, but his complexion now was pasty apart from two spots of hectic color high on his cheeks. His fair hair was untidy and matted in places. He was wearing a green military coat, which looked both dusty and shabby, breeches and linen that must once have been white but were no longer so, and scuffed dusty boots. Even from a slight distance away, Wren could detect an unpleasant odor. She knew even before the butler spoke who he must be.

'Lieutenant Westcott has come home, miss,' Mr Lifford said. 'Miss Heyden is staying here as a guest, sir.'

'*Captain* Westcott,' the young man said almost absently, still frowning, and Wren could see now that his eyes were bright and feverish and rather wild. 'Dash it all, Mama is not here, is she? Or

Cam. Or Abby. They left. It slipped my mind. I remembered yesterday. At least, I think it was yesterday. Who *is* here, Lifford? Anastasia? But she married Avery. Devil take it, I ought not to have come to this house, ought I? I knew that. Forgot.' He was noticeably swaying on his feet.

Wren set her things down on a table beside the door and hurried forward. 'You are Harry Westcott,' she said, taking his arm. 'Have you just come from the Peninsula? Do please sit down again. Mrs Althea Westcott is staying here for the Season with Lady Overfield, but they are out this afternoon. The Earl of Riverdale will be here soon. Mr Lifford, perhaps you would bring the captain a glass of water?' She could tell as soon as she touched him that he was burning up with fever.

The butler hurried away and the young man sank back down onto his seat. 'Riverdale.' He rested one elbow on the arm of the chair and set three fingertips against his forehead. He laughed weakly. 'That used to be me, by Jove, and my father before me. No longer, though. All the time I was on the ship and then in the carriage I remembered. How could I have forgotten as soon as I saw London? If I could only get here and through the door, I thought, I would be home. I even argued with the driver of the hired coach when he told me this was not the address I had given him. I called him a fool.' He grinned and then looked stricken.

'You are home,' Wren told him, setting the backs

221

of her fingers lightly to his cheek to confirm that indeed he was very hot. 'You are with your family.'

'Home.' He closed his eyes. 'The very place where that damned Alex is living. It was not his fault, though, was it?'

'It was not,' she said.

'I expected that they would all be here,' he said. 'Mama and the girls. They are not, though, are they? How the devil could I have forgotten? I remembered when we were at sea before I forgot again. Cam married a dashed schoolteacher because she thought she could do no better. Mama is afraid to show her face anywhere she may be recognized. She is not here, is she?'

The butler had returned and Wren took the glass of water from his tray and held it to the young man's lips as he sipped from it. His hand closed about hers and he drank more greedily. She doubted he had had a chance either to wash or to change his linen since he left the Peninsula, even though he was an officer and one would have expected him to have received preferential treatment among all the other military wounded with whom she supposed he had been shipped home.

'Who are you? I have forgotten,' he said, taking his hand from the glass. 'What did you do to your face? A musket ball glanced past, did it? It looks as if you had a narrow escape.'

'I am Wren Heyden,' she said. 'It is a birthmark.'

'Of course,' he said. 'There are no musket balls

whistling around here, are there? I am in England, aren't I?'

'You are,' Wren said as he sat back in his chair, and she saw that his eyes were suddenly swimming with tears.

'It is one devil of a lark being out there, you know,' he said, grinning at her. 'Mama and the girls are out, are they? I should have sent notice from Dover that I was on my way. But I had a spot of fever again.'

Wren exchanged glances with the butler. 'Mr Lifford,' she said, 'is Captain Westcott's old room unoccupied?'

'It is, miss,' he said.

'Then will you lead the way there?' she said. 'After we get him settled, perhaps you could have a bowl of cold water with some cloths sent up? And will you perhaps send for the family physician? Come, Captain Westcott. Take my arm and we will go up to your room. You may lie down there and be comfortable while I bathe your face and see if I can relieve your fever.'

'Oh, Mama will do that,' he said. 'You need not concern yourself.' But he got to his feet and allowed Wren to take his arm and steer him out of the room and up the stairs. The housekeeper had appeared and come around to the young man's other side to steady him.

'Mr Harry,' she said in a voice thick with emotion, 'you have come home. All in one piece, your mama will be happy to know.'

'She is so happy,' the young man said, 'that she has gone out just when I was expected home and taken the girls with her.'

She clucked her tongue. 'She is at Hinsford, worrying herself silly about you, Mr Harry,' she said. 'And Lady – And Miss Abigail too. They sent you home from that nasty heathen place, then, did they?'

'Kicking and screaming,' he said cheerfully. 'I got a sword cut on my arm again. A mere scratch is all it was, but then it turned putrid and I got the damned fever and dashed near died. When I didn't, they packed me up and sent me home. Colonel's orders until I am better. He doesn't want to see my ugly face for at least two months, he told me. And here I am, fit as a fiddle and half a world away from my men, where I ought to be. It's a lark out there, you know.'

By the time he had finished babbling they had him in his room, had stripped him of his coat and hauled off his boots, and had him lying on his bed. The butler had gone off to send someone running for the physician, the housekeeper had opened a window to let in some fresh air, and two maids had come hurrying in, one with a bowl of water, the other with cloths in her hand and towels over her arm.

Half an hour later Wren was alone with the young man, the door of the bedchamber open behind her. Mr Lifford had gone downstairs to await the arrival of the physician, the maids had gone about their duties, and the housekeeper was in the kitchens supervising the making of nourishing broths and jellies for Captain Westcott. Wren was bathing his face with cool, wet cloths and listening to his increasingly delirious ramblings. His right arm, she had seen through the sleeve of his shirt as soon as his coat came off, was heavily bandaged from shoulder to wrist. If the physician did not come soon, she would have to change those dressings herself. She very much doubted it had been done recently.

She turned with some relief when she heard a light tap on the door, expecting to see either the physician or – please, please – her betrothed. The man standing in the doorway, however, was decidedly not the latter and could not possibly be the former. He was not a tall man. Indeed, he was several inches shorter than she. But he was a man who somehow filled the room with his presence even though he had not stepped quite into it yet. He was blond haired, handsome, exquisitely tailored, and decorated with rings on several fingers, a jewel that winked in his intricately tied neckcloth, and chains and fobs at his waist. He looked gorgeous and powerful and somehow dangerous. He was holding a silver quizzing glass halfway to his eye but beheld the scene before him through lazy, heavy-lidded eyes without its aid. She knew instantly who he must be, just as she had known who Harry Westcott was, and felt more exposed than she had for days and weeks. Her veil might have been a hundred miles away for the amount of good it could do her now. Her hand – the one that was not holding the wet cloth – came up to cover the left side of her face.

'Netherby at your service, Miss Heyden,' he said in a weary voice as he strolled into the room and approached the bed. 'I suppose that is who you are. Lifford sent a runner for me, and apparently the lad really did run. Perhaps Lifford has forgotten that I am no longer Harry's guardian since he passed the age of majority several months ago. But I was in the act of leaving the house when the runner came, so here I am.' He turned his attention then to the young man in the bed. 'You have a bit of a fever, do you, Harry?' He set the backs of perfectly manicured fingers against the captain's brow, Wren having stepped to one side.

'Oh, it's you, is it, Avery?' the captain said irritably. 'If you have come to stop me from enlisting, you can damned well forget it. I *want* to be an army man. I *like* the military life. And you are not my guardian any longer.'

'For which blessing I shall offer up a special prayer of thanks tonight,' the Duke of Netherby said. 'I came to cool your fevered brow, Harry, though Miss Heyden appears to have been doing an admirable job of it without me. I hope you have not been unleashing similar language upon her to what you are using on me.'

'I damned well have not,' Captain Westcott said testily. 'I know how to speak to ladies. If you want to be useful, Avery, stop the wardrobe and the dressing table from walking about the room, will you? It's dashed unnerving.'

'I shall have a word with them,' the duke said, and looked at Wren. 'I take it Cousins Althea and Elizabeth are from home, as well as Riverdale? I apologize for this unexpected intrusion upon your privacy by yet two more members of your betrothed's family, Miss Heyden. I understand that you are something of a recluse.'

'I agreed to meet you all on my wedding day,' Wren said. 'That is only three days away.' She was still holding her hand over the left side of her face.

The duke took the cloth from her other hand, dipped it in the water, squeezed it out, and spread it over the young man's brow. 'We all have things about ourselves that we would rather hide than display,' he said softly, more as if he were speaking to his former ward than to Wren. 'I grew up small, puny, timid, and pretty, and I was unleashed upon a boys' school when I was eleven.'

She could only imagine what that must have been like. Boys' private schools – though they were called paradoxically *public* schools – were reputed to be brutal. She wondered how he had come from there to here, for though he was still small and slight of build and beautiful to look upon, there was not the merest suggestion of puniness or timidity or effeminacy about him. Quite the opposite.

'One either succumbs,' he continued, 'or . . . one does not. I think perhaps you are in the process of not succumbing. Why else would you have agreed to take breakfast on your wedding day with strangers who just happen to be related to your prospective groom?' He dipped the cloth and wrung out the excess water again. 'It sounds as if the physician may have come ambling along at last.'

It was not he, however. It was the Earl of Riverdale who appeared in the doorway, taking in the scene before his eyes.

'How is he?' he asked, flicking a glance at Wren.

'Alex?' Captain Westcott turned his head on the pillow. 'What the devil are you doing here? Is a man's own room not his private domain any longer? I am supposed to resent you, aren't I? Can't remember why, though. I've never had anything against you. Where are Mama and the girls? Why are all these people in my room?'

'Because you have come home safely from the Peninsula, Harry,' the earl said, moving closer to the bed, 'and we are happy to see you. Your mother and Abigail will be here soon. They are coming for my wedding to Miss Heyden in three days' time. At least, I trust they are. Camille is in Bath with her husband and children. I understand from Lifford that a physician has been summoned. Is his fever high?' The last question was directed to Wren.

'Yes,' she said, lowering her hand at last. 'He has a wound on his right arm that needs to be cleansed and dressed again.'

'If you would care to withdraw from the room to spare your blushes, Miss Heyden,' the Duke of Netherby said, 'Riverdale and I will contrive to undress Harry and make him more comfortable. And ourselves too, I hope. You do not exactly smell like a rose, my lad.'

Wren went to her room. A few minutes later she heard what must surely have been the arrival of the physician. Another half hour passed before the Earl of Riverdale tapped on her door.

'How is he?' she asked, opening it wide. 'That poor young man. He was sent home to recover from the recurring fever following a wound that had turned putrid, and in his delirium he thought he really was coming home – to the way things used to be. He expected to find his mother and sisters and his old life here.'

'He has been thoroughly washed from head to toe and put between clean sheets and tended and dosed,' he said. 'Netherby is sitting with him while he rattles on about what a famous lark it is to be over there fighting. He will sleep soon, the physician has assured us, and now that his wound is clean and he can be cared for by a doctor again, the fever should run its course within a few days and stay away. He is going to need some recovery time, however. He will need to be fattened up, but with everyone here who will be eager to fuss over him, that should not take long. Come outside with me to stroll in the garden. It is a bit late for Kew today, I am afraid.'

She did not even stop at the drawing room to pick up her bonnet and other things. She went outside with him, her arm through his, and reveled in the feeling of the warm breeze on her cheeks.

'I really am sorry for all this,' he said as they strolled among the flower beds. 'Your dearest wish was a modest one – someone to wed. Some*one*, not hordes of others associated with him. I promised to protect you from all that and have failed miserably so far. You will be thinking me a fraud and a deceiver.'

'No,' she said.

'Shall I send you home to Withington?' he asked. 'I know you sent your own carriage there after you moved here. Would you like to go back to the quiet privacy to which you are accustomed? Perhaps, if you are kind and prepared to give me a second chance, I could bring the special license to Brambledean when I am released from my responsibilities here, or even sooner if you wish, and we can marry privately there and *live* privately ever after there.'

'And next spring?' she asked. They had come to the small herb garden, which had indeed been set out as an old-fashioned knot garden, each cluster of herbs separated from others by low walls of stone. The smells were as enticing as those of the flowers. 'Would you not need to come back here then and every year?'

'You could remain in the country when I am in Parliament if you wished,' he said.

'That would not be marriage, would it?' she said. 'I have not been forced into anything, Lord Riverdale. You are not responsible for me. I chose to meet Mrs Westcott and Lizzie. And Lady Jessica. I chose to meet the Dowager Duchess of Netherby and the duchess. I agreed to a family wedding when your mother suggested it. I suggested inviting Miss Kingsley and her daughter to our wedding.'

He was smiling at her and drawing her down to sit on a wooden bench near the knot garden. 'And I suppose you chose to meet Harry and Netherby,' he said.

'I met them under unforeseeable circumstances,' she said. 'It was not your fault. And I am glad it is over with. He is very formidable, is he not? I am not sure why, but he is.'

'Netherby?' He laughed. 'I used to think him a bit of a fop and scoffed at those who always seemed to think there was something dangerous about him. And then I discovered that he *is* dangerous, though he almost never needs to prove it.'

She looked at him. 'Well?' she said. 'You cannot tell me that much without explaining yourself.'

'Cousin Camille was betrothed to Viscount Uxbury,' he told her, 'but he forced her to end the betrothal as soon as he discovered she was illegitimate. He was not pleasant about it either. And then he tried to ingratiate himself with Anna. When he turned up uninvited at a ball in her honor and tried to harass her there, Netherby and I kicked him out. The morning after, he challenged

Netherby to a duel in Hyde Park. No doubt he thought it would be an easy victory for him, especially when Netherby, who had the choice of weapons, chose none at all. On the appointed morning he stripped to his breeches and nothing more – not even boots. I was his second and thought him mad. Everyone else there thought him mad. Uxbury laughed at him. And then Netherby proceeded to knock him down – with his bare feet. When Uxbury got up, Netherby launched himself into the air and felled the man with both feet beneath his chin. Uxbury was unconscious for some time. I do believe Netherby went gently on him, however. I was and am strongly of the opinion that he could have killed Uxbury with the greatest ease if he had wanted to. Afterward, he explained he had been trained in various Far Eastern arts by an old Chinese master.'

'Oh,' Wren said, 'how splendid.'

'Bloodthirsty wench.' He grinned at her. 'So Anna thought, and so Lizzie thought. They were both there, hidden up a tree and behind the tree respectively. Ladies never ever go anywhere near duels, I must add. You would have been there too if you had been given the chance, I suppose?'

'Oh, definitely,' she said, and he laughed outright.

'Miss Heyden,' he said, 'you are going to fit right into this family, you know.'

She smiled at him. What a lovely thing to say. Just as if she were no different in many ways from

Lizzie or the Duchess of Netherby. And she realized, like a sharp stab to the heart, that she had always longed for just that – to belong, to fit in.

He lifted one hand to cup the left side of her face and ran his thumb lightly over her cheek. 'Thank you,' he said, 'for tending to Harry, especially when he was smelling so ripe and his language was not any better. He is very precious. Had he retained the title, he would have borne it well. He was very young and a bit wild, but he would have settled down within a year or two and done a far better job than his father did. He is of sound character. His mother saw to that.'

'You are not responsible for him either,' she said. 'I have discovered your character flaw, Lord Riverdale. You mentioned it yourself in Hyde Park. You would take the burdens of the world upon your own shoulders if you could and solve them. You cannot do it, and it is not a good idea even to try. We all have to find our own way in life. It is, I believe, what life is all about.'

'Finding our way?' he said. 'You mean we get to choose? It did not feel that way last year when my life was turned upside down and inside out and all I wanted was the old life back. I had found a way through that and I had followed it with determination and hard work and satisfaction.'

'You had choices even so,' she said. 'You could have chosen to ignore the monstrosity that is Brambledean and continued along your familiar path. You could have chosen to marry for love or not at all. You could have chosen any of the young ladies who have made their preference for you this year clear. You could have ignored my more blatant marriage proposal. You still have choices and always will. So do I. I could leave for Withington tomorrow morning if I chose.'

'And do you choose?' he asked.

'No,' she said. 'I am going to remain here and marry you. I must have met about half your family already. I can surely survive meeting the other half.'

He laughed again and then closed the distance between their mouths. He kissed her warmly, lingeringly, gently. She breathed in the scents of rosemary and sage and mint and thyme and the background fragrances of sweet peas and other flowers and thought that she could forfeit passion for this sense of . . . Of what? She could not put a name to it. Affection, perhaps?

'I should go back up and see how Captain Westcott is doing,' she said regretfully when he lifted his head. 'Perhaps there is something I can do to help.'

'*Captain?*' He got to his feet and offered his hand.

'That is what he said when Mr Lifford called him Lieutenant Westcott,' she said.

'Impressive,' he said. 'You do not need to tend him, you know. There are other—'

'Yes,' she said, interrupting him, 'I *do* know.'

CHAPTER 13

Alexander moved back into the house. The physician gave it as his opinion that there was no need for Harry to be nursed around the clock, but Alexander nevertheless had a truckle bed made up for himself in the dressing room leading off Harry's bedchamber so that he would be within calling distance if he was needed. Netherby approved. Harry grumbled.

Alexander's mother and Elizabeth were relieved to have a supportive male presence, especially because Harry's fever had not yet abated when they returned home and went up to see him. He asked if they were visiting his mother and then frowned and corrected himself.

Miss Heyden was with Alexander in Harry's room that evening, bathing his face with cool cloths, when Cousin Eugenia, the Dowager Countess of Riverdale, Harry's grandmother, called to see him, inevitably bringing Cousin Matilda, her eldest daughter, with her. Their attention was focused entirely upon Harry for some time, as was to be expected. But after a few minutes, Cousin Matilda noticed Miss Heyden, who had moved back to stand by the window, and gazed at her with what looked like fascinated horror.

'My dear young lady,' she said, 'whatever happened to your face? I must beg leave to recommend some ointment that would clear it up in no time.'

'Don't be a fool, Matilda,' her mother commanded. 'It looks to me like a permanent blemish.'

'It is, ma'am,' Miss Heyden said, and Alexander, meeting her eyes, grimaced slightly. She favored him with a fleeting smile.

'Miss Heyden is my betrothed,' he explained, and made the introductions.

'Well, of course she is,' Cousin Matilda said. 'Who else would she be? A veil might make you less self-conscious, Miss Heyden.'

Alexander closed his eyes.

'It does,' Miss Heyden said. 'But I believe it is important that Lord Riverdale's relatives see me as I am.'

'And why would she wear one at all, Matilda?' the dowager said, sounding irritated, as she often did with that particular daughter. 'She is remarkably handsome apart from those purple marks, which I imagine one does not even notice after a while. Alexander has shown great good sense in not allowing such a trivial detail to influence his choice. It is time he married and started to fill his nursery. There is an alarming dearth of heirs in this family.'

Alexander wondered if his prospective bride

would after all bolt for the country tomorrow morning. But she was half smiling at the old lady.

Harry, ignored for the moment, laughed weakly. 'I cannot help in that department. I am sorry, Grandmama,' he said. 'I am a bastard. Why is Mama not here? Everyone else is.'

'Your mind is wandering again,' his grandmother told him bluntly, 'as apparently it was when you arrived this afternoon. It is a good thing Miss Heyden had the presence of mind to cool your face with cold cloths. You need to rest and then get some fat on your bones. Your mother and Abigail are quite possibly coming here for Alexander's wedding. Althea is this very minute writing another letter to urge them to come on your account.'

'Alex's wedding,' he said, draping his uninjured arm across his eyes. 'Well, at least no one is hounding me to marry and produce heirs. That is one advantage of being a bastard.'

'You ought not to use that word in the presence of your grandmother, Harry,' Cousin Matilda said, and he laughed again.

'I am *not* going to apologize again,' Alexander said quietly when the dowager and Cousin Matilda had gone downstairs and Harry had dropped off into a doze. 'Doubtless you would consider me a bore.'

'Doubtless I would,' she agreed. 'There is going to be no one new left for me to meet on my wedding day.'

'Do not forget my mother's family,' he said.

'I am not likely to,' she told him, pulling a face.

'You ought not to be doing this,' he said after she had straightened the bedcovers without waking Harry and rung to have the bowl and cloths taken away and fresh ones brought.

'Why not?' she asked. 'Your mother needed to write to Harry's mother on the chance that she has decided not to come for our wedding, and Lizzie did not feel she could easily get out of the private birthday dinner to which she had been invited. Why not me? I will be a full-fledged member of the family in three days' time.'

And she was being drawn into the family, it seemed, whether she fully realized it or not.

'Harry enlisted as a private soldier the day after that ghastly meeting we all had with his solicitor,' Alexander told her. 'He disappeared, and when Netherby finally found him, he had already taken the king's shilling. How Netherby got him out of it remains a mystery, but he did. He purchased a commission instead, but Harry insisted upon a foot regiment and upon earning his own promotions without any further help from Avery's purse.'

'Then you were right about him,' she said. 'He is a young man of sturdy character who will do well with his life and be strengthened by what has happened to him. Though he is obviously deeply hurt by it all. It will not be easy.'

'No,' he said.

'But you are *not* to blame yourself,' she said even

238

more softly. 'That is what *you* must learn from all of this.'

Harry opened his eyes. 'I say,' he said, looking at Miss Heyden. 'You are going to be my second cousin-in-law. I have just worked it out. Though you may not want to claim me even at that distant relationship.' He gave her the ghost of his old charming, boyish smile. 'It's not a comfortable thing to have a bastard in your family, is it? Or to be one in someone else's. Ask Mama. Ask Cam. Ask Abby.'

'Captain Westcott,' she said, leaning slightly toward him and checking the heat in his cheeks with the backs of her fingers. 'Family ties are too precious to be thrown away for such a slight cause.'

'Slight?' He laughed.

'Yes, slight,' she repeated. 'It is obvious you are loved by your family despite the transgressions of your father. And calling yourself a bastard, you know, hurts them as much as it hurts you. Perhaps more.'

He stared at her with a mix of confusion and awe, and then said, 'Yes, ma'am.' He then promptly drifted off to sleep again.

Alexander gazed at her as she spread a cloth soaked with the freshly brought water across his forehead. *Family ties are too precious to be thrown away for such a slight cause.* What the devil had happened to *her* family? He did not even know her childhood name, did he? *Heyden* was the name of the man her aunt had married. And *Wren*? Was it her baptismal name? Good God, he did not even know her name. In three days' time they were going to be married, yet he was still plagued by one basic question.

Who the devil *was* this woman he was about to marry?

A letter arrived from Viola Kingsley, the former Countess of Riverdale, the following morning. She and her daughter were coming for the wedding. It was too late now to send the letter that had been written to tell her of the arrival of her son.

They arrived at Westcott House the following day to warm hugs and welcomes – and a tearful reunion with Captain Harry Westcott, who had come downstairs, against advice, when their carriage was heard. His fever had ebbed the night before and had not returned this morning, but he was weak and tired and complaining about the broths and jellies the cook was sending up to him.

Wren watched the three of them in a tight hug together in the main hall and blinked her eyes. The ladies had, of course, been taken completely by surprise and were not willing to let him go.

It was easy to see from where Harry had acquired his good looks. His mother was blond and elegant and still beautiful, and his younger sister was fair haired, dainty, and exquisitely pretty.

Miss Kingsley was the first to turn from the group. She approached them with a smile and eyes that were bright with unshed tears. 'Althea,' she

240

said to Mrs Westcott, 'you must think my manners have gone begging. How delightful it is to see you again, and how good it was of you to invite Abby and me to come here for a family wedding when I never feel sure we ought to lay claim to membership. And Elizabeth and Alexander! You are both looking well. Present me to your betrothed if you will, Alexander. I assume this is she.' She turned her attention upon Wren.

'Yes indeed,' the Earl of Riverdale said, drawing Wren's hand through his arm. 'Cousin Viola and Abigail, I have the pleasure of presenting my betrothed, Miss Wren Heyden.'

'I say, Mama,' Captain Westcott said, 'Miss Heyden sat with me throughout the bout of fever I arrived home with. She bathed my face with cool cloths and listened to my ravings without once calling me an idiot. And this morning she sneaked me a piece of toast after I have been tortured with nothing but gruels in which there is not a single lump of meat or vegetables a man could get his teeth into.'

'Physician's orders, Harry,' Elizabeth said, laughing. 'And now that you have betrayed poor Wren I daresay she will be arrested and dragged off within the hour to sit in the stocks.'

'Miss Heyden.' The former countess extended her hand, her eyes roaming over Wren's face. 'I am delighted to make your acquaintance. I thank you for the note you included with Althea's second letter and the personal invitation to your wedding.

241

It tipped the scales in favor of our coming. Did it not, Abby? And now I find that I am even more deeply in your debt. You have been caring for my son and preventing him from devouring beefsteaks and ale when he was feverish, the foolish boy. I will forgive the toast this morning.'

Wren thought about how difficult it must have been for her to come to the wedding of the man who now bore the title that had been her son's. And to come here to the house that had been hers. Yet now she was shaking the hand of the woman who tomorrow would assume the title that had been her own for longer than twenty years, and she was smiling graciously as though she felt no pang at all.

'I think it will soon be time for the beefsteaks and ale,' Wren said. 'You must find your son looking dreadfully thin.'

'Ah but,' she said, her eyes brightening with more tears, 'he is alive.'

'I am pleased to make your acquaintance, Miss Heyden,' Abigail Westcott said, stepping away from her brother's side in order to offer her hand to Wren. 'My cousin Jessica wrote to me about you. She is enormously impressed that you are a businesswoman and a very successful one. I am impressed too. Thank you for looking after my brother.'

'Everyone else has done so too,' Wren told her. 'Mrs Westcott and Lizzie and I have taken turns sitting with him during the day, and Lord Riverdale sleeps in his dressing room at night. The Duke of Netherby has come each day to spend an hour or more with him.'

'And has looked at me through his quizzing glass every time I complain about the food,' the captain said indignantly, 'and informed me I am getting to be a bore. He treats me as though I were a schoolboy again.'

'I cannot *believe* you are here and I am not merely dreaming, Harry,' Abigail said. 'You are not going back to that horrid place, are you? Promise me you are not?'

'The Peninsula?' he said. 'Of course I am going back. I am an officer, Abby. A captain, no less. I was promoted – just after I had almost got my arm sliced off, in fact. I have men counting on me out there and I am not going to let them down. I don't *want* to let them down.'

'I know,' she said, tossing her glance at the ceiling. 'It is all a great lark. Well, I am not going to quarrel with you, Harry. Not today, anyway.'

'Come upstairs to the drawing room,' Mrs Westcott said. 'You must be ready for refreshments.'

'I shall see Harry back to his room,' Lord Riverdale said. 'Would you like to come too, Abigail?'

'I will come in a short while, Harry,' his mother said.

'To tuck me in, I suppose,' he said with a grin.

'Well, I *am* your mama,' she reminded him. She walked beside Wren as they climbed the stairs. 'I am so sorry, Miss Heyden. All the focus of attention ought to be upon you today. You are tomorrow's bride.'

'I am perfectly contented that it be upon Captain Westcott,' Wren said. 'The Duke of Netherby informed us that his captaincy was awarded for an act of extraordinary bravery. How he got that information out of your son, I do not know. He has said nothing to the rest of us. He is a modest young man and I like him exceedingly.'

'You have endeared yourself to a mother's heart,' Miss Kingsley said. 'Again.'

Word spread fast. The Duke of Netherby paid his accustomed call before the morning was out, bringing his stepmother and Lady Jessica with him. Miss Kingsley went up to the captain's room not long after and Abigail came down. She and Lady Jessica met in the middle of the drawing room and hugged each other with exclamations and squeals of joy – the squeals were Lady Jessica's. They sat on the window seat, their heads together as they chattered away, their facial expressions bright with animation.

Wren was not ignored. Quite the contrary. She was drawn into a group with Mrs Westcott and Elizabeth and the dowager duchess, who plied her with questions about the wedding clothes for which she had shopped during the past week. Abigail came to sit beside her later, after her cousin had run upstairs to look in on the captain – 'if I can get past Avery,' she said, pulling a face as she left the room. Abigail wanted to know about the wedding plans. Her mother made much of Wren for the rest of the day and told her how happy she was.

'Alexander has always been one of the nicest people I know even apart from those impossibly romantic good looks of his,' she said, 'and I am delighted to know he is to be happily settled.'

Lord Riverdale himself stayed close to her all evening.

Belowstairs, all was apparently busy in preparation for tomorrow's wedding breakfast.

It was a busy, pleasant wedding eve, Wren told herself all day, and indeed she enjoyed it. Yet she felt horribly lonely through it all. They were a close-knit family, the Westcotts, despite the ghastly upheavals of last year that had shaken them to the roots and threatened to break them asunder. She felt her aloneness, her lack of a family of her own, like a physical weight. Perhaps tomorrow she would feel differently. She would be a member of this family. She would be a Westcott. She would belong.

Or would she?

Even if she did, would her new family ever fill the empty space where her own family – the bride's family – ought to be?

CHAPTER 14

Alexander waited outside St George's Church on Hanover Square, his hands opening and closing at his sides. His was not to be the typical society wedding held here during the months of the Season. There were very few guests and no frills – no organ or choir, no incense or floral arrangements, no flower-bedecked carriage. No groom waiting at the front of the church for his bride to walk toward him along the nave on the arm of her father.

But it felt no less a momentous occasion to him. He had purchased the special license and made the arrangements, and now here he was, as nervous as if there were three hundred guests and three bishops gathered inside.

Instead there were the members of his family on both his mother's and his father's sides, with the exception of Cousin Mildred's three boys and Camille and Joel Cunningham and their adopted children. Harry was here, looking thin and smart, if slightly shabby, in his military uniform, which had been ruthlessly brushed and cleaned.

The situation was very lopsided, of course, for

there was no family on the bride's side. Perhaps after all they should have stuck with the original plan of marrying even more quietly than this. He knew she was feeling the absence of her aunt and uncle quite acutely, but that was not to be helped. What about the rest of her family, though? Was there any? He strongly suspected there was. Surely, she would have told him, no matter how painful the telling, if they had all perished in some disaster when she was a child.

One of these days they were going to have a long talk about her past. And one of these days they must talk about a number of other things too. The week had sped by in such a whirl of activity that they had not even discussed a marriage contract. She had revealed no details of her fortune to him and had extracted no promise from him about how it would be managed and spent. She had once sworn she would not marry before she had protected her interests.

He was just beginning to wonder if she would be late when his carriage turned into the square. He had come earlier with Sidney, from Sid's rooms, where he had spent the night again. He flexed his fingers once more and stepped forward as the carriage drew to a halt at the foot of the steps.

He helped his mother descend first. She took both his hands in hers and squeezed them tightly. 'My dearest boy,' she said. 'What a lovely day. Promise me you will be happy.'

'I promise, Mama.' He kissed her forehead and turned to help Elizabeth alight. They shared a wordless hug, and she went up the steps with their mother and disappeared inside the church while he was handing down his bride.

She was wearing an elegant, perfectly tailored, high-waisted dress in a vivid shade of pink that looked unexpectedly stunning with her dark hair, some of which was visible beneath a cream-colored bonnet with pink satin lining ruched on the underside of the brim and pink rosebuds and greenery in a cluster on one side of the crown. Wide pink satin ribbons held the confection in place and were tied with a large bow beneath her left ear. There was not a veil in sight. She set a hand in his and stepped down carefully.

'You look beautiful,' he told her.

'And so do you,' she said, smiling.

He bowed over her hand, raised it to his lips, and drew it through his arm. They climbed the steps together and stepped inside the church. The few guests gathered at the front were swallowed up by the cold grandeur of their surroundings. The church smelled of candles and old incense and prayer books. In the absence of organ music, his bootheels rang on the stone floor as they made their way forward. He looked at his bride, whose hand rested in the crook of his arm, and felt all the momentous significance of the occasion.

This was his wedding day.

He was about to join himself to this woman for

the rest of their lives. And it felt right. There had been no lengthy courtship, no grand romance, no declaration of love. But there was liking and respect on both sides. He was quite sure of that. There was admiration too on his side.

He looked ahead again to the clergyman, properly vested despite the quiet nature of the wedding. Sid, his best man, bearer of the ring, was facing them, a look of anxiety on his face. The others turned their heads, smiling, as they passed. And they came to a stop before the clergyman.

'Dearly beloved,' he said after a moment of silence, and this was it, Alexander thought. The most solemn, most momentous hour of his life.

And time swept on. Within moments, it seemed, the world as he knew it changed irrevocably with the exchange of vows and the placement of a ring and they were man and wife and moving off to the vestry to sign the register and then returning to greet their guests with handshakes and hugs and kisses. And then they were leading the way back along the nave and out onto the church steps, where Sid and Jessica and Abigail and Harry were awaiting them with handfuls of rose petals and a few curious onlookers, drawn no doubt by the fashionable carriages drawn up before the church.

The sun was shining.

There were more hugs and backslapping and congratulations somewhat louder and more hearty than those offered inside before Alexander handed his bride into his carriage for the drive back to

South Audley Street. They were to ride alone. There were no old boots or pots and pans to clatter along behind them as they moved away from the church – at his insistence. And it was a closed carriage, when the weather was fine enough for an open barouche.

The trappings, the absence of those festive touches that usually drew attention to a bridal conveyance, did not matter. They were married.

He reached for her hand as the carriage rocked into motion. 'Well, my lady,' he said.

'Do you regret not having a grander wedding?' she asked.

'No,' he said. 'Did you regret not having a quieter wedding?'

'No.'

He raised her hand to his lips. 'I believe,' he said, 'I will remember our wedding all my life as something perfect – just as it was.'

'So will I,' she said softly.

But there were times during the day when Wren wished they had kept to the original plan for a private wedding. She almost did not step into the carriage to go to church. It seemed like a physical impossibility. But of course she did. Going inside the church, which she was quite convinced during the journey she would not be able to do, was made easier by the fact that he was outside waiting for her and suddenly it was her wedding day and nothing else mattered. From the moment she set her hand in his to alight from the carriage, she saw only him and then the church and the clergyman awaiting them, and she felt only the solemn joy of the occasion. She was getting *married*. More than that, she was marrying the man with whom she had fallen deeply and unexpectedly – and secretly – in love. Oh, he was more right than he knew when he said in the carriage afterward that their wedding had been perfect. Even the ordeal after they came out of the vestry of facing the Westcott and Radley families en masse, some of whom she had not met before, could not quite mar the perfection. They had all been so very kind.

Joy remained with her during the carriage ride home. And her first sight of the dining room fairly took her breath away and really did bring tears to her eyes. The finest china, crystal, and silverware had been formally set out on a crisp white cloth. An elaborate epergne of summer flowers adorned the center of the table, and a pink rosebud stood in individual crystal vases at each place beside an intricately folded linen napkin. Wall sconces were filled with flowers, leaves and ferns spilling over the sides. Candles in silver holders burned everywhere despite the sunlight beyond the windows. A two-tiered cake iced in white and decorated with pink rosebuds stood alone on a small side table, a silver knife with pink ribbon adorning its handle beside it.

The cause of Wren's tears was the drinking glasses and individual vases. They were Heyden ware. The design was the last one Uncle Reggie had approved.

'Wherever—?' She whirled about to gaze at the Earl of Riverdale. He was smiling back at her, looking smugly pleased with himself.

'I was at one of the shops you visited with Lizzie and Jessica within hours of you leaving it,' he said. 'Fortunately, the shop owner had a complete set of everything I needed. He did complain, though, that I had left him with almost nothing and it might take him weeks to get more.'

'Oh.' And he must have paid the full retail price for them when he might have got them . . . But no. She would not complete that thought, even within her own head.

'Thank you,' she said. 'Oh, how inadequate words are. *Thank* you, Lord Riverdale.'

'Might that be Alexander now?' he said. 'Or even Alex?'

'Yes.' But there was no time to say more. Their guests were arriving.

Sitting through the wedding breakfast with a large number of people, kind as they all were, was excruciatingly difficult for Wren. She had never done anything remotely like it before. Worse, she was very much on display as the bride and was expected to smile and converse without ceasing. None of them could have any idea what an ordeal it was for her. There were speeches and toasts, during which, inexplicably, everyone seemed to look and smile at *her* rather than at the speaker.

And then, when it was all over, they removed to the drawing room and in many ways the situation was worse, for everyone circulated, as she remembered the neighbors doing it at that ghastly tea at Brambledean. But this time she did not have a veil to hide behind.

And yet on balance, Wren did not really regret what she had agreed to. At least she had done it. And now she had met almost the whole of her husband's family and that terror was not still ahead of her.

Her *husband*. Every time that fact was mentioned – and it was mentioned a great deal – she felt an inner welling of joy. When she had made her list back in February and started to interview the gentlemen whose names were on it, she surely had not really believed her dream would come true. Had she?

But it had. Today.

Today was her wedding day.

Everyone left late in the afternoon. Everyone. Harry and Abigail went with Cousin Louise and Jessica to spend the night at Archer House. Cousin Viola went with the dowager countess and Matilda. Alexander's mother and Elizabeth went with Aunt Lilian and Uncle Richard Radley. It had all been planned ahead of time and was accomplished with a great deal of chatter and laughter and hugs as the bride and groom were left alone at Westcott House.

'Would you like a stroll in the park?' Alexander suggested as they waved the last carriage on its way. They both needed some air and exercise, he believed, and he for one was not quite ready yet for the sudden quietness of the house.

'Lovely,' she said. She did not change out of the pink dress she had worn for the wedding, but she did don a plainer bonnet – a straw one he had seen before – and she drew the veil down over her face before they left the house. He raised his eyebrows. 'Please understand. I have felt so dreadfully . . . exposed all day. It is something I have never done before. So many people! Until the day you first came to Withington I had not shown my face to *anyone* except my aunt and uncle and my governess and a few trusted servants in almost twenty years. Not even to anyone at the glassworks from the manager on down. Not to anyone.'

It was incredible to think that she had spent almost twenty years behind a veil – all through her girlhood, all through her early adulthood. 'I am not intending to scold you,' he said as they made their way along South Audley Street. 'You must always do as you choose. I am not going to play tyrant.'

'I know,' she said, and he turned his head to smile at her. It was still a bit dizzying to think that she was his wife, his countess.

'Do you realize,' he said, 'that there is no marriage contract? You once told me you would protect your rights and your options before you married.'

'And do you realize,' she said, 'that you still do not know the extent of my fortune? But marriage is not a business deal, is it? I am accustomed to deals and contracts and the careful protection of my rights and interests. Marriage ought not to be like that.'

'So you decided to trust me?' he said.

She did not answer for a while. 'Yes,' she said then. 'And I think perhaps you did the same thing, Alexander. I could be a pauper or deeply in debt for all you know.'

'Yes,' he agreed. 'But when I proposed marriage to you, it was because I wished to marry *you*, not your money.'

'We are a couple of fools,' she said as they crossed the road to the park. 'Or that is what my business instincts tell me. I tell them to be quiet, however. I always remember something Aunt Megan once told me. Our brains are not in command of our lives unless we let them be, she said. *We* are in command.'

'We are not our brains, then?' he asked.

'No,' she said. 'We possess brains, but sometimes they try to make us believe they possess us. My aunt was a placid lady and did not usually say much, but she had great depths of wisdom.'

'I know that today has been a huge ordeal for you, Wren,' he said as he led her onto the wide lawn between the carriage road and the trees. 'I knew it even before you drew the veil over your face. I just hope it has not been too overwhelming.'

'I very much like your family,' she told him, 'on both sides. You are very fortunate.'

'I am,' he agreed. He hesitated for only a moment. 'Do you have family?'

It was a long time before she answered. 'If by family you mean people with whom I have ties of blood,' she said, 'then I assume so. I do not know for certain. Twenty years is a long time. But if by family you mean ties of affinity and loyalty and affection and all the things that bind the Westcott and Radley families, then no. I have no family. My uncle and aunt are dead.'

He kept his head turned toward her. Carriages and horses and pedestrians passed one another on the main thoroughfare, but here it was quieter. 'Will you tell me about them one day?' he asked her.

'Perhaps,' she said. 'One day.'

'But not yet.'

'No,' she said. 'And perhaps never. It is not a story I want to tell, Alexander, and it is not one you would want to hear.'

'But perhaps you need to tell it,' he said, 'and perhaps I need to hear. No, forget I said that. Please. I will not add yet one more burden to your load.' Although she was his wife, he had no right to her heart and soul. What was inside her was hers to guard or disclose. She had married him out of trust. He would earn that trust, then.

He talked of their wedding and the breakfast, of Harry and Abigail and Camille, of some of the mischief he had got up to with Sid when they were boys. She spoke of her governess and her aunt, of the time when her uncle and aunt had chosen Withington House as their country home, consulting her wishes every step of the way.

They dined together later upon cold cuts and leftovers from the breakfast – at Wren's insistence for the sake of the servants, who had been unusually busy all day – and they spent the evening in the drawing room, talking again. This time she wanted to talk about Brambledean Court and what ought to be done there first now that there were funds.

Alexander felt the awkwardness of his situation. 'I cannot in all conscience make grandiose plans for the spending of your money, Wren,' he said.

'But it is *our* money now,' she told him. 'Not mine, not yours, but ours. We must always decide together what ought to be done – at Brambledean, at Withington, at Riddings Park, at the Staffordshire house, even at the glassworks if you are prepared to take an interest in it. I shall feel uncomfortable about the money if you do, Alexander. I hope you will not. We are *us* now.'

'It sounds ungrammatical,' he said at the same time as he was jolted by the idea of it – *we are* us *now*. 'But I shall try. It will take a little getting used to, though. I have stood alone since my father's death and managed my own affairs. In the normal course of things, I would have continued to do so after my marriage, and I would have provided for my wife too.'

'Then our marriage will be good for you,' she said briskly. 'It will be a necessary lesson in humility. I need to have a say in all the decision making, Alexander, not because the money has come from me – I wish it could be otherwise – but because I want to be involved and like and need to be involved. I am not anyone's idea of a typical lady, as you may have noticed. I can work co-operatively with other people. I did it with my uncle, especially during the last few years of his life when he was a bit weary. We worked together, and it worked well – is that a pun?'

'Probably,' he said. 'Very well, then, let's talk about Brambledean. Everything hinges upon the farms, Wren. Without them, the estate cannot prosper and we cannot prosper. Poor us, one might say, when we have all our other properties and sources of income. But there are many people dependent upon me – upon *us*. And it is for their sakes that the farms need to be made prosperous.'

'Then give me your ideas on what needs to be done first,' she said. 'I know very little about either farming or the running of a vast estate, but I will learn. Be my teacher.'

And they talked and planned for a whole hour – dry, dull stuff that would have driven most brides into hysterics or a coma on their wedding day. She listened, sitting back in her chair, her arms folded beneath her bosom, her head tipped slightly to one side. And occasionally she spoke, either with a pertinent question or with an intelligent comment or suggestion. It was like talking to another man, he thought as he relaxed back in his chair – until he caught himself in the thought and was very glad he had not said it aloud. She was *nothing like* a man, except perhaps in her willingness to use her mind to its full capacity without fear of being considered unfeminine.

She was very feminine actually. There was something surprisingly appealing – sexually, that was – about a woman who demanded to be taken seriously as a whole person. Though whether that was deliberate on her part, he did not know. He would guess not.

Their discussion came to an end when Lifford brought in the tea tray and lit the candles and drew the curtains to shut out the heavy dusk of evening. They talked on more general topics after that until the conversation lagged as they finished their tea.

'I get security with my marriage,' he said at last, 'and the wherewithal to repair the neglect of decades to what I have inherited. And an intelligent wife with a good business head. What do you get in exchange, Wren?' He wished he could rephrase his words as soon as they had been spoken. *An intelligent wife with a good business head.* It was hardly a complimentary way to describe one's bride on her wedding day.

'Marriage,' she said without hesitation, her head tipped slightly to one side. 'It is what I wanted, remember? It is why I invited you to Withington.'

'I passed the tests you set me?' he asked.

'Yes,' she said.

It was impossible to know what else lay beyond the simple answer. Was marriage the be-all and end-all to her? The security of being a wife, of having a shared home and a family? Sex? He knew that was part of it. She had admitted it in so many words before they ever came to London. It was impossible to know what her feelings were for him, and he could not ask, because she might ask the same question of him, and he did not know how he would answer. He did not know the answer. Liking, respect, even admiration did not seem enough.

'Are you ready for bed?' he asked.

'Yes,' she said.

The final chapter of their wedding day still had to be written. He got to his feet and offered his hand. She took it, and he drew her arm through his when she was on her feet. They proceeded upstairs without speaking and stopped outside her new dressing room, which was beside his and linked to it, her new bedchamber on the other side of it.

'I will come to you in half an hour if I may,' he said.

'Yes.'

He took her hand in his and held it to his lips before opening the door and then closing it behind her.

No, he did not know how he felt about her. Perhaps it did not matter if he could not find the appropriate word. She was his bride. That was really all that mattered tonight.

CHAPTER 15

Maude helped Wren out of her dress and took the pins from her hair while telling her that her aunt would be the happiest woman in the world today if she were still alive.

'Well, the *second* happiest woman, I suppose I mean,' she added. 'I suppose you are the happiest. And I am the third happiest, though since she is *not* alive, God rest her soul, I daresay I am the second.'

Wren laughed, wiped away a few tears, and hugged her startled maid before dismissing her. She donned her nightgown, a new one of fine linen Elizabeth had helped her select, and brushed her hair until it shone. Then she waited in the bedchamber to which her belongings had been moved this morning after she left for church. It was a lovely room, large and square and high ceilinged and decorated tastefully in various shades of fawn and ecru and cream and gold. It did not look down upon the garden at the back of the house, as her other room did, but upon the street at the front. It was a pleasant view nevertheless. Even an urban scene could have its charm – just as an industrial workshop could. Beauty came in many forms.

She was not nervous. Perhaps she ought to be. A typical lady would have been, she supposed. But she was filled with elation and expectation. She could hardly wait. And even as she was thinking it there was a light tap on her dressing room door. She had left it ajar, and Alexander came into her room without waiting for her summons. He had looked splendidly handsome in his black-and-white wedding clothes with a silver embroidered waistcoat and lace at his neck and wrists. He looked no less so now in a wine-colored brocaded dressing gown and slippers. It was certainly obvious that the breadth of his shoulders and chest owed nothing to padding.

He looked around the room. 'I have never been in here before,' he said. 'It is lovely, is it not?'

'It is,' she agreed.

'It is a great pity,' he said, 'that my predecessor, the beloved Humphrey, did not lavish the same care upon Brambledean as he did upon Westcott House.'

'Ah,' she said, 'but then he would have deprived us of the pleasure of re-creating it for ourselves.'

His eyes came back to her. 'That is a striking thought,' he said. 'So I may remember the late Earl of Riverdale with some fondness after all, may I? Ah, Wren, I have wondered how long it is.' He was moving toward her.

'My hair?' It was thick and almost straight and

nearly waist length and a rich chestnut brown. She had always thought it her best feature.

'It is beautiful,' he said.

'I considered braiding it,' she told him. 'But I have always worn it loose at night, sometimes to the despair of Maude if she is called upon to brush out the tangles in the morning.'

'You must continue to wear it down,' he said. 'Husband's orders. You did promise to obey me, if you recall. And if Maude complains, I shall dismiss her without a character and demonstrate that I intend to be master in my own home.'

She tipped her head to one side and smiled slowly. His eyes were, of course, laughing. 'I am in fear and trembling,' she said.

'As you ought to be,' he said. 'Wren, I never quite understand why married people of the upper classes have separate rooms. Just to prove that they can, perhaps? It seems especially puzzling when the two people are young and there is pleasure to be had and children to beget. Will you keep this room for your private use during the daytime and consider my bedchamber ours from tonight on?'

She was glad he was talking to her more as an equal than as a timid bride. She was equally glad of his suggestion. Aunt Megan and Uncle Reggie had always shared a room and a big old canopied bed, which sagged slightly in the middle. She had gone there screaming a few times in the early days when she was still suffering from nightmares, and they had taken her in between them and she had slept in warmth and happiness, half squashed and utterly safe.

'Yes,' she said.

'Come, then,' he said, and took up one of the candles from the table beside her and snuffed the others. He led the way through their dressing rooms and into his bedchamber. It was a twin to her room in size and shape, but this one was decorated in rich shades of wine and gold and lit by one branch of candles on the mantel and two candles in wall sconces on either side of the canopied bed. She ran her hand down one of the smooth spirals carved into the thick wooden posts at the foot of the bed.

'This is a fine room too,' she said. 'But we will absolutely have to find a way to outdo it at Brambledean.' She turned a smiling face to him.

'I am in perfect agreement,' he said, setting down the candlestick beside the candelabra. 'But perhaps we can wait until another occasion to discuss it. I find myself distracted tonight, I must confess.'

'Me too,' she said, and he kissed her.

She realized almost immediately that he was going to take his time about it. The bed was beside them, but for now he was ignoring it. He had kissed her before, but each time it had been all too brief for someone who was starved of intimate human contact and yearned for it. She knew very little. Almost nothing, in fact, but she knew enough to understand that there was a whole world of erotic experience that had been denied her – or that she had denied herself. Tonight would begin to set that right, and she was glad he was in no hurry.

He opened her mouth with his own, slid his tongue inside, and proceeded to do things that had her clutching the sides of his dressing gown at the waist and fighting to keep her knees under her. With the lightest of strokes against sensitive surfaces, he sent raw aches shooting through her. But it was not just his mouth. His hands roamed over her, seeming to find curves where she had not thought she had any and to appreciate the curves she had thought inadequate.

His hands spread over her buttocks at last and drew her fully against him. His hard, muscled man's body was enough to make her want to swoon. Not that she would. She had no intention of missing a single moment. She could feel that he was aroused, though she had no experience. She inhaled slowly as she tipped back her head, and his mouth, freed from hers, trailed kisses along her neck.

Please never stop. Oh please, please never stop.

'Come and lie down,' he murmured, his mouth against hers again, his eyes gazing, heavy lidded, into hers.

'Yes.'

'Will you let me remove your nightgown first?' he asked her.

Oh. Really? Now? With so many candles burning?

'Only if I may remove your dressing gown,' she said.

'Agreed.' He laughed softly. 'But me first.'

He edged her nightgown up between them and lifted it off over her head when she raised her arms. He dropped it to the floor and took a step back, his hands cupping her shoulders. Wren found herself curiously unself-conscious, though she did fight the urge to apologize. She was such a shapeless beanpole. Well, not quite shapeless, perhaps, but certainly not shapely. But he had chosen to marry her. He really had. On Easter Sunday she had released him from any sense of obligation he might have been feeling. He had proposed marriage to her here in London entirely of his own volition. He had had options – that pretty and shapely young lady with whom he had been walking in the park, for example.

'You have the physique of an athlete, Wren,' he said. 'If there were women athletes, they would surely aspire to look like you.'

She looked, startled, into his face, and his eyes crinkled at the corners.

'That does not sound like much of a compliment, does it?' he said. 'It was intended as one, though I probably ought not to have spoken aloud. You are magnificent.'

He could not possibly mean it. But he would not lie to her. And if he did, he certainly would not have paid her that particular compliment. She liked it. Oh goodness, she liked it. 'And did you notice tonight?' she asked.

He raised his eyebrows in inquiry.

'Did you *notice?*' she asked again. And she saw understanding dawn as his eyes focused upon the left side of her face.

'In all truth I did not,' he said. 'My gentleman's honor on it, Wren. I did not notice. I do not believe I have noticed all day. Which proves a point, I believe.'

'That you are not much of an observer?' she said. But though she made a joke of it, she felt a great lifting of the spirit. Was it possible that someone could look at her and truly *not notice?* Her aunt and uncle had always said it was so, of course, but they had known her forever. And she had never been quite sure they had not spoken more from the heart than from a strict adherence to the truth.

She untied the sash at his waist and slid her hands beneath his dressing gown at the shoulders. It was only then she realized he was wearing nothing underneath. She pushed the garment off and watched it slither down his arms and body and bunch about his feet. He kicked it away, his slippers with it.

She looked at him as he had looked at her, the candlelight flickering over his body. And . . . oh goodness. There were no words. She ran her hands lightly over his chest and felt the firmness of muscles there. She slid them up to his shoulders and felt their warm, hard solidity. His legs were long and powerful, a little longer than her own. His hips and waist were slender. And – ah yes, he was aroused and ready, as was she. She was aching with longing – or with something stronger and more physical than mere longing, though she could not find a word for it. She raised her eyes to his face before turning to lie down on the bed.

'Do you want me to snuff the candles?' he asked her.

She hesitated. 'No.' She wanted to see as well as feel. She had five senses. Why deliberately eliminate one of them?

When he lay down beside her and turned to her, she did not think she could be any more ready for the consummation. But she could, as she discovered over the next several minutes. And again he was in no hurry. His hands and mouth moved over her, explored her, tasted her, while her own hands, helpless and untutored at first, followed suit, discovering maleness and *otherness* as well as a beauty that might have brought her close once more to swooning if there had not been more powerful feelings to keep her very much aware and present.

He turned her onto her back at last, came over her, spread her legs wide with his own, and slid his hands beneath her while his weight came down on her, almost robbing her of breath but not of need. And she felt him at the most sensitive part of herself, seeking, circling, settling. He came into her. She inhaled slowly and deeply, feeling the hardness of him opening her, stretching her, hurting her, coming deep and deeper, the sharpness of the pain gone, until she was filled with him and filled with wonder.

At last. Ah, at last! At last.

He held still for a few moments and then took some of his weight on his forearms while he gazed down at her, his eyes heavy with an expression she had not seen there before.

'I am sorry,' he murmured.

For the pain? 'I am not,' she said. She would have endured a great deal more of it in order to have this – this joining of her body to a man's, this knowledge that after all she could be fully a woman and fully a person too.

He lowered his head to the pillow beside her own then and began to withdraw from her. *Please don't,* she wanted to say but did not. She was glad a moment later, for he paused at the brink of her and pressed inward again – and then again and again until his movements were firm and swift and rhythmic. And of course. Oh, of course. She was not an utter ignoramus. She had occasionally observed the animal kingdom, and it was not so very different for humans. This was what happened. This was the consummation, the love-making, and it would happen again and again in the nights and weeks and years ahead. This was how they would be man and wife. This was how they would get sons and daughters. She concentrated upon experiencing every strange and new sensation, upon listening to the unexpected wetness of it and their labored breathing, upon breathing in the surprisingly enticing smells of sweat and something else unmistakably carnal, upon seeing dark hair mingling with her own and his muscled shoulders just above her own and his rhythmically moving body as he worked in her.

This, she told herself with very deliberate exultation at last, when the ache of need and pleasure flowed in tandem with her blood, was her wedding night. *Their* wedding night. The first night of their marriage. She was glad she had decided to trust him, not just on the issue of money, but in everything. It would be a good marriage.

After what might have been many long minutes or only a few – time had become meaningless – his movements turned swifter and more urgent until they stopped suddenly when he was deep inside and she felt a gush of liquid heat and knew with only a slight pang of regret that it was over. But only for now. There would be other times. They were married and he was the one who had suggested that they share a room and a bed.

He made a sound of male satisfaction that did not translate into words, relaxed his full weight onto her again, and – if she was not mistaken – fell promptly asleep. The thought amused her and she smiled. He must weigh a ton. But she did not want him to wake up.

Alexander was not sleeping. He had just allowed himself the self-indulgence of total relaxation after his exertions even though he was aware that he must have been crushing her. It had been a long time. Too long. And now he had settled for less than his dream. But that was a disloyal thought, and he moved off to her side and pulled the bedcovers up about them. He felt too lazy to get out of bed to snuff the candles. Her face was turned toward him, shadowed by the flickering candlelight, her dark hair in disarray about her head and over her shoulder and one breast. It made her look much younger and more obviously feminine than usual.

He wondered if he had made the right decision in persuading her to make his bedchamber and his bed her own too. It seemed, strangely, like more of a commitment than simply marrying her had been this morning. It was a loss of privacy, of somewhere to retreat that was entirely his own. But he could no longer think that way and would not. He had made the decision when he offered her marriage. No half measures. No harking back to a dream that could never now be fulfilled. But then most dreams were like that. That was why they were called by that name.

He must get used to having her here in his bed, partly because he did have needs – as did she – but more because he had duties to his title and position over and above the financial ones. Cousin Eugenia, the dowager countess, had stated it baldly not so long ago. There was a great dearth of heirs in the Westcott family. He was it, in fact, yet he was not even the heir. He was the incumbent. If he were to die before producing at least one son, the family tree would have to be climbed to the very topmost branches in order to discover another more fruitful branch, or else the title would have to pass into abeyance. It was his duty to beget several sons and, he hoped, some daughters. He liked the idea of daughters. Yet his wife was almost thirty. They could not delay.

'Did I hurt you?' he asked.

'I did not mind,' she said, though she did not deny it. But no, she would not. She had wanted to be married. She wanted children too. If she had ever dreamed of romantic, passionate love, she too had made the decision to settle for a quieter substitute. It was not necessarily a bad thing. It was not without hope.

'I do not believe it will happen again,' he said. 'The pain, I mean.'

'No.'

'Was I very heavy?' he asked.

'Alexander,' she said. 'I was well pleased. I thought all men above a certain age were experienced enough not to feel such anxieties.'

Good God! He was very glad of the dim, flickering light. He was quite possibly blushing. He had *not* been a virgin tonight. He had had one very satisfactory lover ten years ago when he was at Oxford. She had been a tavern keeper – not one of the barmaids, but the owner herself, a widow twenty years his senior and buxom and hearty and affectionate and very, very skilled in bed. Not that he had had anyone with whom to compare her, it was true, but he had not doubted at the time and did not doubt now that she had been the very best teacher any young man could possibly wish for. They had parted on the best of terms after he graduated, and there had been very few women since then. For one thing, he had been busy at Riddings Park. For another – well, finding women of easy virtue, an unkind euphemism for women who were forced to sell their bodies in order to eat, had always seemed distasteful to him.

'You see,' he said, 'it has always seemed a bit sordid to engage in casual liaisons.'

'So I have rescued you from a life of near celibacy, have I?' she asked him.

This was a strange conversation. 'You have indeed,' he said. 'Wren, thank you for marrying me . . . without a marriage contract. Thank you for trusting me.' According to the law, everything that had been hers, including her very person, was now his. And if that was a disturbing thought even to him, what must it be to her?

She did not say anything for a while but merely gazed at him. 'I learned trust at the age of ten,' she said. 'It was a bit like jumping out of an upstairs window while someone stood below, holding no more than a pillow while the house burned down behind me. I put my faith in the person who saved me and learned that trust and knowing whom to trust are among the most important qualities anyone can cultivate. Without trust there is . . . nothing. A contract would have made me feel that perhaps I ought to have a little bit of doubt, and I chose not to entertain that fear.'

He gazed at her for a long while, wondering if she intended to continue, to tell him what it was in her life that had been like a house burning down behind her. But she did not say any more.

'Nevertheless,' he said, 'we will be visiting a lawyer within the next few days, Wren. I will not have you totally dependent upon my trustworthiness. Besides, some things need to be in writing and properly certified. I could die at any moment.'

'Oh, please do not,' she said.

'I shall try not to.' He smiled at her and raised one hand to push her hair back over her shoulder. She had small breasts, but they were firm and nicely shaped. He moved his hand about the one he had exposed, cupped it from beneath in his palm, and set his thumb over her nipple, which hardened as he stroked it lightly. 'Are you very sore?'

She thought a moment and shook her head.

'Will you think me very greedy?' he asked, feathering light kisses over her forehead, her temple, her cheek, her mouth.

'No,' she said.

She was wet and hot when he entered her this time and closed inner muscles about him while she raised her knees and set her feet flat on the bed. He moved swiftly in her, his eyes closed, the bulk of his weight on his forearms again, feeling greedy despite her denial, and came to a quick climax. He brought her with him this time when he moved off her, not withdrawing from her, keeping his arms about her, and he felt the soft warmth of her body as he settled the covers about them once more, and knew that she was relaxing into sleep, her head nestled on his shoulder.

Yes, he had settled for less than the dream. But so, probably, did almost every other man and woman who married. There could not be very many who were at leisure to search for love, and even fewer who found it. His mind touched upon Anna and Netherby and even upon Camille and Joel Cunningham, but he was not going to start making comparisons. He did not *know* anyway, did he? One surely never did know anyone else's marriage as it really was. No one would know his except the two of them. They would make of it what they chose. It was actually a good thought with which to begin a marriage.

He slept.

CHAPTER 16

'I should perhaps have thought of taking you on a wedding journey,' Alexander said the next morning, holding both of Wren's hands. 'To Scotland. Or the Lakes. Or Wales.'

'We,' she said. '*We* ought to have thought of it. But I do not want a wedding trip. Do you?'

'No,' he said. 'But it feels wrong to have been sitting here composing a letter early in the morning following our wedding and now to be going off to the House of Lords and leaving you alone.'

They had been jointly composing a letter to the steward at Brambledean with instructions on what they wished him to do immediately. Wren supposed it *was* a bit odd to be thus employed, but why not? Working together like this made her feel as much married as what they had done in their bed last night. And she liked the feeling of being married.

'I never mind being alone,' she told him. 'Besides, I have work of my own to do too. There have been reports and queries from the glassworks in the past few days and I need to respond to them without further delay, as I always do. One of them has detailed sketches of a new design for my approval. I am not sure after one quick glance that I *do* approve. I need to give the matter far more concentrated attention.'

She must write a few other letters too, one to her housekeeper at Withington, another to the house in Staffordshire, a third to Philip Croft, her business manager, about the change in her name and status.

'What you are really telling me,' he said, raising one of her hands to his lips, 'is that you cannot wait for me to leave for my work so that you can get to yours.' His eyes were smiling.

'Ah,' she said, 'the gentleman begins to learn.'

He laughed outright. 'You can probably expect a quiet day,' he said.

'Yes.' But she did feel a pang of regret a few minutes later as she watched him leave the house. She would have liked to prolong the sense of togetherness just a little longer.

A quiet day. It seemed ages since she had spent a day alone. She would enjoy this one with the thought that her husband would be coming home later. And that must be one of the loveliest words in the English language – *husband*.

Her day alone started well. She wrote the letters first and then studied the sketches from the glassworks. She still could not make up her mind about the multicolored curlicues that would be cut into the glass on a new batch of drinking glasses if she gave her approval. They would look dazzlingly gorgeous, but would they also be elegant? It was the final measure by which she judged all designs and the one slight difference between her and her uncle. Both of them had liked vivid beauty and both had liked elegance, but while Uncle Reggie had tended to put more emphasis upon the former, she had leaned toward the latter. Usually, of course, the distinction between the two, as now, was such a fine one that a decision was not easy to make.

Half the morning had gone by in total absorption in her work before she made the simple discovery that if the yellow curlicues were omitted – or, better yet, changed to a different color – the whole effect was transformed. Total elegance. But even as she thought it and smiled, the butler appeared with a silver salver piled with the morning's post and, behind him, a maid carried in a tray of coffee and oatmeal biscuits.

'For me?' Wren asked the butler. From whom could she possibly be expecting all these letters?

'Yes, my lady,' he said with an inclination of the head. 'And I took the liberty of setting the morning paper on the tray too.' He and the maid left the room.

Wren picked up the pile of letters and looked quickly through them. Most surely must be for Alexander or for his mother or Elizabeth. But all were addressed either to the Countess of Riverdale or to both the earl and countess. And almost none of them had been franked, she noticed. They must all have been hand-delivered. She picked up the paper, which had been opened to the page of society news before being folded neatly. The announcement of her wedding was there as well as a gossip column about who had attended. In the column Wren had been identified as the fabulously wealthy Heyden glassware heiress. Oh goodness.

The letters were all invitations – to a wide variety of *ton* entertainments over the coming days and weeks, from balls to routs to a picnic to a Venetian breakfast to a musical evening. Oh goodness again. This was the stuff of her worst fears. It was the reason she had withdrawn her offer to Alexander on Easter Sunday. But he had promised . . . Well, she would simply hold him to it. She had gone as far as she intended to go in sociability and further than she had originally intended. She had met most of his family. She had gone walking a few times in Hyde Park – once without a veil. As much as she enjoyed his family, she had been exhausted by those efforts. She craved her privacy now in a visceral way. She would not further expose herself.

She was going to have to reply to all these invitations, she supposed, though she would wait and show them to Alexander first. She sat down, her tranquillity severely ruffled, to drink her coffee. She had taken only two bites out of one of the biscuits, however, when the door opened again to admit Cousin Viola – all the family had urged her yesterday to call them by their given names. So much for her quiet day, Wren thought as she got to her feet. But she could wish some of the others had returned first. She felt extremely awkward this morning greeting the lady who just over a year ago had held the title that was now hers and lived in this house with her children.

Cousin Viola looked just as uncomfortable. 'Am I the first to return?' she asked. 'I am so sorry. I thought to find Althea and Elizabeth here and perhaps Harry and Abby too. I expected that you would have gone out somewhere with Alexander.'

'He felt that he really ought to go to the Lords this morning,' Wren explained.

'On the day after his wedding?' the other lady said, looking startled. But then she laughed. 'Oh, but that sounds just like Alexander.'

'And I had work to do here myself,' Wren added.

'Oh, have I interrupted—'

'No, you have not,' Wren assured her. 'Do come and sit down. The coffee is fresh and there are extra cups. Let me pour you some.'

A minute later they were seated on either side of the fireplace in a room that seemed somehow larger and quieter than it had five minutes ago.

'I find this situation far more awkward than I expected when I suggested inviting you to the wedding,' Wren said. 'And more awkward than it seemed when you first arrived. After yesterday you must – Well, surely you must resent me.'

'You are refreshingly honest,' Viola said. 'For of course I have been sitting here trying not to squirm with discomfort. I do not feel any resentment toward you, Wren, or toward Alexander. Even if you had not been good enough to invite Abby and me to your wedding, and even if you had not been so extraordinarily kind to Harry, I still would not resent you. There is only one person deserving of my resentment and he is dead. I will say no more about that, for he was my husband and I owe him loyalty even in death – and even though the marriage was never a legal one. I am no saint, however. I did feel an intense hatred and resentment of Anastasia for many months even while denying it and understanding how illogical such feelings were. But then I saw how persistently kind and generous she tried to be to my children, her half siblings, and even to me, and I had a good talk with her when we were all in Bath last year. And I am determinedly loving her. That may sound strangely worded, but love is not always a feeling, Wren. Sometimes it is more of a decision. I have decided to love her, and I trust that eventually I will feel it too.'

'I find her delightful, I must confess,' Wren said. 'I find the whole family delightful, in fact. They have welcomed me despite everything.'

'Everything?' Viola regarded her in silence for a few moments, her head tipped to one side. 'Do you mean despite your face? Or do you mean despite your money?'

'A bit of both, I suppose,' Wren said. 'I was described in one of the papers this morning as a fabulously wealthy heiress. Everyone will be saying today that someone with Alexander's good looks would not have married a woman who looks as I do without the money.'

'And do you care what people say?' Viola asked. 'Do you?'

'Touché.' Viola laughed softly. 'Because I have hidden away in the country with Abby and refused to come to London until now? I suppose we all care, Wren, no matter how much we try to tell others and ourselves that we do not. Yes, I care. You cannot know what it is like to lose your very identity when you are already forty years old. Most of us, whether we realize it or not, take our identity from things and other people and circumstances and our very names. It is only when all those identifiers are stripped away that we ask ourselves the question *who am I?* It does not happen to many people, of course. It is more frightening than I can put into words to wonder if in fact one even exists without all those things. I call myself Viola Kingsley because that is who I was as a girl. It does not feel quite who I am today, however. But I beg your pardon. I do not usually talk so shamelessly about myself.'

'I do understand,' Wren told her. 'I was not born with the name Wren Heyden. I acquired both names when I was ten years old and with them a whole new identity. I feel for you even though the transformation happened for me at a quite different point in my life than it did for you. And for me it was a change infinitely for the better.'

'Ten years old,' Viola said. 'Oh, poor little girl. I did not know that about you. I know very little about you except that you are kind and beautiful – yes, you are. There is no point in looking so skeptical. And, little though I know, I have the feeling you are going to be the perfect wife for Alexander. He needs someone as serious minded and intelligent as he. And someone who can make him smile, as he did yesterday.'

'Oh,' Wren said, arrested. 'I think that must be a worthy thing to do for others, must it not? Making them smile?'

They smiled at each other as if to prove the point. She could have a genuine friendship with this woman, Wren thought with a rush of warmth to the heart. First Lizzie, now Viola. Ah, she had missed so much in her life of self-imposed seclusion. Viola had opted out of life last year. Wren had been doing it for almost twenty years.

It was as though Viola read her thoughts. 'You see what comes of conversation?' she said. 'I would have sat here this morning in pained embarrassment, talking about the weather and praying for Althea and Elizabeth or my children to return here soon if you had not chosen to talk openly about the awkwardness we both felt. By talking freely we have each discovered that we are not the only ones who have ever suffered. Sometimes it feels, does it not, as though one had been unfairly singled out while everyone else proceeds with a happy, untroubled life?'

'Indeed.' Wren smiled again, and then moved on to lighter subjects. 'Will you be attending any social functions while you are in town?' she asked. 'Will Abigail?'

'My mother-in-law – *former* mother-in-law – and Matilda are very keen that I do,' Viola said. 'They pointed out last evening that what happened to me was not in any way my fault and most of the *ton* would be perfectly happy to see me again and welcome me back. They believe I ought to make the effort for Abby's sake. They think it is still possible, especially with the combined influence of the family and Avery, for her to have a decent coming-out and to find a husband suited to her upbringing. However, it is Abby who must make that decision, and I cannot predict what she will decide, though I can make an educated guess. If she decides to do it, however, it will not be with me by her side. She will have more powerful advocates. As for myself, I have no real wish to be restored to favor. It is not that I am afraid to show my face, but . . . well' – she smiled – 'perhaps I *am* a little afraid.'

'A stack of invitations arrived this morning,' Wren said, nodding in the direction of the tray. 'I was not expecting them. I daresay I am very naïve. Our wedding was announced and commented upon in today's papers, and I *am* now the Countess of Riverdale. I will refuse them all, of course.'

'Will you?' Viola said. 'I understand you have spent years hiding yourself away and wearing a facial veil when you must go out. Yet you did not wear one yesterday. Will Alexander not try to insist that you attend at least a few of those entertainments?'

'No,' Wren told her.

'You said that with utter confidence,' Viola said. 'So you will have no social life as the Countess of Riverdale?'

'No.' Wren shook her head.

'We are two fearful women, are we not?' Viola pulled a face and then looked speculatively at Wren. 'Are we really going to give in to our fears? Or shall we challenge each other? Shall we show ourselves together to London, even if not to the *ton*? Shall we visit some of the galleries and churches and perhaps the Tower of London together in the next few days before I return home? Strangely, sightseeing is not something a Countess of Riverdale usually does. There are too many parties and other social events to take up her time. I shall run the very real risk of being recognized, and you will run the risk of being seen – for of course, to make the challenge real, you would have to go unveiled. What do you say? Shall we do it?'

Wren hesitated for only a moment. 'What veil?' she said, and they both laughed again.

The door opened once more at that moment to admit Harry and Abigail and Jessica. They seemed to bring youth and energy and sunshine in with them – and chatter and laughter. Harry made his bow, and the young ladies hugged them both.

'Did you like the description of yourself as a

fabulously wealthy heiress?' Jessica asked Wren with a laugh. 'Avery, of course, pointed out that *heiress* is an inaccurate word since you are already the owner of the glassware fortune.'

'I did not like that description at all,' Abigail said, 'implying as it did, ever so slyly, that Alex married you for the fortune and nothing else. Alex has always been a favorite of mine. I have always admired him, and I know it is something he would never, ever do even if he *does* need money to repair all the damage to that heap Papa left him. You looked absolutely beautiful yesterday, Wren, and quite radiant.'

'You still look radiant this morning,' Jessica said, and giggled a bit self-consciously. 'I hope you do not mind that I have come here with Abby and Harry. I suppose Alex has gone off to the House of Lords?'

'I warned you not to bet against me, Jess,' Harry said, flopping into a chair, looking pale and cheerful and rather tired.

'Have you seen Josephine, Wren?' Abigail asked. 'Anastasia and Avery's baby? She is gorgeous. Oh, Mama, you must go and see her. Anastasia says you must. She is disappointed, of course, that I will not be able to go to Morland Abbey for the summer, as she had originally hoped, but she understands that you and I will wish to be in Bath for Camille's confinement. She says she and Avery will probably go there too after the baby is born.'

Harry was yawning.

Mrs Westcott and Elizabeth arrived home a few minutes later, and the buzz of conversation proceeded with more volume and enthusiasm. Wren laughed quietly to herself. Had she really expected a quiet day? Had she really wanted one? She was actually enjoying this sense of family and of being part of it.

'I suppose,' Elizabeth said, 'Alex has taken himself off to the House of Lords. Sometimes I could shake that brother of mine.'

'You look more than usually lovely this morning, Wren,' her mother-in-law said with a little nod of satisfaction, and Wren knew that what she was really saying was that her daughter-in-law looked well and truly bedded. But since the words and the nod had been delivered unobtrusively while everyone else chattered, Wren did not feel unduly embarrassed.

And then the door opened one more time, and it was Alexander himself, looking rather surprised and achingly handsome. Wren got to her feet.

'Ah,' he said, 'a family party while the master of the house is away? Is this what comes of now having a mistress of the house?'

'Actually, Alex,' Elizabeth said, 'your presence is quite superfluous.'

'Hmm,' he said, meeting Wren halfway across the room and raising her hand to his lips. 'I left the Lords early to take you for that drive to Kew you did not have last week. I pictured you languishing here alone.'

'Then you were quite wrong,' she said. 'Today I am a Westcott, my lord, and am enjoying the company of my family.'

He grinned at her.

'That is putting you in your place, Alex,' Harry said, yawning again.

'However,' Wren said, 'I will forgo the further pleasure of their company in order to go for a drive with my husband.'

His grin widened. 'And I am the bearer of another invitation for this evening,' he said. 'Netherby is taking Anna to the theater but declares that his private box is far too spacious for them to rattle about in alone – his words. He wants us to join them there. And he wants Cousin Viola and Abigail to come too and Harry if he feels up to it. I gave him no answer. I did, however, warn him that you would all very possibly decline the invitation. He merely shrugged and looked bored in that way he has. You must none of you feel under any obligation. I shall be perfectly happy to spend the evening at home in present company.'

'Oh.' Wren turned her head to look at Viola and they exchanged identical smirks.

'An even more daunting challenge than the one we devised,' Viola said.

Everyone looked at her blankly – except Wren. 'Do we have the courage?' she asked. And oh goodness, did she? *Ought* she?

Viola lifted her chin, thought a moment, and nodded.

Wren returned her attention to Alexander. 'We would be in a private box?' she asked. 'In a darkened theater?'

He hesitated. 'In a private box, yes,' he said. 'But before the play begins the theater will be well lit and everyone will be looking around to see who else is present and who is with whom and what food for gossip is to be had. You would be very much on display during that time. After this morning's announcement, there would be great curiosity to have that first glimpse of the new Countess of Riverdale – the fabulously wealthy Heyden glassware heiress. And after the events of last year there would be much food for gossip in the reappearance of the former countess and her son and daughter. I am afraid there would be as much focus upon Netherby's box before the performance as there would be on the stage later.'

'You think we ought not to go, then?' she asked him.

'This is not my decision to make,' he said firmly.

'By thunder,' Harry said, 'I would rather face a column of Boney's men on the attack, all yelling *vive l'empereur* between beats of the drum in that unnerving way of theirs. I am not going. Besides, I am going to be ready to crawl off to my bed to sleep the clock around by the time this evening comes.'

'I will go,' Abigail said, 'if Jessica can come too. I was never allowed to attend the theater before I was eighteen, and then I could not. I will go.'

'And so will I, Abby,' Viola said.

Oh, this was not fair, Wren thought. Inch by excruciating inch she was being dragged out into the open, where she had never intended to go. Except that there was no unfairness involved. The invitation had been extended and the decision of whether she would accept it or not was entirely hers.

'I will do it,' she said.

Alexander caught both her hands in his and squeezed tightly while there was a slight cheer behind her and then laughter.

'Oh, bravo, Wren,' Elizabeth said. 'And Viola and Abigail too.'

'I would have won my wager, then,' Alexander said. 'Unfortunately for me, Netherby was unwilling to bet against me.'

Now what had she done? Wren thought, feeling a twinge of panic. Whatever had she done? 'But first,' she said, 'I want to see Kew Gardens.'

CHAPTER 17

T hose who went to the theater in search of
fresh material for gossip as much as entertainment from the stage were to find more
than sufficient that evening without looking farther
than the Duke of Netherby's private box. The duke
and his duchess were there. So was the Earl of
Riverdale with his mysterious new bride, the *fabulously wealthy Heyden glassware heiress*, whom a few
people claimed to have seen with him in Hyde
Park, though none had had a satisfyingly good
look. Some had even said she went about heavily
veiled. The former, dispossessed countess, whom
no one had seen in more than a year, was also in
the box, the old and the new in company together,
and so was her bastard daughter. The Duke of
Netherby's sister, young Lady Jessica Archer,
whose beauty had taken the *ton* by storm during
her come-out this year, was scarcely noticed amid
the sensational appearance of her companions.

As Wren entered the duke's box on her husband's
arm, having already run the gauntlet of other new
arrivals outside the theater and in the foyer and
on the stairs, she was fully aware that she could

not have orchestrated a more public introduction to the *ton* if she had tried. And it seemed to her, in that first dizzying moment, that the other boxes and the galleries and the pit were already crowded with people. It was probably fanciful to suppose that every single eye turned upon them, but perhaps not. This had been madness of epic proportions and would not have happened if she and Viola had not just finished challenging each other to face the world together. But by *world* they had meant London – the place, not the people in it, and specifically not the *ton*.

Alexander smiled at her as he seated her on a chair next to the outer rail of the box so that she would have a clear view of the stage. Fortunately it was her right profile that faced outward to the theater. She was warmed by his smile and clung to that warmth. The visit to Kew Gardens had been splendid. They had talked and laughed and touched frequently, both when they sat side by side in the curricle and when they strolled in the gardens. She had felt that he wanted to be there with her, that he enjoyed her company, that, like her, he was remembering last night's intimacies and anticipating similar pleasure tonight. She had felt . . . well, *married*. She would have felt perfectly, blissfully happy if she had not also been feeling a bit sick with apprehension about this evening.

And here she was, and it was every bit as dreadful as she had feared. It would not take much for her to jump to her feet and bolt. But bolt where?

'You do that awfully well,' Alexander murmured in her ear.

'What is that?' she asked.

'That perfectly poised look, chin raised, eyes directed along the nose,' he said. 'You appear as though you have been a duchess for the last twenty years.'

'Whereas in reality I have been a countess for . . . what? Thirty-three hours?' she said.

'And you are very beautiful, I might add,' he said.

'Flatterer!'

The duchess – Anna – was still on her feet, talking to Viola, whose hand she held in both her own. 'I am *so* pleased you came, Aunt Viola,' she said. 'I am very vexed with Camille and Joel, and I told them so in my last letter. I had my heart set on all of you coming to spend a month or so of the summer at Morland Abbey. I wanted to have lots of time to show off Josephine and to get to know their adopted baby, Sarah. And to see their adopted daughter, Winifred, again. I remember her well from the orphanage and shed tears when Camille and Joel adopted her as well as Sarah. But they have selfishly chosen this summer to have a baby of their own. And so you and Abigail will go to Bath, and Avery and Josephine will have to go there too to see you all.'

Viola and Abigail were both smiling. Anna was teasing, Wren realized. She was also trying to take their minds off these first few minutes of their ordeal at being on display to the *ton* for the first time since their lives changed so catastrophically last year. Joel Cunningham, Camille's husband, Wren had learned, had grown up at the orphanage in Bath with Anna and was her best friend. Wren remembered Viola telling her that she had decided to love Anna, though she could not yet *feel* that love. It was an idea to ponder.

The Duke of Netherby looked even more gorgeous than usual in satin and lace when most gentlemen, Alexander included, were wearing the more fashionable black and white. He was gazing outward across the theater with haughty languor through his quizzing glass. Candlelight glinted and winked off the jewels encrusted in its handle and about its rim and off those on his fingers and at his throat. He was a comforting presence as, she guessed, he fully intended to be this evening. So was Alexander, sitting slightly behind her, his hand beside hers on the velvet rail, their little fingers overlapping. Occasionally his finger stroked hers.

'When will the play begin?' she asked.

'It should be starting now,' Alexander told her. 'But it is always a little late to allow for the arrival of stragglers. The stragglers know it, of course, and arrive even later than they otherwise would.'

'I believe the lateness of the start is also an acknowledgment of the fact that most people come to the theater to see everyone else as much as to watch the play, Alexander,' Viola said.

'Ah, such cynicism,' the duke said on a sigh. 'Who was it who said *the play's the thing*?'

'William Shakespeare,' Jessica said.

'. . . *wherein I'll catch the conscience of the king*,' Abigail added.

'Ah yes,' he said faintly.

Wren was watching a group of people step into the empty box across from theirs, two ladies and four gentlemen. Both ladies were blond and dressed all in sparkling white. They might well have been sisters. One of them seated herself off to one side of the box and one of the gentlemen went to sit beside and slightly behind her. The other lady took a seat in the middle of the box. She looked small and almost fragile amid a court of the other three gentlemen, who hovered about her, one of them positioning her chair, another taking her fan from her hand and plying it gently before her face, the third fetching something, presumably a footstool, from the back of the box and setting it at her feet. She smiled sweetly at them all and turned her attention outward to her court of admirers in the galleries and pit – or so it seemed to Wren, who was inclined at first to be amused.

But there was a strange feeling. A slight light-headedness. A suggestion of a buzzing in the ears. It could not be, of course. Twenty years had passed, and with those years some clarity of memory. But even if her memory had been crystal clear, time – twenty years of time – would have wrought significant changes. The lady raised one white-gloved hand in acknowledgment of the homage being paid her by a cluster of gentlemen in the pit and moved her head in a gracious nod. And there was something about both gestures . . .

'One does wonder how she does it,' Viola was saying, sounding amused.

'With a wig and cosmetics and an army of experts,' Jessica said. 'When you see her close up, Aunt Viola, she looks quite grotesque.'

They might have been talking about anyone. And all talk ceased soon anyway, at least within their own box, as the candlelight dimmed and the play began. It was the first dramatic performance Wren had watched, and she marveled at the scenery, the costumes, the voices and gestures of the actors, the sense of gorgeous unreality that drew her into another world and made her almost forget her own. She would have been enthralled if she could have ignored the erratic fluttering of her heart.

It could not be.

One wonders how she does it.

With a wig and cosmetics and an army of experts.

And, just before silence had fallen in their box, Alexander's voice – *even her daughter is older than I am, perhaps older than Lizzie.*

He might have been talking about anyone. She did not ask.

'Abigail, take my arm,' the Duke of Netherby said when the intermission began, 'and we will stroll outside the box and perhaps even imbibe some lemonade, heaven help us. Jess, take my other arm so that I will be balanced.'

'Ought I?' Abigail asked.

'An unanswerable question,' he said, 'and a thoroughly boring one.'

She took his arm after a glance at her mother and the three of them left the box.

'Shall we go too, Aunt Viola?' Anna suggested.

'Oh, whyever not?' Viola said, getting to her feet.

'Wren?' Alexander stood before her, one hand extended. 'What is your wish? We can merely stretch our legs in here, if you choose.'

'Thank you.' She set her hand in his and stood. She did not turn her head, but with her peripheral vision she was aware that the two ladies in white had remained in their box and that other gentlemen had stepped into it, presumably to pay their respects.

'Are you enjoying the play?' Alexander asked, closing his hand about hers.

'Very much,' she said.

He moved his head a little closer and frowned slightly. 'What is it?' he asked her. 'Are you regretting your decision to come? Is this all a little overwhelming for you?'

'I am fine,' she said. But she was feeling the unfamiliar urge to step closer to him, to bury herself against him, to feel the safety of his arms about her. Perhaps that was all it was. Perhaps she *was* overwhelmed. Too much had happened too fast in her life.

298

He was still looking searchingly at her. But they were interrupted by the opening of the door and the appearance of the Radleys, Alexander's aunt and uncle, who had come with a couple of friends to greet them. They stayed only a few minutes while Aunt Lilian told them how much she had enjoyed the wedding yesterday and the other couple congratulated them and Uncle Richard commented that they were putting Alexander to the blush.

And then they were alone again and Wren turned to resume her seat – and glanced unwillingly across at the box opposite. One lady and gentleman were still seated to the side. Most of the visiting gentlemen were leaving the box with bows for the other lady, while one member of her court had fetched her a glass of something and was presenting it to her with a graceful bow of his own. She was ignoring them all, however. She was holding a jeweled lorgnette to her eyes and looking directly across at their box. So were the other lady and the gentleman with her. Both sides of her face were visible, Wren realized. She sat down hastily and turned her attention toward the empty stage.

'You are attracting attention from over there,' Alexander said. 'I hope it does not bother you. But really you ought to be feeling flattered, Wren. Lady Hodges usually notices no other lady but herself. By all accounts she has been the toast of the *ton* for at least the past thirty years, though her appearances in recent years are rarer and more carefully orchestrated.'

It could not be, Wren thought once more as the others returned to their box in time for the second half of the performance. *It could not be.*

But somehow it was.

Lady Hodges . . .

As far as Alexander was concerned, the evening had gone well. Cousin Viola was quietly dignified, rather as she had always been as far back as Alexander remembered. She nodded to a few people as they left the theater but did not exchange words or smiles with anyone. Abigail was both dignified and shyly smiling. Jessica was exuberant. Anna remarked upon the quality of the performance. Netherby was his usual imperturbable self. Wren spoke with admiration about the play and was warm in her thanks to Anna and Netherby as she hugged the former and shook hands with the latter before climbing into the carriage after Cousin Viola and Abigail.

'Well?' Alexander asked as the carriage moved away. 'I would say you all met the challenge quite magnificently. Are you pleased?' Wren had told him earlier of the agreement she and Cousin Viola had come to, though they had intended a mere sightseeing outing or two together.

'We did it, certainly,' Viola said. She had Abigail's hand in hers, Alexander noticed. 'We have proved something to ourselves and maybe to others too. Abby, was it an experiment to be repeated?'

'It was pleasant,' Abigail said, 'and I do appreciate the effort Anastasia is making to draw us back into the family and even into society. I am sure tonight must have been her idea more than Avery's.'

'Not Jessica's?' her mother asked.

'No,' Abigail said. 'Jessica wants to do quite the opposite, silly thing. She wants to withdraw from society herself in order to be with me. She does not understand that we must both find our place in the world but that those places will necessarily be very different.'

She was quite mature for one so young, Alexander thought. One did not always realize it. She was small and sweet and quiet and a bit fragile looking.

He moved slightly on the seat so that his shoulder was against Wren's. She had fallen silent. Despite her praise for the play after it was finished, he had had the curious feeling during the second half that she was not really seeing it at all. He took her hand in his. She did not withdraw it, but it remained limp and unresponsive.

'No, Mama,' Abigail said. 'I have no craving for more such evenings. Certainly not for parties. Not any longer. It was lovely to come for Alexander and Wren's wedding and to see the family again. And it was wonderful beyond imagining to find Harry here.'

'Shall we go back home within the next few days, then?' Cousin Viola suggested. 'And take Harry with us? He insists he will be well enough to return to the Peninsula within a week or two, but when he was sent home, he was ordered quite specifically by both an army surgeon and his commanding officer not to return for at least two months. We will fatten him up and perhaps take him to Bath to see Camille and Grandmama Kingsley and to meet Joel and Winifred and Sarah.'

'I should like that, Mama,' Abigail said. 'I just have to persuade Jessica that really my world has not ended. Cam's did not end, did it? It *began* last year.'

Alexander's mother and Elizabeth were at home when they arrived, having just returned from a musical evening at the house of one of Elizabeth's friends. They wanted to talk about it, and they wanted to hear about the visit to the theater. They all entered the drawing room together – except Wren, who slipped off upstairs without a word. And Harry had retired even before they left for the theater.

'Has Wren gone to bed?' Elizabeth asked five minutes or so later when she had not returned.

'I am not sure,' Alexander said. 'I think perhaps she needed to be alone. The whole of the last week or so has been overwhelming for her, and this evening was perhaps too much.'

'Has she lived her whole life as a hermit?' Abigail asked. 'And always veiled?'

'Yes,' Alexander said.

Abigail looked a bit surprised as her mother, Viola, said, 'I am sorry, Alexander, if I have been

302

the cause of distress to your wife. I challenged her to face the world with me. I like her exceedingly well, you know.'

'So do we all, Viola,' Alexander's mother said. 'But you must not blame yourself. We have learned Wren has a very firm mind of her own and will not be talked into anything she does not choose to do.'

Five minutes later Alexander was worried. He had expected her to come back down. Surely she would have said good night and offered some excuse of tiredness if she had not intended to do so.

'I will go up and see how she is,' he said.

She was not in bed – not in their bed, anyway. Nor was she in her dressing room or her own room. Or so he thought at first. There were no candles burning in there. Wherever was she, then? He set his candle down on the table beside the window and looked out, almost as though he expected to see her walking down the street. The room behind him was quiet, but there was a prickly feeling along his spine that warned him he was not alone. He turned.

She was on the floor on the far side of the bed, huddled into the corner, her knees drawn up to her chest, her forehead on her knees, one arm wrapped about her legs, the other about her head. She was not making a sound. He felt his stomach lurch and his knees turn a bit weak.

'Wren?' He spoke her name softly.

There was no response.

'Wren?' He moved closer to her and went down on his haunches before her. 'What is it? What has happened?'

The only response this time was a slight tightening of both arms.

'Will you let me help you up from there?' he asked her. 'Will you talk to me?'

She said something, but the words were muffled against her knees.

'I beg your pardon?' he said.

'Go away.' They were clear enough this time.

'But why?' he asked her.

No response.

He squeezed into the space beside her, sitting with his back against the wall, his wrists draped over his raised knees. There was not much room. His left side was pressed against her.

'I have let you down,' he said softly. 'I promised you the life of your choosing, yet at every turn I have encouraged you to do what you are uncomfortable doing. You will say that I forced nothing on you, but my very willingness to allow you to decide each time you are called upon to move further and further into the open has been a form of coercion. For perhaps you have felt you need to prove something to me and to yourself. You do not need to prove anything, Wren. Had I been more forceful on a few occasions and said a firm no myself instead of leaving the decision to you, I might have saved you from this sort of . . . collapse. I ought to have said no to Netherby's invitation today without even mentioning it at home. I will do better in the future, I promise you. Shall we go home to Brambledean? Tomorrow? There you may live as you wish to live, and I will be happy to see you happy. I care, Wren. I really do care.'

And he did, he realized. If he could have taken every last penny of her fortune at that moment and dumped it in the middle of the Atlantic Ocean, he would have done it without any hesitation at all. He cared. For her. He cared deeply.

Still she said nothing. He eased his arm up from between them and wrapped it about her. She was as rigid as a statue.

'Wren,' he said. 'Wren, my love, speak to me.'

She mumbled something.

'I beg your pardon?'

The words were quite distinct this time. 'She is my mother.'

What? He did not say it aloud. But whom could she possibly mean? He frowned in thought. What had happened? Was it just the stress of too much exposure to other people – to strangers? Had she just reached a natural breaking point halfway through this evening? *Halfway.* There had been a difference between the two halves. She had been a bit tense from the start, but she had remained in command of herself, and he believed she had watched the play even if she had not been relaxed enough to be totally absorbed in it. There had been something troubling her during the interval, though she had denied it, and afterward she had been almost silent and . . . absent. She had disappeared upstairs without a word as soon as they came home.

She is my mother.

What the devil had happened? Snippets of the evening came back to him. He remembered then the two women in white who had been staring at Wren so pointedly. He remembered words, a few of them spoken by him.

One does wonder how she does it.

With a wig and cosmetics and an army of experts. When you see her close to . . . she looks quite grotesque.

Even her daughter is older than I am, perhaps older than Lizzie.

You are attracting attention from over there. I hope it does not bother you. But really you ought to be feeling flattered, Wren. Lady Hodges usually notices no other lady but herself. By all accounts she has been the toast of the ton *for at least the past thirty years, though her appearances in recent years are rarer and more carefully orchestrated.*

Good God. Oh, good God!

'Lady Hodges?' he asked.

There was a low moan.

He turned as best he could in the confined space and wrapped his other arm about her too. It was not easy to do when she was curled up into a hard, unyielding ball. 'Oh, good God,' he said aloud. 'My poor darling. Let me hold you, Wren. Let me hold you properly. I am going to pick you up and carry you through to our room and hold you on the bed. Will you let me?'

She said nothing, but when he stood up and leaned down to scoop her into his arms, she released her tight hold on herself and let him get one arm beneath her knees and the other about her back beneath her shoulders. She let her head flop onto his shoulder, her eyes closed. He carried her through the two dressing rooms and set her on the bed, which had been turned down for the night. He eased off the light shoes she had worn to the theater and removed as many of her hairpins as he could find. And he lay down beside her and gathered her close. He did not try to talk to her. Sometimes, he thought, concern and love – yes, *love* – had to speak for themselves.

He did not know Lady Hodges, but he knew some things about her. Everyone did. She was a famous eccentric, if that was the right word to describe her. By all accounts she had been an extraordinarily beautiful girl, daughter of a gentleman of very moderate means. She had taken the *ton* by storm when her father had wangled an invitation from a distant relative to present her at a *ton* ball with his own daughter. Soon after, she married a wealthy baron. She had thereafter made her beauty the business of her life and had enslaved men by the dozens. It would not have been an entirely unusual story, had she not somehow contrived to hang on to her beauty – and her court – even after she had passed her youth and then her young womanhood and even her middle age. Young men were drawn by her wealth and strange fame, and she kept one of her daughters close so that – or so the accepted theory went – she might be flattered when told that they looked like sisters. Some particular flatterers even maintained that she looked like the younger sister. But Jessica had been right. Young and lovely as the woman appeared from a distance or in dim light, from close to she looked like a grotesque parody of youth. The woman's vanity and self-absorption were commonly known to know no bounds.

And she was *Wren's mother.*

CHAPTER 18

Somehow Wren had held herself together through the second half of the performance at the theater, the farewells to the duke and duchess and Jessica, and the carriage ride home. But as she hurried upstairs and into her bedchamber without bothering to take a candle with her or to light any when she got there, she found herself plummeting backward twenty years and more. By the time she reached the corner of the room, hidden beyond the bed, and curled herself up on the floor into as tight a ball as she could manage, those twenty years no longer existed. She was back in her own little childhood room inside her own little childhood self, and the whole world of beauty and dazzle and glamour and laughter and friends and warmth and family and love was beyond her heavily netted window and beyond her door, which as often as not was locked from the other side.

The swiftness of her descent into the past would not have been so total, perhaps, if it had not been for that surreal image in the box across from theirs. For twenty years had passed since Aunt Megan had taken her from Roxingly Park forever. Yet her mother had not changed in all that time. She looked youthful and dainty and almost ethereally lovely. The other woman, the one who had looked so like her but had sat farther off to her side of the box, looking about with proud hauteur, had changed, if, indeed, she was Blanche. Her eldest sister had been sixteen when Wren last saw her and the favorite because she was blond and beautiful like her mother though without her allure. She had been someone to display but never allowed to overshadow.

She had been seen. Wren knew she had been. Perhaps they had looked at first merely out of curiosity, just like everyone else, because she had just married the Earl of Riverdale, but no one knew anything else about her except her ownership of the Heyden glassworks. They could not possibly have recognized her, especially just from her right profile. And they probably would not have recognized her name from the morning papers. Although the adoption certificate showed that Wren's father had given his permission, it was unlikely he had said anything to her mother, who would not have wanted to know.

They had seen her, full face, during the interval when she had looked over to their box to find herself being scrutinized through her mother's lorgnette. And they had understood. There had been something in their faces. But how could she have seen that from such a distance and through the lenses of a lorgnette? She could not, of course.

But she had known. Perhaps it was the language of their bodies she had read more than their facial expressions. She had known that they knew. And she herself had known even before the hammer blow of hearing the name. Lady Hodges.

She was lost deep in memory when she became aware of Alexander's presence in her room. Or perhaps *memory* was the wrong word, since she was not remembering any particular incidents from her childhood. What she was really lost in was identification. She *was* that child again, alone and friendless – *almost* friendless. But even that one thin, frail memory of love did not force its way into the child's identity that held her curled into her corner, arms wrapped about herself for protection and to make her smaller and less visible. If only she could be fully invisible . . .

She heard a name that sounded familiar, just as the voice that spoke it did, though she could not immediately place either.

'Wren?'

They came from far, far in the future, that name and that voice. Mentally she sank deeper into herself. But the future would not let her be.

'Wren? What is it? What has happened?'

What *had* happened? She tightened her hold on herself.

'Will you let me help you up from there? Will you talk to me?'

And she knew suddenly who Wren was and whom the voice belonged to. But it had all been an illusion, that future. *This* was who she was, this child she could not let go of despite the pain of hopeless misery. She could be no one else. It had been a foolish dream.

'Go away,' she said, and repeated the words more clearly when he did not hear the first time. But he did not go. Instead, he squeezed in beside her, between the bed and the wall, and talked to her. She did not hear all his words or feel his arms come about her – she was still locked inside her old self – but she did hear his pain. And perhaps that was her salvation, that was what began to pull her back. For she had learned – her future self, the one called Wren, had learned just recently – that pain was not confined to her alone, that other people suffered, that suffering could either isolate the sufferer or lead her out of the prison of her aloneness into a shared suffering and a shared courage, and an empathy that reached to the ends of the world. Viola. Abigail and Harry. Jessica. And now Alexander. She had pulled him into her darkness, and she heard the pain in his voice.

'Wren,' he said. 'Wren, my love, speak to me.'

And she told him – twice, because he did not hear the first time. She told him. *She is my mother.* And went spiraling downward and inward again.

But he would not let her go. Or, if she must go, then he would not let her go alone. He got to his feet, talking to her, and picked her up and carried her – away from her room and into his own and set her on the bed and did a few things to make her more comfortable before lying down beside her and gathering her to him.

My love, he had called her.

Darling.

He had also spoken her mother's name and she had heard herself moan.

He did not speak now. He was Alexander and this was not his room. It was theirs. He was her husband. He had made love to her here last night – three separate times. With pleasure. It had not been just a dutiful consummation to him. She would have known. She had pleased him. He had gone to the House of Lords this morning, drawn by duty, but he had left early to come home and take her to Kew Gardens. And he had talked with her and touched her without any sign of revulsion. He had been relaxed and happy. He had laughed at the wonder with which she had beheld the pagoda. But it had been affectionate laughter. He had told her she looked like a child to whom the world was a new and wondrous place, and she had told him that he was exactly right. They had both laughed then, and for a while they had walked hand in hand instead of with her hand tucked through the crook of his elbow. He had not fully understood, though, that she was a twenty-nine-year-old experiencing the wonders of childhood for the first time.

He had not understood then. Perhaps he did now.

Oh, Alexander, Alexander, what have I done to you?

The room was in darkness. There were no candles burning, as there had been last night. He was fully clothed except that he was wearing no shoes. She could feel the soft folds of his neckcloth against her cheek and the buttons of his pantaloons against her waist. His lovely evening clothes were going to be creased beyond redemption. So was her new evening gown. He was warm and relaxed, but he was not sleeping. She knew that as she gradually came to herself, Wren again – Wren Westcott, Countess of Riverdale – and no longer Rowena Handrich, youngest daughter and second youngest child of Baron and Lady Hodges. The daughter most people probably did not know existed, except perhaps through rumor as the skeleton in the closet of the perfect life that was Lady Hodges's.

'Alexander,' she said softly, breathing in the warmth and the now-familiar scent of his cologne and of him.

'Yes,' he said.

She kept her eyes closed, allowed the future to flow all the way back into her and become the present, felt the soft comfort of the bed around her, the protective muscled strength of the man against whom she was held from her head right down to her feet, heard the sound of a lone horse clopping past on the street outside and the distant chiming of a clock from somewhere inside, and dared to feel almost safe again. Though she did not know in what way exactly she had felt *unsafe*. It had not been a physical fear of being hurt or snatched away or killed. It had been a far deeper, more primal fear of losing herself or what she had become in the twenty years of distance she had put between herself and that child she had been. Though she had not left the child behind. She could not. And perhaps she would not if she could, for that child had deserved better of life. That child had been innocent.

'I will tell you,' she said. 'But it is a dark tale, and I am afraid of pulling you into my darkness. You do not deserve that. I ought not to have—'

'Wren,' he said against the top of her head, his voice soft and deep. 'I proposed marriage to you, if you will remember. After you had offered it to me, you withdrew your offer. I asked you a week or so ago because I wanted to marry you. And I knew the ten missing years of your life were dark ones. I knew too that eventually I would know about them. I married you anyway.'

She heaved a deep sigh. 'Do you care?' she asked him. 'You said a little while ago that you do.'

'I care,' he said.

'I wish you did not,' she told him. 'You would be able to listen dispassionately and not get drawn in.'

'I hope that is not true,' he said. 'I hope I will always feel compassion for suffering even if I have no personal involvement with the persons concerned. But I have an involvement with you. You are my wife. And I care.'

Ah. He had meant it, then. *He had meant it.* She savored the thought. *He cared.*

'Make love to me first,' she said. 'Please make love to me.'

And he did. Without stopping to unclothe them except in essential places. Without any of the tenderness she would have expected if she had paused long enough to expect anything. Without moving back the bedcovers. Without taking his time – or hers.

They were on one side of the bed and then the other, rolled up in their own clothes and sheets and blankets, pushing impatiently at them, kissing with ferocity enough to devour each other, moving urgent hands over each other, frustrated by clothing, twining and untwining legs. He was on top of her, and then she was on top of him. He set his hands behind her knees, drew them up on either side of him until they hugged his hips, bunched up her skirt between them, held her by the hips and lifted her, and brought her down onto himself until she had his whole hard, long length inside. He said something. She said something. But words were meaningless, so she didn't remember them.

And they rode each other. There was no other word for what happened over the next few minutes. They rode hard onto and into the hot wetness they had created, seeking pleasure, comfort, goodness knew what, reaching and reaching for something that had no word at all. And no thought either. Just reaching. Eyes tightly shut. Muscles clenching tightly and relaxing to the rhythm of their ride. *Please, oh please.* His hands hard on her buttocks, hers on his shoulders, her fingers curled over them, his neckcloth brushing her chin. *Please. Oh please.*

And almost unbearable pleasure-pain as muscles clenched and would not unclench, as movement ceased and eyes pressed more tightly together. The ride was solo now as he drove deep into her, withdrew, and drove inward again – and held. And muscles unclenched and pain shattered and was suddenly, incredibly, not pain at all but so far its opposite that *pleasure* would not encompass it. Someone was sighing out loud with her voice. And then that lovely gush of liquid heat at her core that she remembered from last night.

She was hot. Her hands were slick with sweat. Her bodice and sleeves were clinging to her bosom and arms. His neckcloth and cravat were damp. They were both panting for breath. Wren collapsed down onto him, and he straightened her legs to lie on either side of his and wrapped his arms about her. Strangely, despite the heat and damp and discomfort of tangled fabrics, despite everything, she dozed. But not for long, she guessed when she came back to herself. He was not sleeping. His fingers were combing lightly through her hair. She sighed, but it came out sounding a bit like a moan. He cupped the side of her face with one hand, lifted it with the heel of his hand, and kissed her.

'We need to tidy up,' he said. 'Come. I'll ring for my valet and you must ring for your maid. I'll have tea brought up afterward for you. We will sit and talk.'

All she wanted to do was close her eyes again and sleep. But he was right. They were too uncomfortable to settle for a night's sleep. And if she did not talk tonight, she might never talk again. She might become a veiled, reclusive mute. And that was not even a joke. It would be so easy.

He untangled them from the sheets and blankets, and they got off the bed, brushed ineffectually at their clothes in the near darkness, and moved through to her dressing room. He lit a branch of candles for her before going into his dressing room and closing the door between them. It was not quite midnight, she saw when she glanced at the clock. She had thought it much later. She pulled on the bell rope to summon Maude. She wished then she had asked Alexander to unbutton her at the back so that she could at least have removed her dress. Whatever would Maude think? And about her *hair*?

But she did not much care what Maude thought.

The bed had been made up and then turned down neatly for the night on both sides, Alexander saw when he stepped back into the bedchamber from his dressing room, and the candles had been lit. There was a tray of tea and a decanter of brandy on the table by the hearth with a plate of fruit cake – a part of the wedding cake that had not been iced, he guessed. The servants' hall was probably buzzing with talk about the lusty progress of his marriage. He was wearing a nightshirt with a light silk dressing gown.

Good God, that woman. She looked grotesque from close up, as Jessica had said. From a distance and in the relatively dim light of the theater, she had looked younger than Wren. Yet she was Wren's mother. There was something a bit eerie about it. He poured himself a glass of brandy and downed it. It had made his stomach turn over, seeing Wren huddled into a ball in the corner. And her voice when she had spoken, telling him to go away, telling him that that woman was her mother, had been thin and high pitched, like that of a child. He had been afraid he would not be able to bring her back.

Had he brought her back? In one way, what had happened on that bed half an hour or so ago had been the best sex of his life. It had been uninhibited passion on both their parts. But he must not make the mistake of thinking they had been making love. There had been a desperation in her that had sought a sexual outlet since it had been available. And he had given her what she wanted. It had been wild sex devoid of love. No, not that. He had given her what she wanted *because he cared*. And he cared not just because she was a suffering human being and his wife, but because she was Wren. He had promised liking and respect and the hope of affection, and he had every intention of carrying through on that promise. But there was more. He did not know the how or the where or the when of it, and he was not going to analyze it to death. He was a man, for the love of God. But whatever it was, it was more than just those three solemn aspects of caring he had pledged her when he asked her to marry him.

She came in quietly through his dressing room. She looked neat and pretty in a long, short-sleeved nightgown, her hair brushed smooth and tied loosely at the nape of her neck. Her face was pale, the purple marks on the left side looking darker than usual in contrast. Her eyes were tired and not quite meeting his. He was on the verge of suggesting that they go to bed to sleep, but he held his peace. Let her decide.

'Let me pour you some tea?' he said.

'Thank you.' She came to sit in one of the wing chairs that flanked the fireplace and were hardly ever used since he liked to do his reading downstairs in the drawing room or library and was not a solitary nighttime drinker.

He set her cup and saucer beside her and a plate with a piece of cake. She ignored both and looked at him as he seated himself opposite, though her eyes did not rise above his chin.

'I am sorry, Alexander,' she said, her voice without expression. 'I am horribly, horribly damaged. And I do not mean just my face. It goes far deeper. Too deep to be touched or healed. I am sorry.'

He felt chilled to the heart. Some suffering was beyond help. He knew that. But he would not believe it. Not of Wren. Not of the woman who was becoming more precious to him with every passing day. 'Tell me,' he said.

She shrugged her shoulders and kept them up. She hugged her arms with her hands, running them up and down the bare flesh as though she were cold, though it was a warm night. He got to his feet, moved the table with her cup and plate a bit away from her chair, grabbed the plaid blanket that was folded over the foot of the bed, half lifted her from the chair to slide in beneath her, and held her. It was not as easy to snuggle her as it would have been with a less tall woman, but he managed it, nestling her head on his shoulder and wrapping the blanket about her before resting his cheek against the top of her head.

'Tell me,' he said again, going against his earlier decision to let her decide for herself. But if she did not tell him now, he had the chilling feeling that she might never tell and then she might be forever lost to him. And perhaps to herself too. Ah, good God, what did he know about dealing with damaged people – *horribly, horribly damaged.*

She was silent for a long time before she started speaking in the same toneless voice. 'There are some people who are totally self-absorbed,' she said, 'for whom no one else really exists except as an audience to watch and listen and praise and admire and adore. I believe it must be some kind of sickness. My mother was like that. She was astonishingly beautiful. Perhaps all children feel that way about their mothers. But I think even by objective standards she was lovely beyond compare. She demanded adoration. She gathered about herself people who would adore her – men mostly, though not exclusively. She gathered *beautiful* people. She never seemed to fear competition, but she did seem to feel that anyone less than beautiful reflected poorly on herself.'

Ah. One could see where this was going.

'She doted on her children and displayed them for other people's admiration as an extension of herself,' she said. 'First Blanche and Justin, who were blond and lovely as she was, and then Ruby, who was dark like our father but just as lovely. And then I was born with a great red . . . blob covering one side of my face and head like a giant ripe strawberry. She had me taken away as soon as she set eyes on me. She could not bear to look at me. She saw me as a judgment upon herself for quarreling bitterly with Papa when she discovered she was bearing me. All I was to her was a cruel punishment.'

Alexander opened his mouth to say that surely she must have meant something to her mother, but his words remained unsaid. Somehow he did not doubt that the woman was as narcissistic as Wren had said.

'She and Papa were often away from home,' Wren said. 'She liked being in town attending parties and balls. When they were at home, she liked to have guests, sometimes enough of them for a house party that would last for several weeks. I had to be kept out of sight when she was home. When there were guests, I had to be locked inside my room, lest I wander out and be seen.'

'There was no schoolroom?' he asked. 'No nursery where no adults came? No outings?'

'My sisters and elder brother adored her,' she said. 'They took their cue from her. Ruby would turn her back whenever I came into a room. Justin would make loud retching noises. Blanche would be cross and tell me to go back to my room, where they could forget I existed to spoil life for poor Mama and all of them. The governess just shrugged and pretended I did not exist. I sometimes went out of doors when there was no one at home except us children, but Justin or Blanche would lock me in if any of their friends had come to play.'

'Your father?' he asked.

'I rarely saw him,' she said. 'None of us did. He had no interest in children, I believe. Perhaps he did not know how I was . . . segregated.'

'No one took your part?' he asked.

'Only Colin,' she said. 'He was born four years after me, blond and beautiful and sweet-natured. He would sometimes come into my room, even when it was locked – he learned how to turn the key from the other side – bringing toys and books with him. He would always ask me how my face was and insist upon kissing it better. And he would spread his toys around me and pretend to read his books to me until he really could do it. I could not read myself. Once, we played outside together and ran and climbed trees and . . . laughed. Oh, how good that felt. I used to listen to the others playing and laughing outside . . .'

There was a lengthy silence, during which Alexander held her close and kissed the top of her head. He was chilled at her words, but would not show his horror. 'What happened when you were ten years old?' he asked.

'A few things happened together,' she said. 'Aunt Megan came to stay. She was my mother's sister, but she had never come before. They were as different as day and night. I do not know why she came then. She never said. But she found out about me and came to see me in my room. I remember her holding me and kissing me and wondering why everyone had been making such a fuss about a great strawberry swelling on one side of my head and face. By then the swelling had gone down and the red had mostly turned to purple. Then a day or two later there were people visiting who had children, and no one had locked my door. I did not intend to show myself or try to join in their game, but I did go outside to watch. They were playing some boisterous game on the bank of the lake, and I climbed a tree as close as I could get without being seen. But somehow I lost my balance and fell out. I did not hurt myself, but I frightened the children so much that one of them fell in the lake and the others ran up to the house, screaming hysterically. My sisters ran after them and my elder brother too after warning me that I had done it now. I pulled the child out of the lake – it was shallow and there was no real danger of his drowning – and went back to my room.'

Alexander closed his eyes.

'Aunt Megan came for me after it was dark and told me she was taking me away where I would be safe and loved for the rest of my life,' she said. 'I do not remember feeling much either way. I believe I was exhausted from crying. No one had ever loved me – except Colin – and I liked my aunt and went with her without a murmur. But she was not stealing me away without anyone knowing. As we passed the drawing room, my mother came out onto the landing and told Aunt Megan that she was a fool, that she would regret taking me, that it would be far better to let me be sent to the insane asylum as she had planned to do the next day.'

Alexander sucked in his breath.

'I did not even know what that was,' Wren said. 'I asked when we were on the way to London, but my aunt told me she did not know either.' She took a long, shuddering breath. 'I have neither seen nor heard of my mother or any of them from that day to this – to a few hours ago at the theater. Almost twenty years. And she looks now exactly as she looked then.'

Her breathing was a bit ragged. He held her close.

'She saw me,' she said. 'She knew me.'

'You belong to me now, Wren,' he said. 'I have ownership of you. Not to tyrannize over you, but to keep you safe so that you can be free of these fears and horrors. I look after what is my own. It is more than a promise.'

It sounded ostentatious to his own ears. He was not even quite sure what he meant. How could he both own her and set her free? But he did know that he was speaking straight from the heart and that he would not, by God – not ever, not even in the smallest of ways – betray her trust in him.

'I care,' he told her.

CHAPTER 19

Wren awoke slowly from a deep sleep and was aware of warmth and comfort and daylight and the sounds of wheels and horses and a single human shout from beyond the window, and of the fact that she was nestled in her husband's arms, her head on his shoulder. And then it all came flooding back – yesterday, the first full day of her marriage.

'What time is it?' she asked, drawing back her head, not checking first to see if he was awake.

He was. He was gazing back at her, his hair tousled, his nightshirt open at the neck. She was still wearing her nightgown. A man in his nightshirt, she thought, could look every bit as enticing as the same man naked. This man could, anyway, and he was the only one in whom she was interested.

'Late enough,' he said, 'to satisfy our servants and please our relatives.'

'Oh.'

'It is important,' he said.

'To keep up appearances?'

'I think perhaps it is more than that, is it not?' he asked.

I care, he had told her last night. *You belong to me now, Wren. I have ownership of you. Not to tyrannize over you, but to keep you safe so that you can be free of these fears and horrors. I look after what is my own. It is more than a promise.* Strange words, which might have sounded alarming but had not. For she had believed the intention behind the words. And after they had come back to bed, he had loved her slowly, gently, and surely with tenderness.

'Thank you for listening,' she said. 'I try not to be self-pitying, but last night it all came welling up at your expense. My life has been hugely, wondrously blessed and continues to be. I will not inflict my darkness upon you again.'

'Avoiding self-pity can sometimes mean suppressing what needs to be spoken of and dealt with,' he said.

'You are going to be late for the Lords,' she told him.

'I am not going today,' he said. 'I daresay the country will not fall into total collapse as a result. I am going to spend today with my wife. If she will have me, that is.'

'She will think about it,' she said. She raised her eyes and set one fingertip to her chin. 'She has given the matter due consideration. She will have you.'

'Wren.' He laughed softly and touched his forehead to hers. 'I may find myself capable of missing a day at the Lords, you know, but I am quite incapable of missing my breakfast.'

A short while later they entered the breakfast parlor together. Everyone was still there, though it seemed they had all finished eating. Wren felt acutely self-conscious as all eyes turned their way and was very glad indeed that they had had their wedding night and yesterday's breakfast to themselves. There was a cheerful exchange of greetings.

'I hope I have left you enough sausage and bacon, Alex,' Harry said. 'After twelve hours of unbroken sleep and those few ghastly days of nothing but gruel and jellies, I was ravenous.'

'There is enough for me,' Alexander said, peering into the dishes. 'I am not sure about Wren, though.'

'If you did not leave me two slices of toast, Harry,' Wren said as she seated herself between her mother-in-law and Abigail, 'I shall have to get the cook to put you back on broths.'

'I did. I swear.' He laughed. There was more color in his face this morning, and it was already surely a little fuller than it had been a week ago.

'You were very tired last night, Wren?' her mother-in-law asked, covering one of her hands with her own as the butler poured her coffee and set her toast before her.

'I was,' Wren said. 'But I do apologize for not saying good night before I went upstairs. That was ill-mannered of me.'

'Oh, it was clearly more than just tiredness,' Elizabeth said. 'It was exhaustion, Wren. Going to the theater must have been a huge ordeal for you in addition to everything else.'

'So it was for Viola and Abigail,' Wren said. 'But we did it, and today we may bask in self-congratulation.' *Just please let no one mention my mother.*

'I am taking Wren out for the day,' Alexander said. 'Yesterday was a mistake. Sometimes there are more important things than cold duty.'

'Ah.' Elizabeth laughed. 'There is hope for you yet, Alex.'

'I think, Wren,' their mother said, patting her hand, 'you are already having a positive influence upon my son.'

'You are not leaving for home today, I hope?' Wren asked Viola.

'No.' Viola shook her head. 'Mildred and Thomas have organized a family picnic to Richmond Park.'

'You and Alex are invited too, of course,' Wren's mother-in-law said. 'But if you would prefer a day alone together, I am sure everyone will understand.'

'I think Wren needs a quiet day,' Alexander said.

She wondered how much any of them understood that even just this much was all new to her and a strain on her nerves – this sitting at a table with six other people, part of a conversation. For the past year and a bit there had been almost total silence in her life. But these people were her family now. So were the others – the other Westcotts and the Radleys – and they had been kind to her.

Alexander's quiet day sounded infinitely desirable. But—

'It would be a pity to be the only ones missing from a family picnic,' she said.

He had the loveliest eyes. Not only were they a clear blue, but they had the ability to smile even when the rest of his face did not. 'Yes, it would,' he said.

Was it possible now, Wren wondered, to move forward, to be happy, to be done finally with the past? Now that she had seen her mother again and felt the full force of the pain she had bottled up for twenty years? But she had spoken of it, so could she now forget? Or, if forgetting was impossible, could she at least let go of the feeling that the central core of her being was one bottomless pit of darkness?

Was it possible to be . . . normal?

Richmond Park had been set up as a private deer park during the reign of King Charles I, but although it was still royal property, it was now open for the pleasure of the public. It was a broad expanse of wooded areas and grassland and flower gardens, with a number of small lakes known as the Pen Ponds. It was a lovely piece of the countryside close enough to London to allow for a brief escape to those who must spend most of their days there. It was the perfect place for a picnic, and the weather had cooperated, as it had been doing for several weeks past. The sky was blue with just enough fluffy white clouds to offer occasional shade from the sun.

Alexander was glad to be with the family, though he hoped to be able to wander off for some time alone with Wren. He must make a decision about what to do with his new knowledge, but he needed to sense her mood first. She had slept deeply through the night – he knew because he had not – and had seemed refreshed this morning. She appeared to have recovered her spirits, though he was not foolish enough to believe that now she was healed.

Everyone remained together for a while, seated upon blankets on one expanse of grass, trees behind them, one of the ponds before them. Wren was holding the Netherbys' baby, a bald, plump-cheeked little girl who was just beginning to smile in that wide, toothless way of babies. Anna was beside her on one side, Abby on the other, Elizabeth close by. Wren was totally absorbed in the baby, the child's head on her raised knees, its little hands in hers, its feet pressing against her ribs beneath her bosom. She looked utterly happy, and it struck Alexander that motherhood would agree with her – as fatherhood surely would with him. Soon, he hoped.

Jessica and Harry had wandered close to the water. She was talking animatedly about something. The older people were in a group together, centered about the chair that had been brought for the use of Cousin Eugenia, the dowager countess. Netherby stood a little apart, as he often did, his shoulder propped against a stout tree trunk, his posture indolent and elegant. He was dressed as gorgeously as ever. He was flicking open the lid of a jeweled snuffbox.

Alexander used to dislike him. He had thought him effete and trivial minded, someone who did not take his position and responsibilities seriously. He had felt disliked in return, thought of, no doubt, as stuffy and humorless. Alexander had changed his mind during the last year or so with all the family turmoil that had followed upon the death of the former earl. He doubted he and Netherby would ever be close friends. They were too different in almost every imaginable way. But they respected, even perhaps liked each other, he felt. And they trusted each other. At least, he trusted Netherby. He approached him now, and Netherby closed his snuffbox unused and returned it to his pocket.

'A family picnic in rural England,' he said on a sort of sigh. 'It is deeply affecting, is it not?'

Alexander smiled. Not many minutes ago Netherby had been holding his child and subjecting himself to having his nose grabbed. 'What do you know about Hodges?' he asked.

'*Lord* Hodges?' Netherby pursed his lips. 'What do you wish to know, my dear fellow? His life story? I cannot give it, alas. I was never a keen student of social history.'

'How old would you say he is?' Alexander asked. He did not know Lord Hodges at all, but he had seen him a few times.

'Mid-twenties?' the duke suggested.

'Not mid-thirties?'

'I would say not,' Netherby said, 'unless, like his mother, he has discovered the fountain of youth.'

'What is his first name?' Alexander asked.

Netherby thought. 'Alan? Conan?'

'Not Justin?' Alexander suggested.

'Colin,' Netherby said decisively. 'I assume there is some point to your questions, Riverdale? The sight of an apparently youthful Lady Hodges last evening, perhaps? I do assure you she is the man's mother rather than his wife.'

'Does he live with her?' Alexander asked.

'Hmm.' Netherby raised his quizzing glass and tapped it against his lips. 'Why is it that I know he has rooms very close to White's? Ah, yes, I have it. He made a joke when someone asked him if he had ridden to the club. He said it would be rather pointless, as he could mount on the rump of his horse outside his rooms and dismount from the neck at White's without the horse having to lift a hoof. I assume he somewhat exaggerated unless he owns an extraordinarily long horse.'

'I'll find out,' Alexander said, 'and call on him.'

'You will call on him,' Netherby asked, 'to discover just how long his horse is? Perhaps five people can ride on its back without being crowded. But the poor beast might sag in the middle.'

'He is Wren's brother,' Alexander said.

'Ah.' The world-weary eyes sharpened to regard him shrewdly. 'Which fact would make Lady Hodges her mother and Lady Elwood her sister.'

'Lady Elwood?' Alexander said. 'The other lady in the box last night, do you mean?'

'The same,' Netherby said. 'The lady is gradually growing older than her mother.'

'The father and the older brother must have died,' Alexander said.

'Was there an older brother?' Netherby asked. 'I never had the pleasure of his acquaintance. Your wife said nothing at the theater last evening.'

'No,' Alexander said. They did not speak for a while. Harry and Jessica had returned to the rest of the group, and Harry had stretched out on one of the blankets, one arm draped over his eyes. His mother seated herself beside him and said something to him while she smoothed his hair back from his brow. 'Will Harry go back, do you think?'

'To the Peninsula?' Netherby said. 'Oh, without a doubt. He has been worn to the bone by injuries and fever, but the bone is tough and so is Harry.'

'This has all been the making of him, then?' Alexander asked dubiously.

'*This?*' The duke brooded over his answer, his glass tapping against his lips again. 'Rather, *life* is the making or breaking of all of us, Riverdale. We are all tested in different ways. This is Harry's testing ground.'

It would have seemed a strange answer if Alexander had not already learned that Netherby was not at all as he seemed from the image he projected to the world. He wondered what had been the duke's testing ground. He knew what his had been – and still was. And if Netherby was right, as undoubtedly he was, there was no single test for anyone. Life was a continuous series of tests, all or some or none of which one might pass or fail and learn from or not.

Wren had lifted the baby to sit on her raised knees and was bouncing her gently. Abby was up on her knees beside her, trying to make the baby smile. Anna was smiling happily.

'Wren has neither seen nor heard anything of or from any of them since her aunt took her away when she was ten years old,' Alexander said. 'Her mother was about to commit her to an insane asylum.'

'Because of her face,' Netherby said. It was not a question. 'Because it was imperfect and the lady's very survival depends upon her own beauty and the perfection of everyone connected with her.'

'Yes,' Alexander said.

'Did you want me to come with you?' Netherby asked.

'No,' Alexander said. 'But thank you.'

The baby, happy and smiling and bouncing one moment, was suddenly crying. Anna was on her feet, laughing and taking the child from Wren. The baby still howled with what sounded more like temper than pain.

'Ah,' Netherby said, pushing his shoulder away from the tree, 'it is time to discover a secluded nook, it seems. We should have named our daughter Tyranny rather than Josephine. Eternally Demanding Stomach would have been too much of a mouthful. And I do believe there was a pun in there somewhere.' He went strolling off toward his family.

'Wren,' Alexander said after following him, 'come for a stroll with me?'

They walked among the trees, in a different direction from the one Anna and Avery had taken with Josephine.

'I have never held a baby before,' Wren said. 'Oh, Alexander—' But then she felt foolish. All women were silly about babies, were they not? Perhaps that fact ensured the protection of the young of the human race. She had wanted a family of her own, but her thoughts had centered mostly about being married. Now that she *was* wed, she yearned for motherhood too. Would she never be satisfied?

'Perhaps,' he said, 'you will be holding one of your own within the next year or so, Wren.' He disengaged his arm from hers and set it about her shoulders to draw her against his side. Surprised, she set her own arm about his waist. 'What do you want to do? Do you want to go home? Do you want to stay?'

'I *am* home,' she said, and when he turned his head to look at her, their faces were a mere few inches apart.

'In London?' he said.

'*Here,*' she said, and he tipped his head slightly

to one side. She knew he understood that she did not mean here in Richmond Park. 'I am not running away any longer, Alexander. I instructed Maude before we left the house to make all my veils disappear before I return. I told her she could sell them if she wished. But she said she would burn them with the greatest pleasure.'

'Wren,' he said, and he kissed first her forehead and then her mouth.

'I am as I am,' she said.

He dipped his head closer to hers. 'Those are the loveliest words I have heard you utter,' he said.

Her knees turned weak. *I care,* he had told her last night. And he did care. Those were the loveliest words she had heard *him* utter. But she would not say so aloud. She would reveal too much about herself if she did.

She looked up at an old oak tree by which they had stopped. 'I have not climbed a tree since I fell out of that one the day I left Roxingly,' she said.

'You are not by any chance planning to climb now, are you?' he asked her.

Many of the branches were wide and almost horizontal to the ground. Some of them were low. And some of the higher branches were easily accessible from lower ones. She was not a child. She had not climbed for twenty years, and even then not often. She was wearing a new sprigged muslin dress. She had the body of an athlete, he had told her. She was afraid of heights. But that unoffending tree suddenly looked like all the barriers that had ever stood between her and freedom. It was silly. It was childish. It would ruin her dress and expose her legs. Her shoes were totally unsuitable. She would probably fall again and break every limb she possessed, not to mention her head. She needed to make pro and con lists.

'Why not?' she said, and took her arm from about his waist, shrugged off his arm from her shoulders, and marched to the tree and up it.

Well, she did not exactly *march* up. Indeed, she hauled herself onto the lowest branch in a most ungainly fashion and then stepped gingerly up to the next and crawled inelegantly up to the third before looking down. Her rational mind told her she was still pathetically close to the ground. If Alexander below her stretched up an arm and she stretched down a leg, he would surely be able to grasp her ankle or even her knee. Her irrational mind told her she was in danger of bumping her head on the sky before falling from it like Icarus. She turned with great care and sat on the branch. Her legs felt boneless.

He was grinning at her. He had removed his hat and dropped it to the grass. 'I daresay,' he said, 'it must be almost twenty years since I climbed a tree.'

She grinned back at him before deciding that looking downward was not a good idea. He came up after her until his boot was on the branch beside her and then disappeared upward. He sat on a branch adjacent to her own and slightly above it and draped his wrists over his bent knees.

'I think,' he said, 'it is still almost twenty years since I *climbed* a tree.'

'Do not belittle me,' she said as she edged along to set her own back against the trunk. 'I have one question. How do we get down?'

'I do not know about you,' he said. 'I intend to climb down the way I came up.'

'I thought so,' she said. 'But that is the whole problem.'

'Never fear,' he said. 'When teatime comes, I shall fetch you some food.'

And somehow they found the sheer silliness of their exchange hilariously funny and laughed and snorted with glee.

'And maybe a blanket to keep you warm tonight,' he added.

'And breakfast in the morning?' she asked.

'You are very demanding,' he told her.

'Ah, but—' She tipped her head to look up at him. 'You care.'

Their laughter stopped. He gazed back down at her, his smile lingering, and she wished she had not said that – although *he* had said it first. Last night.

'Yes, I do,' he said. 'You had better tell me what I can fetch you for breakfast, then.'

'Toast and coffee,' she said. 'Marmalade. Milk and sugar.'

'Wren.' He held her gaze. 'Are you regretting any of this?'

She closed her eyes and shook her head. How could she regret it? Yes, marriage was vastly different from what she had expected. It had challenged her in unimaginable ways – and they had only been wed for two days. But how she loved it. And how she loved him.

She would not ask him if *he* was regretting it. It would be a pointless question. If she regretted it, there was something he could do about it. He could take her home and leave her to the hermit's life to which she was accustomed. If he regretted it, however, there was nothing she could do to make life better for him.

'We will stay in London, then, until the end of the session, will we?' he asked. 'And then go home to Brambledean? And perhaps to Staffordshire?'

'You would come there with me?' she asked him.

'Of course,' he said. 'I have no plans to be apart from my wife for longer than a few hours at a time. Besides, I may need to hold your hand when you meet your team of managers and designers and artisans for the first time without a veil.'

Ah, she had not thought of that. 'Yes, we will remain here,' she said.

'But not literally *here*,' he said, and he climbed down from his branch to hers and the one below just as though he were descending stairs in the house. 'Give me your hand. I promise not to let you fall.'

And she set her hand in his and knew somehow that he never would.

CHAPTER 20

Alexander discovered what he wanted to know early the following afternoon when he called in at White's Club. Lord Hodges's rooms were within easy walking distance, though it would have taken a very long horse indeed to span both places. Fortunately for him, he discovered when he rapped the knocker against the door, the man was at home. A servant conducted him upstairs and left him in a square, well-appointed room, tastefully decorated and furnished. Lord Hodges joined him there within five minutes.

And yes, Alexander decided, Netherby was almost certainly right, just as was his own impression from having seen the baron a few times before. He was surely only in his mid-twenties. He was tall and good looking, youthfully slender, with blond hair cut short. He looked at his visitor with polite curiosity as he greeted him and shook his hand.

'To what do I owe the honor?' he asked as he indicated a chair.

Alexander sat. 'I believe,' he said, 'you must be *Colin* Handrich rather than Justin?'

A brief frown creased Lord Hodges's brow. 'My brother died ten years ago,' he said. 'Three years before my father.'

'You have three sisters,' Alexander said.

'Lady Elwood and Mrs Murphy,' the young man said. 'I had a third sister, but she died as a child about twenty years ago. I beg your pardon, Riverdale, but what is the purpose of these questions?'

'I am glad of one thing at least,' Alexander said. 'You did not know. I must enlighten you: Your third sister is not dead. She is the Countess of Riverdale, my wife.'

Hodges stared blankly at him, laughed slightly, then frowned again. 'You are mistaken,' he said.

'No,' Alexander said. 'What do you remember of her?'

'Of Rowena?' Lord Hodges sat back in his chair. 'She was sickly. She rarely came out of her room. She never came into the nursery or the schoolroom or downstairs with the rest of us. She had a great . . . strawberry swelling covering one side of her face and head. I think it must have killed her, though the swelling had started to go down and lose some of its color. My aunt took her away to a doctor who said he could cure her. But she died. I am sorry for the misunderstanding. You have married someone else. I read your wedding announcement a day or two ago. Please accept my congratulations.'

'Thank you,' Alexander said. 'But you were given

the wrong information. Your aunt took your sister to London and called upon a former employer of hers, a Mr Heyden, hoping he could help her find employment. He married her instead and they adopted your sister and changed her name to Wren Heyden. They raised and educated her. Sadly they both died last year, within days of each other, leaving Wren alone and very wealthy.'

'The Heyden glassware heiress,' Hodges said softly, as though to himself. 'That was how your wife was described in the announcement.'

'She has a home not far from Brambledean Court,' Alexander said. 'I met her there earlier this year and married her three days ago.'

The young man stared at him. 'You must be mistaken,' he said.

'No,' Alexander said.

Lord Hodges gripped the arms of his chair. 'Does my mother know?' he asked.

'She may have drawn her own conclusions when she saw my wife across the theater two evenings ago,' Alexander said.

'My aunt *kidnapped* Rowena?' Lord Hodges asked.

'There were plans to send your sister to an insane asylum the following day,' Alexander told him. 'I would use the word *rescued* rather than *kidnapped*. Besides, your mother saw them leave and did nothing to stop them.'

'God.' Hodges had turned noticeably pale. His hands were white-knuckled on the arms of his chair.

'But I remember her well enough to know she was perfectly sane, even though she could not read or write. Did they believe she was not? Was that why she was kept locked up most of the time?'

'I think,' Alexander said, 'it was her appearance.'

Lord Hodges lurched to his feet, crossed the room to a sideboard, picked up a decanter, changed his mind and set it down again, and came to stand facing the fireplace, one hand gripping the mantel above his bowed head. 'I was only five or six when she was taken away,' he said. 'I remember so little about the events surrounding it. I know I cried when I heard she had died and lost faith in the power of prayer and healing. I used to kiss her face better whenever I went to see her and pray for a miracle. I am sorry. That is an embarrassing childhood memory to blurt out. It was her appearance, then? The strawberry mark? It was for that she was locked away and to be sent to an asylum?'

They were not questions that called for answers. Alexander did not offer any. But he did say something. 'Perhaps your childhood prayers *were* answered,' he said. 'Do you remember your aunt?'

'Not really,' Lord Hodges said. 'I remember that she came and then took Rowena away to the doctor a few days later. I cannot recall anything else about her. She was kind to Rowena?'

'She and her husband showered her with love and acceptance,' Alexander said, 'and saw to it that she was properly educated. When she showed an interest in the glassworks, her uncle trained her to take his place and left the business to her in his will. She is a superbly successful businesswoman.'

Lord Hodges said nothing. He had his eyes closed.

'You do not live with your mother,' Alexander said.

'No.' The young man opened his eyes.

'Has she mentioned the evening at the theater?' Alexander asked.

'Not to me,' Lord Hodges told him. 'I do not see a great deal of her. I do not see her at all, in fact, except when I run into her by chance at some entertainment. But I will say no more on that subject. It is a family matter.'

'I understand,' Alexander said.

'A family matter.' Lord Hodges laughed suddenly. 'You *are* family, are you not? You are my brother-in-law.'

Yes. Alexander had not thought of that until now.

'Keep her away from my mother,' Lord Hodges said, his voice low. 'Does she still have the mark?'

'The purple remains of it,' Alexander said. 'She is beautiful.'

The young man half smiled and turned away from the fireplace. 'My mother will not like that,' he said. 'She will allow only unmarred beauty in her orbit, and that beauty she will enslave if she is given the chance. Keep Rowena away from her.'

'For your mother's sake?' Alexander asked.

Lord Hodges drew breath to speak but released it and waited a few moments. 'My father escaped by dying,' he said. 'My elder brother escaped into alcohol and died as a result when he was younger than I am now. My eldest sister is a shell of the woman she might have been. My middle sister married an Irishman when she was seventeen, escaped to Ireland with him, and never returned. I stayed with an uncle and aunt during school holidays after my father died and in Oxford while I was at university. I moved here to these very rooms afterward. Rowena was rescued by Aunt – God, I do not even recall her name.'

'Megan,' Alexander said.

'By Aunt Megan,' Hodges said. 'Keep her away from my mother. That is dashed unfilial, Riverdale, and I always try to preserve decorum, even inside my own head. Honor your mother and father and all that. But Rowena is my sister and you are my brother-in-law. Keep her away.' He returned to his chair and sank down onto it while Alexander regarded him silently. 'Is it true, then? Is she really alive? Has she been alive all these years?'

'Will you come and meet her?' Alexander asked.

'Oh, God,' Lord Hodges said. 'She must hate me.'

'She remembers you,' Alexander told him, 'as the only person in her first ten years who ever showed her kindness. She remembers the kisses on the damaged side of her face. She remembers you turning the key in her door and coming in to play with her. She remembers playing outside with you once.'

'I was told I must never do it again.' The young

man was frowning in thought. 'I had forgotten. I was told she was ill and must not go out. I remember reading stories to her because she could not read herself. I must have only just learned.' He looked at Alexander. 'Will she hate me?'

'No.' Alexander got to his feet. 'I am going home now. Will you come with me? I cannot promise she will be there, of course.'

'I will come.' Lord Hodges stood too. 'I was on my way out somewhere, but I cannot for the life of me remember where. I will come. God. *Rowena.*'

Alexander had no idea if he was doing the right thing. He would find out, he supposed.

Viola and Abigail were to return home the following day, taking Harry with them. Today Wren had gone to see the Tower of London with Viola and Lizzie while her mother-in-law called on her brother and sister-in-law and Abigail went to spend the morning with Jessica and to see the baby – her niece – once more. Harry was borne off by the Duke of Netherby to practice some light swordplay in an effort to get the strength back in his arm, which was otherwise healing nicely. They were all back home by the middle of the afternoon, however. Jessica had come with Abigail and was going later with her and Viola and Harry to dine with the dowager countess and Cousin Matilda.

Wren was feeling a bit exhausted, as she did much of the time these days. She had gone out unveiled but not unnoticed. And at home she seemed always to be surrounded by people – well-meaning people, it was true, people of whom she was growing increasingly fond, but people none-theless. Elizabeth and her mother were to attend a soiree this evening. Perhaps, Wren thought hope-fully as the drawing room about her buzzed with cheerful teatime conversation, she would have the chance of a quiet evening alone with Alexander. How blissful that would be. And she did not believe he would mind. He had told her that for several years he had hardly come to London at all but had spent his time at Riddings Park. He still preferred the quiet of country life to the bustle of life in town.

She sat back in her chair, sipped her tea, enjoyed the company, and longed for the evening. When the drawing room door opened and she saw Alexander, her heart lifted. But he did not close the door behind him or advance far into the room as he greeted everyone.

'Wren,' he said, 'will you come down to the library with me? There is someone I would like you to meet.'

Again? Who now? she wondered in some dismay. Had she not met enough strangers in the last week or so to last a lifetime? He was surely being unfair.

'Of course,' she said, getting to her feet. She would not reproach him in front of everyone else. She almost asked him who it was when they were on their way downstairs, but she would soon see for herself.

He was a young man, tall and slender, smartly dressed, blond haired, and very handsome. He was turning from a bookcase when they entered the library, and he was looking as ill at ease as Wren was feeling. She was feeling something else too – dread? His eyes were riveted upon her from the first moment.

'Roe?' he said, his voice little more than a whisper.

Only one person had ever called her that – one little mop-haired blond child with his toys and his books and his healing kisses. This man—

'*Colin?*' Her fingers curled into her palms at her sides.

His eyes stilled on the left side of her face and then focused on her own eyes. 'Roe,' he said again. 'It is you. *It is you?*'

Wren felt as though the blood were draining from her head. She felt as though she were gazing down a long tunnel. A warm hand grasped her firmly by the elbow.

'I have brought Lord Hodges to meet you, Wren,' Alexander said.

Lord Hodges? He was not Papa. He was not – no, surely he was not Justin.

'Yes, I am Colin,' he said, crossing the room toward her in a few long strides and taking both her hands in a bruising clasp. 'Roe. Oh, good God, Roe. I thought you were dead. I thought you died twenty years ago.'

A little six-year-old. A happy little boy with his

toys and books and get-better kisses who always seemed to skip happily wherever he went. The only person who had loved her during her own childhood.

'Oh, God,' he said, 'they told me you were dead.'

If he squeezed her hands any more tightly, he was going to break a few fingers. 'You used to kiss my face to make it better,' she said. 'Do you remember, Colin? You did make it better. See? It never did go quite away, but it is better. And everything else got better too. Except that you were lost to me. And I have always wondered . . . My heart has always ached.'

'I survived too,' he said, and when he smiled, she could see – oh, surely she could see that radiant little boy, though she had to look up an inch or two at him now. 'I still cannot believe it, Roe. You are *alive*. All these years . . .'

I survived too . . . A strange choice of words.

'Perhaps we should all sit down,' Alexander suggested.

He poured them each a glass of wine while Wren sat with Colin on the deep leather sofa that faced the fireplace. He took both her hands in his again as soon as they were seated, as though he feared she would disappear if he did not hold on to her. Alexander sat in one of the armchairs flanking the hearth.

'No, it never did go quite away,' Colin said, tipping his head to look at the side of her face, 'but it does not matter, Roe. Riverdale was right.

351

You are beautiful. And you were the fortunate one. If you had not been blemished, she would have kept you. Did Aunt Megan treat you well? Riverdale says she did.'

'She was an angel,' Wren said. 'And I use the word with all sincerity. So was Uncle Reggie, whom she married. But, Colin – *Lord Hodges*?'

'Were you cut off from all knowledge of us, then?' he asked her. 'Papa died seven years ago of a weak heart. Justin died three years before him. There is an official story of the cause, but the truth is that he drank himself to death. You probably do not know anything else about us either, do you? Blanche married Sir Nelson Elwood. They live with our mother. There are no children. Ruby married Sean Murphy when she was seventeen and went to Ireland with him. She never comes back, but I have been there a few times. I have – you and I have three nephews and a niece. I have rooms here in London, where I live year-round.'

'Not with . . . Mother?' she asked.

'No.' He released her hands and reached for his glass of wine. 'I suppose you were not sickly as a child, were you? That was not why you rarely came out of your room.'

'No,' she said.

'I suppose you were kept there,' he said, 'because you were a blemish upon her beautiful world. Young children are very gullible. They believe everything they are told. I suppose that is natural. They have to grow gradually into discernment – and cynicism. I was proud of myself when I learned to turn that key. I can remember turning it so that I could come and play with you. I never thought to question why a sickly sister had to be locked into her room. But, Wren, you were able to escape when you were still young. If you had not had that strawberry blemish, you would have been sucked up like the rest of us, for you *are* beautiful and probably were even as a child. But forgive me. Nothing must have seemed like a blessing in those days.'

'Oh, *you* did,' she told him.

Both he and Alexander smiled at her, and she looked from one to the other of them and felt a great welling of love.

'The rest of us had identity only as her beautiful offspring,' Colin said. 'I had a bit of a lisp as a child. I was not allowed to grow out of it until I almost was unable to do so. And I was not allowed to cut my hair in what I considered a decently boyish style because it was blond and curly and people used to pat me on the head and coo over me. And I was told you had died. I can remember going to your room the night after I heard and tucking my favorite cloth tiger beneath your bedcovers to keep you warm and putting the book you most liked me to read on your pillow to keep you company. But it seems I stayed there to do both myself. I believe I fell asleep crying. There was a bit of a hue and cry the next morning when I was not in my own bed.'

'Thank you,' she said. 'Even though I did not know it, thank you, Colin.'

'Why *Wren*?' he asked her.

She smiled. 'It is what Uncle Reggie called me the first time he saw me,' she said. 'He said I was all thin and big-eyed and looked like a little bird. Soon Aunt Megan was calling me Wren too and I liked it. When they adopted me, I became Wren Heyden, the name I bore until three days ago, when I became Wren Westcott.' She glanced at Alexander and smiled again.

'I do not believe I could get used to saying it,' Colin said, 'though it is pretty.'

'Oh no,' she said. 'You must always call me Roe. Only you have ever done so, and I associate it with brightness and comfort and love.'

He sighed and looked from her to Alexander. 'I want to know so much,' he said. 'I want to know everything. And I suppose I want to *tell* you everything. There are so many missing years. But I must not take up more of your time today. Riverdale, I owe you a debt of gratitude I may never be able to repay. I would never have known. I read your marriage announcement, but the name *Wren Heyden* meant nothing to me. I would not have known even if I had seen her, for her face is different now from the way I remember it. I would have gone through the rest of my life believing my sister to be dead.'

'But you must stay,' Wren said, forgetting her earlier longing to be alone with Alexander for the evening. 'Stay for dinner. Meet my mother- and sister-in-law and cousins. I daresay you know some of them already.'

'Alas, I cannot,' he said. 'I have an engagement I cannot break. A friend of mine has a sister who needs an escort to Vauxhall, and I am he. She is a shy girl and has not taken well with the *ton* so far this year.'

'Then you certainly must go,' Wren said as he got to his feet and offered both his hands to draw her up before him.

'Roe,' he said, tightening his grip, 'stay away from her. She is my mother – *our* mother – and I would not utter one disloyal word about her to anyone outside the family. I said the same thing to Riverdale earlier about staying away from her, but only after he convinced me that he was indeed my brother-in-law. She is poison, Roe. There is only one person in her world – herself. Everyone else is part of a stage set about her or the audience to gaze upon her with wonder and awe. She can be vicious to anyone who will not play his or her appointed part. I am almost choking on such disloyal words about my own mother, but she is your mother too and she will *not* be happy if she comes face-to-face with you. She will fear exposure as someone who is not quite perfect after all. Stay away from her. Forget about her. But I daresay you already intend to do just that.'

'Colin.' She smiled at him. 'Something in me has healed today. There *was* goodness in those years.'

'I am sure I will be waking up tonight imagining this is all a dream,' he said. 'And for once I will enjoy waking all the way up to realize it is not. You are *alive*.'

'Yes,' she said. 'Enjoy Vauxhall.'

'Oh, I will.' He grinned. 'Miss Parmiter may be shy, with the result that the *ton* has taken little notice of her. But I have. Roe, may I kiss it better again?'

'Oh yes, please.' She laughed as he kissed her left cheek and then pulled her into a tight hug. She hugged him back and thought that darkness was never quite dark. Her first ten years had come very close, so close that she had almost forgotten the one thin thread of light that had made all the difference – the bright-faced little boy who had grown into this handsome young man. Her brother.

They saw him on his way, she and Alexander, after he had agreed to return the following day. Then they returned to the library. He had her hand in his, she realized, their fingers laced. He drew her down onto the sofa and wrapped one arm about her. She rested her head on his shoulder and closed her eyes. She felt his free hand wipe her cheeks gently with a handkerchief.

'If he had turned out to be the other brother,' he said, 'I would not have told him.'

'Justin?' she said. 'I suppose he suffered too. One does not drink oneself to death for the pleasure of it.'

'He was cruel to you,' he said.

'He was just a boy,' she told him. 'Blanche and Ruby were just girls. I have to forgive, Alexander, even if only in my own mind. If one of them had looked as I did and I had looked as one of them did and been under the influence of my mother, who is to say I would not have behaved in just the way they did?'

He bent his head and kissed her.

'I am going to go and see her,' she said.

The arm about her shoulders tightened. 'Your *mother*?' he said.

'Yes.'

'*Why*?' he asked. 'Wren, there is no need for that. Your brother advises against it, and he ought to know. He was quite adamant about it, in fact. You do not need to do this. Let me take you home. I am longing to go myself. Let's go home.'

'Do you know where she lives?' she asked.

'No.' He sighed. 'But it should not be hard to find out.'

'Will you do that, please?' she asked him. 'I am going.'

He did not ask why again, which was just as well. She did not know why. Except that her past had been opened up at last, beginning with the visit to the theater and the outpouring of her story later. And now this. She had to finish what had been started or it would forever fester inside her. She was not looking for healing. She was not sure that was possible – just as perhaps it was not for Colin and her sisters. She just wanted to face her memories, including those that were too deep to be dragged up into her conscious mind. That was all. That was why.

'Wren.' Both his arms were about her. His cheek was resting against her head. 'What am I going to do with you? No, don't answer. I know what I am going to be doing with you within the next day or two. I am going to be going with you to call upon Lady Hodges.'

'Yes,' she said. 'Thank you. And soon, Alexander. Then I want to go home with you.'

CHAPTER 21

Viola left the following morning after breakfast, with Harry and Abigail. All was noise and bustle for a while and hugs and kisses and even a few tears.

'I say, Wren,' Harry said when he was taking his leave of her. 'I do hope you will not hold the first day or so of our acquaintance against me. I seem to remember asking rudely who you were and demanding Mama and bumbling on about walking furniture. And I dread to think what I must have looked like – and smelled like.'

'All is forgotten except the joy of realizing who you were,' she said, laughing as she patted his good arm. 'Enjoy your relaxation time in the country.' She somehow doubted he would relax as much as his mother and sister hoped. Already he was looking wiry and restless and altogether more healthy than he had looked a week ago.

'Thank you for all you have done for me,' he said, catching her up in a tight hug, 'and for inviting Mama and Abby here. I understand it was your idea to use your wedding as an extra inducement. Thank you, Wren.'

Abigail hugged her too. 'Yes, thank you,' she said. 'It was important I come for poor Jess's sake. She has taken the changes in my fortune very much to heart. I have been able to spend our few days here explaining that I am at peace with it all, that I am not a tragic figure for whom she should sacrifice her own hopes and happiness. It has been easier to convince her person-to-person than by letter. And it has been lovely seeing everyone again and meeting you. I think you are quite perfect for Alex. For one thing, you are almost as tall as he is.' She laughed. 'Thank you, Wren, for everything.'

Viola took one of her hands between both of her own. 'Thank you,' she said, 'for the tender care you lavished upon my son. Thank you for giving Abby and Jessica the chance to spend some time together. In many ways they are more like sisters than cousins and the events of the past year or so have been hard on them. And thank you, Wren, for . . . friendship. I feel that I have found a friend in you, and that is not something I say to many people. You have inspired me with your quiet courage.'

'That,' Wren told her, 'is one of the loveliest things anyone could possibly say to me. And please know how happy I am to be able to call you friend as well. Enjoy your month or two with Harry. I will write, and hope to see you again soon.'

'I shall you as well.' And they hugged each other amid the noise and fuss of general farewells.

Harry had drawn Alexander into a hug too, Wren noticed, and was slapping his back. She even overheard what he said. 'I don't resent you, Alex,' he said, 'despite what I know you half believe. When I see you going off to the Lords, I think how dreary it would be if that were me. Give me a battleground instead any day of the week.'

Then everyone was moving out onto the pavement and Alexander was handing the ladies into their waiting carriage and Harry was climbing in after them. Two minutes later the carriage disappeared along South Audley Street, and those who remained stood gazing after it.

'Viola has changed,' Wren's mother-in-law said. 'I was always very fond of her. She was so elegant and dignified and gracious, as she still is, but there used to be a certain aloofness about her too. She seems a little warmer now.'

'I believe the aloofness could be attributed to the wretchedness of her marriage, Mama,' Elizabeth said. 'You did not miss anything in not knowing Cousin Humphrey, Wren.'

'I like her very well indeed,' Wren said as they entered the house again. 'And Abigail is very sweet. She is mature beyond her years.'

'I would wager Harry will be back in the Peninsula before his two months are up if he has any say in the matter,' Alexander said. 'He told me the life of an officer suits him better than that of an earl. Perhaps he even believes it.'

'Wren?' Elizabeth linked an arm through hers as they climbed the stairs. 'Lord Hodges is your brother?'

Alexander had told his mother and sister about the relationship. 'Yes,' Wren said. 'Colin was six when I left home. I adored him. He was told I had died.'

Her mother-in-law, coming up behind them on Alexander's arm, drew in a sharp breath, though she did not say anything.

'His shock was greater than mine yesterday,' Wren said. 'My greatest shock was knowing he is *Lord Hodges*. My father was alive when I left home. So was my elder brother.'

'Oh,' Elizabeth said.

'I am going to see her,' Wren said as they entered the drawing room.

'Lady Hodges?' Her mother-in-law looked shocked. 'Oh, my dear. You are going with your brother?'

'No,' Wren said. 'He has no dealings with her and has strongly advised me to stay away.'

'But you are going anyway?' her mother-in-law said. 'Wren, is it wise?'

Elizabeth released her arm before they sat down. 'I can understand that she must go, Mama,' she said. 'I do not know your story, Wren, but I can perhaps imagine some of it, for I do know a bit about – But she is your mother and the least said the better. Yes, of course, you must go, and I applaud your courage. Alex is going with you?'

'Kicking and screaming,' he said, looking from one to the other of them, a frown on his face. He had not sat down. 'This must be a woman's logic at work. To both Hodges and me it is madness. And I *do* know Wren's story, Lizzie – or some of it anyway. I daresay there is far more. Yes, I am going with her. Tomorrow morning if the lady is at home. And then I am going to miss what remains of the parliamentary session. I am going to take Wren home. No, correction. Wren and I will be going home together. To Brambledean.'

'With my blessing,' his mother said. 'And *home* is the right word. Wren will make it home for you, Alex.'

'Now if you will all excuse me,' Alexander said, 'I have some business to attend to.'

Wren went to see him on his way.

Lady Hodges lived with her eldest daughter and son-in-law on Curzon Street, in a home owned but not inhabited by her son. She did not go out a great deal, and when she did it was to a place, like the theater, where she would be fully on display but not exposed to sunlight or direct light of any sort – and, preferably, where she would be set a little apart from her beholders. At home she occupied rooms in which the curtains were drawn permanently across the windows and the lights, though many, were artfully arranged to give an impression of warmth and brightness and to twinkle off jewels without illumining the lady herself. She surrounded herself there with beautiful young men who were drawn by the gifts she lavished upon them and by the fame of her beauty, which had persisted for more than thirty years and become legend. Her eldest daughter, still lovely though she was now in her middle thirties, had stayed with her, though the others had left for various reasons, her elder son by reason of death. She liked to have Blanche with her so that people might flatter her by believing they must be sisters.

Her vanity knew no bounds. When she looked in her mirror – and she did so only after spending a couple of hours each day in the hands of a small army of maids and wigmakers and stylists and manicurists and cosmetics artists – she saw the seventeen-year-old who had once taken the *ton* by storm. She had captivated a dozen or more gentlemen, most notably a married duke who had offered her carte blanche and riches galore and a wealthy, handsome baron who had offered her marriage. Her only regret when she chose the latter had been that she could not switch the ranks of the two men. She would have liked to be a duchess.

She was at home and in the middle of her toilette when a footman tapped on the door of her dressing room and murmured a message to one of the maids who then informed a more senior maid who informed my lady that the Earl and Countess of Riverdale had called and asked to pay their respects to her.

She was surprised. Indeed, she was amazed and not at all pleased. It was the very last thing she had expected. She had heard – who had not? – of the ugly woman with a purple face whom the Earl of Riverdale had been forced to marry, poor gentleman, because his pockets were sadly to let and she was fabulously wealthy. She had looked curiously at the woman when she had seen her in the box across from her own at the theater, as no doubt everyone else had done. And at first she had wondered, with a twinge of disappointment, why the reports of the woman's looks had been so inaccurate.

Then during the interval she had seen the countess full face. Blanche had seen her too. And Lady Hodges had felt a great unease. For the woman's face was indeed purple – *on the left side*. And she was not unlike . . . But she preferred not to see the resemblance, which was doubtless imagined anyway.

But that night while she lay in bed memories flickered to life. Lord Riverdale had married Miss Wren Heyden, heiress to the Heyden glassware fortune. Megan had once shamed the family by taking employment as companion to an invalid – a Mrs Heyden, wife of a very wealthy man. At least, she believed the name had been Heyden. The woman had died after a few years. What if . . .?

What if anyone ever suspected that the hideously ugly Countess of Riverdale had come from *her* body as a punishment because she had ranted and railed against Hodges for burdening her with yet another pregnancy and because she had tried everything within her power to abort it?

Her first instinct was to deny her presence. But

what if the rebuff set them to talking out of sheer spite? The woman surely was not expecting to be welcomed with open arms and kisses, was she? Had she come to make trouble? Was she really Rowena? Had plain, dumpy Megan really snared a wealthy husband? And kept Rowena and even changed her name? What sort of name was *Wren*? Was Megan still alive? Lady Hodges had neither seen her nor heard from her since that night when she had gone marching off with Rowena, all righteous indignation, the day before the child was to be taken to the asylum, where she ought to have been confined since her infancy.

'Have them shown into the rose salon and inform them I shall be down directly,' she said.

She was still no more than halfway through her toilette, but let them wait. She was certainly not going to urge anyone to hurry. This was the most important part of her day. 'And have Sir Nelson and Lady Elwood instructed to be ready to accompany me. And Mr Wragley and Mr Tobin too as soon as they arrive.'

They sat side by side in silence, Alexander's fingers resting lightly on her wrist as her hand clasped the other in her lap. Wren would not turn her head to look at him. Her mind was focusing, as it did when she went to work on anything to do with her business. It was not going to be allowed to admit distractions.

And Alexander *was* a distraction – supportive

and silently disapproving. No, that was not quite the right word. *Caring* would be more accurate – silently caring. She knew he feared for her and wished with all his being to protect her from hurt. She knew too that he would not interfere, that he would let her do what she must do, that he would support her no matter what.

It was endearing. It warmed her heart. But it was a distraction.

She felt a little as though they had stepped onto a stage set. The room was in semidarkness – just as her own sitting room had been when she summoned the first three gentlemen on her list of potential candidates for husband. But because the curtains were a rose pink, so was the room, lit by many candles set in gilded candelabra and wall sconces. There were a number of other chairs in the room apart from the sofa to which they had been specifically directed by the butler, but one of them stood apart from the rest. It could be described, Wren thought, only as a throne. It was lusciously upholstered in rose-colored velvet, but its arms and back and legs were intricately carved and gilded, and the legs were longer than those on the other chairs. Two low velvet steps led up to it. It was quite extraordinary. Somehow the light gleamed off the gold, but left the chair itself in shadow. It all seemed uncannily familiar, though how it could when she had spent most of her childhood in her room Wren did not know.

A dozen times it occurred to her that her mother

was playing games with them, that perhaps she intended to keep them here all day. A few times she was on the brink of getting to her feet and suggesting that they go back home. Each time she returned to her focus.

Alexander did not say a word, bless his heart, though his fingertips sometimes stroked lightly instead of remaining motionless on her wrist.

And then the door opened and five people came into the room – the younger of the two ladies who had occupied the theater box opposite their own, whom Wren now knew to be Blanche; the man who had been with her there, presumably her husband; two very young gentlemen, who were handsome almost to the point of prettiness; and . . . her mother.

Alexander got to his feet and bowed stiffly. Wren remained seated and looked at each of the three principal figures in turn. Blanche had not changed much except that she looked her age. She was tall, slim, blond, and very good looking. Her husband was also a handsome man, though he had the florid, slightly puffy complexion of someone who had been drinking too much for too many years. Her mother . . . Well, she had the slender figure of a girl, though there was evidence of stays tightly laced. Her white muslin dress was fussy with frills and flounces, with long, gauzy sleeves and lacy frills that covered her hands to the tips of her fingers. Rings glittered and gleamed on those fingers with their long, painted nails. A lacy white stole was draped artfully to cover her bosom and neck. Her hair was blond and youthful and artfully dressed high on her head with curls feathering over her neck and temples. It was without a doubt a wig. Her complexion was delicately pale, her eyes wide and guileless and fringed with long lashes a few shades darker than her hair and as artificial as it was. Her lips were plump and pink.

In the dim rose-hued light of the room she looked young and delicate and beautiful and so unreal that . . . Ah, yes. Jessica's word sprang to mind. She looked grotesque. A woman who must have been in her mid- to late fifties ought not to look like a girl newly stepping out into the world of the *ton*.

The whole performance was extraordinary. Not a word was spoken as the five moved across the room and the two pretty gentlemen offered a hand each to assist Lady Hodges to mount her throne before one of them picked up a rose pink feathered fan from a table beside her and handed it to the other, who wafted it before her face. Sir Nelson Elwood meanwhile was seating Blanche in one of the more lowly chairs.

'Lord and Lady Riverdale,' Lady Hodges said in a sweet girl's voice, which immediately sent shivers of memory down Wren's spine, 'I understand congratulations are in order. Young love is always a pleasure to look upon.'

Alexander had sat down again.

'Thank you, Mother,' Wren said.

The lady gestured elegantly and the man holding the fan lowered it to his side. 'Ah,' she said, 'so you *are* Rowena. Your looks have improved a little. It is a good thing, however, that you were left a fortune. I wish you happy in your marriage.'

'Thank you,' Wren said again.

'And what may I do for you,' her mother asked, 'apart from wishing you well?'

'Nothing,' Wren said. 'And even your good wishes are unnecessary. I came because I needed to come, because I needed to look upon you once more as an adult who has learned self-worth. I needed to confront the darkness of a childhood no child should ever have to endure, with no hint of love from anyone except my younger brother, with whom I was reunited yesterday, to great joy on both sides. Your cruelty to him in telling him I had died was only surpassed by your prolonged cruelty to a child who, through no fault of her own, was born with a facial blemish. I wanted to look you in the eye and tell you that you have missed so much joy you might have had in your life by putting your trust in self-worship and in physical beauty, which never lasts, at least not in its youthful blooming. You have ignored all the love and comfort you might have enjoyed with your family and others. All I ever wanted was to love and to be loved. I do not hate you. I have suffered enough and will probably never be quite free of the effects of what happened to me. I will not add hatred to that burden, which I will determinedly work toward dissipating for the rest of my life. I feel sorrow instead, for perhaps you cannot help your character any more than I can help the birthmark on my face.'

Alexander's fingertips were on her wrist again.

'My dear Rowena.' Her mother had taken the feathers in her own hand and was fanning her face again. 'I kept you and cared for you for ten long years when you were hideous to look upon and everyone begged me to send you somewhere where only those well paid to do so would have to look at you. It is trial enough to look at you now – I feel for Lord Riverdale – but perhaps you do not remember how you looked then. Megan made a martyr of herself by taking you in, it seems, and persuaded that old man, doubtless still grief-stricken after the death of his wife, to marry her and take on the burden of you. I assume she is dead now? Poor Megan. But you are rich and have been able to purchase a husband and even a title. I congratulate you again. You should be thanking me, not heaping recriminations upon my head. Mr Wragley, my vinaigrette, if you please.'

One of the young men picked it up from the table and handed it to her.

'Blanche,' Wren said, moving her attention to her sister, 'I never knew you well. I was never given the chance. I would be happy to get to know you as a sister if you would like.'

Blanche looked at her with cool disdain. 'No,

371

thank you,' she said, and her husband, who had not been introduced, set a hand on her shoulder.

Wren got to her feet. 'That is all,' she said. 'I shall not trouble you again, Mother. And I shall not deliberately expose your ugly secret, though I daresay it will soon be known that I am Lord Hodges's sister. Colin and I loved each other dearly as children. We will love each other again now and on into the future.'

Alexander was on his feet beside her and spoke now for the first time in more than an hour. 'I thank you for receiving us, ma'am,' he said. 'It was important to my wife to see you and speak with you again. She will be happier now, I believe. And her happiness is important to me. Of greater importance than anything else in my life, in fact. I certainly did not marry her for her money. I love her, you see.' With that, he turned and offered his arm to his wife. 'Wren?'

He escorted her from the room and down the stairs to the hall. A footman held the door open for them. They would no doubt have stepped out of the house without speaking again if someone had not called Wren's name. They turned. Both young men were hurrying down after them. They did not speak again until they were down in the hall too.

'You have upset Lady Hodges,' one of them said.

'Ugliness upsets her,' the other explained.

'And when she is upset, then we are upset,' the first man said.

It was the second man's turn. 'It is our express wish,' he said, 'that you stay away from her in the future.'

'We and her other devoted friends always see to it that her wishes are granted,' the first young man said. 'And it would be in your own interest, Lady Riverdale, to keep silent about your relationship to—'

He did not have a chance to finish. The other young man did not have a chance to chime in with his next remark. It all happened so quickly that Wren had no time even to blink. First the current speaker was grabbed by the neckcloth and then the other, and both were walked backward until there was no farther to go. They were hoisted upward, their backs to the wall, their elegantly booted feet only just scraping the tiled floor, their faces turning an identical shade of blue.

'Wren,' Alexander said, his voice pleasant, 'go outside, my love, and await me in the carriage.'

But she stayed and gazed in amazement. He did not appear to have exerted a great deal of energy or power, and his voice was not breathless. He looked from one to the other of the young men he held in place.

'I do not like the sound of my wife's name on your lips,' he said, his voice soft but curiously menacing. 'I do not remember giving either of you permission to address her directly. I do not recall her ladyship giving such permission. Such permission is withheld. My wife's name will not pass your lips ever again anywhere I might hear of it.

You will utter no warnings or threats against her *ever again*. You will offer no public opinion about her. If you ever encounter her again, you will lower your eyes and button your lips. If you are given orders to the contrary, you will obey those orders at your peril. And you will pass on this message to your cohorts so that I may avoid the tedium of having to repeat them. Do you understand?'

Feet and hands dangled. Eyes popped. Neither young man seemed able to mount any defense against a one-handed hold. Nor did they seem quite able to draw breath.

'It was not a rhetorical question,' Alexander said when there was no answer. 'It requires an answer.'

'Yes,' the first gentleman squeaked.

'Understood,' the second wheezed simultaneously.

Alexander opened his fingers and let them drop. They both crumpled to the floor, then rose awkwardly and fled in ungainly haste back up the stairs. Alexander brushed his hands together as though they were somehow soiled. He turned to glance at the footman, who was still holding the door open and gawking. His eyes alit upon Wren.

'Ah,' he said, 'the ever-obedient wife. Come. We are done here, I believe.'

She took his arm without saying a word.

CHAPTER 22

Before Alexander climbed into the carriage after his wife, he told his coachman to keep driving until he was notified otherwise.

She sat with rigidly correct posture on her side of the carriage seat, her face slightly turned away to gaze out of the window. She had taken him by surprise during that visit. He had expected that she would ask questions of her mother to try to understand the *why* of her childhood and the way she had been treated. He had expected her to plead for some sort of reconciliation, for some sign that her mother had maternal feelings after all and some feelings of remorse. He had expected emotion, tears, drama – *some* outpouring of passion and pain.

Instead she had been magnificent. And he understood why she had gone against his advice and that of her brother. *I came because I needed to come, because I needed to look upon you once more as an adult who has learned self-worth. I needed to confront the darkness of a childhood no child should ever have to endure . . . . I wanted to look you in the eye and tell you that you have missed so much joy you might have had in your life. . . . I do not hate you . . . I feel sorrow instead, for perhaps you cannot help your character any more than I can help the birthmark on my face.*

But he could not ignore the fact that that woman with her eerily youthful appearance and little girl voice was Wren's mother.

He took her gloveless hand in his. It was cold and lifeless at first. But it curled into his almost immediately, and the carriage jerked slightly as it moved off.

'Thank you,' she said. 'How did you manage to do that? There were two of them.'

'They were a grave disappointment,' he said. 'I was itching for a fight, but all they could do was dangle.'

'It is . . . hurtful to be told that one was hideous to look upon,' she said, 'even when one is assured that there has been a slight improvement and even when one despises the person who speaks such words.'

'But she is your mother,' he said.

'Yes.' She closed her eyes for a few moments and leaned slightly toward him until their shoulders touched. 'There is an image that leaps to mind with the word *mother* – *your* mother, your aunt Lilian, Cousin Louise, Anna. But there is no compulsion on a woman to fit that image just because she has borne a child, is there? My mother is . . . Is there something wrong with her, Alexander? Can she really not help who she is, or *how* she is? Or can she? No. Don't answer that.'

She slid her hand beneath his arm and moved closer. 'It does not matter. I went there so that I would be free of her at last. I am not naive enough to believe it will be as simple as that, of course, but calling on her was an important step and I have taken it. I am not going to puzzle over her. She is as she is. And Blanche is as she is.' With that, she sighed deeply. 'Alexander, what a burden I have proved to be to you.'

'I have not felt even a moment's regret,' he said quite truthfully.

'Thank you,' she said again after a brief silence. 'Thank you for telling her my happiness is important to you.'

'It is,' he said.

'And thank you for saying you love me,' she said.

'I do.'

'I know.' She wriggled her hand in his until their fingers were laced. 'Thank you.'

But she did not know. She did not know that something had happened to him when he had spoken those words. Any red-blooded male would have said the same thing under the circumstances, of course. But the thing was, the words had not come from his head as his other words had. They had come from somewhere else, some unconscious part of himself, and had struck him with their truth just as though he had been struck over the head with a large mallet. He loved her. Not just loved, but *loved*. Whatever the devil that meant.

She thought, of course, that he spoke of affection,

and she was quite right. But it was not *just* affection. He was not particularly good with words except the practical ones with which he dealt with everyday life. He could deliver a coherent, even forceful speech in the House of Lords without having to have a secretary write it for him. But he did not have the words to explain even to himself what he had just discovered about his feelings for his wife. *Love* encompassed it but was woefully inadequate.

The words had come straight from his heart, he supposed, but the heart was not strong on language. Only on feelings. He was a man, for the love of God. He was not accustomed to analyzing his feelings. And if he kept trying he was going to give himself a headache.

'Thank you,' she said again into the silence that had fallen between them. 'My heart is full, and all I can think of to say is those two words. They can be virtually meaningless or they can be powerful. I mean them powerfully.'

Just as he meant *I love you* powerfully.

'We will go home,' he said. 'Tomorrow.'

She turned her face toward him and smiled. 'To peace,' she said, 'and quiet and the challenge of all the work we need to do there.'

'Yes,' he said. 'To our new life together. We will make a home of Brambledean, Wren, and a prosperous estate, and eventually there will be a beautifully landscaped park that will employ many people and a fully staffed house worthy of its grandeur. But more than anything it will be a *home*. Ours. And our children's if we are so fortunate.'

'It sounds like bliss,' she said. 'It sounds like heaven. Tomorrow?'

'Tomorrow,' he said. He leaned forward to tap upon the panel as a signal to his coachman to take them back to South Audley Street. He did not know where they had been going since they left Curzon Street. He had not been paying attention.

'The House is still in session,' she said.

'I do not mind missing—' he began, but she interrupted.

'No,' she said. 'I have been thinking about that, Alexander. It is your duty to remain, and duty has always been important to you. It is one thing I have always liked and admired about you – that you have felt guilt even at missing a few days since you met me again. Marriage should not change anyone in fundamentals, only enhance what is already there.'

'I would rather take you home tomorrow,' he said. 'I also have a duty to you.'

'I want to see more of Colin,' she said. 'Much more. We have twenty years to make up for. I want to know everything about him. I want him to know everything about me. He is my *brother*.'

He sighed but said nothing.

'I scarcely know your aunt Lilian and uncle Richard,' she said, 'or Sidney or Susan and Alvin.

I liked them when I met them on our wedding day and would wish to see more of them. I want to spend some time with Cousin Eugenia, the dowager countess. I want to hear stories about her long life. I want to see more of Cousin Matilda, who annoys her mother by fussing over her and loving her to distraction. I scarcely know Cousins Mildred and Thomas. I want to know more about their boys, who are still at school and sound like a handful of mischief. I want to know Cousin Louise better and Avery. And Anna and the baby. I want to know how Jessica is faring now that she has seen Abby again. And I want to get to know your mother and Lizzie better. They are the only mother and sister I will ever know, and I intend to cherish them.'

He laughed softly. 'All this,' he asked, 'to persuade me to do my duty and attend the House of Lords until the end of the session?'

'Well, that too,' she said. 'But I mean everything else as well. I have lived in a well-padded and comfortable cocoon for twenty years after living in a cell for ten. Now I have taken a few tentative steps out into the world, and I need to take a few more before retreating to the peace and quiet of Brambledean. If we go home now, Alexander, I may never leave again.'

'I thought that was what you wanted,' he said.

'It was,' she said. 'It is. But I have learned something about myself recently. It is what Uncle Reggie always used to say about me. I am stubborn to a fault. I stubbornly refused to face the world while he lived. Now I stubbornly refuse *not* to.'

'Ah,' he said. 'I have married a stubborn woman, have I? That sounds like a challenge. Next you will be telling me you wish to attend a grand *ton* ball.'

There was a silence. But silence can have a quality. Not all silences are equal. The carriage rocked to a halt outside Westcott House. One of the horses snorted and stamped. Two people were talking to each other out on the street. Somewhere a dog was barking. Inside the carriage there was silence.

'Yes,' she said.

The Westcott and Radley families and Lord Hodges had been invited to tea at Westcott House. The dining room table had been set with all the best china and loaded with a sumptuous variety of sandwiches and scones and cakes.

'This has all the appearance of a family meeting, Althea,' Cousin Matilda said after they were all settled and had taken the edge off their hunger. Lady Josephine Archer, whom a chorus of protesting voices had saved from being taken away by her nurse, was being passed from person to person to be bounced on knees, cuddled and rocked in arms, and dangled above heads.

'We cannot come together just to celebrate family?' Wren's mother-in-law said. 'We cannot have a welcome-to-the-family party for Lord Hodges? You are quite right, though, Matilda. We invited you all not *just* to celebrate. We need to plan a ball to introduce Wren to the *ton*.'

All eyes turned Wren's way. Colin, seated beside her, raised his eyebrows and grinned at her.

'I have been saying so from the start,' Matilda said. 'She is the Countess of Riverdale, a position of great prestige. But I was informed that she is a recluse and that Alexander has chosen to humor her whims.'

'To respect her decisions, Matilda,' her mother said sharply, 'as any husband worthy of the name ought. Clearly Wren has changed her mind.'

'Mama and I are quite delighted,' Elizabeth said.

'And so am I,' Aunt Lilian said. 'What is the point of having an earl and a countess in the family if there is no public occasion at which we can show them off to our friends and neighbors?' Her eyes twinkled at Wren and Alexander and there was general laughter.

'My feelings precisely,' Uncle Richard said.

'Do you dance, Wren?' Cousin Mildred asked. 'If you do not, or if you need to brush up on your steps, I know a dancing master who would—'

'Not, one would hope,' Avery said, sounding pained, 'the man who was employed to teach Anna to dance last year, Aunt?'

'Mr Robertson, yes,' she said.

'If I had not intervened while he was teaching the waltz,' he said, 'I daresay he would still be trying to teach Anna just how to position her left hand on his shoulder with each finger held just so and her head at just such an angle with just such an expression on her face.'

'And if Lizzie and Alex had not demonstrated how it ought to be done,' Anna added, laughing. 'And if *you* had not then danced it with me, Avery, breaking every rule poor Mr Robertson had just taught. I would have to agree – I am sorry, Aunt Mildred – that meticulous as Mr Robertson's instructions are, he can also be intimidating to someone who just wishes to be able to enjoy dancing without tripping and falling all over her partner's feet. Practicing various dances in advance of your first ball is probably a good idea, though, Wren. Aunt Mildred is quite right about that. Lizzie and Alex will help you. Shall Avery and I come too? And perhaps Lord Hodges?'

'Oh, and us,' Susan Cole said. 'May we, Alex? It would be great fun. And we will bring Sidney with us. Lady Jessica will perhaps be willing to make the numbers even.'

'Who is going to provide the music?' Cousin Louise asked. 'And let no one look at me. Our music teacher always told Mama when I was a girl that I was all thumbs, though I thought they were particularly nimble thumbs. Mildred is better. Matilda is the best.'

'I am out of practice,' Cousin Matilda protested. 'And I never did hold much with the waltz. I know no suitable tunes.'

'My brother is a skilled pianist,' Wren's mother-in-law said. 'Can we persuade you, Richard?'

'With a little arm twisting, Althea,' he said amiably. 'If, that is, Wren feels the need of a few practice sessions. She has not voiced an opinion on the matter yet.'

'Well,' Wren said, 'I was taught to dance by a governess who was very strict and probably as meticulous about the details as is the Mr Robertson you speak of. But that was a long time ago and did not include the waltz. And I only ever danced with her or with my aunt or my uncle. There were never other people to make up sets.'

'Then we have work to do,' Cousin Matilda said. 'And where, Althea, is the ball to be held?'

'Here, I thought,' Alexander answered. 'With the doors folded back between the drawing room and the music room and most of the furniture and carpets removed, we can create quite a sizable—'

'I understood, Riverdale,' Avery said, 'that it is a *ton* ball we have been summoned here to plan, not some sort of assembly for a limited few. The venue will, of course, be the ballroom at Archer House. We held a ball there for Anna last year, you will recall, and for Jessica this year. We are becoming quite experienced ball givers, though it pains me to admit it. And when I say *we*, I must confess that I mean mainly my stepmother and Anna and my poor, long-suffering secretary. My dear Wren, if you wish to display yourself to the beau monde, you must do it in a grand manner and invite everyone who is anyone and squeeze them into one of London's largest ballrooms and its accompanying public salons and have the whole spectacle spoken of admiringly the next day as a sad squeeze. Anything less would be unworthy of your courage.'

Courage. Was that what had impelled her? Had that one little word spelled her doom? *Next you will be telling me you wish to attend a grand* ton *ball,* Alexander had said in the carriage by way of a jest. And she had spoken that other little word – *yes.* It had been spoken on a whim, in a burst of stubborn determination not to allow her mother to destroy the rest of her life, not to allow her any further influence at all upon it, in fact.

She would remain in London a while longer because duty was important to her husband. And she would become better acquainted with his family and her brother Colin while she was still here. She would not be driven away to Brambledean just because of a need to hide and heal. She would go there when it was time to go. She would be busy there, and she would reach out to get to know their neighbors better, her first acquaintance with some of them at Alexander's tea not having been an auspicious start.

She was going to be as normal as it was possible for her to be.

But a ton *ball?*

At Archer House?

Colin, she realized suddenly, was holding her

hand tightly on the table between them. Alexander, at the head of the table, was looking at her with that expression of his she loved best – apparently grave but with smiling eyes.

'You may choose the assembly for a limited few here, as Netherby describes it, if you wish, Wren,' he said. 'And if anyone has anything to say about your courage, the remark may be addressed to me.'

Avery, Wren noticed, raised his quizzing glass all the way to his eye and examined Alexander through it while Anna laughed and set a hand on his arm.

'A hit, Avery, you must confess,' Elizabeth said, a laugh in her voice.

'If you had the courage to call upon our mother, Roe,' Colin said quietly, for her ears only, 'you can do anything.'

'I want to waltz,' she said to the whole table. 'And to waltz properly, I have heard, one needs space. I daresay the ballroom at Archer House offers a great deal of that. Thank you, Avery and Anna – and Cousin Louise. Mama and Lizzie and I will help with the planning. Is it proper for a lady to ask a gentleman to dance with her? I know the answer, of course. My governess would have had heart palpitations at the very idea. I am doing it anyway. I want to waltz with Alexander.'

'You are a woman of discernment, Wren,' Cousin Mildred said, clapping her hands. 'Alex is the best dancer among us – oh, with the possible exception of Thomas and Avery. And Mr Radley and

Mr Sidney Radley, I daresay, and Mr Cole. And perhaps Lord Hodges.'

'You may take your foot out of your mouth now, Mil,' Cousin Thomas said to general laughter.

The smile in Alexander's eyes had deepened and spread to the rest of his face as he held Wren's gaze. 'I will teach you,' he said. 'And yes, Wren, we will waltz together at your coming-out ball. I will insist upon it. A husband really must assert his authority occasionally.'

Wren would have been in her element during the following two weeks planning the ball. However, her mother-in-law and Cousin Louise assumed happy ownership of that task while Mr Goddard, Avery's secretary, quietly and efficiently did all that needed to be done. If he ever wished to leave the duke's employ, Wren thought privately, though it was extremely unlikely, she had a job to offer him in Staffordshire.

Meanwhile she was not idle. There was a modiste to be visited with Elizabeth, for despite being in possession of several evening gowns she had thought suitable for any occasion, apparently she was wrong. And if she was to have a new gown to wear, then she must have everything else new to go with it – undergarments, stays, slippers, silk stockings, gloves, a fan, and a jeweled headband with feathered plumes, though she was not at all sure she would actually wear that last purchase.

There were two families with whom to become

more fully acquainted. She called upon them all, usually in company with Elizabeth. She went strolling in Hyde Park with various combinations of relatives. She wrote to Viola. She even wrote a letter to introduce herself to Camille and Joel. She hoped, she said in it, to go to Bath soon with Alexander to meet them and their daughters and the baby due in the near future.

Colin came to the house almost daily. Sometimes they sat in the library, just the two of them, talking about all the missing years, getting to know each other, coming to feel like brother and sister. Sometimes he sat with her in the drawing room or dining room with Alexander and her mother-in-law and Elizabeth. Once, he took her in his curricle for a drive in Hyde Park, though he avoided the areas where they were most likely to meet crowds of people. Always he took his leave of her by kissing her left cheek better while they both laughed.

During one of their private talks in the library she broached a topic she had discussed with Alexander the night before. 'Colin,' she said, 'you told me you live here in London all year. I suppose that means you do not feel comfortable going home to Roxingly even though it is yours. Would you consider living at Withington House in Wiltshire? It is just eight miles or so from Brambledean. I have thought of selling it, but I do love it. It holds fond memories for me. I would far prefer to see a family member there.'

He looked consideringly at her. 'I have thought of purchasing a place of my own in the country,' he admitted. 'Maybe I will buy it from you, Roe. I like the idea of having a place close to you.'

'No.' She held up one finger. 'You do not need to buy it. I will give it to you. Alexander will approve.'

But he was adamant, of course. If he was going to move to Withington, he was not going to do it on her charity.

'Then let us compromise,' she said. 'Come there this summer if you will and stay as long as you like. Pay the servants' wages and the other expenses. After a year, decide if it is somewhere you wish to make your home and then purchase it if it is. But only if it is, Colin. No obligations.'

He grinned at her and held out his hand to shake on the deal.

'Oh, I do love you, Colin,' she said.

'Roe,' he said, her hand still clasped in his, 'will you write to Ruby? I think it will please her to discover that you are alive and that you are willing to hold out an olive branch. I recall her telling me just before she married Sean Murphy and went off to Ireland that the biggest regret of her life was never having stood up for you while you were still alive.'

Wren looked down at their clasped hands and heaved an audible sigh. She hesitated for a long time. 'Very well,' she said at last. 'Because you ask it of me, Colin. The worst she can do is ignore the letter. Or answer it.'

'Were they very nasty to you?' he asked.

She shook her head. 'I will write to Ruby,' she said.

'Thank you.' He raised her hand to his lips.

During those weeks she dealt with all the reports that came from the glassworks. Her suggestion of one minor color change to the new design had been well received, and soon she would have samples of the finished product before it was put on the market.

And she learned to dance. It was quickly apparent that the skills she thought she had were woefully inadequate, but she set to with a will. Uncle Richard on the pianoforte showed a great deal of patience. So did all the other dancers who had volunteered their time to come to Westcott House almost every afternoon to help her. And learn she did, to the accompaniment of a great deal of laughter and some serious work. The relatives who were not actually dancing often turned up to watch and give their advice and encouragement. Alexander's mother was always there, smiling and laughing and nodding her head in time to the music. Cousin Matilda announced that she was coming around to the waltz on the afternoon when Wren finally got it as she performed the steps with Alexander. Elizabeth was dancing with Sidney, Anna with Avery, Susan with Alvin, and Colin with Jessica.

'Though I would question its appropriateness for any couple who are not related by blood or married or at the very least betrothed,' she added to the obvious discomfort of Jessica and Colin.

'If I were but fifty years younger,' the dowager countess said, 'I would not waste my time waltzing with a brother or father or even a husband. I will never forgive whoever invented the waltz for not doing so half a century sooner.'

'Perfect.' Alexander was smiling at Wren, her hand still in his, his other arm still about her waist. 'Either I am a perfect teacher or you are a perfect pupil.'

'Or both,' she said.

'Or both,' he agreed.

Those two weeks were busy and a bit frightening as she wondered more and more what she had unleashed. They were blissful too. For there were always the nights to look forward to, that span of hours when she was alone with her husband. She loved lying in bed with him, sometimes in darkness, occasionally with candles burning. They did not always make love, though usually they did, and sometimes they made love both at night and in the early morning. But they always talked, their arms about each other, and they always slept deeply and well. She knew he liked her, respected her, cared for her. No, more than cared. She knew he had an affection for her. And it was enough. It was what she had dreamed of and more than that. She only hoped it would continue, that they were not just in a honeymoon stage of their marriage that would wear off in time. But she would not believe it. It was up to her to make sure it continued, never to grow complacent or lazy.

She was going to make her marriage work, just as she was going to make her life work.

If only there was not a ball to be faced first. And *everybody who was anybody,* as Avery had put it, was going to be there. Of all the invitations they had sent out, only three had been refused, with regrets. Only three. It was enough to give her heart palpitations.

But she was going to waltz with Alexander.

CHAPTER 23

'I would say she looks stunningly beautiful,' Alexander said, 'but I may, of course, be biased. What would you say, Maude?'

He had stepped into his wife's dressing room to see if she was ready for the ball. Clearly she was. She was standing before the pier glass in a gown of primrose yellow silk overlaid with fine lace, looking youthful and vibrant. It was high waisted, low necked, and short sleeved. It was deeply ruched and scalloped about the hem. Her gloves and slippers were ivory colored. Her dark hair was dressed in elaborate curls on the top of her head, adding to her height, with tendrils curling along her neck and over her temples. Ah, but she was not quite ready. Her pearl necklace still lay on the dressing table.

'I said the same thing five minutes before you even came in here,' Maude said. 'This time I think she believes me. Us. My lord.'

'Well, I do.' Wren laughed. 'I think I am the most beautiful woman in the world.' She twirled once about, and her skirt twirled with her. 'There. Are you both satisfied?'

'Sit down again,' Maude said. 'We forgot your pearls.'

'I will see to that,' Alexander said. 'You may go and have your dinner, Maude. I daresay you missed it at the proper time.'

'You go to the ball, then,' Maude said, addressing Wren. 'And just remember what Mr Heyden always used to say to you. There is nothing you can't do if you set your mind to it.'

'I will remember, Maude,' Wren said. 'Thank you.'

She looked ruefully at Alexander after her maid had left. 'She is more nervous than I am,' she said.

'You are not nervous?' he asked.

'Not nervous,' she said. 'Terrified.'

He smiled at her. He was a bit surprised that she had chosen delicacy over boldness for her gown. She and his mother and Lizzie had been involved in a conspiracy of secrecy about it. He had imagined she would choose royal blue or a vivid rose pink or even bright red, bold colors to bolster her courage. The yellow was inspired. Actually it was a little brighter than primrose. And then he understood. Of course.

'Daffodils in June?' he said, indicating her gown with both hands. 'Trumpets of hope?'

'I have danced alone among them at Withington,' she said. 'Tonight I will be one of them and dance in company.'

'Yes, you will,' he said. 'Sit down while I will put on your necklace.'

She sat, handed him the pearls, and bowed her head. He slipped the pearls into a pocket, drew out a diamond necklace from another, and clasped it about her neck. He set his hands on her shoulders.

'Thank you.' She lifted her head to look in the mirror, raising a hand at the same time to touch the necklace. Her hand froze before it arrived. The chain was gold. It was dotted with small diamonds along its whole length with a larger one at the center, hanging just above the neckline of her dress. 'Oh,' she said, and one finger ran lightly over the right side of the chain. 'Oh.'

'They will never outshine the daffodils,' he said. 'But it is high time I gave you a wedding gift.'

'It must be the most beautiful necklace ever,' she said. 'Oh, thank you, Alexander. But how inadequate words can be.'

'There are earbobs too,' he said.

She turned on the stool to look up at him. 'I have never worn any,' she said as he drew them out of his pocket to display on his palm – two single diamonds, a little smaller than the one at the center of the necklace, set in gold. 'How exquisite they are. See how the light glints off them. I do not even know how to put them on.'

'Neither do I,' he said. 'I have never worn any either. Can we work it out together, do you suppose, on the theory that two brains are more effective than one?'

'And four hands better than two?' she said as her own hovered over his while he clipped the first to her left ear. She lowered her hands to her lap while he clipped on the second, and then she stood and wrapped her arms about his neck. 'Alexander, thank you. I am so glad the first two gentlemen on my list did not come up to snuff.' She laughed. Actually, it was more of a giggle.

'And I am very glad,' he said, 'that I was not number four on your list. Number three might have taken your fancy before I had a chance.'

'Never,' she said. 'Alexander? You do not ever regret—'

He set a finger across her lips. 'You must ask again? Do I behave like a man who regrets anything he has done recently?' he asked her. 'Should we perhaps consider going downstairs? It would be a huge embarrassment, do you not think, to arrive at Archer House too late to stand in the receiving line for the ball that is in your honor?'

Her eyes widened in alarm. 'There is no danger of that, is there?' she asked.

'Well,' he said, drawing her arm through his, 'Mama and Lizzie may be starting to think we have climbed out of the window and gone without them.'

She reached for her filmy wrap and fan on the side of the dressing table, and Alexander heard her draw and hold a deep breath before releasing it and turning to smile at him.

Wren's heart was in her throat from the moment of their arrival at Archer House, when she saw the red carpet that had been run out over the steps and across the pavement. And inside there was the grand hall and stairway bedecked with white and yellow and orange flowers and copious amounts of greenery. There were more than the usual number of footmen in gorgeous livery that included pale gold satin coats, white knee breeches and stockings and gloves, buckled shoes, and powdered wigs. Upstairs there were salons whose open doors gave glimpses of lavish floral arrangements within and candelabra and tables covered with starched white cloths. Some seemed designed for quiet relaxation for guests wishing to escape the noise and bustle of the dancing for a while. Others had been set up for cardplayers. One large salon next to the ballroom was ready for the refreshments that would be served despite the fact that there was to be a proper supper late in the evening.

Everything suggested a grand occasion, and *it was all in her honor.*

And there was the ballroom itself. Wren had seen it on an earlier visit and had been awed by its size and magnificence. Now it looked unfamiliar in all the splendor of banks of flowers and chandeliers and wall sconces in which hundreds of candles burned and a freshly polished floor that gleamed in the candlelight and chairs upholstered in dark green velvet arranged in a double row around the perimeter.

She had never in her life felt more intimidated. Just three months ago she had been living the life of a virtual recluse, carefully veiled on the rare occasions when she ventured beyond her own home. Even indoors she had worn her veil when any stranger intruded. She had lifted it to a stranger for the first time in almost twenty years when the Earl of Riverdale came to Withington at her invitation. Was it possible that was only three months ago? How could she possibly have come from that to this in so short a time? And why was she doing *this*? It was everything she had been quite adamant she would never do.

She had moved a few paces into the ballroom while all the others – her own family group, Avery and Anna, Cousin Louise and Jessica, Cousins Mildred and Thomas, the dowager countess and Cousin Matilda – were clustered outside, talking while they awaited the appearance of the first guests. Why *was* she doing it? No one had pressured her. Indeed, no one had even suggested a ball in her honor – they had all respected her desire for privacy. Even Alexander had not been suggesting it that afternoon in the carriage. Was it her mother, then? Had her mother goaded her into doing something beyond her wildest imaginings? Had seeing her again and listening to her made Wren believe that the only way to be free of her past was to open wide the door of her childhood prison and step out into the widest of wide worlds? Was a *ton* ball the most blatant way it could be done? And *would* she then be free? Was she *now* free?

She supposed not. But miracles did not always

come in a single flash of time. Sometimes they came with every step forward one took when every instinct urged two steps back. Sometimes they came with the simple courage to say *no longer, no more.* She raised one hand to touch the side of her bare, unveiled face and felt the stirrings of panic. And so she took one step farther into the room.

An arm came through her own on her right side, and almost simultaneously another arm linked itself through hers on the left.

'I wonder,' Anna said, 'if you are feeling the sort of paralyzing terror I was feeling in this very room last year, Wren. I daresay you are, though you look as cool and poised as you always look.'

'It is a good thing we wear our skirts long,' Wren said. 'You cannot see my shaking knees.'

'If it is any consolation to you,' Anna said, 'I will add that my first ball here will always be one of my most treasured memories.'

'You were right about the colors, Wren, though I was dubious,' Elizabeth said. 'Your gown is perfect. As Mama said before we left home, you look like a piece of both springtime and summer.'

'And I was right about Alexander, Lizzie,' Wren said. 'He *did* recognize the reference to daffodils without having to be told.'

And then, long before she was quite ready – but would she ever be? – the guests began to arrive and it was time to form the receiving line while the uniformed majordomo stepped into place beyond the ballroom doors to announce the guests as they came to the top of the stairs. Anna and Avery stood inside the doors, Wren and Alexander next to them, Elizabeth and her mother beyond them.

And Wren stood there, smiling and inclining her head, shaking hands, even presenting her cheek for the occasional kiss for a whole hour while close to three hundred of the crème de la crème of society filed past and greeted her and took a good look at her. She made no attempt to hide the left side of her face. She behaved as though there were no damage there at all. There were several lingering looks, a few raised eyebrows, one raised lorgnette, and two open grimaces. That was all. Everyone else greeted her with smiles and polite remarks. Several were even warm in their greetings. The raised lorgnette, Wren realized only after it had passed into the ballroom with its owner, belonged to the older of the two ladies who had been walking by the Serpentine with Alexander on the day of her own arrival in London.

'I believe it is time to proceed with the dancing,' Avery said at last. An elaborately jeweled quizzing glass was halfway to his eye. 'I must congratulate you and thank you effusively, Wren. This third ball at Archer House during my tenure as duke is clearly destined to be as sad a squeeze as the other two. Such success can only enhance my reputation.'

Wren laughed, as she was intended to do, she

realized from the keen, amused glance he cast her way. And she turned her laughing face to Alexander, who had somehow contrived to look even more handsome than usual tonight in his black tailed evening coat and silver satin knee breeches and silver embroidered waistcoat with white stockings and linen and elaborately tied neckcloth and lace at his cuffs.

'The first act of the drama is over,' she said. 'Now for the second – the dancing.'

'It is always worth remembering,' he said just before he led her out onto the floor to form a set for the first country dance of the evening, 'that most other people will be dancing too and focused upon their own little world, and that those who are not dancing will be either engrossed in conversation with one another or watching any of a hundred or so of the other dancers. We always tend to believe that everyone is watching us. It is very rarely so.'

'Ah.' She laughed. 'A timely lesson in humility.' Even so, she was not convinced. Alexander must have drawn more than his fair share of eyes wherever he went, and so, surely, would she tonight for a variety of reasons. The ball was in her honor. She was the new Countess of Riverdale but unknown to the *ton*. Word must have spread about her facial blemish, and, even if it had not, everyone would have had a good look at it tonight. She was unusually tall. She had been described in the morning papers the day after her wedding as the vastly wealthy Heyden glassware heiress. She was the newly discovered sister of Lord Hodges. Therefore, she must be the daughter of the famous – or infamous – Lady Hodges. Oh, there were any number of reasons to be skeptical of the comfort Alexander had tried to offer. But no matter. She was here and she was not going to take two steps back now – or even one. She was not even going to continue to stand in the same spot. She stepped forward on her husband's arm, her spine straight, her chin raised, a smile on her face, and – lest the smile look too much like a grimace – a sparkle in her eyes.

The worst was over. Everyone had seen her.

No, it was not. The dancing was yet to come. And she could not remember a single dance or what steps and figures went with the dances she could not remember. Her legs felt wooden, her knees half locked, her feet too large for the ends of her legs.

'Wren,' Alexander said, setting his free hand over hers on his sleeve, 'I do admire you, you know. More than I have admired anyone else in my whole life.'

But how was that going to help?

Netherby would certainly be able to boast that his third ball at Archer House was as successful as the other two, Alexander thought as the evening progressed, and undoubtedly would do so at the end of the evening just to get a smile out of Wren.

Not that smiles needed to be coaxed out of her tonight. She had not stopped smiling since the first guest appeared in the doorway of the ball-room. And it was not just a sociable smile. It sparkled. She looked like the happiest person at the ball, her shoulders back, her head high. And she danced every set – with him, with Sidney, with her brother, with one of her brother's friends, with Netherby, with strangers to whom she had been introduced for the first time in the receiving line. And she danced with precision and apparent enjoyment. She went in to supper on Uncle Richard's arm.

Perhaps only he understood just how much courage it was taking her to get through the evening. Or perhaps not. His mother and Lizzie surely understood. So, he suspected, did Anna and Netherby and . . . well, all his family. So did Hodges. He even came to talk about it with Alexander during the break between two sets after supper.

'How can Roe be such a smashing success tonight after being a hermit for twenty years?' he asked. 'Where does she find the poise and courage, Riverdale? I honestly do not feel worthy to be her brother.'

'Or I to be her husband,' Alexander said with a laugh. 'Her uncle gave her the name Wren apparently because she looked like a caged bird. I think she has finally discovered that the door of the cage has been open all these years, and she has fluttered outside and found that freedom is worth fighting for.'

'Yes,' her brother agreed. 'She is fighting, is she not?'

'Oh yes,' Alexander said. 'This ballroom is her battleground.'

'I have engaged Miss Parmiter's hand for the next set,' Hodges said. 'I must go and claim her. It is a waltz and she has only this week been approved by one of the patronesses of Almack's to dance it.'

Wren had been granted no such approval, though several of the patronesses were present this evening and doubtless would oblige if asked. But she was almost thirty years old and the Countess of Riverdale and did not need anyone's approval for anything. She had already waltzed this evening with her brother, and it had pained Alexander not to partner her himself. But etiquette decreed that he dance with his wife no more than twice this evening and he had preferred to wait for the waltz later in the evening – now, in fact. He had danced every set with different partners, but this was the one for which he had waited. He had reserved it with her. It would have been disastrous to arrive at her side only to discover that someone else had claimed it.

She smiled when she saw him come. To a casual observer it would have seemed that her expression had not changed, for she had smiled all evening. But he could see a greater depth to her eyes, a warmth of regard she reserved for him alone. And it was time, surely, for both of them to acknowledge what had happened since that first ghastly meeting at Withington, since her withdrawal of her offer on Easter Sunday, since his sensible, rational offer in Hyde Park. For *something* had happened. Everything had happened, in fact, and he was sure it could not have happened just to him.

'Ma'am,' he said, reaching for her hand and bowing over it as he kept his eyes on hers, 'this is my dance, I believe.'

Elizabeth, beside her, was fanning her face and looking amused.

'Sir,' Wren said, 'I believe it is. And I can almost promise,' she added after he had led her onto the floor, 'not to tread all over your feet. I did not tread on Colin's even once earlier.'

'Wren,' he said as one of the violinists was still tuning his instrument and other dancers gathered about them, 'you have done it. You have stepped out fearlessly into the world and proved that you can do anything you choose to do.'

'Ah, not fearlessly,' she said.

'Courageously, then,' he said. 'No courage is needed if there is no fear, after all, and you are the most courageous woman – no, *person* – I have ever known.'

'And I do not believe I could swim across the English Channel to France,' she said.

'But would you choose to try?' he asked.

'No.' They both laughed.

And the music began. They waltzed tentatively at first, concentrating upon performing the correct steps and finding a shared rhythm. Then he twirled her into a spin and she raised a flushed, smiling face to his. Her spine arched inward with the pressure of his hand at her waist. Her left hand rested on his shoulder while her right hand was clasped in his. And the world was a wonderful place, and happiness was a real thing even if it welled up only occasionally into conscious moments of joy like this one. His family – and hers – and friends and peers and acquaintances danced around them with a shared pleasure in this celebration of life and friendship and laughter. And his wife was in his arms and they were at the very beginning of a marriage that would, God willing, bring them contentment and more on down the years to old age and perhaps even beyond.

Other couples twirled about them, candlelight wheeled above them, flowers gave off their heady perfumes, and the music seeped into their very bones, or so it seemed.

She smiled at him and he smiled back and really nothing else mattered, nothing else existed but her – and him. Them.

'Ah,' she said on a sigh when the music finally came to an end, 'so soon?'

'Come,' he said. He did not know if she had promised the next set. He did not really care. He led her out onto the balcony beyond the French windows and down the steps to the garden below.

It was lit with colored lanterns strung among the trees, though not many people strolled there. He stopped walking when they were beneath a willow tree beside a fountain, out of sight of the house. 'Happy?' he asked.

'Mmm,' she said, clinging to his arm. 'It is beautifully cool out here.'

'I suppose,' he said, 'you are still going to insist that we wait to go home to Brambledean until after the parliamentary session is over.'

'Yes,' she said. 'Because your duty here is important. To you. And therefore to me.'

'We will leave the very day after,' he said. 'At the crack of dawn. I want to be home. With you.'

'It does sound heavenly, does it not?' she said.

'Wren.' He turned to face her and cupped her face in his hands. 'I am guilty of a terrible deception. Of myself as much as of you. I surely suspected when you insisted upon ending things between us at Brambledean. I surely knew when I saw you again by the Serpentine. The truth must have been staring me in the face and knocking on my brow when I offered you marriage on that woodland path. It has been clamoring for my attention ever since.'

She raised both her hands and set them over the backs of his. 'What?' she half whispered. Lamplight was swaying across her face in the breeze.

'I love you,' he said. 'I wish there were a better word. But maybe it is the best after all, for it encompasses everything else and reaches beyond.

407

I love you more than . . . Well, I am really not good with words. I love you.'

Her smile was soft and warm and radiant in the dim light. 'Oh,' she said, her voice hushed with wonder. 'But you have chosen the most precious word in the English language, Alexander. I love you too, you see. I think I have known my own feelings since the moment you walked into my drawing room at Withington and looked so disconcerted not to find it full of other guests. I have certainly known since Easter Sunday. It broke my heart to let you go, but it would have been worse to continue – or so I thought. After we met again I chose to settle for the hope of affection, and it has been good knowing that you do indeed care. I have tried to tell myself it is enough. I have tried not to be greedy. But now . . . Oh, Alexander, now . . .'

He touched his forehead to hers. 'And it is at least a few weeks since I last noticed, you know,' he said. 'Is it still there? I wonder.' He lifted his head and gazed with a frown of concentration at the left side of her face. 'Indeed it is. The birthmark is still there. How could I possibly not have noticed?'

She was laughing. 'Perhaps,' she said, 'because you were noticing me instead.'

'Ah,' he said. 'Undoubtedly that is it.'

They smiled at each other, and she pressed her hands warmly against his as he kissed her.

. . . *because you were noticing me instead.*

Ah, Wren.

Yes.